To my mother and father
And to the memory of Lev Davidovich Bronstein

Critical Theory and Science Fiction

Critical Theory
and
Science Fiction

Carl Freedman

Wesleyan University Press

Published by University Press of New England

Hanover and London

Wesleyan University Press
Published by University Press of New England, Hanover, NH 03755
© 2000 by Carl Freedman
All rights reserved
Printed in the United States of America   5 4 3 2 1
CIP data appear at the end of the book

To change the world is not to explore the moon. It is to make the revolution and build socialism without regressing back to capitalism.

The rest, including the moon, will be given to us in addition.

—LOUIS ALTHUSSER

Se vuol ballare,
Signor Contino,
Il chitarrino
Le suonerò.

—LORENZO DA PONTE

A map of the world that does not include Utopia is not worth even glancing at, for it leaves out the one country at which Humanity is always landing. And when Humanity lands there, it looks out, and, seeing a better country, sets sail. Progress is the realisation of Utopias.

—OSCAR WILDE

Contents

Acknowledgments

I have been working on this essay, in one way or another, for a long time. Indeed, in composing and revising the text I have often been struck by how much preparation was accomplished on occasions when I had no conscious notion that any such project was under way. Inevitably, then, I have incurred many debts, to institutions, and to individuals. All I can do here is discuss, very briefly, some of the more obvious ones and extend my apologies to those who have accidentally gone unmentioned.

My institutional obligations are relatively straightforward. Various sorts of financial or other support have been provided by the following: the Marxist Literary Group at Yale University from 1977 to 1984; the Center for the Humanities of Wesleyan University; the Department of English, the College of Arts and Sciences, and the Office of Research, all of Louisiana State University; the Eaton Science Fiction Collection at the University of California at Riverside, and the annual conferences and critical anthologies sponsored by the Eaton Collection; the journal *Science-Fiction Studies*; and, last but certainly not least, the Wesleyan University Press. To all, my thanks.

My debts to individuals are far more numerous and more difficult to keep track of; the following account is doubtless highly selective.

In a sense, my first debt is to my father for introducing me to science fiction. When I was in my early teens, he recommended Isaac Asimov's *I, Robot*, which I read at once and enjoyed hugely. I proceeded to read through most of the rest of Asimov's science fiction (and much of his nonfiction), and have preserved a special fondness for Asimov ever since. Relatively little is said about Asimov's work in the main text, and he certainly does not loom nearly so large in my conception of science fiction as he once did; nonetheless I am glad of the chance to record my admiration for him.

My adolescent enthusiasm for science fiction lasted only a few years. I returned to SF during my graduate student years, when I first began to think systematically about both critical theory and science fiction. My chief mentor in both instances was Fredric Jameson, to whose teaching and writing I am even more indebted than my frequent references to him will probably indicate.

I am no less grateful to many graduate school colleagues with whom I discussed critical theory and science fiction almost endlessly. I have especially vivid memories of valuable conversations with the late Rena Grant, with Jonathan Haynes, with John Rieder, with Steven Shaviro, and, above all, with Christopher Kendrick, my old theoretical alter ego. More recently, Chris Kendrick provided me with a complete set of critical annotations of the manuscript as it was being produced; his comments were invariably intelligent and interesting, usually of direct use, and occasionally legible as well.

Another complete set of annotations was provided by Carl Gardner, my friend of more than three decades, who read the manuscript not only as a lifelong aficionado of science fiction but also as a professional physicist and applied mathematician. Yet another complete set of comments on the manuscript was provided by Robin Roberts, my colleague at LSU, from whom I have also learned much in the undergraduate courses on science fiction that we have taught together.

I have, indeed, taught many courses, graduate and undergraduate, on both critical theory and science fiction, and a huge collective debt is owed to my students. Special recognition is due the members of the best class I have ever seen: the students of my graduate seminar "Critical Theory and Science Fiction," taught in the LSU English Department during the spring semester of 1997.

Khachig Tölölyan has done me so many personal and professional good turns over the years that I have almost come to take his consistent generosity and support for granted. He has been important to my academic endeavors in more ways than I could particularize here.

I mentioned the journal *Science-Fiction Studies* above. Although I have the highest praise for the members of its current collective editorship, I must here single out the former editor, Robert Philmus, during whose tenure I became formally associated with the journal. It was while working with Robert that I became a professional critic of science fiction; among many other good turns, he commissioned me to write the article "Science Fiction and Critical Theory," out of which this book grew.

Somewhat similarly, I must single out George Slusser as the curator of the Eaton Collection and the first guiding genius of the Eaton conferences; his support over the years is an instance of that disinterested academic integrity that leads him to sponsor and subsidize the expression of views (like mine) with which he strongly disagrees.

My LSU colleague John Lowe read a draft of the concluding section on the postmodern, and contributed many careful and useful comments

Suzanna Tamminen, the editor-in-chief of the Wesleyan University Press, has been a source of help and good humor, and her enthusiasm for this project from manuscript to hard covers has been a real inspiration to me. If Robert Philmus first taught me how much good editors of scholarly journals contribute to our intellectual culture, Suzanna taught me the same about good editors at university presses.

Alcena Rogan has consistently provided astute criticism, generous support, and love. Of all the things she has done for me, I will mention only her most tangible contribution to this volume, namely, the preparation of the index. An index of concepts as well as of proper names can be vital to the reader of an essay like this, and it is brilliantly presented here.

My greatest of all debts, however, is to someone too young to have made any *direct* contribution to this project: my daughter Rosa. Both critical theory and science fiction are ultimately oriented toward the future, as I will argue at some length, and Rosa is my main personal reason for being interested in the future. She will live to see the second half of the twenty-first century, by which time, I hope, the world will be more like what most of the theorists and novelists discussed in this volume would desire than like the late twentieth-century world into which Rosa was born.

July 1999   C.F.

Preface

Like any other writer, I am often asked about my current project. During the time that I thought of the following essay as my current project, I sometimes responded simply by giving the title. On other occasions, however, when a little more detail seemed to be called for, I usually employed one of two prepared responses. The short, playful response was to say that my thesis about critical theory and science fiction is that each is a version of the other. This, of course, is more aphorism than answer, but I remain rather attached to it as an aphorism. It seems to me to have some of the provocative elegance of a Möbius strip—a figure, indeed, that tends to turn up rather often in science fiction.

My longer, more serious response began by saying that my aim was to do for science fiction what Georg Lukács does for historical fiction in *The Historical Novel*. The comparison is immodest indeed, since, in my opinion, *The Historical Novel* remains, for all its imperfections and ambiguities, the finest literary-critical account of any particular fictional genre. Leaving aside, however, the question of to what degree I succeed in emulating the brilliance of Lukács's achievement, there should be no question that the fundamental intention of this volume is strictly parallel to that of Lukács's great work. Just as Lukács argues that the historical novel is a privileged and paradigmatic genre for Marxism, so I argue that science fiction enjoys—and ought to be recognized as enjoying—such a position not only for Marxism but for critical theory in general. Sometimes though by no means always a "popular" literature (like historical fiction), science fiction is of all forms of fiction today the one that bears the deepest and most interesting affinity with the rigors of dialectical thinking. Lukács demonstrates that a great deal of light can be thrown on the historical novel by studying it in conjunction with historical materialism. Likewise, I maintain that we can learn a great deal about the work of such science-fiction authors as Philip K. Dick, Ursula Le Guin, Stanisław Lem, and Samuel Delany by studying it together with the theoretical production of writers like Mikhail Bakhtin, Jacques Lacan, Ernst Bloch, Theodor Adorno, and

Lukács himself. But there is no question of merely "applying" critical theory to science fiction, and I also argue that understanding these two modes of discourse together can reveal much about both. The equivalent of this position is perhaps not quite overt in Lukács's own text, though I believe it is implicit in the general logic of his argument.

It may be useful to sketch out here how my general argument is advanced in the different components of the essay to follow. Chapter 1, "Definitions," focuses on the two terms of my title. I define critical theory as something broader than Critical Theory in the Frankfurt School usage but not unrelated to it. I use the term to designate the traditions of dialectical and self-reflective thought initiated during the historical moment of Kant and Hegel. Insofar as twentieth-century work is concerned, I maintain a certain privilege for specific forms of critical thinking: Marxism above all, but also psychoanalysis and the best work of such postdialectical theorists as Foucault and Derrida. As to science fiction, here I lean heavily on Darko Suvin's pathbreaking definition that science fiction is the literature of cognitive estrangement. Although this insight seems to me the starting point for any genuine understanding of science fiction, I do suggest some modifications and elaborations of Suvin's account. I establish a distinction between cognition proper and what I call the literary *cognition effect*. I also insist that the category of science fiction, like any other generic category, is best used to analyze tendencies within a literary work rather than to classify entire works in one or another pigeonhole. Like Suvin, I make clear that the estrangements of science fiction need not be limited to the technological estrangements popularly associated with the genre.

Chapter 1, then, is concerned simply with establishing the two categories that dominate the volume. Chapter 2, "Articulations," is concerned with setting these categories in motion, so to speak, with regard to each other. In the chapter's first section, I offer some general theorizing on the nature of reading and canon-formation, arguing that every kind of reading implicitly or explicitly privileges its own canon. In the next three sections—which constitute the conceptual center of the volume as a whole—I move to my fundamental argument that critical theory, as a mode of reading, tends to privilege science fiction (though usually, so far, implicitly and even unconsciously). To prefigure here the core sentences of the entire book: I maintain that science fiction, like critical theory, insists upon historical mutability, material reducibility, and utopian possibility. Of all genres, science fiction is thus the one most devoted to the historical concreteness and rigorous self-reflectiveness of critical theory. The science-fictional world is not only one different in time or place from our own, but one whose chief interest is precisely the difference that such difference makes. It is also a world whose difference is concretized within a cognitive continuum with the actual—thus sharply distinguishing science fiction from the irrationalist estrangements of fantasy or Gothic literature (which may secretly work to ratify the mundane status quo by presenting no alternative to the latter other than inexplicable discontinuities).

The second, third, and fourth sections of chapter 2 make and substantiate this general argument in different ways. The second section operates on the micrological level of style, and attempts to demonstrate the affinity between critical theory and science fiction by analyzing the prose of Philip K. Dick. I necessarily engage the question of style in the novel generally, and bring to bear on it the work of Bakhtin, who provides what I take to be the most critically informed discussion of novelistic style to date. In the third and fourth sections of the chapter I turn from the micrological to the macrological level, and focus on the narrative structure of science fiction with regard to the latter's affinity with critical theory. More specifically, in the third section I discuss this question by examining the relations between science fiction and historical fiction. To do so it is necessary to provide a historicizing account of science fiction itself and, of course, to offer a full-scale engagement with Lukács's theory of the historical novel. In the following section I concentrate on science fiction and utopia, producing a narrative of the relations between science fiction and utopia as forms in the context of Bloch's hermeneutic philosophy of utopia. Chapter 2 concludes with a brief fifth section in which I give a perspective on how the deep affinity between critical theory and science fiction has been largely occluded by what might be called the internal political economy of critical thought.

Chapters 1 and 2 operate on a quite comprehensive level. Though a great many individual works are briefly discussed, and though a few passages are analyzed closely, the overall aim of these two chapters is not to provide any detailed readings but to make a general argument about the relations of critical theory and science fiction. In chapter 3, "Excursuses," I continue the argument through fairly extensive analyses of five major science-fiction novels. I deliberately employ the somewhat unusual term, "excursus" (which I take from a similar usage in *Dialectic of Enlightenment* by Adorno and Max Horkheimer), in order to emphasize that the readings are not intended to provide "proof" (in any empiricist sense) of the argument in chapter 2 but rather to extend the argument in a somewhat different way.

Each of the novels considered in chapter 3 resonates strongly with concerns proper to critical theory. In my reading of *Solaris* I explore how the text uses science fiction to foreground the problems of cognition and estrangement themselves, and to deconstruct positivistic science in order to stress the dialectical provisionality of all knowledge; I also argue that the crucial category of Otherness can be illuminated by comparing its treatment in Lem's novel with that in Lacanian psychoanalysis. In the analysis of *The Dispossessed* that follows, I turn from a cognitive-epistemological emphasis to an ethical-political one. I consider how Le Guin's achievement is nothing less than the reinvention of the positive utopia after many years of eclipse by negative versions of the Orwell-Huxley sort. I maintain that the novel's insistence upon the unavoidable complexities and ambivalences of social organization coexists with a definite radical commitment, and that in many ways the text's most consequential intellectual kinship is less with the anarchist thought of the author's own political lineage than with the more critical, dialectical Marxist thought of Trotsky. Joanna Russ's *The Two of Them* then provides the occasion for a consideration of feminism as a unique area of critical theory, one in which, as I suggest, theory and narrative bear an unusually close and complex relationship to each other. More specifically, I show how the novel radically recasts many of the masculinist conventions of pulp science fiction in order to demonstrate the special compatibility of feminist critical thought with science fiction. I then approach Delany's *Stars in My Pocket Like Grains of Sand*, showing how the text's awesomely ambitious representations of cultural and biological difference can be understood in connection with the critical philosophies of difference constructed by Jacques Derrida and, even more, by Adorno. Delany is perhaps the living American novelist most personally familiar with the texts of critical theory, and his greatest work (which I believe *Stars in My Pocket* to be) may be the most intellectually impressive single achievement in current American fiction. Chapter 3 ends by returning to Philip K. Dick (for me the greatest of all science-fiction writers). Reading *The Man in the High Castle*, I revisit the problem of the relations between science fiction and historical fiction; I show how certain of the novel's concerns are related to the Adornian concept of the dialectic of enlightenment; and I argue that the text critically interrogates (both implicitly and explicitly) the generic form of science fiction itself.

Finally, the book as a whole concludes with a coda in which I coordinate both critical theory and science fiction with the historical category of the postmodern in order to produce some speculations about the future of both modes of discourse.

Such, in outline, is what this essay sets itself to do. How original a project do I take it to be? Though the theoretically engaged criticism of science fiction in the American academy often feels like a lonely activity indeed — beset both by those who dismiss science fiction altogether and, more insidiously, by those who maintain a purely empiricist interest in it as an instance of "popular culture" — I am far from the first to insist that science fiction ought to be read with much closer and more alert attention than it usually has been. Indeed, for more than half a century there have been distinguished critics — not primarily associated professionally with the study of science fiction — who have on occasion bravely spoken out to make serious claims for the genre; I am thinking — to take just a few instances — of such diverse figures as C. S. Lewis, Raymond Williams, Robert Scholes, Leslie Fiedler, Fredric Jameson, and Donna Haraway. Furthermore, for about a quarter-century there has been a developing tradition of professional science-fiction criticism frequently (if by no means invariably) informed by the perspectives of critical theory; the two most important (and not unrelated) enabling events in this regard are the founding of the journal *Science-Fiction Studies* in 1973 by the late Dale Mullen (perhaps the most underappreciated hero of the serious study of the genre) and the publication in 1979 of Darko Suvin's *Metamorphoses of Science Fiction*. Because I depend heavily on Suvin's work, and because I write frequently for *Science-Fiction Studies* and serve on the journal's board of editorial consultants, it seems clear that it is in this evolving tradition (among other places) that the current volume places itself.

But I do not know that anyone else has yet attempted to make and systematically support claims for science fiction in quite the encompassing and explicit way that I do. I do not know that critical theory and science fiction have ever before been examined together with the same level of detail that I bring to *both* kinds of discourse. Though the general relationship between critical theory and science fiction is certainly well established, it is in my view insufficiently recognized and very inadequately understood; that is the situation that I mean to remedy. Thus, although the current volume plainly owes much to work that has come before (most notably the work of Suvin and Jameson among my own contemporaries), it has some claims to originality too.

I conclude these prefatory comments with a few pointers that I hope may be useful in orienting the reader about what can and cannot be expected in the pages to follow.

First, I emphasize as strongly as possible a point briefly suggested above: that the main project of this volume is *not* what the title would imply to many readers, namely, the "application" of critical theory to science fiction. Sometimes, of course, I do bring critical theory to bear on science fiction, just as sometimes I bring science fiction to bear on critical theory. Both operations are necessary moments in my general argument, but that argument centers on the *structural* affinities between the two modes of discourse. Even the readings of science-fiction novels in chapter 3 are designed to illuminate the work of Lacan, Trotsky, and Adorno, as well as that of Lem, Le Guin, and Delany.

Second, I therefore warn against the tendency to assume that, when a title contains two or more terms, the more or most specific term (which most readers, in this case, will take to be science fiction) conveys what the book is "really" about. This is a book about critical theory as much as about science fiction, and the order in which I have placed the two terms is not an accident. The following pages, after all, contain detailed discussions of critical theorists who never overtly concerned themselves with science fiction, and examinations of problems (such as the intellectual effects of socioeconomic modernity, and the nature and value of literary style) that are by no means limited, in their relevance, to science fiction. One practical issue here concerns my intended audience. I am sure that many readers who approach this text will have extensive familiarity with science fiction and the secondary literature on it. I hope also, however, to attract readers who are interested in critical theory but who have hitherto paid little or no attention to science fiction. My point, of course, is that they ought to be very interested in science fiction indeed.

Third, I want to stress the essayistic—as opposed to encyclopedic—character of this project. The joint terrain of critical theory and science fiction is so vast that a really exhaustive demonstration of my basic argument would fill a shelf of thick volumes. So I have had to practice a strict economy. One consequence is that a number of theorists (like Lenin, Sartre, Walter Benjamin, and Louis Althusser) and a number of fiction writers (like J. G. Ballard, Thomas Disch, and "James Tiptree, Jr." [Alice Sheldon]) whom I would like to have discussed at length are mentioned only in passing. Nonetheless, I hope that I have made my general argument with enough rigor and lucidity to establish what Althusser would call a *problematic*—that is, a conceptual framework within which further research and analysis can be conducted. In the future I will probably discuss, in the spirit of this essay, more texts of critical theory and of science fiction. Perhaps others will too.

The vastness of critical theory and of science fiction means, of course, that the pertinent secondary literature is vast as well. And I have tried to be economical not only in the main text but also in the footnotes—partly for reasons of space, but also because of a long-standing dislike of the pseudoscholarly practice of citing works merely in order to suggest (truthfully or not) that one has read them. Obviously, genuine intellectual debts ought to be acknowledged as a matter of basic honesty, and this I have done to the best of my ability. But it should not be assumed (to paraphrase C. S. Lewis) that I must be ignorant or contemptuous of the articles and books that I do not mention.

Finally, I should like to state one affirmation that, I hope, clearly animates nearly every page to come. Despite all the immense difficulties and complexities, I do believe that both critical theory and science fiction have the potential to play a role in the liberation of humanity from oppression. That (to adapt a similar remark by Terry Eagleton) is why I have thought the book worth writing.

Critical Theory and Science Fiction

1. Definitions

Critical Theory

If *theory* is taken to mean an intellectual framework, a problematic that, by the form of its questions even more than by the content of its answers, defines a certain conceptual terrain, then all thought is theoretical. This proposition is, indeed, virtually tautological, since a theory or intellectual problematic is not that which merely shapes or contains thought (as though the latter somehow possessed an unshaped, uncontained earlier existence) but that which gives rise to the possibility of thought in the first place. It may be added that few theories are more narrow and dogmatic than those (like Anglo-American "common sense") that remain oblivious or even hostile to their status as theories. Keynes's aphorism about his colleagues—that those economists who think they dislike theory are simply attached to an older theory—is applicable in other fields as well.[1] *Critical* theory, however, has, or ought to have, a considerably more specific meaning. The term is by no means unfamiliar in current academic discourse; nonetheless, it is not always used with great precision. I shall begin by defining just what difference the adjective makes.

The word *critical* can be etymologically traced to Greek and even Indo-European roots (a tracing that leads ultimately to the concepts of cutting and separation),[2] and the Oxford English Dictionary finds that *critical* in the sense of "involving or exercising careful judgment or observation" is used in English as early as 1650 (by Sir Thomas Browne). With the three *Critiques* of Kant, however, the meaning of the word undergoes a radical,

1. An excellent demonstration of this principle (which I deliberately choose from a context far removed from any of my immediate current concerns) is provided by Garry Wills's brilliant deconstruction of the orthodox political liberalism of Arthur Schlesinger, particularly in the latter's revealing opposition of "ideas" to "ideology"; see Wills, *Nixon Agonistes*, exp. ed. (New York: New American Library, 1979), 311–326.

2. My authority here is, of course, the *American Heritage Dictionary*.

irrevocable transformation. This is not the place for a full-scale rehearsal of Kantian philosophy, which few today would regard in any case as adequate to current theoretical exigencies. But it is important to remember Kant not only as the founder of German idealism and the paradigmatic exponent of a contemplative metaphysics (and aesthetics), but also as the thinker who first clearly establishes what might be called the priority of *interpretation*. The whole concept of the thing-in-itself and the separation of the latter from the phenomenal world of theoretical or scientific investigation (however inadequate and however widely challenged since Kant's own day) is a pioneering attempt to provide an alternative both to theological dogmatism and to the vulgar empiricism that assumes an untroubled adequacy of knowing subject to known object. Indeed, it is only with Kant that the affinity between dogmatism and empiricism, as varieties of an unreflexive philosophical realism, becomes fully visible. The Kantian alternative is to insist upon the active interpretive function of human cognition, whose various components — understanding, judgment, and reason, in Kant's division — regulate the phenomenal world a priori but (in sharp contrast to the subjectivism and irrationality into which so much later idealism has fallen) with a validity guaranteed by the integrity of the phenomenal world, which exists on this side, so to speak, of the thing-in-itself. The thing-in-itself remains strictly unknowable; at the same time, however, cognition achieves genuine knowledge of the phenomena, which cognition plays an active role in constructing. A passage from the introduction to *Critique of Judgment* (1790) is especially pertinent to the status of Kantian critique with regard to theoretical investigation in both the natural and human sciences:[3]

Our cognitive power as a whole has two domains, that of the concepts of nature and that of the concept of freedom, because it legislates a priori by means of both kinds of concept. Now philosophy too divides, according to these legislations, into theoretical and practical. And yet the territory on which its domain is set up and on which it *exercises* its legislation is still always confined to the sum total of the objects of all possible experience, insofar as they are considered nothing more than mere phenomena, since otherwise it would be inconceivable that the understanding could legislate with regard to them. (emphasis in original)

This scheme is vulnerable to materialist refutation because the ineffability of the thing-in-itself ultimately resolves thought into mere contemplation, despite the shaping dialectical vigor that interpretation exercises on the phenomenal plane. The classic analysis here remains that of Lukács, for whom the problem of the thing-in-itself is actually the problem of capitalist reification and the consequent opaqueness of the commodity to bourgeois consciousness; and Lukács's critique of Kant has been interestingly reworked by

3. Immanuel Kant, *Critique of Judgment*, trans. Werner S. Pluhar (Indianapolis: Hackett, 1987), 13; translation modified.

many more recent commentators[4] Nonetheless, with Kant the notion of critique and critical thought breaks from the problematic of knowing as a merely *extractive* process (the necessary illusion of all philosophical realism and, indeed, precisely the "careful observation" suggested by the OED) and is resituated as the project of making visible the absolute presuppositions of any knowledge whatever. With the advent of critique and the critical in the Kantian and post-Kantian sense, theory decisively loses its innocence; henceforth any mode of thought that declines to interrogate its own presuppositions and to engage its own role in the construction of the objects of its own knowledge may appropriately be stigmatized with the adjective *precritical*. Precritical theory has certainly continued to exist to this day, but there is a real sense in which it represents a regression to an intellectual prehistory that ought to have been permanently transcended.

And yet to speak of an intellectual prehistory that "ought" to have been transcended is, in itself, inadequate; just as it is inadequate to describe the moment of critical theory as Kantian and post-Kantian, if such a description is taken to imply that what is solely or mainly at stake are the abstract narratives of intellectual history. A fully concrete historicization of the critical would in the end probably involve nothing less than the reconstruction of modernity itself (using that term both in the conventional sense of the decisively postmedieval and imperialist phase of Western civilization but also in Habermas's sense of a project that remains "incomplete" even in our own "postmodern" era).[5] Among the extremely various historical determinants of the critical moment, however, there are at least two that have special relevance to the particular interests of this essay.

One is the triumph of the natural sciences. It is well known that science was an explicitly pressing issue for Kant himself, who in many ways counts as the last major speculative philosopher for whom the ancient link between philosophy and science remains fully vital: the entire edifice of Kant's critical philosophy rests on the presupposition that the results obtained by natural science are valid, though in ways that pre-Kantian philosophy had not succeeded in formulating with precision. But the relevance of science to the advent of critique has a significance far wider than that particular bit of intellectual "influence." For science—even though many of its practitioners have historically thought their way forward in empiricist and, later, specifically positivist terms

---

4. See Georg Lukács, *History and Class Consciousness*, trans. Rodney Livingstone (Cambridge, Mass.: MIT Press, 1971), esp. 114–140. Some interesting neo-Lukácsian remarks on Kant may be found in Fredric Jameson, *Postmodernism* (Durham: Duke University Press, 1991), 248ff. Terry Eagleton incisively rewrites Lukács's analysis in somewhat deconstructive terms: "The thing in itself is thus a kind of empty signifier of that total knowledge which the bourgeoisie never ceases to dream of, but which its own fragmenting, dissevering activities continually frustrate"; Eagleton, *The Ideology of the Aesthetic* (Oxford: Blackwell, 1990), 77.

5. See Jürgen Habermas, "Modernity—An Incomplete Project," trans. Seyla Ben-Habib, in *The Anti-Aesthetic*, ed. Hal Foster (Port Townsend, Wash.: Bay, 1983), 3–15.

—possesses a fundamentally critical, nonempiricist charge in its ceaseless questioning of the given, in its refusal to repose in any material or intellectual status quo. By the late eighteenth century the practical transformations wrought by the scientific project, which had been blessed by official sanction a century earlier in England through the formation of the Royal Society, had become sufficiently urgent to help stimulate and in turn be stimulated by critical theory in the modern sense—theory, that is, engaged in fundamental interrogation and self-interrogation, theory decisively free of conservative epistemological canons of tradition, appearance, or logic in the merely formal sense.

Nor is textual evidence of the link between the natural sciences and critical thought to be located only in academic philosophy such as Kant's. In the current context it is especially pertinent to recall that hardly more than a generation after the appearance of *Critique of Judgement* came Mary Shelley's *Frankenstein* (1818), which has not only been listed in many genealogies of the genre as the first science-fiction novel (a context in which we shall later return to it) but which also probably counts as the first important work of fiction to engage modern science seriously and to feature a scientist as its protagonist.[6] Indeed, the intellectual significance of *Frankenstein* is actually underscored by consideration of an obvious but superficial objection to its status as *science fiction*, in the sense of fiction in some way allied to science: namely, that its ethical stance is ultimately conservative and hostile to science. So it is: but such hostility by no means cancels the *epistemological* radicalism of the novel, its sense that the most fundamental of material and intellectual categories—condensed into the problem of life itself—can no longer be taken for granted but are now somehow up for grabs and can be challenged and rethought. Victor Frankenstein's experiment is monstrous, to be sure, but its viability amounts to intellectual revolution, to an awareness that what the text itself might designate a moment of "Promethean" critical thought is at hand.

A convenient literary index of the hegemony that science attained sometime between the turn of the eighteenth century and that of the nineteenth is the contrast of Mary Shelley's hostility to science with that of Swift in book 3 of *Gulliver's Travels*, published ninety-two years before *Frankenstein*. In 1726, it was still possible for a serious mind (though, admittedly, Swift's mind was intellectually reactionary even by the standards of the time) to refuse to take science seriously, to lampoon it as a series of frivolous, self-referential games in which no authentic intellectual activity was taking place and no practical

6. Goethe's *Faust* (whose composition extended from 1770 to 1831) might be mentioned in this context; the transformative power of science is certainly in many ways a powerful presence in the text. Yet Goethe's project is curiously overdetermined by his choice of a medieval legend as its source, so that Faust exhibits many of the attributes of the modern Promethean scientist without wholly ceasing to be a general "scholar" of the medieval type. The great opening monologue invokes the four medieval faculties of philosophy, law, medicine, and theology—in dissatisfaction, to be sure, but a general orientation is nonetheless implied from which Victor Frankenstein is quite free.

consequences were at issue.[7] This attitude is inconceivable in the mental universe of *Frankenstein*. From Mary Shelley—perhaps from Goethe—onward, serious objections to science must be based on the assumption that the latter is not trivial but *dangerous*; and such a sense of danger is inseparable from the awareness that fundamental questions are at stake, questions that demand the dialectical reflexivity of critical theory in the strongest sense. Indeed, although, as we shall see, many later versions of critical theory have remained as friendly to natural science as Kant's, it is striking that a rather post-Mary-Shelleyan unease with science is central to the most prominent instance of critical theory as a named movement: the Critical Theory of the Frankfurt School (another matter to which we shall return).

In the emergence of critical thought, however, probably even more important than the rise of the physical sciences was the invention of political modernity in the French Revolution and its aftermath. Here, of course, there is little question of direct influence on Kantian critical philosophy; the third of the great critiques was published only one year after the fall of the Bastille and the Declaration of the Rights of Man and Citizen. It is nonetheless appropriate to consider critique as representing, on the philosophical plane, what T. S. Eliot might have called an "objective correlative" to the almost contemporary innovations of sociopolitical revolution. Revolution might be understood as enacting a reduction of inherited sociopolitical categories from the noumenal to the phenomenal level, as inaugurating a transformative (as contradistinguished from contemplative) stance toward social reality as irrevocably as science was performing much the same operation with regard to natural reality. The great events effected or announced in 1789—not only the Declaration itself but also the Tennis Court Oath, the repeal of social class as a legal category, the demotion of the king from sovereign to first magistrate, and the expropriation of the church—effectively destroyed the status quo as a self-legitimating mechanism and made it necessary to retheorize the most fundamental categories of social and political life. As in the sphere of nature, what had been settled was now capable of being put in question and practically altered: so that 1789 (building on the precedent of 1776 in America) enabled not only the development of liberal and revolutionary political thought but also conservatism itself, since the latter is strictly unthinkable unless not conserving the given is somehow on the agenda. Though this sociopolitical matrix did not give rise to critique in the textual sense, it did create a situation in which critical thought possessed immediate political urgency.

The general importance of the French Revolution can also be expressed—and here the philosophical objective correlative becomes less Kantian than

7. It may be noted in passing that the stance that in Swift's day could be adopted by a man of towering literary genius has now sunk so low on the intellectual scale that it is almost never encountered in life-forms higher than the sort of politicians and journalists who sometimes ridicule the titles of scientific research projects supported by public funds.

Hegelian—by crediting it with the invention of *history* itself, or (what in critical terms amounts to the same thing) the enabling of radically historical thought. Here Lukács's account is definitive: "It was the French Revolution, the revolutionary wars and the rise and fall of Napoleon, which for the first time made history a *mass experience*, and moreover on a European scale" (emphasis in original).[8] Prior to 1789 (and with the immense but finally ambiguous exception of the English Revolution of the 1640s) the political history of Europe had constituted a *(relatively)* unimportant narrative and one of indifference to the great majority of the population. But revolution necessitates that the masses be "invited" into history, as the leaders of the French Revolution did; their successors and enemies were virtually compelled to follow suit, particularly with regard to the mass (often conscript) armies that replaced the small mercenary and professional bands of the prerevolutionary era. For the first time, significant historical change took place not only during the lifetime but within the actual lived experience of the average (especially male and adult) person; it is this greatly accelerated and expanded pace of events that amounts to history in the sense that has been known ever since. As Lukács puts it: "Hence the concrete possibilities for men to comprehend their own existence as something historically conditioned, for them to see in history something which deeply affects their daily lives and immediately concerns them" (*Historical Novel* 24). In this context, critical theory inevitably takes a historical turn, as the historical dialectics of Hegel (who was of course concerned with justifying the "necessity" of the French Revolution) supersede the essentially static conception of human nature assumed by Kant and other earlier thinkers. If, then, the Kantian invention of critique constitutes the priority of interpretation, of the dialectical "interinanimation" (to adapt Donne's useful coinage) of subject and object, then the Hegelian moment may be defined as the recasting of critique into the radically historical form it has taken ever since the age of the democratic revolution. The historicization of dialectical critique, it should be added, also means that henceforth social formations must be seen not as inherited collections of natural habits but as systemic and mutable totalities (though for Hegel, of course, such mutability is wholly idealist in character).

Natural science and the French Revolution: it is worthwhile to consider the political connotations that attach to these two crucial determinants of the critical moment. Both innovations are of course fundamental to modernity itself, and in particular to the hegemony of the Western (though no longer only the Western) nation-state organized on the economic basis of industrial capitalism (or, until recently, Stalinist socialism). In that sense, science and the

---

8. Georg Lukács, *The Historical Novel*, trans. Hannah and Stanley Mitchell (London: Merlin, 1962), 23. Though I am indebted to Lukács for this discussion of the intellectual consequences of the French Revolution, the far larger debt that the current work owes to The *Historical Novel* will gradually become evident.

traditions of 1789 would seem to be virtually unassailable; and so they are on the levels of economic or, to a lesser degree, political production. And yet (in a case of "uneven development" whose significance Habermas has been almost alone among current thinkers in estimating) the matter falls out rather differently on the ideological or cultural plane, where modernity *as a concept* (or, in Raymond Williams's sense, as a structure of feeling) has never attained complete security. Indeed, the contemporary cultural landscape is littered with antimodern protests and in particular with instances of ideological resistance to natural science and to the politics of 1789. Consider, on one educational level, the persistent campaigns against evolutionary biology in the public school curriculum, or, on a somewhat different educational level, the journalistic acclaim often granted to any treatment of the French Revolution that recycles neo-Burkean platitudes (for example, Simon Schama's *Citizens* [1989]). Such attacks are generally made from the political right, as these examples suggest, though more complex variations on the antimodern thesis have sometimes been attempted from the left (by far the most powerful such attempt being Horkheimer and Adorno's *Dialectic of Enlightenment* [1947], which identifies Auschwitz as the culminating and paradigmatic project of enlightened modernity). There would seem, then, to be something in the very nature of modernity with which the modern world is never completely comfortable, and which can hardly be satisfactorily explained as mere regressive nostalgia (as though the actual restoration of a Catholic feudal past were an even apparently viable option).

The "something" in question may, at least to a considerable degree, be identified with critique, or critical theory, itself. Inseparable from the foundation of modernity, critical theory can nonetheless expect no dependable gratitude from it; for the critical refusal of all repose must call into question the structures of "actually existing" modernity itself—and this is equally true whether one is thinking of structures in the economic sense (the capitalist mode of production) or in the psychological sense (the unified bourgeois ego). Accordingly, the persistence of precritical thinking cannot be understood as mere atavism, nor as ineffectual error to be remedied by a course of reading in Kant, Hegel, and their successors, nor even, exclusively, as expressing a fully serious wish for prescientific modes of knowledge and predemocratic political organization. Precritical thought is rather the "intellectual equivalent" (to invert Plekhanov's famous formulation of the "social equivalent" of the work of art) of *any* status quo. It is a nonirritable condition of mental ease to which *every* mind is highly susceptible, and the inevitable Other with which critique must dialogically contend in any arena however modern. (The real force of *Dialectic of Enlightenment*, as well as of the celebrated opening essay "Cultural Criticism and Society" in Adorno's *Prisms* [1955], depends on understanding that the Frankfurt School critique of modernity—crucially a critique of critique—is thus also an implacable *self*-critique and in that sense thoroughly modern after all.) Critical theory, to use a currently fashionable term, is unswervingly *oppositional*.[9]

The various definitional strands suggested thus far may now be woven, at least provisionally, into a more extensive definition of critical theory. Critical theory is dialectical thought: that is, thought which (in principle) can take nothing less than the totality of the human world or social field for its object. And yet, not only does critical theory regard the latter as a *historical* process, constantly in material flux; it also conceptualizes its own methodology as deeply involved in that flux rather than as a passive intellectual instrument by means of which an unproblematic (as-if-Cartesian) subject extracts absolute knowledge from pregiven objects. Furthermore, by dissolving the reified static categories of the ideological status quo, critical theory constantly shows that things are not what they seem to be *and* that things need not eternally be as they are. Thus it maintains a cutting edge of social subversion even at its most rarefied and abstract.

It is not my present purpose to suggest an inventory of those theories since Kant and Hegel that can be regarded as genuinely critical. Such discriminations will be made ad hoc throughout the current study, but a full-scale catalogue would be far too cumbersome (even leaving aside the difficulties of undialectical genre theory—to be discussed in the following section of this chapter—that a merely *classificatory* approach would entail: critical and precritical elements may well coexist even within the same text, to say nothing of the same "school"). Nonetheless, I do want to discuss briefly three areas of theoretical discourse that seem to me privileged.[10]

Marxism remains the central instance of post-Hegelian critical thought. I admit at once, however, that Marxism is undergoing a certain crisis today, though not precisely in any of the ways that it is currently fashionable to maintain. For example, the neoliberal notion that the totalizing intellectual dynamic of Marxism is somehow obsolete can hardly be taken seriously save as a symptom of how the increasingly pervasive regime of commodification and exchange-value makes it increasingly difficult to resist the empiricist splintering of knowledge into monographic "specialities." Indeed, the ever more thorough penetration of the social field by exchange-value is itself a function of the progressive globalization of capital, which in turn renders a perspective capable of grasping social formations as totalities more urgent, though doubtless

9. Cf. Horkheimer in the founding text of the Frankfurt usage, "Traditional and Critical Theory": "The hostility to theory as such which prevails in contemporary public life is really directed against the transformative activity associated with critical thinking. Opposition starts as soon as theorists fail to limit themselves to verification and classification by means of categories which are as neutral as possible, that is, categories which are indispensable to inherited ways of life"; Horkheimer, *Critical Theory*, trans. Matthew J. O'Connell et al. (New York: Herder and Herder, 1972), 232.

10. By far the most noteworthy absence in what immediately follows is the lack of any discussion of feminism—a theory (or constellation of theories) that presents special problems, with which I grapple in the third section of chapter 3.

also more difficult, than ever. It is important in this context to remember that, as Ernest Mandel and others have frequently pointed out,[11] capitalism today resembles Marx's abstract or "pure" model of the capitalist mode of production much *more closely* than did the capitalism that actually existed during Marx's own lifetime; the increasingly "totalitarian" character of capitalism as a world system paradoxically makes it increasingly difficult to feel or even to theorize either capitalism in general or particular capitalist societies as wholes (just as fish, for instance, presumably do not feel wet and, even if endowed with rational faculties, would have great difficulty in producing the concept of wetness).

Still, the neoliberal objection to totalizing thought looks almost sophisticated compared to the conservative assumption that Marxism is invalidated by the collapse of Eastern European and Soviet Stalinism. The real point here is not simply that authentic critical Marxism has always been antithetical to Stalinism, but also that the long-term incoherence and unworkability of the latter have since the 1920s constituted an object of trenchant Marxist analysis, especially within the Trotskyist tradition (probably the richest variety of Marxist thought insofar as specifically political and political-historical writing is concerned). The actual crisis in Marxism is, however, distantly related to the false problems posed by conservatism and neoliberalism: it is the extremely problematic status of the Marxist theory of *revolution*. Although Marxism has always maintained an internationalist perspective, and although the world market occupies a crucial place in Marx's construction of the capitalist mode of production, the late twentieth century does seem to have produced a perhaps fatal incommensurability between the extent of the globalization (or multinationalization) of capital and the economic primacy of the nation-state assumed by the classic model of socialist revolution. Exactly how the proletariat can seize control of the means of production when the latter are, to an ever-growing extent, organized on a transcontinental basis is a problem yet to be seriously addressed. It may prove solvable, and the current crisis is perhaps best seen as one of Marxism-*Leninism* rather than Marxism proper. Still, if Marxist critical theory is understood as the combination of a science (historical materialism), a philosophy (dialectical materialism), and a politics (scientific socialism), then it must be conceded that the current blockage of the third element is a serious symptom indeed.

At the same time, however—and any paradox here is apparent rather than real—the fact that capitalism has proved much stronger and more resilient than Marx envisaged also renders the method of critical analysis that bears his name more rather than less pertinent. What Marx achieved (primarily in the three volumes of *Capital* [1867–1894]) by recasting the historical dialectics of

11. See, for example, Mandel's introduction to Karl Marx, *Capital*, trans. Ben Fowkes (Harmondsworth: Penguin, 1976), 1:82–83.

Hegel into materialist form—and whether one understands this recasting in Lukácsian terms, as development, or in Althusserian terms, as rupture—was the method needed for genuine critique of the social field as the latter is defined by the production and reproduction of capital. This is not to suggest that *Capital* or subsequent critical analysis in the tradition of that founding text are at all contaminated by the economic determinism or economic reductionism traditionally associated with "vulgar Marxism." But the reproduction of capital does, "in the last instance," establish the arena in which human activity in a capitalist society takes place, in the sense, that is, that the theory capable of authentic critique of capitalist society as a radically heterogeneous whole must be able to construct and account for the motions of capital. This is the real sense of Sartre's famous assertion that Marxism is "the one philosophy of our time which we cannot go beyond,"[12] a maxim too often taken to be a voluntaristic (hence, finally, metaphysical) slogan. But Sartre's point is that Marxism, as the critical analysis of capital and class, cannot be genuinely transcended *during the capitalist era* (though he was certainly well aware that it is possible to repackage a pre-Marxist idea as the hottest new theory "after" Marxism).[13] Accordingly, the currently irresistible expansion, both spatial and temporal, of the regime of capital, with all the intolerable self-contradictions attendant thereto, creates greatly enlarged theoretical terrain for the methods of dialectical-historical-materialist analysis. The unprecedented "cunning" that capital now displays on the global stage renders Marxism more urgent than ever. Indeed, the very impasse confronted by Marxist politics demands creative new elaborations of Marxist critique—a demand by no means unmet.[14]

Second only to Marxism as a variety of critical theory I would name psychoanalysis. The two discourses have, indeed, long been felt to be analogous to one another. Both are materialisms oriented toward praxis; that is, toward theoretically informed political or therapeutic work. Both, as Althusser has suggestively maintained, can be understood as "conflictual sciences," as theoretical discourses of unprecedented critical rigor in areas previously dominated by ideologies more or less in harmony with the rule and general outlook

12. Jean-Paul Sartre, *Search for a Method*, trans. Hazel E. Barnes (New York: Vintage, 1968), xxxiv.

13. "As soon as there will exist *for everyone* a margin of *real* freedom beyond the production of life, Marxism will have lived out its span; a philosophy of freedom will take its place. But we have no means, no intellectual instrument, no concrete experience which allows us to conceive of this freedom or of this philosophy" (ibid., 34; emphasis in original). This suggests, incidentally, one of the fundamental errors in any assimilation of Marxism to religion: whereas the religious believer desires the categories of his or her religion to be of *eternal* relevance, the Marxist desires nothing so much as a state of affairs in which the categories of Marxism will finally be obsolete.

14. In the field of cultural studies, Jameson's immense critique of postmodernism (cited above) seems to me an important instance. Although Jameson, in my view, exaggerates the extent to which postmodernism (in both aesthetic and other terms) can usefully be considered the "cultural dominant" of the current age, his study is nonetheless a pathbreaking attempt to coordinate current cultural production with the dynamics of what Mandel has analyzed as late capitalism.

of the bourgeoisie.[15] Furthermore, there has been a whole series of interesting attempts to integrate psychoanalysis and Marxism with one another, beginning with the pioneering social psychology of Wilhelm Reich and attaining most advanced form mainly in work done within the Frankfurt School or by the Althusserians. Though no particular version of Freudo-Marxism can yet claim to be definitive, the hyphen of the term is, I think, indelibly inscribed on the critical agenda: there is now something inevitably archaic in a Marxism that does not somehow try to enlist Freudian theoretical resources to develop the potentially powerful but extremely embryonic concept of subjectivity implied by both the description of commodity fetishism in *Capital* and the analysis of political representation in *The Eighteenth Brumaire of Louis Bonaparte* (1852). Equally, it is difficult to take with full seriousness any version of psychoanalysis that does not somehow (whether in the manner obliquely suggested by Lacan in *The Four Fundamental Concepts of Psycho-Analysis* [1973] or otherwise) attempt to historicize the Freudian ego and to go beyond Freud's own suggestive but sketchy notions as to how the subject of psychoanalysis is formed with respect to the economic and political relations of modern class society.

What needs to be stressed in the current context, however, is the extent to which the major categories of psychoanalysis—above all the unconscious, of course, but also the drives, the transference, and the Oedipus and castration complexes—are profoundly dialectical. The psyche for Freud, like the social formation for Marx, is a complexly structured whole: neither an assemblage of reified particulars nor a centered unity monocausally determined by some single essence, but a formation governed by the dialectical process of *overdetermination* (to invoke the term invented by Freud but, significantly, appropriated by Althusser in order to theorize the Marxist dialectic itself); that is, by the causative conjuncture of radically heterogeneous factors, few of which are fully conscious and none of which can be inferred from or reduced to any of the others. Furthermore, what might be called the epistemology of psychoanalysis is radically critical and antirealist. The analyst is engaged in a process of interpretation, a reading of signs (dreams, parapraxes, symptoms, and the like); and these signs must finally be understood as raw material out of which, in that dialectical process of knowing which Freud designates the transference, psychic meaning is (in quintessentially post-Kantian fashion) constructed. It is the *de-centering* of the subject—this critical interrogation of the human psyche that forever renders unacceptable the notion of the latter as the unproblematically knowable conscious unity of the older precritical psychology—that remains the enduring "scandal" of psychoanalysis, far more than the much advertised emphasis on sexuality (just as, according to D. H. Lawrence,

15. See Louis Althusser, "On Marx and Freud," trans. Warren Montag, *Rethinking Marxism* 4 (Spring 1991): 17–30.

bourgeois taste in painting can welcome any number of conventionally senti-mentalized nudes but finds the postimpressionist apples of Cézanne to be pro-foundly immoral). Though Freudian vocabulary can certainly be appropri-ated for precritical purposes (for example, a kind of vulgar-Freudian one-dimensional sexual determinism that is the rough equivalent of the eco-nomic determinism of vulgar Marxism), psychoanalysis in full dialectical rigor is a critique of almost unsurpassed richness and subtlety.

Though less important in my view than either Marxism or psychoanalysis, one other area of critical theory deserves attention: that body of work—heav-ily indebted to Nietzsche, mainly of French provenance, and extremely in-fluential during the past three decades—most strongly instanced by Jacques Derrida's analyses of cultural, especially linguistic, sedimentation and by Michel Foucault's investigations of the microtechnologies of power. The common term for such work is, of course, poststructuralism, a designation that is accurate from the viewpoint of intellectual history as narrowly con-structed and is in that way superior to such increasingly meaningless rubrics as "postmodern discourse." A more adequate term for such theory, however, might well be *postdialectical*. In many ways, poststructuralism, at least in its stronger forms, continues the classic dialectical project. Its approach is gener-ally interpretative and antirealist in the post-Kantian way, and is frequently radically historical as well. The latter point is quite obviously true of Foucault (who in disciplinary terms can be considered, as he sometimes considered himself, a historian) but is really no less true of Derrida as well. For Derrida, deconstruction is not an ahistorical property intrinsic to writing itself (though Paul de Man's domesticated American version of deconstruction does come close to this position). Rather, it is a critical operation enabled by a certain moment in the *history* of writing, a moment defined by such diverse develop-ments as the rise of cybernetic technology and the growing awareness by Western of non-Western cultures.[16] Indeed, in some cases the basic strategy of *post*structuralism can be understood as the restoration of a dialectical (and temporal) dimension to the increasingly claustrophobic static structures of classical or "high" structuralism: witness, paradigmatically, Derrida's critique of the Saussurian sign, a critique that in many ways parallels Bakhtin's (or Volosinov's) explicitly dialectical and dialogic "deconstruction" of structural-ist linguistics.

If, however, this body of thought must be considered postdialectical rather than dialectical proper, it is not only because of the strategic distance that fig-ures like Foucault and Derrida have usually maintained from Marx and Freud (and even leaving aside that, in the particular French intellectual for-mation relevant here, the names of Marx and Freud have often served as code

16. See, for example, the opening pages of Jacques Derrida, *Of Grammatology*, trans. Gayatri Chakravorty Spivak (Baltimore: Johns Hopkins University Press, 1976).

words for Althusser and Lacan). More important, though not unrelated, is the suspicion that virtually all versions of poststructuralism have cast on the indispensable dialectical category of totality. This is the point of contact between poststructuralism and neoliberalism (or, sometimes, neoconservatism), a contact grotesquely illustrated in, for example, the editorial history of *Tel Quel*.[17] Still, it must be stressed that much poststructuralism has remained faithful to the principle of *relationality*, which is a crucial component of totality as dialectically understood, and which is partly detachable from the issue of an overdeterminationist dynamic that would guarantee the integrity of totality as such. It should also be stressed that, in general, the attitude toward totality of thinkers like Foucault and Derrida is a great deal more complex than the vulgar slogans about "wars on totality" fashionable in much weaker varieties of poststructuralism. It is possible to maintain irreducible reservations about even the most rigorous versions of contemporary postdialectical thought while nonetheless appreciating the intellectual creativity and usefulness of the latter.

Such, then, is my understanding of critical theory—not exhaustive, of course (such an attempt would be preposterous), but sufficient to provide some conceptual mapping for the study that lies ahead. In what follows I shall be concerned with critical theory mainly in its cultural and, still more, its literary contexts. But any Procrustean disciplinary division is of course profoundly contrary to the spirit of critical theory itself.

Science Fiction

It is symptomatic of the complexity of science fiction as a generic category that critical discussion of it tends to devote considerable attention to the problem of definition—much more so than is the case with such superficially analogous genres as mystery fiction or romance, and perhaps even more than with such larger categories as epic or the novel itself. No definitional consensus exists. There are narrow and broad definitions, eulogistic and dyslogistic definitions, definitions that position science fiction in a variety of ways with regard to its customary generic Others (notably fantasy, on the one hand, and "mainstream" or realistic fiction on the other) and, finally, antidefinitions that proclaim the problem of definition to be insoluble. Indeed, not only the question of definition proper but even the looser matter of *description*—of deciding, even in the most rough-and-ready way, approximately which texts are to be

17. The "negative dialectic" of Adorno is a rather different matter. Adorno is not so much epistemologically suspicious of totality as he is hostile to the social phenomenon of total administration, which he sometimes silently conflates with totality as a Marxist and Lukácsian category; see Carl Freedman and Neil Lazarus, "The Mandarin Marxism of Theodor Adorno," *Rethinking Marxism* 1 (Winter 1988): 85–111.

designated by the rubric of science fiction — is a matter of widespread disagreement. We may begin the definitional task by considering the two poles of opinion in the matter of simple description.

Science fiction can be construed very strictly to refer only to that body of work in, or that grows directly out of, the American pulp tradition established in 1926 when Hugo Gernsback founded *Amazing Stories*. This is, of course, an extremely narrow construction of science fiction, one that excludes even such close precursors as Mary Shelley, Poe, Verne, and H. G. Wells (works by the latter three were reprinted by Gernsback in his inaugural issue), not to mention contemporary British work by writers like Stapledon, C. S. Lewis, and Aldous Huxley, as well as the rich Russian and East European traditions. Though obviously deflationary from the viewpoint of anyone, like myself, who wishes to make large literary and theoretical claims for the genre, the strict construction of science fiction does have two merits. One is popular currency. For the general public (as well as for the commercial marketing system employed by publishers, bookshops, and the vendors of the newer electronic media), the name of science fiction has always suggested the pulp tradition, today largely as the latter has been transmogrified into such filmic and televisional equivalents of pulp as *Stars Wars* (1977–onward) and *Star Trek* (1966–onward). The other merit, not unrelated to the first, is philological correctness. It is certainly true that the term, originally in the more cumbersome form of "scientifiction" and then as "science fiction," was invented in the pulps (by Gernsback himself, according to some accounts), and that any wider use involves deliberate semantic change. Mary Shelley never heard the expression; Wells very likely never heard it; and even Lewis, who had some interest in and sympathy for the American magazines, hardly belonged to the world of pulp, instead taking his inspiration mainly from Stapledon and Wells directly (as well as from the entire tradition of Christian heroic and fantastic literature from *Beowulf* [c. 750] onward). Accordingly, whatever critics like myself may propose, it seems unlikely that the narrow usage will ever completely vanish.

Yet it suffers not only from general critical inutility but from immense self-contradiction: the list of authors who have directly and self-consciously succeeded Gernsbackian pulp includes (to pick only a small fraction of the names that could be adduced) Americans like Alfred Bester, Theodore Sturgeon, Walter M. Miller, Philip K. Dick, Ursula Le Guin, Alice Sheldon, Samuel Delany, Joanna Russ, Joe Haldeman, Thomas Disch, Norman Spinrad, Kate Wilhelm, Vonda McIntyre, and William Gibson, and probably also such British figures as Brian Aldiss, J. G. Ballard, and Michael Moorcock. Accordingly — and unless science fiction is construed not only narrowly but defamatorily, so that by definition only bad fiction can bear the label — the body of work suggested by such names must be science fiction even by the strictest philological standards. But it is ludicrous to consider writers of such caliber

as simply and solely the literary sons and daughters of Hugo Gernsback and
E. E. "Doc" Smith, as we are logically obliged to do if science fiction is understood purely in terms of pulp. Mighty oaks may grow from tiny acorns, but
novels like Le Guin's *The Dispossessed* (1974) or Delany's *Stars in My Pocket
Like Grains of Sand* (1984) cannot be understood as merely the fulfillment of
a promise implicit in Gernsback's *Ralph 124C 41+* (1911) or Doc Smith's *The
Skylark of Space* (1928). There is here something of an analogy with the history
of novel criticism in general. The latter was able to attain some real seriousness and rigor when it became evident, in the light of the major achievements
of the nineteenth-century novel, that the form had a vital lineage—particularly, as Lukács and others pointed out, in epic itself[18]—that far transcended
the relatively crude Renaissance prose narratives that supplied the name. Similarly, if the likes of Le Guin and Delany write science fiction, as they incon-
testably do, then it is clear that current Anglo-American science fiction draws
on far more than the pulp tradition that constitutes *one* of its filiations; in that
case it may well be both useful and legitimate to employ the term in a much
wider sense than mere philology would allow.

Accordingly, we may consider a construction of science fiction as broad as
the pulp-centered construction is narrow. The term can be taken to include—
to pick just a few examples—the whole tradition of arealistic travel literature
from Lucian to Rabelais, Cyrano, and beyond; the classic utopian line from
More onward; a modernist and postmodernist tradition of work not actually
marketed as science fiction, from Kafka and even Joyce to Samuel Beckett and
Thomas Pynchon; and even such world-class epic poets as Dante and Milton.
The latter two examples are especially worth pondering for a moment, not
least because of their prestige value (a factor that will not be dismissed by anyone who has struggled to obtain academic recognition for science fiction).
The point is not simply that, by the contemporary standards of rationality,
Dante offers plausible scientific speculation as to the geography of hell in relation to that of earth (and purgatory), and that Milton does the same with regard to the substance of which angels are supposed to be made. On this level,
indeed, one might even argue that Dante and Milton, in the active interest
they took in the scientific developments of their own times and places, are
considerably more akin to Isaac Asimov and Arthur C. Clarke than to Words-
worth and T. S. Eliot. The larger point, however, is that many of the major literary values for which science fiction is generally read are very much at work
in Dante's and Milton's efforts to take the reader far beyond the boundaries of
his or her own mundane environment, into strange, awe-inspiring realms
thought to be in fact unknown, or at least largely unknown, but not in principle unknowable. It is in this sense of creating rich, complex, but not ultimately

18. See especially Georg Lukács, *The Theory of the Novel*, trans. Anna Bostock (Cambridge,
Mass.: MIT Press, 1971).

fantastic alternative worlds that Dante and Milton can be said to write science fiction. The matter can be put the other way around, as it were, by suggesting that if one were to seek, in older literature, qualities similar to those found in the multisecular historic sweep of Asimov's *Foundation* (1951–1953) series or the cosmic awe at the conclusion of Clarke's *Childhood's End* (1954), one would probably do far better to go to Dante and Milton than to Romantic or post-Romantic verse, or to the realistic novel. It would seem, then, justifiable to accept the classification of *Paradise Lost* (1667) and *Inferno* (c. 1315) as science fiction.

It would not, however, be difficult to make similar arguments with regard to a great many other texts that do not arrive in the bookshop with the rubric of "science fiction" printed on the dust jackets or back covers. The very ease with which the broadest construction of science fiction can be justified may itself arouse suspicion. As we argue that the qualities that govern texts universally agreed to be science fiction can be found to govern other texts as well, it may be difficult to see just where the argument will stop. It may even begin to appear that ultimately nearly *all* fiction—perhaps even including realism itself—will be found to be science fiction. Does not that conclusion preclude success in defining science fiction as a recognizable *kind* of fiction? In fact, I do believe that all fiction is, in a sense, science fiction. It is even salutary, I think, sometimes to put the matter in more deliberately provocative, paradoxical form, and to maintain that fiction is a subcategory of science fiction rather than the other way around. Nonetheless, the capacity of such formulations to illuminate depends upon a more conceptually specific notion of science fiction than we have suggested thus far. Merely descriptive concepts have proved adequate to expanding the term beyond the narrow pulp-centered notion; having failed to *limit* the category of science fiction by descriptive means, however, we are now in urgent need of a genuinely critical, analytic, definitional principle.

By far the most helpful such principle yet suggested is that of Darko Suvin. Science fiction, he defines, is "a literary genre whose necessary and sufficient conditions are the presence and interaction of estrangement and cognition, and whose main formal device is an imaginative framework alternative to the author's empirical environment" (emphasis deleted). He goes on to add that estrangement "differentiates [science fiction] from the 'realistic' literary mainstream," while cognition differentiates it from myth, the folk tale, and fantasy.[19] In this understanding, then—though Suvin does not put the matter in exactly this way—science fiction is determined by the *dialectic* between estrangement and cognition. The first term refers to the creation of an alternative fictional world that, by refusing to take our mundane environment for

    19. Darko Suvin, *Metamorphoses of Science Fiction* (New Haven: Yale University Press, 1979), 7–8.

granted, implicitly or explicitly performs an estranging critical interrogation of the latter. But the *critical* character of the interrogation is guaranteed by the operation of cognition, which enables the science-fictional text to account rationally for its imagined world and for the connections as well as the disconnections of the latter to our own empirical world. If the dialectic is flattened out to mere cognition, then the result is "realistic" or mundane fiction, which can cognitively account for its imaginings but performs no estrangement; if the dialectic is flattened out to mere estrangement (or, it might be argued, pseudo-estrangement), then the result is fantasy, which estranges, or appears to estrange, but in an irrationalist, theoretically illegitimate way.

This definition seems to me not only fundamentally sound but indispensable. Yet in Suvin's own formulations the concept of science fiction as the fiction of cognitive estrangement involves at least two serious problems—both of which, however, may well be mere inadvertencies and both of which can in any case be solved *within* the basic Suvinian problematic (which can itself thus be enriched).

The first problem is that the category of cognition appears to commit the literary critic to making generic distinctions on the basis of matters far removed from literature and genre. The awkwardness does not transpire so long as we are thinking, say, of Heinlein's *The Man Who Sold the Moon* (1950) as paradigmatic of (cognitive) science fiction and Tolkien's *The Lord of the Rings* (1954–1955) as paradigmatic of (noncognitive) fantasy. The rational connections that link D. D. Harriman's world to our own are clear and direct, while the evident absence of any such connections between our world and that of the hobbits and orcs is equally clear. Yet there is a great deal of literature— some of it commonly labeled science fiction, some commonly labeled fantasy, and some, significantly, labeled both—that is based neither on the careful, straightforward extrapolation of Heinlein's novella nor on the sharp break with known empirical reality of Tolkien's trilogy. Joanna Russ's *The Female Man* (1975) is considered science fiction, but few physicists would unhesitatingly affirm that the notion of parallel universes on which Russ's novel depends is a valid cognitive option. Must we wait for a scientific consensus on the matter before deciding whether the text is science fiction or fantasy? H. P. Lovecraft has been described both as a science-fiction writer and as a writer of horror fantasy. Do "The Shadow over Innsmouth" (1936) and "The Dunwich Horror" (1939) earn the title of science fiction because their monstrosities have their origin not in the admitted supernatural but in vulgar pseudo-Darwinian notions of racial degeneration? What of C. S. Lewis's *Out of the Silent Planet* (1938) and the following two novels in the Ransom trilogy? If theology is a science (if, to put it bluntly, Christianity is true) then the powerful estrangements produced by Ransom's adventures on Mars are wholly cognitive; if religious dogma, however, is in fact as precritical as most critical theorists would insist, then Lewis's epistemology is not really cognitive at all.

All these examples suggest that cognition proper is *not*, in the strictest terms, exactly the quality that defines science fiction. What is rather at stake is what we might term (following a familiar Barthesian precedent) the *cognition effect*. The crucial issue for generic discrimination is not any epistemological judgment external to the text itself on the rationality or irrationality of the latter's imaginings, but rather (as some of Suvin's language does, in fact, imply, but never makes entirely clear) the attitude *of the text itself* to the kind of estrangements being performed. Comparison between Lewis and Tolkien is especially illuminating in this context, because both trilogies are concerned with conveying almost precisely similar orthodox Christian values. *The Lord of the Rings* is understood as fantasy and *Out of the Silent Planet* and its sequels as science fiction: not because it would necessarily be less rational to believe in hobbits and orcs than in planetary angels and Merlin redivivus, but because of the formal stances adopted by the texts themselves. Tolkien's trilogy proclaims in its very letter a noncognitive disjunction from the mundane world (the kind of disjunction in fact suggested by Tolkien's own central critical category of literary production as "sub-creation"),[20] while Lewis's trilogy considers that principles it regards as cognitively valid cannot exclude events like the action fictionally portrayed from occurring within the author's actual environment. Lewis, accordingly, produces a cognition effect, while Tolkien quite deliberately does not.

Unless the distinction between cognition and cognition effect is kept steadily in view, the definition of science fiction as cognitive estrangement can lead to patent absurdities. For example, one of Asimov's science-fiction mystery stories ("The Dying Night," originally published in 1956) depends for its plot resolution on the assumption that Mercury has a "captured" rotation; that is, that it turns on its axis at precisely the same rate that it revolves around the sun, and therefore that it contains areas where night is permanent. This assumption was faithful to common astronomical wisdom at the time of the story's composition, but was disproved in 1965; the planet, evidently, does rotate much more rapidly than it revolves, and all parts of it are at one time or another exposed to sunlight. In an afterword to one reprinting of the story, Asimov humorously complained, "I wish astronomers would get these things right to begin with," and he refused "to change the story to suit *their* whims" (emphasis in original).[21] Fortunately, the "whims" of astronomers have nothing to do with the cognition effect of the story (by an author, indeed, who is unusually consistent and insistent in producing the cognition effect), and there is no question of the story's suddenly being reclassified as fantasy nine years after its initial appearance. Once the formal distinction is clear, however, between cognition and cognition effect, we should not exaggerate its practical significance: the

20. See J. R. R. Tolkien, "On Fairy-Stories," in *Essays Presented to Charles Williams*, ed. C. S. Lewis (London: Oxford, 1947).
21. Isaac Asimov, *The Best of Isaac Asimov* (London: Sphere Books, 1973), 274.

readiest means of producing a cognition effect is precisely through cognition itself; that is, through rationality as the latter is understood from a critical point of view. Science fiction of Lewis's or Lovecraft's sort remains relatively atypical of the genre, while the solidity of the cognition effect in Russ or Asimov is by no means unrelated to the fact that Russ's device *may* be cognitively legitimate, while Asimov's once *was*. Science fiction is, overwhelmingly though not necessarily, a genuinely cognitive literature.

The second difficulty with defining science fiction as the literature of cognitive estrangement is rather more complex; it may be approached by noting that, taken literally, Suvin's definition suffers from an immense sacrifice of descriptive to eulogistic force. It is one thing to transcend philology by expanding the concept of science fiction far beyond the largely forgettable pulp texts for which the term was originally invented, and even beyond the texts written in direct succession to pulp. But cognitive estrangement as a definitional principle seems not merely to transcend but to overturn both philology and common usage, largely denying the title of science fiction to most of the pulp tradition while granting it to works produced very far from the influence of the latter. I do not think it can be fruitfully maintained that many very complex or interesting cognitive estrangements are produced in Doc Smith's Skylark series, or in the *Star Wars* films, or in most of that vast galaxy of television programs, films, stories, and novels designated *Star Trek*. Can we really accept a definition by the logic of which such work is not science fiction at all but the plays of Brecht—to take the obvious instance—are? It is true, of course, that for Brecht historical materialism is not only cognitive but scientific in the strongest sense, and Marx just as much the founder of a science as Galileo. Nor is there necessarily any reason (and here an old Kantian problem resurfaces) why the natural sciences should be cognitively privileged over the human sciences—even leaving aside that much of the science fiction that seems most explicitly wedded to the so-called hard sciences (for example, much of Heinlein) often turns out, upon inspection, to involve not science at all but engineering. Nonetheless, Suvin does, in fact, seem to find Brecht a difficult case: well aware of the latter's status as the preeminent theorist and practitioner of literary estrangement *(Verfremdung)*, he remarks that estrangement is "used by Brecht in a different way, within a still predominantly 'realistic' context" *(Metamorphoses* 7). The assertion is surely false, for Brecht is in no sense a literary realist, not even allowing for the quotation marks—as Lukács angrily charged and as Brecht himself proudly admitted.[22] In order to

22. The terminological situation here is complicated, since Brecht, when arguing *against* Lukács, did occasionally call himself a realist. He used the term tactically, however, and meant it not in any literary or generic sense but in the sense of one concerned with reality—a concern, in Brecht's view, that necessitated a sharp break with the literary realism praised and prescribed by Lukács. For a useful summary of the Brecht-Lukács controversy, see Henri Arvon, *Marxist Esthetics*, trans. Helen Lane (Ithaca: Cornell University Press, 1973), 100–112. Some of the relevant documents in the controversy are collected, along with some related material and a retrospective

clarify the issues at stake here, it is necessary to clarify the dynamics of genre criticism itself.[23]

Genre has often been considered a suspect category because of the static, merely classificatory intellectual framework that it seems to imply: the various genres are understood as a row of so many pigeonholes, and each literary text is expected to fit more or less unproblematically into one of them (allowing, of course, for the inevitable ambiguous or borderline cases). But it is possible to conceptualize genre in a radically different and thoroughly dialectical way. In this understanding, a genre is not a classification but an element or, better still, a *tendency* that, in combination with other relatively autonomous generic elements or tendencies, is active to a greater or lesser degree within a literary text that is itself understood as a complexly structured totality. In other words: a text is not filed under a generic category; instead, a generic tendency is something that happens within a text.

It is a priori likely that most texts display the activity of numerous different genres, and that few or no texts can be adequately described in terms of one genre alone. Genre in this sense is analogous to the Marxist concept of the mode of production as the latter has gained new explanatory force by being contrasted, in the Althusserian vocabulary, with the category of social forma-tion—a term that is preferred to the more familiar notion of society, because the latter connotes a relatively homogeneous unity, whereas the former is meant to suggest an overdetermined combination of *different* modes of pro-duction at work in the same place and during the same time. Though it is thus impossible simply to equate a given social formation with a given mode of pro-duction, it is nonetheless legitimate to affirm that (for instance) the United States "is" capitalist, so long as we understand that the copulative signifies not true equation or identity but rather conveys that, of the various and relatively autonomous modes of production active within the U.S. social formation, capitalism enjoys a position of *dominance*. In the same way, the dialectical re-thinking of genre does not in the least preclude generic discrimination. We may validly describe a particular text as science fiction if we understand the formulation to mean that cognitive estrangement is the dominant generic ten-dency within the overdetermined textual whole.

Accordingly, there is probably no text that is a perfect and pure embodi-ment of science fiction (no text, that is to say, in which science fiction is the

analysis by Fredric Jameson, in *Aesthetics and Politics*, ed. Ronald Taylor (London: New Left Books, 1977).

23. In the following discussion of genre I am indebted to Fredric Jameson, *The Political Un-conscious* (Ithaca: Cornell University Press, 1981), esp. 103–150, and equally to Etienne Balibar, "The Basic Concepts of Historical Materialism," in *Reading Capital*, by Louis Althusser and Etienne Balibar, trans. Ben Brewster (London: Verso, 1979), 201–308. It is something of a mystery why Balibar's pathbreaking reconceptualization of the crucial Marxist category of mode of pro-duction (surely one of the most original, fruitful innovations in critical theory during the past few decades) has never, in my view, received quite the celebrity that it deserves.

only generic tendency operative) but also no text in which the science-fiction tendency is altogether absent. Indeed, it might be argued that this tendency is the precondition for the constitution of fictionality—and even of representation—itself. For the construction of an alternative world is the very definition of fiction: owing to the character of representation as a nontransparent process that necessarily involves not only similarity but *difference* between representation and the "referent" of the latter, an irreducible degree of alterity and estrangement is bound to obtain even in the case of the most "realistic" fiction imaginable. The appearance of transparency in that paradigmatic realist Balzac has been famously exposed as an illusion;[24] nonetheless, it is important to understand the operation of alterity in realism not as the failure of the latter, but as the sign of the estranging tendency of science fiction that supplies (if secretly) some of the power of great realistic fiction.[25] Furthermore, just as some degree of alterity and hence estrangement is fundamental to all fiction, finally including realism itself, so the same is true (but here the limit case is fantasy) of that other dialectical half of the science-fiction tendency: cognition. The latter is after all an unavoidable operation of the human mind (however precritical, and even if clinically schizophrenic) and must exercise a determinant presence for literary production to take place at all. Even in *The Lord of the Rings*—to consider again what is perhaps the most thoroughgoing fantasy we possess, by an author who stands to fantasy rather as Balzac stands to realism—cognition is quite strongly and overtly operative on at least one level: namely that of the moral and theological values that the text is concerned to enforce.[26]

It is, then, in this very special sense that the apparently wild assertions that all fiction is science fiction and even that the latter is a wider term than the former may be justified: cognition and estrangement, which together

24. The reference, of course, is to Roland Barthes, *S/Z*, trans. Richard Miller (New York: Hill and Wang, 1974).

25. Consider the following Samuel Delany anecdote, concisely summarized by Paul K. Alkon: "A historian gradually stopped reading anything but science fiction in his spare time. Finally he began to doubt that he could ever again read anything else. Worried, he picked up an old favorite, *Pride and Prejudice*, to see what might happen. To his relief, he enjoyed it more than ever. But he saw it in a different way: whereas before he appreciated Austen for her masterful portraits of human nature acting as it might in the real world, now, as he read he asked himself what kind of world must be postulated in order for the events of her story to have happened as she relates them. The answer, somewhat to his surprise as an expert in early nineteenth-century history, was that for the tale of Elizabeth and Darcy to unfold as it does in *Pride and Prejudice* one must assume a world quite different from that in which Jane Austen actually lived"; Alkon, "*Gulliver* and the Origins of Science Fiction," in *The Genres of "Gulliver's Travels,"* ed. Frederik N. Smith (Newark: University of Delaware Press, 1990), 163. In my terms, what happened to Delany's friend is that, trained by reading a great deal of literature in which science fiction was the dominant generic tendency, he was able to appreciate its presence in a text where it played a subordinate but significant role. The relation of science fiction to realism will be discussed further in the third section of chapter 2.

26. Cf. C. S. Lewis, who maintains that, while in *The Lord of the Rings* "the direct debt . . . which every author must owe to the actual universe is here deliberately reduced to the minimum," it is nonetheless true that "as for escapism, what we chiefly escape is the illusions of our ordinary life"; Lewis, *On Stories*, ed. Walter Hooper (New York: Harcourt, 1982), 84–85.

constitute the generic tendency of science fiction, are not only actually present in all fiction, but are structurally crucial to the possibility of fiction and even of representation in the first place. Yet in more routine usage, the term of science fiction ought, as I have maintained above, to be reserved for those texts in which cognitive estrangement is not only present but dominant. And it is with this dialectical understanding of genre that we may now reconsider the apparently difficult cases of Brecht, on the one hand, and *Star Wars* on the other.

Brecht is indeed an author in whose work the science-fiction tendency is often not only strong but dominant. Masterpieces like *Mother Courage* (1941) and *The Good Person of Szechwan* (1943) are essentially thought experiments that may well recall that most famous slogan of pulp science fiction during the Campbellian "Golden Age" of the 1940s and 1950s: the idea as hero. (Brecht might well have added, recasting one of his own most famous maxims: unhappy is the fiction or drama that *needs* heroes beyond ideas.) Only tenuously or hardly at all anchored in their nominal settings of seventeenth-century Germany or twentieth-century China, these works evoke arealistic loci alternative to the author's mundane environment in order to enforce not only cognitive but critical Marxian estrangements of Western capitalist society with regard to such fundamental issues as war, love, family, commerce, and morality. What distinguishes Brechtian estrangement from the estrangements more familiar in texts explicitly marketed as science fiction is not that Brecht is more closely allied to literary realism but simply that he is relatively uninterested in those specifically *technological* versions of estrangement that have traditionally figured (though to a decreasing degree since the 1960s) in science fiction that derives directly from the pulp line. Conversely, *Star Wars* (and its sequels) might be understood as activating the science-fiction tendency only weakly and fitfully in most regards—in cognitive terms, the diachronic sequence from John W. Campbell, or even Doc Smith, to George Lucas is a narrative of regression—but with a spectacular hypertrophy of the specifically *visual* dimension associated with science-fictional tales of space travel. (Given the centrality of the visual dimension to film as a medium, it might even be argued that this one factor establishes the generic dominance of science fiction in the filmic text.)[27] Both Brecht and Lucas, then, might be described as producers of science fiction, but in quite different ways, which a dialectical generic approach allows us to specify with some precision.

27. Cf. John Rieder, "Embracing the Alien: Science Fiction in Mass Culture," *Science-Fiction Studies* 9 (March 1982): 26–37. Rieder persuasively argues that the *Star Wars* films are superior to most other blockbuster Hollywood science-fictional films of the recent past in the *totalizing* (as opposed to epiphanic) role that visual and auditory special effects play—a role, he maintains, that enables the special effects to convey considerable utopian energy despite the banality of the narrative line. For a somewhat different analysis of special effects in science-fiction film, see Carl Freedman, "Kubrick's *2001* and the Possibility of a Science-Fiction Cinema," *Science-Fiction Studies* 25 (July 1998): 300–318.

It is this basically Suvinian definition of science fiction as the fiction of cognitive estrangement—but modified so as to emphasize the dialectical character of genre and the centrality of the cognition effect—that will enable further such discriminations to be made throughout the remainder of this essay. Having thus defined, at least provisionally, my two central categories of concern, I will now, in the following and necessarily much longer chapter, articulate the two categories together. My aim is not to read science fiction "in the light of" critical theory (itself a suspiciously positivistic metaphor), but to articulate certain *structural* affinities between the two terms. Although critically informed readings of particular science-fictional texts will inevitably play a part in the following chapters (especially chapter 3), my chief intent is to show that the conjunction of critical theory and science fiction is not fortuitous but fundamental.

2. Articulations

Genre, Theory, and Phases of Canon-Formation

The question of the canon is one of the liveliest and most hotly debated in literary studies today, and the—at best—marginal position that science fiction occupies with regard to the most widely influential canons of literary value makes explicit consideration of canon-formation urgent. It is not difficult to understand why challenges to the received canon and even critical investigations into the mechanics of canon-formation have provoked precritical ire. John Guillory, one of the most acute theorists of canonization, has pointed out that despite the social decline of aristocracy, "the canon has retained its self-image as an aristocracy of texts," and that "the pure authority of great literature may be the only image of pure authority we have."[1] He further notes: "The canon participates centrally in the establishment of consensus as the embodiment of a collective valuation. Hence it is in the interest of canonical reformations to erase the conflictual prehistory of canon-formation or to represent such history as the narrative of error" (358). The quasi-reverence with which the canon is widely regarded in conservative and precritical literary ideologies can be further elucidated by giving Guillory's thesis a more specifically institutional inflection. For the whole position of the humanities in the modern—especially the modern American—university cannot be understood apart from the invidious position that humanities departments occupy with relation to the much better funded and more publicly respected departments that specialize in the natural sciences. The latter owe their prestige not only to industrial and military utility but also to the image of solidity that they project, to the objective public knowledge that scientific investigation is widely supposed to attain. Literary studies can display nothing precisely comparable, because none of its more or less rigorous methods—from Germanic

1. John Guillory, "The Ideology of Canon-Formation: T. S. Eliot and Cleanth Brooks," in *Canons*, ed. Robert von Hallberg (Chicago: University of Chicago Press, 1984), 339.

philology and positivistic literary history to New Criticism and even some varieties of critical theory itself—has won endorsement or respect comparable to
that enjoyed by natural science. In this situation, the canon, as an "aristocracy
of texts" projecting an "image of pure authority" may well seem the most solid
thing that literary studies has to offer. There is a real sense, then, in which the
question of the canon must be at the heart of any critical literary investigation.

Much conservative ideology would forbid the question from even being
asked. Nonetheless, sufficient critical energy has been directed to this matter
during the recent past that not only have we witnessed a great deal of reform-
ist tinkering with and revision of the canon, but—more important—we also
possess a considerable body of work that radically problematizes canon-
formation itself. Writers like Guillory, Paul Lauter, Herbert Lindenberger,
Richard Ohmann, and Lillian Robinson (among others)[2] have investigated
various ways in which canonization does not simply respond to the degree of
"value" immanent in texts but rather refracts (if not necessarily reflects) a wide
variety of objective interests—personal and, more especially, social—dependent upon the specificities of particular times and places. In other words, genuinely critical analysis of the canon does not simply display the "unfair" exclusion of certain texts maintained to be "great" according to the same criteria by
which other texts are included. Nor does it, in a weird parody of affirmative
action, lobby for the inclusion of texts in order to "represent" the various
groups responsible for the production of the texts. Instead, it interrogates the
presuppositions implicitly governing the criteria and mechanisms of canon-
formation itself. What is most radically at stake is not the empirical content of
any particular canon but the *form* of canonization. As with much else in current critical theory, the founding insight of rigorous canon critique was originally voiced (with characteristic hyperbole) by Nietzsche: "As in the case of
other wars, so in that of the aesthetic wars which artists provoke with their
works and their apologias for them the outcome is, unhappily, decided in the
end by power and not by reason. All the world now accepts it as a historical
fact that Gluck was in the right in his struggle with Piccini: in any event he
won; power was on his side" (emphasis in original).[3] It seems to me, however,
that what might thus be designated neo-Nietzschean canon critique, although
it has grasped that the structure of canon-formation is a more fundamental
issue than the content of specific canons, has not been sufficiently sensitive to

2. See, for example, Guillory, "Ideology," and perhaps a few other pieces from the same gath-
ering; most of Paul Lauter's *Canons and Contexts* (New York: Oxford University Press, 1991);
chaps. 1, 2, 6, and 7 of Herbert Lindenberger's *The History in Literature* (New York: Columbia
University Press, 1990); chaps. 4 and 5 of Richard Ohmann's *Politics of Letters* (Middletown: Wesleyan University Press, 1987); and Lillian Robinson's "Treason Our Text: Feminist Challenges to
the Literary Canon," in *The New Feminist Criticism*, ed. Elaine Showalter (New York: Pantheon,
1985), 105–121. Many other titles could easily be cited, but this selection should give an adequate
idea of the *kind* of canon theory to which I am indebted and upon which I wish to expand.

3. Friedrich Nietzsche, *Human, All Too Human*, trans. R. J. Hollingdale (Cambridge: Cambridge University Press, 1986), 347–348; translation modified.

the canonical importance of the structure—particularly the *generic* structure—of individual texts themselves. For genre is not in the least a politically innocent category, and if—as is now fairly widely accepted—the ideology of a text inheres at least as much in its form as its manifest content, then genre must surely be reckoned at least as important a factor for canonization as, say, the stated "moral" of a poem or the kind of life experience that ultimately provides the raw material for an autobiographical novel. In any case, because my concern here is partly with a particular genre—science fiction—the problem of the canon with regard to the latter cannot be considered apart from the relation between canon-formation and genre.

We can approach this matter by recalling that the process of reading itself, though by no means always critical, is inevitably theoretical; no better illustration of this point can be cited than the frequently noticed tendency of any school of reading (critical or precritical) to privilege, whether implicitly or explicitly, a particular area of the literary terrain. Two widely diverse examples may be noted. Lukácsian criticism, which is certainly a critical theory, is overwhelmingly oriented toward the novel of classical realism. Balzac and Tolstoy provide Lukács with his essential models, and, despite the immense range of his empirical erudition, he seldom strays far from them in any conceptual sense. His intense admiration for Thomas Mann—one of the most consistent enthusiasms of Lukács's very long career—is based on his ability to theoretically construct Mann as the authentic successor of the nineteenth-century realists. Conversely, literary modernism seldom figures in his work save as an object of denunciation or (as with his late recognition of Brecht) an object assimilable to the basic principles of realism after all. Lyric poetry scarcely even exists for Lukács.

But lyric poetry (to take our second example), especially the lyric poetry of T. S. Eliot and his seventeenth-century precursors, is the central genre for American New Criticism, a school of considerable technical sophistication but one whose conceptual orientation is predominantly precritical. (There is some irony here, as the more philosophically schooled of the New Critics were directly indebted to Kant himself. But they tended to understand Kantian aesthetic contemplation as the empiricist apprehension of works existing on a Wimsattian "objective" level, rather than as constructive or *radically* interpretative in character.) Engaged in working out pedagogically convenient styles of "close reading" on short and highly wrought poetic artifacts, the New Critics have far less to say about prose fiction (Cleanth Brooks's work on Faulkner is exceptional and not, indeed, a particularly New Critical project), and they would be hopelessly at sea with a work like *Finnegans Wake* (1939), not to mention, say, Trotsky's *History of the Russian Revolution* (1932–33).

There is, of course, a major difference between Lukács and the New Critics. Genuinely critical in the sense defined in the preceding chapter, Lukács knows what he is doing with clear self-consciousness. He is constructing a theory

of realism for determinate ends both philosophical (the justification of orthodox Marxism as Lukács understands the latter to be the heir of the classical
metaphysical line from Aristotle to Hegel) and political (the struggle against
fascism). The New Critics, by contrast, seem to imagine, though doubtless
with some degree of neo-Agrarian *mauvaise foi*, that they are simply and inno-
cently "reading." But it is noteworthy how both posit a privileged generic
space, and it could readily be shown how equivalent generic spaces are assumed or stated by other schools as well: organicist English fiction, especially
that of Lawrence, by the *Scrutiny* school; symbolist poetry like Mallarmé's by
Derridean deconstruction; high modernist drama and fiction by the Frankfurt
School and by Althusserian Marxism; the Bible and the Prophetic Books of
Blake (as well as much Shakespearean and Spenserian romance) by the myth
criticism of Northrop Frye; Romantic and neo-Romantic poetry by the influence criticism of Harold Bloom; and so forth. Science fiction, it must be
noted, has been overtly privileged by relatively few influential readers.

What this pattern of generic privileging suggests, I think, is not simply the
importance of genre to the reading of literature but a way in which genre
must be thought as a more fundamental category than literature itself. Genre
is a substantive property of discourse and its context, a tendential mode
whereby signifying practices are organized. Literature, by contrast (understanding the term in any sense more specific than that of all written documents whatever) is a formally arbitrary and socially determinate category. Literature, in other words, is a wholly *functional* term.[4] Those works are
literature that are designated literature by the minority of readers who, in a
given time and place, possess the social and institutional *power* (as Nietzsche
would say) that enables their views on the matter to prevail. In our present
historical situation, these authoritative readers include academic critics and
teachers, publishing executives, librarians, editors of journals and reviews,
and others. Such agents, acting in a determinate social context and toward
determinate (if often unconscious) ends, decide that a certain relatively small
number of texts, out of the much vaster number that actually exist, shall be
considered—that is, shall be canonized—as literature. They judge, for instance, that the poems, essays, and some of the letters written by Wallace Stevens are literature, while the insurance policies and office memoranda also
written by him are not. But, of course, such judgments vary greatly in various
historical situations, as the most cursory acquaintance with literary history reveals. *Paradise Lost* (1667), to be sure, was literature on the day of its first publication and remains so today. In 1776, on the other hand, Adam Smith's *The
Wealth of Nations* was literature in a sense in which it probably no longer is
and in which the last scholarly publication by the most recent winner of the

4. See Terry Eagleton, *Literary Theory*, 2d ed. (Minneapolis: University of Minnesota Press,
1996), 1–14, for an elegant argument to this effect.

Nobel Prize in economics almost certainly is not. Conversely, the plays of Shakespeare have progressed from being minimally or hardly at all literature to being more centrally literature than any other texts in the language.[5] The attempt to construct an essential or transhistorically substantive definition of literature is, accordingly, in vain. Reading, one might say, does not merely respond to literature: reading (of a certain sort) *creates* literature.

This kind of reading, then—this process of creation—may be understood as at one with the process of canon-formation itself, which, as becomes evident, comprises three overlapping but distinct phases, in each of which genre plays an important role. In the primary phase of canonization—the construction of the very category of literature out of all verbal documents extant—genre is a nearly all-powerful factor. To put it another way, in this phase the ideology of canon-formation makes itself felt mainly through generic mediation. So it is that the business memoranda of so conservative and respectable an author as Stevens are denied the title of literature, while a poem by a militant and unknown slumdweller, if it obeyed a few simple conventions, would not be denied the title. It is in this sense that genre must be understood as a category logically prior to literature: the very existence of the latter is radically enabled by the former. Indeed, generic determination operates so functionally on this primary level of canon-formation that the same verbal construction may be literary or nonliterary depending upon the material context. The sentence, *Walk with light,* would be literature in a book of spiritual aphorisms but not on a metal sign at a street intersection.

Most works of literature, however—like the slumdweller's poem, probably—are generally considered bad or negligible literature, and are relegated to near-invisibility at the periphery of the canon. There is, then, a secondary phase of the canon-constructing process, which is devoted to forming a secondary canon: a canon-within-the-canon that distinguishes "good" literature, literature that deserves to be taken seriously, literature that is literature in more than the bare bibliographic sense, literature worth studying and teaching and writing articles about. Though nongeneric ideological considerations are more important here than in the primary phase of the process, the power of genre is still strong. Shakespeare's contemporaries were generally convinced of his personal genius, and there was a dawning awareness that the scripts of English stage plays might in some sense be literature; there was, however, widespread resistance to considering such scripts as literature in quite the same honorific sense that applied to ancient drama or to English odes and sonnets. The boom in Shakespeare's reputation was directly dependent upon the collapse of this

5. A nice anecdote in illustration concerns the Bodleian Library of Oxford University, which was presented with a copy of the First Folio of Shakespeare (1623) upon publication but discarded it shortly thereafter during routine housecleaning: a book of English scripts was hardly considered appropriate for a proper university library. In more recent years, however, the prevailing Oxford attitude toward Shakespeare has changed.

inhibition. Somewhat similarly perhaps, academic critics in our own time seem to be deciding that autobiography belongs more centrally to the literary canon than they would have allowed only a generation or two ago. In practice, there is bound to be overlapping between the primary and secondary phases of canon-formation, if only because of the inevitable semantic slippage between the concept of membership in a grouping and the concept of exemplifying the grouping favorably; all groupings have a tendency to absolutize themselves, to deconstruct the distinction between descriptive and eulogistic (or dyslogistic) signification. Still, the two phases remain in principle tolerably discrete.

Finally, there is a tertiary phase of canon-formation as well: the tendency, already discussed above, of every distinct school of reading to privilege a distinct kind of reading matter. This phase of the process, which distinguishes not merely literature or even "good" literature but the *best*, the most important literature, is, as we have seen, also largely governed by generic factors (though no doubt more crudely ideological forces are here stronger than in either the primary or secondary phases). Science fiction is certainly literature in the primary sense, but often not in the secondary and—in any explicit fashion—very rarely in the tertiary sense.

Two conclusions may, then, be drawn. First, it is evident that the affinity a mode of reading has for a particular literary object is by no means a matter of taste or judgment within an unproblematically predetermined field of literature. Rather, it is the most subtle moment or what I have called the tertiary phase within the project of constructing literature itself, of determining, out of all the verbal material available for inspection, which works possess the peculiar power that all respecters of literature from Plato to Paul de Man have attributed to the object of their devotion or fear—which is to say that it is, like the primary phase of the same process, a functional act involving, in the long run, determinate social ends. Genre plays a large role in all phases of the canon-forming process, and genre is of course (as shall be discussed in some detail below) not in the least an ideologically neutral factor. Accordingly, if science fiction has rarely been a privileged genre, this means that the literary powers-that-be have not wished science fiction to function with the social prestige that literature in the stronger senses enjoys. It cannot be too emphatically stated that the marginally or dubiously canonical status of science fiction has nothing to do with a series of unfavorable judgments on a series of individual texts—as a conservative empiricist ideology of canon-formation might imagine—but results from a wholesale *generic* dismissal of a kind organic to canonization as a practice. Plausible reasons for the general disinclination to eulogize science fiction will become clear in the course of this study.

The second conclusion involves recognizing that, at least in the most rarefied—the tertiary—phase of the canon-forming process, the operative generic judgments may be implicit rather than explicit. Usually, this distinction is relevant when considering both the positive and negative choices of precritical schools of reading. The Leavisites, for instance, would have hotly denied that they had any special (or certainly any *ideological*) attachment to the sort of fiction produced by George Eliot or D. H. Lawrence, except insofar as such a preference expressed an innocent recognition of what was worth reading at all (and favorable, of course, to "life"). But what I maintain here—and this is, indeed, the central claim of the entire current essay—is that critical theory itself, especially in its most central, Marxian version, does implicitly privilege a certain genre; and the genre is science fiction. This is a large claim. But it should be clear that I am not trying to "revalue" any particular canon in order to beg admission for science fiction. Instead, I have described canon-formation itself, and I now maintain that the most conceptually advanced forms of criticism unconsciously privilege a genre that has been widely despised and ghettoized.

Such an assertion raises two difficult questions. How and why does critical theory privilege science fiction? And, if it does, why do most critical theorists seem to have been unaware of the fact? I tackle the first question in the following three sections of this chapter, in which I explore various dimensions of the affinity between critical theory and science fiction. I then take up the second question in the final section, where the question of the canon once again becomes paramount.

The Critical Dynamic: Science Fiction and Style

In examining the affinity between critical theory and science fiction, there is tactical as well as methodological economy in beginning with the specifically *stylistic* dimension of science fiction. Style is widely taken to be a privileged category in the analysis of any literary kind, a kind of touchstone of the literary itself. The critical or precritical status of this privileging, and its special relevance to the study of science fiction, will be discussed below. But the precise language characteristic of a genre can hardly fail to be a salient aspect of the latter, and we may begin by analyzing the language of the following passage, which opens a major science-fiction novel, Philip K. Dick's *Do Androids Dream of Electric Sheep?* (1968):[6]

> A merry little surge of electricity piped by automatic alarm from the mood organ beside his bed awakened Rick Deckard. Surprised—it always surprised him to find himself awake without prior notice—he rose from the bed, stood up in his multicolored pajamas, and stretched. Now, in her bed, his wife Iran opened her gray, unmerry eyes, blinked, then groaned and shut her eyes again.

In some of its particulars, the passage could be the straightforward opening of a mundane novel (that is, a novel in which the generic tendency of science

6. Philip K. Dick, *Do Androids Dream of Electric Sheep?* (New York: Ballantine, 1982), 1.

fiction is reduced to the barest minimum): a married man, lying in bed beside his wife, awakes and is, presumably, about to start the day. The stylistic register of the paragraph, however, marks it as unmistakably science fiction. The key factor here is the reference to the mood organ—evidently a technical device somehow connected to emotional states and one that, though unknown in our own empirical environment, is an ordinary accoutrement of everyday life in the world of the text.

In fact, the mood organ does figure as an important motif in Dick's novel as a whole. But in the context of the opening paragraph, its chief function is to signal the science-fictional character of the language, and thus to impel us to read the latter differently than we would read the language of mundane fiction.[7] Because technology and emotions are apparently connected in ways unfamiliar to us (though not *wholly* unfamiliar or unpredictable, because we do know of mood-altering drugs, not to mention television itself), the adjective *merry*, as applied to a surge of electricity, may have a sense other than the expected metaphorical one. What does it mean to be "awake without prior notice"? We understand the difference between being jerked from deep sleep to full consciousness and gradually passing through intermediate stages; but the context suggests that a more specific meaning may be operative. Nor is the grammatically simple phrase "his wife Iran" free of ambiguities. Are we here in a world where a man can be married to an entire country? And what of the fact that Rick and Iran seem to sleep in different beds? As in mundane fiction, it may be a detail without profound significance, or it may signify certain sexual problems between the couple. It might, however, also signify some completely novel arrangement of sexual relations that is normal in the society portrayed. In any case, the whole topic of human feelings, sexual and otherwise, is estranged, and the question of a technology of emotion is posed. A few lines following the above paragraph is this bit of conversation:

"Get your crude cop's hand away," Iran said.
"I'm not a cop." He felt irritable, now, although he hadn't dialed for it.

This exchange might be completely mundane, until the final clause. But that clause, though formally subordinate, makes the crucial science-fictional point.

It would be possible, in a full-scale reading of the novel, to show how the first paragraph does function as an appropriate overture. Of course, not all of the possibilities raised there are actually developed. But the relations between technology and emotion do constitute the principal focus of the text, not only

7. At this point my argument is somewhat indebted to Samuel Delany's numerous discussions of science-fictional language, most valuably in his *The Jewel-Hinged Jaw* (New York: Berkley Windhover Books, 1978). See also the interview with him in Charles Platt, *Dream Makers* (New York: Berkley Books, 1980), 69–75. Interesting work in the same area may also be found in Kathleen L. Spencer, "'The Red Sun is High, the Blue Low': Towards a Stylistic Description of Science Fiction," *Science-Fiction Studies* 10 (1983): 35–49.

with regard to such household appliances as the mood organ, but also in connection with the state of virtual war between human authorities and androids, the latter presumed (though one cannot be *completely* certain) to have no emotions at all. But the opening of the novel may also stand alone as paradigmatic, on the molecular level, of the science-fictional generic tendency. The point to be stressed about the language is its profoundly critical, dialectical character. For undialectical theory, the most familiar emotions—love, affection, hatred, anger, and so forth—tend to be unproblematic categories, assumed to be much the same in all times and places, and to exist on an irreducibly subjective level. They may of course manifest themselves in a practically infinite number of permutations, and the precritical reader may relish such psychological fiction as that of Dostoevsky or Flaubert for the subtlety and acuteness with which those authors portray the (presumably universal and static) varieties of affective experience. A dialectical approach, on the other hand, would adopt the kind of perspective suggested by Dick. Because the paragraph shows an emotional dynamic of a future age operating quite differently from what we ourselves empirically experience, the question of the *historicity* of feelings is raised, and the possibility of a historical periodization of emotion in coordination with other aspects of social development (such as technology) is at least implied. The technical emphasis of the paragraph also tends to remove emotion from idealist notions of spirituality or the unproblematically individual, and to suggest that psychic states may be reducible to concrete and transindividual material realities—a reduction that Freud, after all, held to be the ultimate conceptual goal of psychoanalysis and that Lacan (substituting language for neurobiology as the grounding of psychoanalytic materialism) claimed to have achieved through the mediation of neo-Saussurian linguistics. We may also note that, if the phrase I used above, "technology of emotion," has a strongly Foucauldian ring, it is not by chance. Dick's paragraph does indeed resonate with Foucault's concern to show that power does not merely repress or distort the subjectivity of individuals, but actually *constitutes* human subjectivity, from the ground up, so to speak, and in historically variable ways.

Historical materialism, psychoanalysis, Foucauldian archeology: I do not suggest that such elaborate theoretical structures are actually present, even embryonically, in the short and apparently unpretentious paragraph that opens *Do Androids Dream of Electric Sheep?*. It is, rather, a matter of the shared perspectives—here as manifest on the level of style itself—between critical theory and science fiction. What is crucial is the dialectical standpoint of the science-fictional tendency, with its insistence upon historical mutability, material reducibility, and, at least implicitly, utopian possibility. Yet it must be noticed that the quoted sample of Dick's prose, like the prose of most (though certainly not all) science fiction, is far from what is ordinarily considered "fine" writing or the work of a "stylist" in the usual eulogistic sense. If, then, a deep affinity between critical theory and science fiction can be detected on the molecular level of style, the question of stylistic *quality* or value must somehow be engaged. Although science fiction is certainly not without its "stylists" in the normative sense—Ursula Le Guin and Samuel Delany come readily to mind—most of the prose in most of the works where the tendency of science fiction is strongest has rarely received stylistic commendation; indeed, canonical hostility to science fiction has often justified itself on specifically stylistic grounds.

It is necessary, then, to analyze the nature and function of literary style, most urgently in the general context of the ideology of style that has developed within hegemonic criteria of literary value. If a genuinely critical dynamic is to be understood in the conjunction of the categories of style and science fiction, then *both* categories must be subject to dialectical interrogation. With regard to science fiction, such interrogation was offered in the second section of chapter 1. We may now turn to the category of literary style.

A convenient point of departure is provided in an essay by C. S. Lewis about what today would be described as the problem of the canon or the crisis of literary canonization. Lewis claims to know how "the plain man" distinguishes between those texts that are "real Literature" and those that are not (the distinction evidently corresponds to what in the preceding section was designated the secondary phase of canon-formation). Texts that fail to make the higher grade, it seems, "'haven't got style' or 'style and all that,'" in normal lowbrow opinion. As a robustly neo-Christian critic and novelist, Lewis maintains an antiformalist viewpoint, and he therefore goes on to chastise his imaginary lowbrow friend for "a radically false conception of style."[8]

Despite Lewis's tone of class-based condescension, it is nonetheless worth noting that the apparently hapless "plain man," far more than Lewis himself, is supported by the most influential (if, as we shall see, largely precritical) modern theories of literary form. The key reference here is to Russian Formalism, with its extremely various, detailed, and ingenious attempts to prove that the essence (or necessary and sufficient condition) of literature as such is a certain specifically "literary" use of language formally distinguishable from all nonliterary uses and definable in properly stylistic ways. (And here, of course, we are dealing with the primary as well as the secondary phases of the canon-constructing process). Only relatively recently, to be sure, have the particular innovations of Viktor Shklovsky and his colleagues attained a worldwide impact commensurate to their intrinsic intellectual force. But ideas related directly or indirectly to Russian Formalism, especially with regard to the conviction of the latter that literature must be understood in terms internal and specific to itself, without dependence on the referential status of the literary

8. C. S. Lewis, "High and Low Brows," in his *Selected Literary Essays*, ed. Walter Hooper (Cambridge: Cambridge University Press, 1969), 270–271.

text, have resonated throughout most of the most widely prestigious Anglo-American literary theorizing of this century: from certain elements in the work of I. A. Richards, through much of American New Criticism, to such a relatively late epigone of Russian Formalism as Paul de Man—who, in one of his most widely known oracular gestures, proclaims that he does "not hesitate to equate the rhetorical, figural potentiality of language with literature itself." Indeed, it is in just this context that de Man significantly contrasts what he himself terms "the sub-literature of the mass media"[9] (specifically, an episode of *All in the Family*) with *real* literature like *A la recherche du temps perdu* (1913–1928). The operative distinction is precisely that Proust's novel, unlike (or at least far more than) the dialogues of Archie and Edith Bunker, possesses style and all that.

Of course, the category of style, as the defining canonical criterion of literary value, must be historicized in order to be truly intelligible; and such historicization must first of all notice that the de Manian use (like a great many other current uses) of the term *rhetoric* involves a certain historical imprecision. As Fredric Jameson has suggested,[10] style is a specifically modern phenomenon, an effect of the bourgeois cultural revolution; although it is in some ways the successor to rhetoric, it operates in a manner *antithetical* to that of rhetoric in the strict sense. The older term implies a storehouse of linguistic figures, each with its predetermined formal integrity and all available to all aspiring rhetoricians. Actual rhetorical practice must of course vary with the various aims and abilities of different practitioners, but the shared figural infrastructure of all rhetoric guarantees a considerable degree of pan-rhetorical community. Furthermore, those differences that do emerge among rhetorical performances are understood as rhetorical differences simply and solely, as variations in the practice of a common art. They are not taken to be outward embodiments of profound dissimilarities in character or personality, as indices to the variety of human souls. But such is precisely the case with style. Style is generally assumed to be the direct expression of the middle-class ego and must be created anew and almost ex nihilo by every stylist. Fundamentally, it has little in common with such a characteristically collective and transpersonal project of the precapitalist order as rhetoric. On the contrary, it is part and parcel of the whole celebration of personal subjectivity so typical of cultural modernity—not only in the sense that the individual stylist is personally and almost solely responsible for every act of stylistic production, but also in that every particular style (understood here as an overall pattern perceptible in the work of any given stylist) is taken to be profoundly revealing of the author not merely as producer of style but as a human subjectivity in toto. The style *is* the person, as the well-known French proverb has it.

9. Paul de Man, *Allegories of Reading* (New Haven: Yale University Press, 1979), 9–10.
10. See Fredric Jameson, *Marxism and Form* (Princeton: Princeton University Press, 1971), 332–335.

Accordingly, it is not difficult to understand the primacy widely accorded to style in the formalist constructions of literature and literary value. On the one hand, because style, in formalist stylistics, is taken to inhere in language itself, in the medium in which literature has its very existence, a stylistic emphasis enables the immense methodological economy of a quasi- (or pseudo-) scientific taxonomy of literature as an autonomous system sufficient unto itself and structurally describable without necessary reference to extraformal categories. On the other hand, the danger of a merely technicist aridity that such a stylistics might imply is avoided through the considerable affective force and richness that derive from the privileged relationship assumed between style and the soul of the stylist. It is significant that the ultimate context of C. S. Lewis's rejection of formalist stylistics is nothing other than a considered *denial* of the viability of the distinction between literature and what Lewis's invented lowbrow calls not real Literature (or what Paul de Man calls subliterature).[11] Lewis's position is a minority one. More mainstream and formalist theorists, like de Man or Lewis's plain man, are generally convinced that the distinction is indeed viable and that its essence is style and all that.

It is in this context that we may return to the prose of Philip K. Dick. I choose to focus on Dick because I consider him to be the preeminent author of modern science fiction, "the Shakespeare of science fiction,"[12] in Jameson's phrase. By this I suggest not only his general stature within science fiction and beyond it (as the creator of an oeuvre that an increasing body of critical opinion holds to be the most interesting and important produced by any North American novelist since Faulkner), but also the extent to which his greatness, like Shakespeare's among Renaissance dramatists, is bound up with his being radically *typical* of his genre—and not least on stylistic grounds, as our examination of the opening passage of *Do Androids Dream of Electric Sheep?* indicates. Yet Dick's style, while deeply science-fictional, does not, as we have already begun to see, characteristically display the evident polish, the syntactic elegance, and the allusive resonance that are stylistically valorized by hegemonic formalist criteria of value. The plain man of Lewis's imagination would probably hesitate to attribute "style and all that" to Dick's work, and de Man might well rank it closer in aesthetic value to Archie Bunker than to Proust. What is thus called into question, then, is not only the caliber of Dick's style but also, given the formalist stress on style as the defining characteristic of literary canonicity itself, the magnitude of his achievement in general. We have to deal here with a contradiction between what I have argued to be the *critical*

11. The reference here is not only to the essay cited above but, even more important, to Lewis's later and full-length *Experiment in Criticism* (Cambridge: Cambridge University Press, 1961), in which he argues that the operative distinction ought to be between modes of reading rather than between texts.

12. Fredric Jameson, "Futurist visions that tell us about right now," *In These Times* 6, no. 23 (5–11 May 1982): 17.

superiority of Dick's style and its apparent inferiority (or mediocrity) by ordinary received canons of literariness and literary value. A further stylistic analysis of Dick's prose is necessary, then, not merely to shed light on Dick and on science-fictional style generally, but to examine more dialectically the category of style itself.

The following passage condenses the opening of Ubik (1969), the novel that I take to be probably Dick's finest:[13]

At three-thirty a.m. on the night of June 5, 1992, the top telepath in the Sol System fell off the map in the offices of Runciter Associates in New York City. That started vidphones ringing. The Runciter organization had lost track of too many of Hollis' psis during the last two months; this added disappearance wouldn't do. . . .

Sleepily, Runciter grated, "Who? I can't keep in mind at all times which inertials are following what teep or precog. . . . What? Melipone's gone? . . . You're sure the teep was Melipone? Nobody seems to know what he looks like; he must use a different physiognomic template every month. What about his field?"

"We asked Joe Chip to go in there and run tests on the magnitude and minitude of the field being generated there at the Bonds of Erotic Polymorphic Experience Motel. Chip says it registered, at its height, 68.2 blr units of telepathic aura, which only Melipone, among all the known telepaths, can produce." . . .

Runciter said, "I'll consult my dead wife."

"It's the middle of the night. The moratoriums are closed now."

As with the passage from Do Androids Dream of Electric Sheep?, the prose is not at all conspicuously "literary." There does not appear to be any attempt, in the proper formalist manner, to use language in a state of intensified depth, density, and difficulty. On the contrary, the style (heavily influenced by Robert Heinlein and, perhaps more distantly, by Hemingway) seems marked by little more than routine serviceability; it fluently adequates itself to the adventure narrative and does not at all scorn the characteristic formulations of the field. Something "wouldn't do"; a character states that "nobody seems to know" something and asks "what about" something else; something is said to be true "among all the known" examples relevant. Such devices do convey a certain degree of urgency and breathlessness, but not, apparently, in a manner more complex than that attained by an action-adventure cartoon strip. The prose, it would seem, is, in de Man's term, subliterary. Philip K. Dick is not a stylist.

Or is he? We may first of all note that in Ubik, as in Do Androids Dream of Electric Sheep?, science fiction does manifest its generic presence not only on the molar level of plot structure but also with regard to the molecular operations of language itself. The date in the opening clause suggests a sciencefictional framework temporally, and the solar perspective opened up in the following clause does the same thing in spatial terms. There follow a flood of

13. Philip K. Dick, Ubik (Garden City, N.Y.: Doubleday, 1969), 1–2. An article of mine (see note 14) provides specific reasons for the high place I give to this novel among Dick's fictions.

neologisms—this device being perhaps the most paradigmatic expression of science-fictional diction—that suggest the new resources of a brave new world, whether technological ("vidphones," "moratoriums") or human ("psis," "inertials") or, indeed, in terms that implicitly offer to deconstruct that all-too-familiar binary opposition ("a different physiognomic template every month," "68.2 blr units of telepathic aura"). More generally, the passage clearly establishes, in strategically casual phrasing but also with noteworthy economy, that the setting of the novel is one in which such uncanny phenomena as extrasensory perception and communication with the dead (not to mention polymorphously perverse sexuality) have not only become routine but have been thoroughly integrated, economically, into the consumer capitalism of the 1990s. The language of the passage, in sum, emphatically establishes what we have seen to be the sine qua non of every text in which the tendency of science fiction is strong: cognitive estrangement, a clear otherness vis-à-vis the mundane empirical world where the text was produced—which is, however, connected (at least in principle) to that world in rational, nonfantastic ways.

A somewhat closer examination of the passage may reveal the workings of otherness to be yet more complex than we have seen thus far. Most crucial here is the way that the style of the passage critically *manages* difference and differences, the way in which the unfamiliar and the familiar are held in suspension and related to one another through the operations of a radically heterogeneous and polyvalent prose. The overall critical agendum of *Ubik* as a whole—the satiric and rationally paranoid estrangement of the commodity structure of monopoly capitalism[14]—is here enforced through a complex multiaccentuality on the level of sentence production. For example: "'We asked Joe Chip to go in there and run tests on the magnitude and minitude of the field being generated there at the Bonds of Erotic Polymorphic Experience Motel.'" On the simplest plane, this is a casual, serviceable, unadorned bit of adventure fiction, the loyally efficient report of Runciter's subordinate concerning the field operations of Runciter's top subordinate, Joe Chip. At the same time, the sentence introduces such novelties as the quantification of telepathic power and the institutionalization of polymorphic perversity, the air of things new and strange supported by the logical but striking coinage "minitude." What is even more complex and important, however, is the way that casualness and estrangement work together to suggest the routine commodification of telepathy, anti-telepathy, and perversity, and therefore the assimilation of these moments of uncanniness to the quasi-familiar commercial structure that includes Runciter Associates, Hollis's competing organization, and the incidentally mentioned motel. The strange is to some degree thus de-estranged, but the more powerful tendency is the

14. See Carl Freedman, "Towards a Theory of Paranoia: The Science Fiction of Philip K. Dick," *Science-Fiction Studies* 11 (March 1984): 15–24.

complementary one to estrange commodification itself, to evoke the fetishistic weirdness on which this superficially familiar process is based.[15]

A similar stylistic heterogeneity may be detected in this seemingly very simple sentence a few lines later: "Runciter said, 'I'll consult my dead wife.'" Again, the unadorned functionality of neo-Heinleinian prose—the boss is taking decisive but fairly routine action to deal with a crisis—clashes with what is for the reader the intensely strange content of the action. Also again, however, this multiaccentuality problematizes the relation of familiar to unfamiliar in two directions at once. As the sentence introduces communication with the dead, but only in the context of corporate management, it suggests that the commodity structure can make even the reversal (or partial reversal) of the ultimate finality of death seem routine; at the same time it reminds us that this very commodity structure is after all a fundamentally weird network in which dead and living labor interact with one another. It may be added that the point is reiterated almost immediately by the reference in the following line to "moratoriums," which turn out to be commercial enterprises for the maintenance of "half-lifers" like Mrs. Runciter. In this passage, then, Dick's style does more than move his plot along and insinuate the general cognitive estrangements that generically define science fiction. Even more important, the style, in its heterogeneous complexity, enacts on the molecular level the most searching critical-theoretical juxtapositions and interrogations that the novel in toto is concerned with implementing. If this style be "subliterary," then that category itself certainly needs to be rethought—especially within the general context of science fiction. It is time, in fact, to consider more deeply the ideological functions of formalist canons of stylistic value.

Such a rethinking is implicit in the work of the Russian critic who in recent years has emerged as the most eminent modern theorist of novelistic style: Mikhail Bakhtin. The essence of what I have suggested concerning the style of Dick's science fiction can be conveniently expressed in the terms given critical currency by Bakhtin. Dick's is a radically *dialogic* use of language, one that exploits to the utmost what Bakhtin calls *heteroglossia*; that is, the primacy of linguistic polyvalency, of the irreducible multiaccentuality of meaning, as against any concept of singular, closed, monologic discourse. Furthermore, the foregrounding in Dick of the interinanimation of form and content, of text and context, of sentence production and the economic realities of generalized commodity production, strongly recalls Bakhtin's insistence on the impossibility of detaching style from the sociality that it registers and his correlative brilliance in relating the smallest linguistic turns to the most general movements of culture and society. For Dick and Bakhtin, style is an intrinsically *social* category.

15. The main critical-theoretical reference here is of course Marx; see esp. Karl Marx, *Capital*, trans. Ben Fowkes (Harmondsworth: Penguin, 1976), 1:163–177.

This privileging of the contextual, however, this rejection of any attempt to construct literature as a self-sufficient autonomous system, is only one way in which both Dick and Bakhtin mount a powerful challenge to all formalist conceptions of style. For both, the internal structure of style is no less important than, while closely related to, its radical referentiality. With regard to the former, it has far too rarely been noticed that formalist accounts of a specifically literary use of language, from the Russian Formalists themselves onward, have tended to assume an unacknowledged synonymy between the literary and the *poetic*, and thus a putative superiority on the part of the older literary mode: an assumed superiority whose presence can be heard to this day in the eulogistic accent that almost invariably accompanies the descriptive use of terms like "poetry" and "poetic." Bakhtin, however—an unswerving though respectful opponent of the Russian Formalists who were his contemporaries and compatriots—reverses the conventional hierarchization of poetry over prose, arguing that poetic style, for all its apparent verbal richness, tends by its lyrical, rhythmic flow to repress otherness, to occlude difference, and thus to approximate to the authoritarian single-mindedness of monologue: "The natural dialogization of the word is not put to artistic use, the word is sufficient unto itself and does not presume alien utterances beyond its own boundaries. Poetic style is by convention suspended from any mutual interaction with alien discourse."[16] In fundamental contrast, the style of the prose novel is one that welcomes and glories in heteroglossia, highlighting and contextualizing rather than repressing otherness: the novelistic word "break[s] through to its own meaning and its own expression across an environment full of alien words . . . variously evaluating accents, harmonizing with some of the elements in this environment and striking a dissonance with others" (*Dialogic Imagination* 277). These words exactly describe the style of the opening of *Ubik*. Bakhtin's stress on harmony and dissonance corresponds with complete precision to the Dickian dialectic of familiarity and strangeness. Though Bakhtin may never have heard of Dick and seems to have had little or no personal interest in science fiction as such, his insurgently critical standards of novelistic style might well have been formulated specifically to justify Dick's science-fictional style.

Accordingly, it follows that novelistic style, when most capable and most powerfully novelistic (and in that sense, indeed, most *literary*) may eschew certain properties of polish, of well-roundedness, of fluently controlled density and resonance proper to the poetic; and, correspondingly, that novelistic prose that does display such qualities, however "literary" it may seem in normative terms, is perhaps to be suspected of contamination by the monologic authoritarianism of poetry. Returning to the terms most generally privileged in the

16. M. M. Bakhtin, *The Dialogic Imagination*, ed. Michael Holquist, trans. Caryl Emerson and Michael Holquist (Austin: University of Texas Press, 1981), 285.

current essay, we can say that Bakhtin's ultimate critique of formalistic stylistics—and in particular of the precise ways that style is valorized by the latter—is that formalism, for all its technical richness and complexity, remains essentially *precritical*. Its aesthetic preference for poetic monologism is the final, inevitable result of the idealist and empiricist epistemology that absolutely autonomizes literature and concomitantly forecloses context and referentiality. The stylistic markers most commonly taken as indices of the literary in the eulogistic senses may, in fact, therefore be signifiers of conceptual conservatism and regression. Conversely, the dialogic, novelistic style endorsed by Bakhtin and exemplified by Dick is above all critical and dialectical; its "prosaic" quality may signal substantive, as opposed to merely technical, complexity. Indeed, the entire category of the dialogic in Bakhtin's sense is in the end nothing other than the (primarily Marxian) dialectic as manifest in literary (and linguistic) form.

To avoid misunderstanding, we must note one further point about the Bakhtinian problematic. Bakhtin's exaltation of novelistic prose over poetry cannot be entirely separated from the general historical circumstances of early twentieth-century literary criticism, in which the supremacy of poetry among literary forms was still a commonplace, and the novel was still widely regarded as something of a scruffy parvenu. The critical revolution that would challenge this hierarchy had been launched as early as Turgenev, Flaubert, and Henry James, but was far from victorious. Though it is a matter of some controversy to what degree such victory has been won even now, yet it is certainly true that the undialectical binarism—the flat, somewhat reactive privileging of prose over verse—toward which Bakhtin's dialectic too often tends must be seriously qualified, especially in our late twentieth-century theoretical universe where, on the one hand, the post-Flaubertian "art novel" of modernism and postmodernism is a commonly accepted part of the literary landscape, as are, on the other hand, the efforts by poets from T. S. Eliot, Brecht, and William Carlos Williams onward to expand the accents of poetry beyond the sonorous monologism that for Bakhtin was particularly associated with verse of the late-Romantic type. In other words—and applying, in effect, a Bakhtinian critique to the letter of Bakhtin's own work—monologism and dialogism cannot be taken as simple attributes of poetry and prose respectively. Both (in this way like genre itself as discussed in chapter 1) must be understood as *tendencies* strongly or weakly operative within texts and classes of texts; and there is less reason now than in Bakhtin's time to associate monologism with poetry and dialogism with novelistic prose to quite the same extent that Bakhtin himself frequently suggests. Yet such historical adjustment is largely unnecessary in the context of science fiction, the scruffiness of which remains prominent. Indeed, the place assigned to the science-fiction novel by currently hegemonic aesthetic ideology is in many ways remarkably comparable to the place of the novel generally during the period when Bakhtin's insurgent views were formed; thus Bakhtin may be considered in many ways a science-fiction critic *avant la lettre*. Bakhtin requires that style be understood in a radically social, referential way, as attuned to the heterogeneous roughness of discourse and history so significantly foregrounded by Dick. Not only the general spirit of Bakhtin's work but even many of his original formulations still directly apply to the prose of Dick and his science-fiction colleagues. The link between dialectics and the dialogic is, as we have seen, more than merely etymological; if science fiction enjoys a privileged affinity with critical, dialectical theory, then it is only to be expected that its style should be, in Bakhtinian terms, most radically novelistic.

Bakhtin's emphasis on the embracing of the *alien* in novelistic style has an obvious special relevance to the language of science fiction, and it is in this light that I shall consider one more sample of Dickian prose. In the following passage of free indirect discourse from *A Scanner Darkly* (1977), which Dick himself considered his masterpiece, the protagonist, an undercover police drug agent named Bob Arctor, muses on the installation of police scanning devices in his own home:[17]

> To my own house, he thought. Arctor's house. Up the street at the house I am Bob Arctor, the heavy doper suspect being scanned without his knowledge, and then every couple of days I find a pretext to slip down the street and into the apartment where I am Fred replaying miles and miles of tape to see what I did, and this whole business, he thought, depresses me. Except for the protection—and valuable personal information—it will give me.
>
> Probably whoever's hunting me will be caught by the holo-scanners within the first week.
>
> Realizing that, he felt mellow.

Like the passages from *Ubik* and *Do Androids Dream of Electric Sheep?*, this one seems, on the most evident level, to be little more than solidly competent. It differs in registering not much in the way of technological innovation, the only noteworthy item in that regard being the scanners (themselves only a revision and updating of the Orwellian telescreens in *Nineteen Eighty-four* [1949], or, indeed, of the police listening devices so familiar in Dick's world and ours). Nonetheless, its style is profoundly dialogic. As with the other Dick novels examined above, the play of heteroglossia, the presence of the alien and of alienation, involves both the conceptual structure of the novel as a whole and an elaborate network of extratextual referentiality—although the key historical reference here is less the economic reality of commodification (as in *Ubik*) than the political reality of conspiracy. Much of the complexity of the style derives from the ironic fine-tuning possible in free indirect discourse, an instrument that Dick can at times play with near-Flaubertian precision. In the earlier sentences of the passage, the accent of the narrator and

17. Philip K. Dick, *A Scanner Darkly* (New York: Ballantine, 1977), 110.

that of Arctor himself seem almost at one, the evident identity wholly appropriate to the novel's sympathetic treatment of its hero. At the same time, however, the discourse is fissured by the paradox of self-alienation at the heart of the narrative. Not only does Arctor possess a doubled self as both hippie and nark; in these sentences he envisions the practically infinite replication of himself on holographic tape. The repressive state apparatus that employs Arctor assigns him to survey himself, and this assignment amounts to a hyper-Lacanian splitting of the subject, a construction of the very self as alien. This construction is to be understood, in a more general sense, as paradigmatic for the subjects of a conspiratorial, bureaucratized regime. Arctor's musings thus have an estranging significance beyond his own intentions as a character, which are here limited to his personal situation.

The regime of conspiracy is estranged even more complexly, however, as the style switches gears, so to speak, with the last sentence of the first paragraph quoted above. At this point the narrator begins to withdraw his ratification of Arctor's viewpoint, not out of lack of sympathy but on account of superior knowledge. Arctor believes himself to be persecuted by a single enemy, and hopes the scanning of his house will reveal the enemy's identity. The hope is naive, and the text regards it ironically. It is Arctor, not the novel, who believes the information acquired from scanners to be "valuable," and in the following two sentences the dialogic irony trained upon Arctor intensifies, climaxing with the word "mellow," which is scripted as if from within a drug haze in this deeply antidrug text. The irony thus powerfully anticipates the ultimate plot development of the novel; that is, the collusion of the highest levels of the police with the criminal drug syndicate and their joint conspiracy to destroy the mind of Bob Arctor. The shifting voices in this passage resonate strongly with Dick's overall attempt in A Scanner Darkly to estrange the bureaucratic conspiracies of both the state and the latter's nominal opponents, and to trace the connection between such conspiracy and the alienation (ultimately the obliteration) of the hapless individual subject. The stylistic device of free indirect discourse, in the science-fictional inflection given it here by Dick, in this way conveys, on the molecular level, Dick's overall and highly innovative attempt to suggest a critical political theory of conspiracy and bureaucracy in the late-capitalist state.[18]

In conclusion, our examination of Dick's prose—so unstriking to the casually formalist or precritical reading and in this way, as in others, so profoundly characteristic of science-fictional prose generally—powerfully suggests the extent to which, even (or perhaps especially) according to the stylistic grounds on which it has traditionally been judged most harshly, science fiction maintains a critical superiority, a privileged relationship with critical theory itself.

18. For more on the specifically *critical* nature of Dick's view of conspiracy, see Freedman, "Towards a Theory of Paranoia."

One more point in this connection may be emphasized. As we have seen, the dialectic since Hegel has an irreducibly *historical* character; thus the dialogic multiaccentuality of science-fictional style must amount to a radically historical style as well. This point is abundantly illustrated by the three major Dick novels discussed above: not only in the sense that these texts all bear unmistakable historical traces of their productive matrix in the cultural and political radicalism of the American 1960s and 1970s, but, more importantly, in the sense that their novelistic representations, even including the smallest details of everyday subjectivity from Rick Deckard's irritability to Bob Arctor's mellowness, are repeatedly shown, on a sentence-by-sentence basis, to depend upon the material realities of specific (and estranged) times and places.

But the historicity of science-fictional style can also be illustrated much more briefly, for instance with this sentence that concludes one of the best novels by Dick's stylistic precursor, Heinlein: "My word, I'm not even a hundred yet."[19] The tone of lighthearted optimism is of course appropriate to what *The Moon Is a Harsh Mistress* (1966) regards as the comic conclusion of the bourgeois revolution (loosely patterned after the American War of Independence) staged in and by the text. The more saliently science-fictional point, however, is that this optimism is no metaphysical or merely individual attitude; rather, it is directly based on the historic specificities of life on twenty-first-century Luna, specificities that include significant alterations in human life expectancy and other biomedical realities. In general, indeed, we may go so far as to say that, stylistically and otherwise, science fiction is of all genres the most devoted to historical concreteness: for, after all, the science-fictional world is not only one different in time or place from our own, but one whose chief interest is precisely the difference that such difference makes, and, in addition, one whose difference is nonetheless concretized within a cognitive continuum with the actual (thus, as we have seen, sharply distinguishing science fiction from the irrationalist estrangements of such essentially ahistorical modes as fantasy or the Gothic, which may secretly work to ratify the mundane status quo by presenting no alternative to the latter other than inexplicable discontinuities).

It may appear, then, that science fiction is, perhaps paradoxically, a version of historical fiction, and that the affinity for which I argue between science fiction and critical theory is a rewriting of the privileged relationship maintained by Lukács between Marxism and the historical novel. This analogy does, in fact, imply a good deal of what the current essay is concerned to establish. And, in advancing my argument for the critical impulse of science fiction from the molecular level of style to the molar level of narrative structure, it is indeed necessary to engage the problems of critical insight and novelistic form posed most tellingly by Lukács. Such will be the initial task of the following section.

19. Robert A. Heinlein, *The Moon Is a Harsh Mistress* (New York: Berkley Books, 1968), 302.

The Critical Dynamic: Science Fiction and the Historical Novel

Though Georg Lukács's *The Historical Novel* remains the most completely achieved critical analysis of any particular novelistic genre, its accomplishment is closely connected to Lukács's considered *denial* that the historical novel is really a special genre at all.[20] More precisely, Lukács maintains that the historical novel becomes a specialized genre only in its decadence, when it has lost the critical features that define its classical, fully vital phase. For Lukács, the classical historical novel as practiced by Sir Walter Scott and his authentic successors understands historicity in a *dialectical*, as opposed to an antiquarian, way. History, for the historical novelist, is no matter of exoticism or inert factuality; rather, it involves a dialectic of difference and identity (though Lukács himself does not employ those terms), a sense of both change and continuity. The society of the past is portrayed with full awareness of the temporal and social distance that separates it from the society in which the novel is produced, but with equally full awareness of the driving historical forces that link the two eras in a concrete continuum that is social, economic, political, and cultural in nature.[21] Thus it is, for example, that Scott's representations of eighteenth-century and medieval Scotland stress the enormous differences between his country's gentile Highland past and the bourgeois, largely Anglicized Lowland society in which the novelist himself lived—but never in a way that makes the former a mere matter of costume and scenery. The Highland past is never a mere binary (and thus, in the long run, stigmatized) Other counterpointed to the Scotland of Scott's own day. On the contrary, Scott's main focus is consistently on the historical forces that rendered irresistible the supersession of gentile by bourgeois Scotland and—respectable Tory gentleman though Scott was—without glossing over the terrible cost in human suffering. The historical novel, then, is, to use the term that the philosophically erudite Lukács himself repeatedly employs with full intent, an eminently *critical* form, a form that constructs societies as radically historicized and complexly determined totalities.

20. The account that follows of Georg Lukács, *The Historical Novel*, trans. Hannah and Stanley Mitchell (London: Merlin, 1962) refers primarily, though not exclusively, to pages 19–88 and 171–250. For more about Lukács's theory of realism and the novel, the following works by him, all closely allied to *The Historical Novel*, are especially pertinent: *Studies in European Realism* (New York: Grosset and Dunlap, 1964); *Realism in Our Time*, trans. John and Necke Mander (New York: Harper and Row, 1964); *Essays on Thomas Mann*, trans. Stanley Mitchell (London: Merlin, 1964); *Writer and Critic*, ed. and trans. Arthur Kahn (London: Merlin 1978); *Essays on Realism*, ed. Rodney Livingstone, trans. David Fernbach (Cambridge, Mass.: MIT Press, 1981).

21. The distinction here between the dialectical and the antiquarian approaches to history almost precisely corresponds to the opposition that Walter Benjamin defines between historical materialism and historicism in "Theses on the Philosophy of History"; see Walter Benjamin, *Illuminations*, ed. Hannah Arendt, trans. Harry Zohn (New York: Schocken, 1969), 253–264. In order to avoid terminological confusion, however, it should be noted that Lukács himself uses "historicism" in a far more eulogistic sense, one that denotes a much more critical, dialectical view of history.

All this is to say that the historical novel, when fully itself, represents for Lukács a triumph of *realism*, and the latter, not the former, is in Lukácsian terms the most salient generic category. For the defining characteristics of historical realism like Scott's are equally to be found in the genuinely realistic novel set in a society contemporary to the novel's production. The novel of contemporary realism understands the historicity of the present; that is, it represents contemporary society as a mutable, historical totality, the result of complex but comprehensible social developments and one that has by no means arrived at any sort of finality or stasis. Despite the extreme closeness of contemporary society, a realistic representation does not cast it as "natural" or unproblematically given, but as part and parcel of the historical flux. Of course, there are obviously all sorts of minor differences between novels set in the past and those set in the present, but not what Lukács would define as an essential difference, or what we might designate a radically generic difference. Thus it is that Lukács considers Balzac to be the most legitimate immediate heir to Scott (a relationship, indeed, of which the French novelist was quite consciously aware). Thus it is—to choose perhaps the most prominent single example—that Tolstoy practices fundamentally the same kind of art in *Anna Karenina* (1878) as in *War and Peace* (1866).

There is, however, a radical break in the history of the novel as construed by Lukács. It comes not between historical and contemporary realism, but between realism itself and what might be termed the postrealist novel that emerges out of what Lukács sees as the disintegration of realism into naturalism (and later, into impressionism and modernism). The crucial loss here—closely connected, in Lukács's reading, to the increasingly reactionary role assumed by the European bourgeoisie after the failed revolutions of 1848, and the concomitant abandoning of the progressive, democratic elements within bourgeois ideology—is the occlusion of the vital critical perspective of totality. Instead of portraying society as an interconnected whole in which objective and subjective elements are dialectically bound together—thus making possible the "typical" characters of realism; that is, psychologically individuated characters who also incarnate objective trends of sociohistorical development[22]—the postrealist understands objectivity and subjectivity as incommensurate with each other. Thus, in Lukács's view, arise both the lifeless external factuality of naturalism and also the solipsistic abstract psychologism of later literary schools.

Perhaps the worst distortions of postrealism, however, in Lukács's perspective, are to be found in the historical novel proper. The latter now becomes a special and clearly distinct genre, though it would be more accurate, in Lukácsian terms, to designate its new form the *pseudo*historical novel. The

---

22. For an appreciative critique of this concept and its place in the history of literary criticism, see Darko Suvin, "Lukács: Horizons and Implications of the 'Typical Character,'" *Social Text*, no. 16 (1986–87): 97–123.

dialectic of difference and identity to be found in *Waverley* (1814) or *War and Peace* is shattered, and the two terms are both voided of concrete meaning as they become fatally detached from one another. No longer can past and present, objectivity and subjectivity, individuality and sociality, be grasped as dialectically connected parts of a living totality. Instead—and Lukács takes as his chief examples the Flaubert of *Salammbô* (1862) and, even more pertinently, the great German-Swiss novelist Conrad Ferdinand Meyer—both difference and identity hypertrophy, as each assumes a bloated, abstract, and thus false presence in the text. On the one hand, difference becomes an exercise in undialectical archeology, a piling-up of external exotic details that, however accurate in the merely factual sense, remain lifeless and unconnected to present-day society. Conversely, identity takes the form of an ahistorical psychological modernization, so that the subjectivities of Flaubert's Carthage or Meyer's medieval Italy are flatly and silently equated with those of Flaubert's France and Meyer's Switzerland. Whereas the classical historical novel constructs a concrete interinanimation of change and continuity, the "new" or postrealist genre cannot convey either, save in the most abstract and two-dimensional fashion. The only way, Lukács insists, that historical fiction can regain vitality is by the reactivation of critical realism—a development of which he does see some hopeful signs in such authors as Anatole France, Heinrich Mann, and Romain Rolland.

In general terms, then, it is clear that for Lukács novelistic realism—and in particular the realism of the classical historical novel—possesses much the same kind of superiority that novelistic style does for Bakhtin. In both cases the superiority is essentially critical: both aspects of the novel as a form are shown by these two very different but wonderfully complementary critical theorists to enjoy a close kinship with the dialectic of historical materialism. However, whereas Bakhtin's theory of style has a direct and obvious relevance to the reading of science fiction (especially to such central, paradigmatic science-fiction stylists as Dick and Heinlein), any use of Lukács's theory of realism in science-fiction criticism must proceed more indirectly. The problem is not so much that Lukács himself (like Bakhtin) displays little or no personal interest in science fiction as such, but rather that realism itself has generally been taken as opposite rather than allied to science fiction. We have indeed had some hints in chapter 1 that the opposition may not be so stark as first appears, and even that something science-fictional may be at work in the texts of so solidly realistic a novelist as Jane Austen (whom Lukács happens to ignore but who was esteemed highly by Lukács's hero, Walter Scott). Yet nothing in our argument to this point has indicated more than a distant relationship between science fiction and historical realism. Is there a closer affinity?

We may begin by noting that the main theoretical content of *The Historical Novel*, as distilled above, does at several points suggest elements in our earlier discussions of science fiction. Generically, realism is for Lukács essentially a *tendential* category, a literary mode that, coexisting with other modes, may be active to a greater or lesser extent within a particular novelistic text. Indeed, among the chief aesthetic pleasures of *The Historical Novel* are the fineness and multiplicity of the discriminations that Lukács draws among an astonishingly wide range of historical novels—discriminations that generally turn on the precise degree to which and way in which realism operates within the novels under consideration. In this way, then, Lukácsian realism functions in a manner strictly parallel to science fiction as defined in chapter 1. To declare that, say, Manzoni's *I Promessi Sposi* (1826) "is" a work of historical realism is precisely like saying that *The Moon Is a Harsh Mistress* is a work of science fiction. One need not deny that other genres may well, even inevitably, be at work; but for Manzoni realism, and for Heinlein science fiction, is held to be the *dominant* generic tendency within a complexly structured text. Furthermore, though Lukács himself never explicitly poses the question, it is, as we shall see, very dubious, at best, whether in a truly Lukácsian problematic any actual text could be declared to consist simply and solely of realism as a generic tendency—just as we have already alluded to the improbability (at best) of science fiction's constituting the totality of a literary text.

But to demonstrate the parallel functioning of Lukácsian realism and science fiction as genres in a dialectical, tendential sense does not directly engage the question of the relationship between them. Such structural parallels are suggestive, as, of course, is the privileged relationship claimed between each generic tendency and critical theory. Nonetheless, in order to describe the *direct* relationship between the two genres, in order to explore further how science fiction and the historical novel can be articulated with regard to one another, it is first of all necessary to historicize science fiction itself.

Here again, *The Historical Novel* is invaluable as model and inspiration. Lukács's achievement is not only to delineate the various ways that history and historicity are represented within the various forms of the historical novel, but also to map the literary history of the latter against the larger social, economic, and political history of the modern era. As we have seen, Lukács credits the French Revolution (and its immediate aftermath in the Napoleonic Wars) with the invention of history itself, in the sense that history becomes for the first time a mass experience and historical change for the first time intervenes directly in the everyday life of ordinary men and women. Thus it is that the novel (the first major genre capable of dealing at length with ordinary life among the mass of humanity and itself, significantly, a thoroughly modern, though somewhat earlier, invention) is driven to deal with that dialectic of historical identity and difference that characterizes the historical novel in what Lukács regards as its vital, realistic phase. So long as the past is apprehended in merely external fashion, the historicity of past and present alike cannot really be represented, though of course stories taken from an (as-if-indeterminate) past, which are understood and felt as tales of events *in illo tempore,* may provide the subject matter of major literature (for example, Chaucer's *Troilus* [c. 1388], or, in a rather more complicated way, the Roman plays of Shakespeare). By the early nineteenth century, however, history is widely understood both objectively and subjectively, as both a social and an individual category; historical change (change, that is, actualized by continuity) can emerge as a concrete presence within the novelistic text, at once critically regarded and sensuously felt.

To put it another way, the "invitation" of the masses into history—that fundamental social transformation of the age of the bourgeois-democratic revolution—also amounts to *the invitation of history into literature*, and especially into the novel, the kind of literature most able to deal with mass experience. It is thus quite fitting that *Waverley* is published in 1814, at the end of the Napoleonic era, as the social changes and dislocations wrought by the capitalist and bourgeois-democratic era are being radically registered. It is also, we might add, "not accidental" (to use one of Lukács's favorite expressions) that *Waverley* was published in Edinburgh. For the Lowland Scotland of Walter Scott's time was an almost ideal coign of vantage for the observation of historical change, placed as it was—geographically and in other senses as well—between the increasingly capital-driven England (at that time easily the most aggressively modern social formation in the world) and the Scots Highlands (perhaps the most archaic region of western Europe, which within living memory had supported the authentically pre-feudal society of the clans, the latter an authentically gentile formation without urban centers or a middle class).[23] Scott was, then, extraordinarily well situated in place as well as in time to inaugurate the tradition of historical realism. Indeed, many of his immediate successors enjoyed somewhat similar positional advantages: for instance, Fenimore Cooper's vantage point between the increasingly commercial civilization of the white European settlers of North America and their creole progeny, on the one hand, and the tribal societies of the indigenous American population, on the other. It is on such social determinations, and not merely on the contingency of individual genius, that what Lukács sees as the great line of historical realism depends.

Four years after *Waverley* was published in Edinburgh, *Frankenstein* was published in London. We have already discussed this latter text as it registers a Promethean intellectual moment, a decisively modern critical impulse; it is thus not surprising that it was produced by the most technically and culturally advanced nation of the post-Napoleonic world. Now, however, we must consider Mary Shelley's novel in more strictly generic terms, as the "first" work of science fiction, or, more precisely, as the first work in which the science-fictional tendency reaches a certain level of self-consciousness, thus enabling a line of fiction that, at least in retrospect, can be construed as the early history

23. The most useful account of Scotland's role within the development of capitalism in general and British capitalism in particular is Tom Nairn, *The Break-up of Britain*, 2d ed. (London: Verso, 1981), esp. 11–195.

of science fiction proper—that is, fiction in which the tendency of science fiction is clearly dominant. The major landmarks here are easily identifiable, from Mary Shelley to Edgar Allan Poe and then to Verne and Wells, and finally to Wells's immediate successors both in Britain (Stapledon, Aldous Huxley, C. S. Lewis) and in the America of the pulp magazines.

The generic structure of *Frankenstein* can best be understood if we realize that the text marks the *end* (or at least obsolescence) of one genre even as it inaugurates another. Captain Walton, who initially appears to be the protagonist of the work, is in fact the hero of an old-fashioned travel narrative—a form with an ancient lineage that in Mary Shelley's own lifetime had reached a brilliant culmination in Coleridge's "Ancient Mariner" (1798), whose influence on the arctic sections of *Frankenstein* is of course pervasive. When Walton takes Victor Frankenstein aboard his ship and turns himself into the latter's amanuensis—thus bringing to a close the prefatory letters from Walton to his sister and beginning chapter 1 of the main text—he in effect resigns the office of protagonist and hands it over to the new friend for whom he feels such a keen affinity. The affinity is real enough, for Walton and Frankenstein are both quasi-Faustian overreachers—but in crucially different ways. Walton is an explorer in an unproblematically *spatial* way, a discoverer of regions that may appear new and strange to the European observer but that in fact are assumed to have always existed in pretty much the condition that Walton finds. By contrast, Frankenstein—the properly science-fictional hero, whose emergence as protagonist transforms the narrative into a predominantly science-fictional one—is concerned with pushing back the frontiers not of space but of *time*.

This does not appear to be true in the most narrow grammatical sense; for grammatically, of course, the story of Frankenstein and his monstrous creation (like much of the best nineteenth-century science fiction, notably that of Poe and Verne) is set in an alternative present and recent past. In more substantive terms, however, the alternative time frame suggests that such an experiment as Frankenstein's is a concrete possibility for the (near) future and thus turns the actual present—the empirical present of the reader—into a potential and historicized past. In other words, Frankenstein's experiment and its consequences, introduced into an apparently otherwise mundane setting, constitute such a *radical* (or, as we shall discuss in the following section, Blochian) novelty as to reconfigure in time the surrounding world of the novel, to turn apparent present into potential future. Among the results, for example, is that the implicit future projected by the monster's very existence serves (perhaps rather against the author's conscious intentions) to estrange and undermine the almost suffocatingly bourgeois-romantic egoism of the title character. The classic travel narrative—like Walton's—is an essentially ahistorical form that displays "timeless" wonders, often explicitly natural (the arctic seascape, for instance) though sometimes also in the form of naturalized "exotic" cultures inhabited by "people without history." Science fiction, by contrast, engages the whole Hegelian and post-Hegelian problematic of historicity by projecting (even if implicitly, as in *Frankenstein*) a future significantly different from the empirical present while also in concrete continuity with it.

We may conclude, then, that science fiction and the novel of historical realism both involve a Lukácsian dialectic of historical identity and historical difference, and are both produced from much the same historical matrix. Both forms emerge as unmistakably themselves—in the work of Walter Scott and Mary Shelley—during the period when historicity itself is first apprehended (or invented), at the close of the Napoleonic era in the early nineteenth century (which, of course, is also and not incidentally the moment when the industrial revolution and the march of the applied natural sciences assume new force and a quickened pace). Both science fiction and the historical novel are thus, *inter alia*, among the most quintessentially *modern* genres. One notable difference is that the historical novel, which is more concerned with the actual past, is often produced in proximity to archaic social formations such as those of the Scots Highlanders or the Native Americans; whereas science fiction, the more future-oriented genre, is typically at home in the most metropolitan regions of the most advanced nations (initially Britain, the United States, and France). A perhaps more complicated difference between science fiction and the historical novel is that the latter makes a triumphant entrance upon the stage of literary history with the numerous major works of Scott and his immediate successors. Science fiction enters more haltingly, with Mary Shelley's single great novel; and nothing really equivalent to the *tradition* founded by Scott is established until the end of the century. It may be that the futuristic orientation of science fiction requires a lengthier, more difficult gestation period, a more prolonged exposure to the ever more intense effects of technical and cultural modernity. Or, in somewhat different terms, the dramatization of the historicity of the present in relation to the future may be a more difficult critical operation than the comparable dramatization in relation to the past. It is certainly the case that the generic struggle in *Frankenstein* between (relatively ahistorical) travel narrative and (relatively historicizing) science fiction does not end with that novel, but continues to haunt much largely science-fictional work of the nineteenth century. The establishment of the crucial *temporal* standpoint of science fiction is not achieved at a stroke.

Accordingly, many of Poe's best tales that are commonly described as science fiction—"MS. Found in a Bottle" (1833), "A Descent into the Maelström" (1841), "The Balloon-Hoax" (1844), even that early classic of lunar-travel fiction, "The Unparalleled Adventure of One Hans Pfaal" (1835) —probably owe more to the strictly geographic narrative than to science fiction itself (and the latter two stories owe as much to the genre of neo-Swiftian satire). "The Balloon-Hoax," for instance, contains certain prefigurations of the "hard" (or engineering) science fiction of the Heinlein-Asimov sort. Yet both the technology and social relations portrayed are so mundane that relatively little estrangement of Poe's empirical environment—relatively little historicization of Poe's present—is achieved. Only once, perhaps, in his late story "The Facts in the Case of M. Valdemar" (1845), does Poe produce a major fiction in which science fiction is clearly and overwhelmingly the predominant genre. This story (often listed as Poe's best work of science fiction) introduces, in the particular inflection given to mesmerism, a genuinely radical novelty, and thus insinuates a genuine dialectic between present and future. At the same time, it exploits the cognitive (or as-if-cognitive) resources of the new science in order to estrange nothing less than the temporality of death itself.

Still more complicated and important for the history of science fiction than Poe is Poe's French disciple, Jules Verne, the first author of a truly substantial body of major work that can unhesitatingly be described as science fiction. It is striking that the very title Verne gives to his novels as a whole—*Extraordinary Voyages: Known and Unknown Worlds*—seems to foreground the generic tendency of the travel narrative; and the narrative device of the alternative recent past is even more elaborately insisted upon than in Mary Shelley or Poe. Yet Verne is more thoroughly science-fictional than either. We need here to consider that the most specific historical force that doomed the ordinary travel narrative to obsolescence is *imperialism*. As the major Western powers—principally Britain and France—tightened their grip throughout the nineteenth century on hitherto "exotic" lands, the kind of extraordinary voyage in earthly space that had been relatively (though only relatively) innocent for More or Swift became not only increasingly sinister but, even more important in this context, fatally quotidian. A *truly* extraordinary voyage, then, can now only move in that dimension that is in any case being generally foregrounded by the ever-increasing rate of revolutionary historical change both political and technological: time. Such is, in fact, the essential strategy of the largely anti-imperialist Verne (who, on the matter of imperialism as in some other ways, is perhaps closer to Captain Nemo than to any of his other heroes). But, as in *Frankenstein* or "M. Valdemar," the futurism of Verne's orientation is left mainly implicit, and, indeed, the whole temporal dimension is most cunningly recast in *spatial* terms. In Verne science fiction separates itself from the comparatively static, ahistorical travel narrative by actually *disguising* itself as the latter.

Verne accomplishes this remarkably subtle maneuver by staging his voyages in areas that are of no interest to the empirical cartographies of European imperialism and that, indeed, are physically inaccessible in the absence of new knowledge and technology: the subterranean regions of *Journey to the Center of the Earth* (1864), the outer space of *From the Earth to the Moon* (1865), the submarine districts of *Twenty Thousand Leagues Under the Sea* (1870). Though the quality of the actual science behind these journeys varies considerably (Nemo's project, for example, is technically a good deal more plausible than Lidenbrock's), in each case a carefully wrought cognition effect is achieved. The various extraordinary voyages are concretized as possibilities for the (near) future of the reader's actual present—which is thereby estranged and historicized as a possible past. If *Twenty Thousand Leagues* remains the most durably powerful of Verne's novels, it is primarily because the technological achievement of the *Nautilus* enables an unusually high degree of self-sufficiency among the extraordinary voyagers. This self-sufficiency in turn makes possible an unusually clear and estranging contrast between the empirical present of European imperialism and the Novum (as Ernst Bloch would say) of some more humane potential future: a temporal, historical contrast that the imagery of the novel spatializes as the contrast between dry land, where treachery and greed rule and where Nemo has sworn never again to walk, and the *Nautilus* itself, a realm of solidarity and egalitarian (if homoerotic) compassion.

On the other hand, the most prominent partial exception to the fundamentally temporal and futurist orientation of Verne's work is, of course, *Around the World in Eighty Days* (1872). It is the most seriously geographical or spatial and the most lightly science-fictional of Verne's major works; significantly, it boasts the Vernian hero who is most like an imperialist, notably as Fogg crosses *British* India and rescues a Hindu widow (whom he eventually marries) from a suttee. Yet even Fogg's voyage is not without a hidden temporal aspect. Fogg, who is frequently described in mechanical terms, has no interest, after all, in conventional geography as such: he "was not travelling, but only describing a circumference . . . ; he was a solid body, traversing an orbit around the terrestrial globe, according to the laws of rational mechanics."[24] In other words, Fogg and to a considerable degree the text itself are concerned less with the spatial extent of the journey than with its temporal duration (on which the outcome of the great wager depends). The interest lies less in the actual content of the lands crossed than in the technological and social innovations of increasingly rapid travel, so that the text points clearly, if implicitly, to the new forms of transportation and yet greater speeds of the future. It is not accidental that Verne's tale and title have often been rewritten in overtly science-fictional frameworks, with Verne's days replaced by smaller and smaller units of time.

With the work of Verne, we have almost arrived at the borders of modern science fiction. A substantial tradition of science fiction, comparable to the tradition of historical fiction established by Scott, Cooper, Manzoni, Pushkin, and others is almost in view. The final step is taken by H. G. Wells—"the English Jules Verne," as he was known in the 1890s, much to the annoyance of both men. With *The Time Machine* (1895), the crucial temporal dimension of

24. Jules Verne, *Around the World in Eighty Days*, trans. G. M. Towle (New York: Bantam, 1984), 35.

science fiction is finally made explicit, and the device of the apparently geographical narrative can decisively be left behind. Wells, indeed, almost seems to display deliberate contempt for the older kind of travel story by taking some pains, in *The Time Machine*, to convey how *little*, in purely spatial terms, the Time Traveller's vehicle moves during a voyage more extraordinary than any recorded by Verne.

But it is not only or even mainly because of his excursions in overt futurology—four years after *The Time Machine*, for example, he published both *A Story of the Days to Come* and *When the Sleeper Wakes*; and in 1936 he collaborated with the director William Cameron Menzies to make *Things to Come*, one of the earliest masterworks of science-fiction cinema—that Wells must be considered the culmination of a predominantly science-fictional line begun some eight decades earlier by Mary Shelley. Even when not writing actual future history (a subgenre of science fiction whose apex is reached, unsurprisingly, by the writer who was Wells's most devoted disciple, Olaf Stapledon), Wells displays a more developed and critical historical understanding than any other science-fiction author to date, a greater ability to construct historicizing estrangements of his own imperialist European present. In *The War of the Worlds* (1898), for instance, Wells antedates Forster and Orwell in producing a genuinely anti-imperialist novel. Though the text can, indeed, be read as licensing xenophobic fear of the cultural Other as biologically and astronomically alien, its more powerful tendency is to estrange British colonialism by showing Britain itself in the (then but not later) almost unimaginable position of colonial victim—a theme pursued so intently that the Martians, somewhat inexplicably, concentrate their invasion on the one small island, evidently ignoring Continental Europe, the United States, and even Ireland. The result is a critical interrogation of imperialism that (at least) matches *A Passage to India* (1924) or *Burmese Days* (1934).

In what is perhaps Wells's finest fiction, *The Island of Dr. Moreau* (1896), he does choose the kind of setting—a little obscure island somewhere in the vast Pacific Ocean—typical of the old-fashioned geographical narrative. But there is no question here of even a superficial resemblance to the older form. The island on which Prendick lands is not represented as being of any real interest prior to the recent arrival of the biotechnological imperialist named in the title, and what the text displays are not timeless "marvels" but one of the most searching examinations of racial and class attitudes that Victorian England produced. Indeed, the novel, with its Prospero-like hero and its many other echoes of *The Tempest* (1612), not only questions several traditional notions of human hierarchy, but, in its Darwinian deconstruction of the binary opposition between human and beast, somewhat undermines anthropocentrism itself. Wells has often been compared, with respect to class background and general social attitudes, to Dickens, an author of Lukácsian realism though neglected by Lukács himself. In Wells's best science fiction there is indeed a critical consciousness of historical development that is not unworthy of comparison with that in *Bleak House* (1853) or *Little Dorritt* (1857)—and that is considerably superior to that displayed in Wells's own nonfictional *The Outline of History* (1920) or in his naturalistic novels.

We are now in a position to delineate more precisely the affinities and differences between science fiction and the historical novel. Both manifest a radically critical impulse, for both are radically dialectical and historicizing literary tendencies, and both are determinate products of the capitalist-revolutionary dynamic that produced history (in the modern sense) itself. Both operate by means of a post-Hegelian dialectic of historical identity and historical difference: in both, that is, the empirical present of the reader and of the text's own production is put into contrast with an alternative significantly different from the former, yet different in a way that remains rationally accountable. In the historical novel, however, the alternative to actuality is located in a knowable (and generally national) past; there is a real sense in which the novel—not, of course, in substance or detail, but in outline—is prewritten before it ever begins. The outcome of the Jacobite rebellion of 1745, or of the Napoleonic invasion of Russia, are known before the reader ever picks up *Waverley* or *War and Peace*, and cannot be altered by the intellectual fertility of Scott or Tolstoy. Estrangement, accordingly, plays a comparatively limited role in the novel of historical realism. In science fiction, by contrast, cognitive estrangement is central: the mundane status quo shared by author and reader is contrasted, while also connected, to a potential future that is indeed historically determinate (at least in literary effect) but of its very nature less factually preset than any established past. As we have seen, the presence of the (typically international) future in the science-fictional text may be merely implicit in strictly chronological terms, though it is more often explicit during the twentieth-century history of the genre. In either case, however, the dialectical freedom of the writer, though limited and actualized by the cognitive integrity of the genre, is at a critical maximum. Indeed, if nineteenth-century science fiction takes longer to establish itself than nineteenth-century historical realism, despite the fact that both are stimulated by the same general set of historical circumstances, it may well be at least in part because of the greater difficulty of creatively managing the freedom that science fiction demands.

To contrast science fiction and the historical novel along the axis of future and past may, however, be seriously misleading unless the contrast is itself understood in a dialectical rather than a binary way. Two points are especially important here. In the first place, the futurism of science fiction must not be confused with factual forecasting of the real, empirical future. To be sure, many science-fiction authors, especially those with scientific or technical training, have had a taste for futurological predictions, and a few notable hits have been scored: Verne's submarine, Wells's tank, Arthur C. Clarke's communications satellite (an idea that, had Clarke been able to patent it when he first devised it in the 1940s, might conceivably have become the most lucrative insight of the century). But such details are marginal, at best, to science fiction as a genre. The future is crucial to science fiction not as a specific chronological register, but as a locus of radical *alterity* to the mundane status quo, which is thus estranged and historicized as the concrete past of potential future.[25] The potential future in science fiction exists, one might say, primarily for the sake of the actual present; in this sense all science fiction is covered by J. G. Ballard's wonderful maxim that the future in his work has never been more than five minutes away.

Indeed, the historical and (as we shall see) utopian force that the future possesses in major science fiction does not, on the whole, cohere particularly well with positivistic chronological forecasting. For instance, the great negative utopias of modern literature—*We* (1921), *Brave New World* (1932), *Nineteen Eighty-four* (1949)—are drained of much of their power if we attempt to read them not as complexly critical estrangements of certain actual tendencies in Soviet and Anglo-American society, but instead as factual futurology, rating Zamyatin, Huxley, and Orwell as though they were contestants in a guessing game (a habit of reading that is unfortunately encouraged by the final title of the work that Orwell during composition designated *The Last Man in Europe*). Or consider *Last and First Men* (1931), a more complicated and important work than any of that triad. If the early chapters of Stapledon's science-fictional epic are the weakest and least memorable, it is not at all, as some have felt, because they are the most "political." Rather it is because, in dealing with the relatively near future, Stapledon has allowed a good deal of empirical and generally erroneous guesswork—for instance, about the religious forms of competition between China and America—to distract from the more general historico-philosophical design (the latter is typified, in the earlier chapters, by the great vision of an Americanized planet). By the time we reach the fall of the First Men, the temptation to such weather forecasting has been left behind, and the grand design of eighteen human civilizations, each actualizing different aspects of what Stapledon sees as the total potential of the species, is unencumbered. The result—only superficially paradoxical—is that the latter chapters contain the most effective estrangements and, indeed, the most deeply *political* historicizations of Stapledon's present.

There is a further parallel here between science fiction and historical realism: in the latter the past, while of course more fixedly determinate than the future in science fiction, is of value not so much for its literal accuracy in all detail (Scott's slips are as notorious as Flaubert's pedantry) as for its role in

25. Cf. Fredric Jameson, "Progress Versus Utopia; or, Can We Imagine the Future?" *Science-Fiction Studies* 9 (1982): 152. "I would argue . . . that the most characteristic SF does not seriously attempt to imagine the 'real' future of our social system. Rather, its multiple mock futures serve the quite different function of transforming our own present into the determinate past of something yet to come."

establishing the historicity of the present—in the sense of denaturalizing the present by showing it to be neither arbitrary nor inevitable but the conjunctural result of complex, knowable material processes. To compare science fiction and the historical novel in this way brings us to our second qualification of their contrast according to the temporal axis of future and past. We recall that, generically, science fiction and historical realism are after all *tendencies* that in any actual text operate in overdetermined combination with other comparatively autonomous generic tendencies. The close kinship that we have articulated between the two tendencies makes it unsurprising that the two should frequently—perhaps typically—combine together. In other words, works that are predominantly science-fictional may also evince the dialectic of present and *past* that defines historical realism; conversely, historical novels may participate in a properly science-fictional dialectic of present and future. Much science fiction, for instance, contains a subordinate element that might be called disguised historical fiction. Asimov's *Foundation* (1951; the first and best novel of the Foundation series) relates an effective secession from the Galactic Empire by the followers of Hari Seldon and their establishment of a new civilization on the remote planet of Terminus—a new civilization whose history largely recapitulates that of European capitalism, with a strong emphasis on the mercantile and entrepreneurial phases of the latter. Despite the chronological setting of all the action in the remote future, and despite the presence of many genuinely science-fictional elements, the novel thus also establishes an implicit contrast between its own present—the increasingly arid culture of the monopoly-capitalist American Empire of Truman and Joseph McCarthy—and what are imagined as more swashbuckling, more affectively rich, stages in the past development of bourgeois civilization. The present is, as it were, estranged from two temporal directions—from future and past—at once.

On the other hand, for the operation of science-fictional alterity in the historical novel we may return to Lukács's prototypical work of historical realism, Walter Scott's *Waverley*. The critical reconstruction of the Jacobite rising is in fact quite different in method from that of middle-class historiography; while firmly rooted in the Highland past, it at some points approximates to the In-Front-of-Us (to borrow Ernst Bloch's term) of science-fictional estrangement. Consider the great trial scene (chapter 68). When Fergus Mac-Ivor, the Highland chieftain, is condemned to death for his part in the rebellion, he accepts his fate bravely; nonetheless there is a clear sense that his consciousness and motives are not completely dissimilar from those of his judges. For Fergus, despite his clan background, has always displayed a certain cool worldliness and capacity for political calculation. He is, in fact, a transitional figure between his nation's heroic gentile past and the bourgeois Anglicized order, with attendant *Realpolitik*, that renders the pre-feudal past hopelessly archaic. Wholly alien to the bourgeois mind-set, however, is Fergus's retainer, Evan Dhu Maccombich.

When Evan Dhu rises to speak, the English spectators expect that he will beg to be pardoned on account of having been misled by Fergus; instead, he asks that he and several of his fellows be put to death in exchange for Fergus's release. Scott may well be touching here on extremely archaic processes of Highland subject-formation. Even so, Evan Dhu's selflessness also provides a quasi–science-fictional estrangement of normative middle-class rationality, and, with some adjustments (mainly de-hierarchization), could stand as a properly utopian and future-oriented figure of communal solidarity.

Having then sketched the major conceptual parallels and direct relations—as well as contrasts—between science fiction and historical realism, I now resume the task of historicizing the two generic tendencies in relation to each other. Thus far, one major issue in this connection has been left untouched. We have not yet considered science fiction in coordination with what Lukács regards as the emergence of the pseudohistorical novel after the general decline of great realism in the second half of the nineteenth century (a decline, in Lukács's judgment, only occasionally reversed during the twentieth). Without rehearsing Lukács's specific criticisms of such major figures as Meyer or Flaubert—and certainly without necessarily endorsing his astringent condemnations of naturalism and the various modernisms—we can nonetheless concede that the dangers he diagnoses in the (pseudo-)historical novel as a specialized genre are real enough. Paradoxically, historical fiction is of all forms especially vulnerable to an undialectical and *un*historical fetishism of the (as-if-dead) past, a reified and reifying antiquarianism in which the merely aesthetic relish of costume and exotic factuality triumphs over the genuinely critical issues of historical specificity and difference. And such work—amply illustrated by the "historical" novels that regularly figure in current best-seller lists—almost inevitably betrays the kind of psychological modernization indicted by Lukács. Furthermore, it is noteworthy that, although science fiction and historical realism first appear almost simultaneously, with *Waverley* and *Frankenstein*, by the time a substantial science-fictional tradition has been established—by the time, that is, of Verne and Wells—Europe has passed into the post-1848 period that Lukács associates with historical realism's decline. How does science fiction relate to this decline?

It seems to me that the (or a) historic role of science fiction from Verne onward might be described as keeping alive critical historical consciousness as the historical novel proper becomes increasingly problematic. It is not, of course, that science-fiction authors are somehow magically immune from the "false consciousness" that Lukács identifies in an increasingly reactionary bourgeoisie ever more disinclined to know its own history. Rather, what is at stake is a certain relative autonomy of *form* itself. As knowledge (in the sense of *connaissance* even more than in that of *savoir*) of the past becomes ideologically more and more difficult to attain, the historical novel, necessarily tied as it is to such knowledge, is bound to become increasingly susceptible to reification. But science fiction is comparatively free of the burden of the past, at least in the particular way relevant here. Its primary orientation, as we have seen, is toward the future; it is thus capable of engaging the matter of historicity without the same kind of post-1848 ideological baggage that the historical novelist carries. Precisely because the genre itself necessitates much less involvement in what increasingly function as the minefields of the early history and prehistory of the European bourgeoisie, science fiction remains more capable of maintaining a clear critical outlook, of seeing the overall development of human society in dialectical, historicizing terms.

No doubt science fiction pays a certain price for this greater freedom: its historicizations generally display a certain kind (but not the worst kind) of *abstraction* owing to the greater autonomy and distance from the stuff of real history. As evocations of imperialism, for example, *The War of the Worlds* cannot compete with *Burmese Days*—two novels, it should be noted, by authors with many similarities in personal, ideological, and even specifically literary terms—in conveying the sights, the smells, or the contingent personal emotions of the European imperialist project. Yet Orwell's novel (which provides almost a textbook Lukácsian case of the naturalist separation between factual objectivity and psychological subjectivity) suffers from a more damaging variety of abstraction, in that the proliferation of smells and emotions often threatens to overwhelm the larger, genuinely conceptual issues of imperialism that are so trenchantly—and, in that sense, so concretely—estranged by Wells's science-fictional treatment.

In a somewhat similar vein, we might contrast *Last and First Men* with a historical novel also English and almost exactly contemporary with it, Robert Graves's *I, Claudius* (1934). There is no question about Graves's erudition or good faith, and it is certainly true that he conveys the everyday life of a patrician Roman during the early imperial period with much greater force and clarity than that with which Stapledon conveys the everyday life of, say, one of the Fifth Men. Indeed, the essayistic abstraction with which *Last and First Men* is narrated—and that in certain generic ways makes it closer to a philosophically informed work of scholarship than to the conventional novel—is notorious. Yet Stapledon's book is, in every radical sense, overwhelmingly the more historical of the two. The central place that art occupies in the life of the Fifth Men (one of Stapledon's more utopian varieties of the human species) suggests, for instance, an astringent comment on existing philistine England. Equally, the Fifth Men's Wild Continent, a kind of reservation of the primitive, amounts to a most prescient critical estrangement of the increasing asphyxiation of the natural in Stapledon's own repressed society (as well as a shrewd tactical defense against the conservative notion that scientific utopia must develop in the excessively artificial way that negative utopians like Zamyatin and Huxley stigmatize). By contrast, *I, Claudius*, for all its scholarly detail and technical brilliance, never really engages any world-historical issues of either Claudius's or Graves's society. Except in one or two isolated passages, the development of imperial Rome is effectively reduced to an intricate but trivial network of erotic and careerist intrigue; and the psychological motivations displayed are, as Lukács would lead us to expect, glaringly modern. Though there may be external evidence that Graves intended to satirize the patrician class of his own imperial nation (in which the Roman Empire was, after all, taken as the preeminent historical model for the British Empire), the workings of imperialism never come sufficiently into view for the satire to function in that way. The novel, one might say, evinces much *savoir* but little historical *connaissance*. Indeed, Stapledon's narration of the way that the Fifth Men come to possess incomparable historical knowledge by projecting their consciousnesses into those of earlier humans provides, on one level, a parody but, on a deeper level, a critique of Graves's project, which is superficially similar to that of the Fifth Men but—in that it yields little real insight into the Roman past—fundamentally quite different.

In recent years, however, a form of the historical novel has evolved that was quite unforeseen by Lukács. It responds to the problem of reification (the problem of the ossification of a critically vital historical sense) in a manner quite different from *Burmese Days* or *I, Claudius*, with their evasions of recent and ancient history respectively. This new inflection of the genre—which we may provisionally call the postmodern historical novel, though the term probably creates more problems than it solves—is in one way a dialectical sublation of the problem identified by Lukács: that is, it takes the difficulty of knowing the past, of thinking and feeling historically, as novelistic subject matter in its own right.

The already classic example is E. L. Doctorow's *Ragtime* (1975), which on one level seems to be "about" the crucial transitional period of American history to which the title alludes, but which on a more basic level conveys, by numerous subtle stylistic and other formal paths, the extreme difficulty of knowing any longer what turn-of-the-century America was like, especially in its rich but finally occluded traditions of social radicalism.[26] The dialectical paradox of the novel, however, is that in rigorously testing a certain blockage of historicity, *Ragtime* indirectly establishes a sense of the historical American past after all. For the ultimate object of the text must be taken to be that complex constellation of sociopolitical-historical forces (indicated most crudely and obviously by such proper nouns as "McCarthyism" and "Reaganism") that have largely erased the living memory of Emma Goldman's America. There is a real sense, then, in which a work like *Ragtime* is more allied to the classical realistic tradition of the historical novel associated with Walter Scott than to the later naturalistic decadence of the form.

26. See Fredric Jameson, *Postmodernism* (Durham: Duke University Press, 1991), 21–25, for a reading of the novel to this effect.

The same is true of a perhaps even more pertinent instance of postmodern historical fiction, Don DeLillo's *Libra* (1988). The most cunning strategy of the novel lies not simply in taking the Kennedy assassination of 1963 and its attendant mysteries as the perfect synecdoche for recent American history, but, even more, in finding the exact "objective correlative" for the unknowability of that crucial historical event: namely, the historiographic project of the protagonist, Nicholas Branch, a retired CIA analyst who is at work on a secret history of the assassination. The CIA promises that Branch, alone among historians, will have full access to all relevant documentation, though the price for this access is that his history will not be allowed to circulate beyond the walls of the agency itself. Even this very limited attempt at knowing fails. Though Branch (and, behind him, DeLillo) builds up a most complex, fascinating, plausible account of Lee Oswald, his direct and indirect associates, and the whole political and cultural environment, the reliability of the account remains dubious, at least in detail. Branch eventually seems to fall under suspicion by his agency superiors, and he himself begins to suspect that the anonymous, faceless "Curator" (of CIA archives) is withholding material from him. What does remain clear is that the epistemological blockage is no merely textual or even (in the narrow sense) conspiratorial matter. Rather, it is deeply linked to many right-wing propertied interests that lie far beyond the ken of any single individual and of which the CIA itself is only one comparatively bland bureaucratic embodiment. The perspective, in other words, is properly critical, and the basic problems are structural. *Libra* does not regard knowledge of the Kennedy assassination as a potential "golden key" that could unlock all the secrets of recent American history.[27] Instead, it takes the murkiness surrounding the assassination as a characteristic instance of how difficult historical knowledge has become under the regime of monopoly capital and a vast national-security state, even from the vantage point of one so institutionally privileged as Branch. *Waverley* conveys the sense (fully intended by Scott) that the reader is learning a great deal about the 1745 rebellion. Reading *Libra* may well make one feel that one now knows *less* about the 1963 assassination (in the sense of being more uncertain about the various possibilities and details). But the novel also suggests why one is in that curious (and perhaps postmodern) epistemological predicament.

What should be stressed in the current context is the way that novels like *Libra* and *Ragtime* are radically science-fictional. After functioning in roughly parallel fashion for nearly two centuries (and frequently, as we have seen, operating within the same texts) the generic tendencies of science fiction and

27. Cf. Alexander Cockburn on Oliver Stone's *JFK* (1991): "There's no 'golden key' (e.g., the 'truth' about the Kennedy assassination; 'proof' that George Bush flew to Paris on October 20, 1980) that will suddenly render the overall system transparent and vulnerable. People who look for golden keys are akin to those poor souls who thought the future could be decoded by measurements in the Great Pyramid"; *The Nation* (9 March 1992), 320.

historical fiction finally merge in the postmodern, or, as it may more precisely be called, the science-fictional historical novel. For authors such as Doctorow and DeLillo, the study of history, one might say, finally itself becomes a science. Precisely in their self-conscious and rigorous interrogations of the blockages and difficulties that tend to repress historical knowing, these novels engage historiography as a properly critical and interpretive discourse in the full post-Kantian sense. In other words, they not only deal with history as material but also with historiography as theoretical structure.

In this way, perhaps, more than in any other, the science-fictional historical novel marks a fundamental conceptual advance over the naturalistic historical novel typified by *I, Claudius* or *Burmese Days.* Texts of this latter sort tend to view history in predominantly empiricist fashion, as stuff or raw material out of which a novelistic pattern may be shaped. *I, Claudius* may not, as we have seen, really know very much about Rome, but it does not know that it does not know: it does not recognize historical knowing as itself a cognitive problem. For the science-fictional historical novel, historical knowing is the *central* conceptual problem, and the principal cognitive estrangement produced by the form is the defamiliarization of historical knowledge, which is shown to be, for determinate ideological and political reasons, deeply problematic and the reverse of transparent or metaphysically sanctioned. A certain multiplicity and, indeed, a certain overdetermination of historical science are thus suggested. Science fiction has long been familiar with the novel of alternative reality, such as Kingsley Amis's *The Alteration* (1976) or (the masterwork of the kind) Philip K. Dick's *The Man in the High Castle* (1962), in which history is rewritten with one huge difference (the Reformation never occurred, or the Axis won the Second World War) in order to foreground the contingency and mutability of the historical actual. The science-fictional historical novel is a closely related subgenre, though here the estrangement of history—the shattering of the overfamiliarity and taken-for-grantedness of the received narrative of the past—is effected not so much by departing from known historical reality as by questioning how and to what extent historical reality is, after all, known. When Doctorow conducts such famous historical figures as Houdini and J. P. Morgan through fictional events and in and out of the lives of fictional characters, and when DeLillo constructs the *Entwicklungsroman* of a presidential assassin, they are indeed creating "alternative" histories, narratives that are complex and plausible but that insinuate in their very letter the ideological and epistemological problems in establishing their own relationship to historical truth.

With the merger of science fiction and the historical novel in works like *Libra* and *Ragtime,* my historicization of the two similar and largely parallel (yet significantly different) generic tendencies, and my examination of the critical dynamic of science fiction in relation to the historical novel, are nearly complete. One last question, broached in passing much earlier, remains.

Though Lukács never, I think, frames the question in quite this way, the logic of his general critical position suggests an important reason why historical realism, as a generic tendency, has never been able to constitute the totality of a novelistic text. A text that was simply and solely realistic would presumably be one that enacts a perfect historicization of the society represented in relation to the society in which the text was produced. Such flawlessly critical historical perspective would presuppose a coign of vantage in which all significant sociohistorical forces and relations were completely transparent—in other words, a perfected utopia. A purely realistic historical novel, then, would be a strictly utopian text, in both the representations and the provenance of the latter.

Would the same, in principle, be true of a purely science-fictional text? The question is clearly pertinent to this study, especially with regard to the critical dynamic implicit in science-fictional narrative structure; it cannot, however, be answered without an extended consideration of the category of utopia itself. The term has, indeed, already been encountered in this chapter. But there are several important ways in which much of the preceding analysis of the critical dynamic of science fiction, in relation to its style and to its position vis-à-vis the historical novel, can be further developed by investigating the issue of science fiction and utopia.

The Critical Dynamic: Science Fiction and Utopia

Thomas More's neo-Greek coinage, *utopia*, is one of the most successful such inventions in linguistic history; merely to list and discriminate among the major usages of the term and the various senses that it has been made to bear would require a substantial book. This success is of course relevant to the current study, as is the fact that today the dominant Anglo-American colloquial meaning of the word is mildly pejorative: to describe an idea or plan as utopian usually connotes that it is naive and wildly impractical, though perhaps well-intended. For our own purposes, however, there are three distinct (though related) principal meanings: in chronological order, a generic meaning, a political-economic meaning, and a philosophical and hermeneutic meaning. The chief burden of this section will be to investigate the critical relationship between science fiction and utopia by coordinating each of these senses of the latter term with science fiction as defined and analyzed thus far.

Generically, of course, the term refers to the form invented in 1516 (almost exactly three centuries before *Frankenstein*) when More published *Utopia*, and the form has been at least intermittently popular ever since. There is no question here of even a very brief survey of the genre, but it is worth noting that there is probably no other comparably abundant literary kind that can be traced so unambiguously—and often explicitly—to a single text. In *Gulliver's Travels* (1726; probably the finest utopian work produced in the two centuries after More) Swift is careful to include overt mention of his precursor in the prefatory letter.[28] And a number of later authors have recorded their direct debt in their very titles: Wells's *A Modern Utopia* (1905); William Morris's *News from Nowhere* (1890), in which More's neo-Greek is translated into English; Samuel Butler's *Erewhon* (1872), in which More's term is translated and then scrambled; and, much more recently, Ursula Le Guin's *The Dispossessed* (1974), which is subtitled "An Ambiguous Utopia." As the example of Le Guin suggests, utopias today are typically written within an explicitly science-fictional context.

The second, political-economic sense of utopia is doubtless less familiar to most readers. It refers mainly to the polemical writings of Marx and Engels in which the founders of historical materialism deprecate certain alternative conceptions of socialism as "utopian," in contrast to their own scientific version. Suffice it for the moment to note that, when Marx and Engels declare themselves to be against the idea of utopia, they object not (primarily) to the actual contents of any imagined better society, nor to the form that the imagining of such a society might take, and least of all to the idealism and good faith of at least some of those whom they characterize as utopian socialists. Instead, the main object of their attack is the putative means of *transition* from actuality to utopia. Utopia in this sense has no direct connection to science fiction, though its indirect relevance will become apparent.

Finally, utopia has an important hermeneutic sense. The reference here is to a group of philosophers in, or on the margins of, the original Institute for Social Research in Frankfurt, as well as later commentators directly influenced by the Frankfurt School. Key authors include Walter Benjamin, Theodor Adorno, Herbert Marcuse, and, among later figures, Fredric Jameson. But far and away the most important philosopher of utopian interpretation is one already mentioned in passing: Ernst Bloch, and most significantly as he is represented by his immense magnum opus, *Das Prinzip Hoffnung* (1959), an almost unclassifiable work that combines cultural and aesthetic commentary, philosophical and theological speculation, and political polemic, all the while remaining a kind of vast prose poem in its own right.[29] For Bloch, utopia is not

28. "If the censure of yahoos could any way affect me, I should have great reason to complain that some of them are so bold as to think my book of travels a mere fiction out of mine own brain; and have gone so far as to drop hints that the Houyhnhnms and Yahoos have no more existence than the inhabitants of Utopia"; Jonathan Swift, *Gulliver's Travels and Other Writings*, ed. Louis Landa (Boston: Houghton Mifflin, 1960).

29. My references to this work are to the three-volume translation by Neville Plaice, Stephen Plaice, and Paul Knight (Cambridge, Mass.: MIT Press, 1986). The translators have called their version *The Principle of Hope*, but Bloch's title is in fact untranslatable into idiomatic English. Some have suggested that "Hope the Principle," while awkward, is closer to Bloch's German. "The Hope Principle" is at least as awkward but arguably closer yet, at least insofar as it suggests that, for Bloch, hope is a principle analogous to (but also in contrast to) the pleasure principle and reality principle of Freud. Bloch insists that we are *driven* by hope just as inevitably as psychoanalysis holds us to be driven by the search for pleasure, the avoidance of pain, and the recognized strictures of reality.

so much a matter of description or planning as it is a way of thinking and of reading: a utopian hermeneutic construes fragmentary prefigurations of an unalienated (communist) future in the cultural artifacts of the past and present, including many that on the surface may not seem particularly progressive. Though it is possible to contrast critique and utopia, the latter, as we shall see, can also be understood as an aspect of critique. Furthermore, as was suggested in the preceding section and will be argued at much greater length here, the hermeneutic of utopia provides an especially powerful and appropriate way of reading the texts of science fiction. Before examining this particular conjuncture of science fiction and utopia, however, it is necessary to appreciate some of the critical richness of utopia in the Blochian sense.

For Bloch, the central truth of utopia is paradoxical. On the one hand, utopia is never fully present in the here-and-now, and necessarily eludes all attempts to locate it with complete empirical precision. It depends upon what Bloch calls the Novum, that is, the *radically* (though not purely) new, which by definition cannot be exhaustively or definitively mapped. Utopia is to be found in the Not-Yet, or the Not-Yet-Being, or the In-Front-of-Us, or simply the Front, as Bloch variously designates it. Utopia can never be fixed in the perspective of the present, because it exists, to a considerable degree, in the dimension of futurity: not, however, in the future as the latter is imagined by mere chronological forecasting, or in mechanistic and philistine notions of bourgeois "progress," but rather as the future is the object of *hope*, of our deepest and most radical longings. These are longings that can never be satisfied by the fulfillment of any individual wish (say, for personal wealth) but that demand, rather, a revolutionary reconfiguration of the world as a totality. Utopian hope or longing, in other words, possesses an inherently collective character and at bottom has nothing in common with individualist impulses like greed.

Indeed, it is only the dimension of collectivity that guarantees the future-orientedness of utopia; the merely self-interested wish always amounts to a desire that the status quo of the present should remain essentially unaltered while one's own personal lot within it is improved. Yet, precisely because utopian longings are irreducible in human psychology as Bloch understands it—because the hope principle drives us no less ineluctably, if more subtly and less palpably, than the Freudian pleasure principle does—utopia, which in one sense is always *elsewhere*, always escaping our actual horizons, is in another and no less important sense inscribed in the innermost core of our being. As Bloch puts it in the sublime conclusion to *Das Prinzip Hoffnung*:

Marx describes as his final concern "the development of the wealth of human nature"; this *human* wealth as well as that of *nature* as a whole lies solely in the tendency-latency in which the world finds itself—vis-à-vis de tout. This glance therefore confirms that man everywhere is still living in prehistory, indeed all and everything still stands before the creation of the world, of a right world. *True genesis is not at the beginning but at the end,* and it starts to begin only when society and existence become radical, i.e. grasp their roots. But the root of history is the working, creating human being who reshapes and overhauls the given facts. Once he has grasped himself and established what is his, without expropriation and alienation, in real democracy, there arises in the world something which shines into the childhood of all and in which no one has yet been: homeland. (3:1375–1376; emphasis in original)

Every valid theoretical description of utopia is thus paradoxical. Utopia is the homeland where no one has ever been but where alone we are authentically at home. It is the promised land that can only be attained by means of exodus: "the thus designated realm of freedom develops not as return, but as exodus— though into the always intended promised land, promised by process" (*Prinzip Hoffnung* 1:205). Utopia is fundamental to our being, but being is itself a matter of Not-Yet-Being: "The being that conditions consciousness, and the consciousness that processes being, is understood ultimately only out of that and in that from which and towards which it tends. Essential being is not Beenness; on the contrary: the essential being of the world lies itself on the Front" (1:18; emphasis deleted). Such paradoxes are by no means merely verbal. They correspond to the dialectic of immanence and transcendence that constitutes utopia, and, ultimately, to the inescapably dialectical, contradictory nature of post-Kantian and post-Hegelian reality itself.

It is important to understand that this concept of utopia is not only a theory of sociality—of the unalienated classless homeland of a postrevolutionary future—but, no less fundamentally, of psychology as well. The hope principle, incessantly driving us back to where we have never been, constitutes the human psyche as intrinsically *divided.* There is some kinship between this idea and Lacan's concept of the splitting of the subject. Indeed, a psychoanalytic reading of Bloch could readily rewrite utopian positivity as primary narcissism, or, in more strictly Lacanian terms, as pre-Imaginary plenitude. But the differences between Bloch and Lacan are important. Lacan shares Freud's harsh pessimism. For both, plenitude is primarily an illusion, and the Lacanian splitting of the subject is irreducibly structured on a *lack* or privation that can, at best, be somewhat palliated through psychoanalytic practice but can never be radically healed or even challenged. For Bloch, by contrast, plenitude is much more than an illusion; it corresponds to the positive fulfillment of utopian longing. Lack is in one way no less crucial for Bloch than for Freud and Lacan (Bloch certainly does not *deny* the bleakest prospects of psychic self-alienation and the reality principle), but Bloch, unlike the psychoanalysts, understands lack as not simply itself but also as always implying its own positivity. To understand lack or nullity in this paradoxical way is, indeed, the supreme hermeneutic achievement of utopian thought on both the psychic and social levels. It is in this context that Marx can be seen as the greatest of utopian philosophers: "The zero point of extremest alienation which the proletariat represents now at last becomes the dialectical point of change; Marx teaches us to find out All precisely in the Nothing of this zero point" (*Prinzip Hoffnung* 3:1358). Utopian plenitude, one might say, is (*pace* psychoanalysis) a kind of truth, though—again the inevitable paradox—such plenitude can be truly apprehended only in fragmentary form.

It follows, then, that utopia is a form of *cognition* and, indeed, a version of critical theory itself. Bloch's dialectical synthesis of utopia as a category at once social and psychological works to foreground the post-Kantian and post-Hegelian primacy of interpretation and thus to transcend any mechanistic binary opposition between (abstractly positivistic) "objectivity" and (abstractly psychologistic) "subjectivity." Utopian thought cannot display the results of its investigations in the shape of quantified data; nonetheless it retains a cognitive integrity and validity grounded in the very nature of critique. Utopian hermeneutic is after all a kind of *labor*, a political practice, which makes no claim to empiricist "reflection" but construes its objects in an avowedly interested—a collectively interested—way. The construction of utopia among the terrible reifications of actuality is *true*, not in the sense of attaining unproblematic correspondence with pregiven reality, but in the sense of construing that which is at some level(s) only coming into being.[30]

One of the most striking examples in the entirety of *Das Prinzip Hoffnung* is Bloch's long analysis of "wishful images" (1:337–447), which extend from the happy endings of popular films and romances to the communal longings of Nazi Germany and the Ku Klux Klan. Bloch provides a devastating critique of such mendaciously pseudo-utopian desires, and he exposes the concrete continuum that links something as apparently innocuous as beautification through lipstick with something as openly grotesque as the racist fulfillment achieved through the terrorism of the masked night-rider. Both involve a wishful image in the mirror, the desire, as Bloch says, to make ourselves appear more "beautiful" than we really are. Yet the critique is not merely dismissive: the regressive pseudo-utopian wish contains some measure of utopia itself. At the same time that Bloch exposes and negates, he also emphasizes the authentic positivity buried within even the worst fascist distortions of the utopian ideal of collectivity. Accordingly, he maintains that the wish for a happy ending (however trivial or barbaric in form) must be respected and resituated as well as demystified: "For this reason there is more possible pleasure in the idea of a converted Nazi than from all the cynics and nihilists" (1:446). The dialectical poise displayed here is exemplary, since, for the Jewish and Marxist Bloch, Nazism is of course the limit case, the most extreme instance of degradation and nullity. Yet even here the utopian hermeneutic is capable of construing

30. Cf. Ernst Bloch, *A Philosophy of the Future*, trans. John Cumming (New York: Herder and Herder, 1970), 96: "Utopian consciousness remains *wholly without deception* inasmuch as the monument of its fulfillment is still outstanding—and certainly not for sceptical or agnostic reasons. . . . The world-substance . . . is not yet finished and complete, but persists in a utopian-open state, i.e. a state in which its self-identity is not yet manifest" (my emphasis).

plenitude out of privation, of reading, in the hideous pseudo-Wagnerian cele-
brations of murderous Aryan brotherhood, a very partial prefiguration of true
collectivity. Indeed, it is no accident that Bloch typically refers to the utopia of
unalienated postrevolutionary classlessness as our homeland, or, in the original German, *Heimat*—a term that he quite deliberately attempts to rehabili-
tate out of the strongly Nazi sense that it bore between 1933 and 1945.

As a version of critical theory, then, the utopian hermeneutic of Bloch not
only ranks in importance with Bakhtinian stylistics and Lukácsian genre analysis but illustrates more emphatically than they do a crucial dialectical doubleness at the heart of the whole critical-theoretical project. On the one hand,
utopia, the supreme *positive* value, nonetheless implies a ruthless negation
and demystification of actuality: "The essential function of utopia is a critique
of what is present. If we had not already gone beyond the barriers, we could
not even perceive them as barriers."[31] The perspective of utopia alone makes
completely clear how banal and corrupt are the barriers of the status quo that
utopia works to transcend. Indeed, the fact that utopian plenitude can only be
apprehended in the most elusive and fragmentary anticipations—that utopia
emerges only in the teeth, as it were, of the mundane—is the most devastating
commentary upon the latter. On the other hand, the specifically negative dimension of the utopian dialectic—the dimension of critique in the familiar
sense of astringent demystification—can never, as we have seen, remain wholly
self-identical: in every concrete instance it points to a corresponding positivity
and plenitude, that is, to authentic utopian fulfillment.

Of course, a substantially similar dialectic does operate in the theories of
Bakhtin and Lukács. For the former, the critical heteroglossia or multiaccentuality of novelistic style—as opposed to the closed monologism of the
poetic—possesses a potentially revolutionary charge in its grasp of the diverse
and contradictory interconnectedness of the social field. Indeed, one might
even argue that, for Bakhtin, the open, polyvalent style of the novel actually
functions, in Blochian terms, as a utopian figure of a multicultural liberated
humanity. For Lukács, authentic critical realism, through its concrete
historical-materialist ontology and epistemology that negate (and sublate) the
abstractions of naturalism and psychologism, directly serves the revolutionary
project; as we have already seen, a purely realistic text could only be composed from the standpoint of utopia—the standpoint, that is, of the transparency that only a postrevolutionary classless society could enable. Indeed, we
can go so far as to say that the telos of critical theory in general can only be
the transformation (in thought, language, and action) of reality into utopia.
The elaborate demystifying apparatuses of Marxist (and, though to a lesser
degree, Freudian and even some poststructuralist) thought exist, ultimately,

31. Ernst Bloch, *The Utopian Function of Art and Literature*, trans. Jack Zipes and Frank
Mecklenburg (Cambridge, Mass.: MIT Press, 1988), 12.

in order to clear space upon which positive alternatives to the existent can be constructed. Of all versions of critical theory, however, it is perhaps Bloch's that provides the amplest, most explicit demonstration of the reciprocity and indispensability of the negative *and* positive moments of the critical dialectic; not accidentally, it may well be Bloch's utopian hermeneutic that bears the deepest affinity with science fiction.

For Bloch all genuine art—virtually by definition—finds its true significance in utopian construing.[32] Nevertheless, there are discriminations to be made, not only among individual artworks but, perhaps more pertinently, among whole genres, some of which participate more fully in the utopian dialectic than others. Though Bloch (like Bakhtin and Lukács) exhibits little or no personal acquaintance with science fiction as such, he indirectly provides a guide to the utopian dimension of science fiction in his two great companion essays in genre criticism, "A Philosophical View of the Detective Novel," and "A Philosophical View of the Novel of the Artist."[33] Bloch sees the two genres as comparable, frequently "popular" forms (but such a juxtaposition might more likely pair detective fiction with science fiction), which are, however, philosophically antithetical. Detective fiction is a deeply conservative form in which utopia is at a minimum. The essentially Oedipal structure of the detective novel is oriented decisively toward the *past*, when the crime that constitutes the chief datum of the text was committed. The plot of the novel is thus devoted to the strictly reactionary project of solving the crime and identifying the culprit in order that the status quo ante—the as-if-unproblematic condition of the detective's society prior to the (singular) crime—may be restored. Now, although Bloch himself does not pursue this line of thought, there is no doubt that a comprehensively Blochian reading would be capable of constructing anticipatory pre-illuminations of utopian collectivity even from such regressive Tory loci as a rural English village in Agatha Christie or an Oxford college in Dorothy Sayers. What Bloch actually stresses, however, is the much greater utopian energy at work in the novel of the artist. Here the chief structuring datum is a real Novum, namely, the imaginary works of art that give the protagonist his generic identity *as* an artist, but that can be located only on the Front, as works that may be coming into being but possess no established empirical validation yet. "Whereas the detective novel," as Bloch summarizes, "requires a process of collecting evidence, penetrating backward to a past crime, the novel of the artist requires recognition of an interest in the creative person who brings out something new instead of something past" (*Utopian Function* 267).

32. Cf. Bloch, *A Philosophy of the Future*, 94: "The permanence and greatness of major works of art consist precisely in their operation through a fulness of pre-semblance and of realms of utopian significance. These reside, so to speak, in the windows of such works; and always in windows which open in the direction of ultimate anticipation: driving forward, soaring, or achieving towards a goal—which is never a mere land in the clouds above."

33. Bloch, *The Utopian Function of Art and Literature*, 245–278.

For the German-speaking Bloch, Mann's *Doctor Faustus* (1947) is the principal exemplar of the novel of the artist, but Joyce's *A Portrait of the Artist as a Young Man* (1916), which probably occurs more readily to the English-speaking reader, provides an even more pertinent illustration of the Blochian point. Stephen Dedalus, after all, is not, precisely, an artist (for that title cannot be earned by a single haunting villanelle), but a *future* artist, an artist *as a young man*. The great artworks that constitute Stephen as the hero of a *Bildungsroman* about an artist are not only imaginary but, even within the world of the text, exist only on the level of the Not-Yet, as pure though concrete potentiality. In strictly utopian manner, it is the future—the fractional anticipations of that which is coming into existence—that structures Stephen: and not only him individually but, as he himself suggests in his determination to "forge in the smithy of my soul the uncreated conscience of my race,"[34] our entire view of the society that his artistic achievements will retroactively redefine.

Bloch's fundamental generic point about the novel of the artist is even more relevant to science fiction. The estranging novelties that characterize the genre correspond precisely to the Blochian Novum—which, as we have seen, is never a single new element inserted into an essentially unchanged mundane environment, but is instead such a *radical* novelty as to reconstitute the entire surrounding world and thus, in a sense, to create (though certainly not ex nihilo) a new world. Likewise, the science-fictional text is, as we have also seen, defined by its creation of a new world whose radical novelty estranges the empirical world of the status quo. And this is equally true whether the Novum of science fiction is expressed by the wholesale production of new worlds (as in *Last and First Men* or its even more wide-ranging sequel, *Star Maker* [1937]), or whether (as in *Frankenstein*) the Novum manifests itself as one novelty of such radical and profound newness that (as was discussed in the preceding section) the superficially mundane context is dynamically reconstituted as a potential future, new and strange. Furthermore, the utopian aspect of such science-fictional futures is heightened by the cognitive and critical nature of science-fictional estrangement. Although (as Bloch himself makes clear) the longings expressed in fantasies and fairy tales may well possess authentic utopian value, utopia cannot finally be understood as simply cut off from the empirical world of actuality. It is the *transformation* of actuality into utopia that constitutes the practical end of utopian critique and the ultimate object of utopian hope. In other words, such shards of utopia as may be found in fantastic representations of Cockaigne or Never-Never Land involve the recasting of utopia into irrationalist form. By contrast, the cognitive rationality (at least in literary effect) of science fiction allows utopia to emerge as more fully itself, genuinely critical and transformative. In this way, the dynamic of science fiction can on one level be identified with the hope principle itself.

34. James Joyce, *A Portrait of the Artist as a Young Man* (New York: Penguin Books, 1977), 253.

The reading of science fiction drives us into lands where we have never set foot and yet which—because they are cognitively linked to the world we do know and are invested with our actual longings—do indeed amount to a kind of homeland. Even more than in the novel of the artist, the defining features of science fiction are located on the In-Front-of-Us, at the level of the Not-Yet-Being, and in the dimension of utopian futurity.

It is strategically convenient to take a few examples from science-fictional works that may not appear to be particularly progressive or utopian in content. For instance, one of the defining ideologies of Asimov's most important work—the *Foundation* trilogy (1951–1953) and the robot stories, most notably those collected in *I, Robot* (1950)—is a flat quasi-Skinnerian rationalism (*not* rationality). These texts invest enormously in the notion of both mass and in-dividual behavior as predictable in purely positivistic terms that admit of no dialectical complexity. Thus are generated the highly influential Three Laws of Robotics—in which the Kantian and post-Kantian ethical problems posed by the categorical imperative are largely waived by reducing the questions at issue to the level of engineering technique—and, even more strikingly, the "psychohistory" of Hari Seldon and his colleagues, which amounts to a deter-ministic pseudo-Marxism apparently drained of critical and utopian content, and thus flattened out to as-if-actuarial calculation.[35] Quite different from this mechanistic behaviorism, but equally unpromising—on the surface—for the hermeneutic of utopia, is the synthesis of romantic technologism with vulgar-Nietzschean evolutionism that characterizes such of Clarke's major works as *Childhood's End* (1953) or *2001* (1968). The ideological tendency here is to short-circuit the genuinely conceptual questions of political change and social totality by projecting a supermundane future dependent on a march of techni-cal progress understood as autonomous of politics *and* on a sub-Stapledonian materialist "spirituality" absolutely transcendent of political categories.

Yet, even while these works do make major retreats from the conceptual radicalism intrinsic to the generic tendency of science fiction, the apparent nullity of utopia also hides a considerable reserve of utopian energy, and it is the latter that supplies the power so many readers have found in Asimov's and Clarke's finest fiction. In historical situation, the antiethical and antipolitical tendencies of these texts must be understood as, at least in large part, a refusal to join in the manichaean Cold War anti-Communism that had so impover-ished intellectual culture in America and (to a smaller degree) in Britain by largely monopolizing the discourses of ethics and politics. In this context, Asi-mov and Clarke achieve genuine utopian force by projecting potential futures of freedom and positive human fulfillment—the benign world state at the end of *I, Robot*; the epoch-making triumph of the psychohistorians at work in the

35. See Carl Freedman, "Remembering the Future: Science and Positivism From Isaac Asi-mov to Gregory Benford," *Extrapolation* 34, no. 2 (Summer 1998): 128–138.

Second Foundation; the godlike powers of Clarke's Overmind or of his Star Child—in ways that cannot be made to cohere with (even though they do not directly challenge) Cold War dogma. Nor is this achievement merely a matter of historical contextualization in the narrow (or historicist, as Benjamin would say) sense. The Clarkian and Asimovian images of liberation from material necessity and, at some points, of authentic if highly qualified human solidarity achieve a power that outlives its original social matrix. The fragmentary construction of utopia in these images remains true, despite the largely shabby, precritical ideologies by means of which Clarke and Asimov think their various science-fictional Novums. And these Novums, it must be emphasized, owe less to the conventional, if genial, liberalism of Asimov and Clarke as biographical individuals than to the defining characteristics of science fiction as a genre.

Indeed, we might emulate Bloch's brief examination of Ku Klux rhetoric by glancing at a science-fictional text much further removed (in overt terms) from utopian hope than even the Clarkian and Asimovian masterpieces: *Farnham's Freehold* (1964), one of Heinlein's most hatefully militaristic works (and one which is ferociously sexist and somewhat more mildly racist as well). First published in the context of Goldwaterite fanaticism, it was appropriately revived in the 1980s as a cult book of the neofascist survivalist movement. In sharp contrast to Asimov's and Clarke's strategic evasions of Cold War anti-Communism, Heinlein explicitly and enthusiastically embraces the latter. Yet even this text contains, in the science-fictional Novums that structure it, a significant measure of utopian potential. The postnuclear "freehold" of the title supplies images of real human solidarity, however patriarchal and authoritarian the forms by which this solidarity is organized. Indeed, the main significance of Hubert Farnham's original project of surviving thermonuclear war is that it is conceived in explicitly communal, collective terms. Furthermore, what finally transpires to be the novel's ontological premise involves the possibility of time travel and the alteration of the past—frequent Heinlein themes, of course, which are also quintessentially science-fictional. There is thus an oblique suggestion of the potentially utopian mutability of history itself (a mutability also inferrable, in a different way, from the nostalgia implied by the text's very title). It is such largely but not totally occluded moments of utopian positivity that account for the intense, if demented, love that *Farnham's Freehold* (which I take as a somewhat extreme but not radically uncharacteristic instance of Heinleinian right-wing science fiction) has inspired in many readers.

Chapter 3 will feature detailed analyses of science-fictional texts characterized by much greater utopian energy than anything by Asimov or Clarke, to say nothing of Heinlein. But this discussion of work by the so-called Big Three, who largely dominated American (and, though to a lesser extent, Anglo-American) science fiction during the 1940s, the 1950s, and well into the 1960s, should serve to emphasize the particularly complex affinity between science fiction and critical theory in its Blochian version. Science fiction as an aesthetic form is, even more than the novel of the artist, a privileged object of utopian hermeneutic. The structural constitution of the genre on the Front, on the ontological level of Not-Yet-Being, renders science fiction a perhaps uniquely fertile field for the location of fragments of an unalienated futurity, of our postrevolutionary *Heimat*—even despite the regressive ideologies that may help to form (and deform) many science-fictional texts. Yet if science fiction is a privileged *object* for the critical theory of utopia, it is so largely because the genre functions as a *subject* of such theory as well; that is, the cognitive estrangements of the genre work in the manner of utopian critique to foreground and demystify the actual, and thereby to point toward some authentic plenitude with which the deprivations of mundane reality are contrasted. Accordingly, we are now in a position to answer the question posed at the end of the preceding section: Would a purely science-fictional text be a strictly utopian text? Just as the logic of Lukácsian genre criticism suggests that a pure product of historical realism could only be produced in the context of pure and perfected utopia, so the same is indeed true—but more complexly so—of the generic tendency of science fiction. A purely science-fictional text would not only estrange our empirical environment absolutely but would do so in such a perfectly cognitive fashion that the utopian alternative to actuality would not merely be suggested but delineated in complete and precise detail. The project of composing such a text is thus impossible not only in the sense that no asymptote can ever be actually attained (as in the case of the purely realistic text), but also in the sense that the situation of such a project is inherently self-contradictory (and again we encounter the paradoxical nature of utopia itself). For the perfected knowledge of utopia required to compose a purely science-fictional text could only be obtained by the kind of residence *in* utopia that would leave one without a nonutopian actuality to be estranged.

We are bound to notice, however, that, whatever the problems of such a project, the detailed delineation of utopia *does* appear to be the aim of utopia in the *generic* sense established by More. It is now time to coordinate utopia in this meaning with science fiction and with utopia in the sense of philosophical critique.

Bloch himself is in fact somewhat (and, as I shall argue, rightly) skeptical of utopia as a literary kind, and for reasons directly suggested by our hypothetical case of the purely science-fictional text. Precisely because utopia in the Blochian sense—that is, the unalienated homeland where we have never lived—can only be apprehended obliquely and partially, there is some cause to be suspicious of those quasi-cartographic projects that offer a full representation of utopia for direct view. Because utopia is necessarily in large part transcendent of the empirical here-and-now, there would seem to be a crucial falsity in any compositional project that aims to give utopia unproblematic textual immanence. Utopia, in the philosophical and hermeneutic sense, cannot be seen straight on, but only in fractional prefigurations. Yet such a "straight" rendering of utopia seems to be precisely what utopia as a literary genre attempts.

This essentially Blochian point has been influentially rethought and re-stated, in a different vocabulary and with the aid of a quite distinct theoretical lineage, by Louis Marin, the most noteworthy modern student of utopia in the generic sense. Strongly influenced by the sharp Althusserian distinction between ideology and (critical) theory, and by Pierre Macherey's application of this distinction to the study of literature *as* ideology,[36] Marin proposes that utopia as a literary kind is "an ideological critique of ideology."[37] Utopia remains ideological for Marin because it does not, in the manner of Althusserian theory, "produce the theory of its production" (*Utopics* 196). In other words, it is not a properly critical and self-reflexive metadiscourse, but (like literature in general for Macherey) remains a relatively immediate or first-order discursive practice; as such, it is incapable of breaking decisively with the imaginary relations that ultimately define ideology as such. At the same time, however, Marin insists (what Bloch by no means wholly denies) that the literary utopia does nonetheless possess a certain kind of critical (or, perhaps more precisely, quasi-critical) force. Operating from within ideological boundaries, the utopia does not offer, in paradigmatically ideological manner, a totalizing justification of as-if-pregiven reality, but rather a *displacement* of the latter into fictional discourse that works to foreground and to demystify its own ideological presuppositions (again, the influence of Macherey is clearly decisive). Utopic discourse, as Marin summarizes, is "ideological discourse that [alone among ideological discourses, evidently] can anticipate in a theoretical way" (199). Adapting this position to the dominant vocabulary of this study, I will say that the literary utopia lacks the *radical* affinity with critical theory that I have claimed for science fiction, but nevertheless enjoys a somewhat privileged, if subordinate, relationship with critical theory.

We can articulate this point with regard to the definition of science fiction by suggesting that the literary utopia—the pre–science-fictional literary utopia, that is—is in large part defined by a disjunction between relatively strong estrangement and relatively weak cognition. The preeminent example here is of course More's pioneering text: the most powerful tendency of which has

36. The most important references here are to Louis Althusser and Etienne Balibar, *Reading Capital*, trans. Ben Brewster (London: NLB, 1970), 11–69; Louis Althusser, *For Marx*, trans. Ben Brewster (London: NLB, 1977), 87–128 and 161–247; Louis Althusser, *Essays on Ideology* (London: Verso, 1984); and Pierre Macherey, *A Theory of Literary Production*, trans. Geoffrey Wall (London: Routledge, 1978), 3–101.

37. Louis Marin, *Utopics: Spatial Play*, trans. Robert Vollrath (Atlantic Highlands, N.J.: Humanities, 1984), 195. For an influential presentation of and commentary on Marin's theory, see Fredric Jameson, "Of Islands and Trenches: Neutralization and the Production of Utopian Discourse," in his *The Ideologies of Theory: Essays 1971–1986*, vol. 2, *The Syntax of History* (Minneapolis: University of Minnesota Press, 1988), 75–101.

less to do with the particular social content of the island of Utopia than with the unprecedentedly radical way that More's England is estranged by being thrown into contrast with a country that is literally *nowhere*, in the sense of no-where empirically locatable. The putative superiority of Utopia to England is, as many commentators have pointed out, problematic and highly qualified; the implied meaning of "eutopia," or good place, is strictly secondary to the al-ternative meaning of "outopia," or no place.[38] What mainly gives the text its force and its almost matchless generic fertility is the innovative estrangement of actuality according to standards that do not depend upon the conservatism of precedent or tradition, and that, indeed, pronounce, on a quite literal level, a *disclaimer* of empirical validation. This is the radicalism that enables *Utopia* to function, in Marin's vocabulary, as a critique of ideology, and to this degree the generic tendency of science fiction is strongly at work with More's text. To name but one outstanding example, the use of gold and silver in Utopia for purposes of degradation makes no sense as a practical policy suggestion for how the precious metals should be used in More's own society: "If gold in Uto-pia were plentiful enough to be so used, gold in Utopia would not be a pre-cious metal," as C. S. Lewis somewhat pedantically explained.[39] But the real point, of course, is to estrange the nascent fetishism of the money relation in More's England, and in this way the device succeeds brilliantly—right down to the astonishing proto-Freudian prescience with which More's golden chamber pots suggest the connections among excrement, anal eroticism, and money, the universal equivalent of commodity exchange.

Yet, as we saw in chapter 1, the ultimate integrity and validity of literary es-trangement depend upon its cognitive, critical character. When we interro-gate the cognitive dimension of *Utopia*—when, in other words, we ask just what, if not empirical precedent, constitutes the matrix of the values by which the estrangements of the text function—Bloch's and Marin's reservations about utopia as a genre become especially relevant. More's Utopia is, to be sure, far from wholly fantastic. It is not a version of Cockaigne, but is to some extent (especially in book 1) connected with English and European reality; given the speculative, unfinished character of geography as a sixteenth-century science, one might even argue that a certain cognition effect is at-tained with regard to the island's putative existence. But it is a weak cognition

38. The primacy of outopia over eutopia—the primacy, that is, of estrangement over a com-parison of the merits of real and fictional societies—is valid not only for More's text but for the en-tire generic tradition. The popular solecism "dystopia," or bad place, ought therefore to be re-sisted, as it tends to foreground the good/bad comparison and thus to distract attention from the estranging dynamic of utopian fictions, whether positive or negative in their relation to the actual environments in which they were produced.

39. C. S. Lewis, *English Literature in the Sixteenth Century, Excluding Drama* (London: Ox-ford University Press, 1973), 170. Strictly speaking, Lewis's point here is not only pedantic but (at least according to Marxian economic theory) slightly inaccurate: he seems to assume that the law of demand and supply is the primary, or even the sole, determinant of exchange-value.

effect. Much in this (frequently playful and comic) text, not least the title it-self, presents the rational viability of Utopia as, at most, a bare technical pos-sibility, not a really concrete potentiality. If Utopia and actuality are not wholly severed from one another in the manner of fantasy, neither do they par-ticipate in a truly plausible science-fictional continuum. Thus the nature of the critical claim, if any, that Utopia may have upon actuality is left unclear.

The problem here is historical. We have seen how science fiction, like the historical novel and like critical theory itself, is born out of the age of the dem-ocratic revolution, the age in which history itself may fairly be said to be in-vented—which is also to say, the age in which *futurity* in anything other than an abstract or metaphysical sense first comes into being, and, therefore, the age in which anticipatory pre-illuminations of postrevolutionary utopian col-lectivity in the Blochian sense become fully possible. To say that More's age is a precritical (and pre-Kantian) one is also to say that the category of futurity is unavailable to him and thus cannot serve as the cognitive grounding of literary estrangement. But futurity, as Bloch would argue, is the *only* standpoint from which a radical estrangement of the status quo can be genuinely—that is, crit-ically—attained. Unable to assume this standpoint, *Utopia* performs estrange-ments whose epistemological status wavers uneasily between the science-fictional and the fantastic, between cognition and the admittedly irrational. The imaginings of the text cannot be energized in the cognitive manner of sci-ence fiction, and fragmentary anticipations of utopia in the philosophical and hermeneutic meaning of the term are accordingly at a comparatively low level. Furthermore, the very fact that More's text does not and cannot per-form, to a degree comparable with science fiction, the critical labor of utopian hermeneutic leaves it unconstrained by the rigorous demands of the latter. The text therefore attains a certain kind of freedom (or rather pseudofreedom) to delineate utopia not in fractional obliquities but in the direct and full detail that itself, as we have seen, provides some ground for suspicion. And the delin-eation that thus emerges (especially in book 2) is necessarily two-dimensional, precritical, and, as Bakhtin would say, relatively *monologic* and undialectical.

It remains to ask exactly how then, if not in a fully critical or future-oriented way, the estrangements of More's text *do* work. What, in other words, are the historical and ideological presuppositions of this precritical but still im-mensely vital and innovative book? The most adequate answer, I think, has been offered by Christopher Kendrick in perhaps the most useful commen-tary on *Utopia* since Marin's own.[40] Kendrick proposes that the estrangements of the text are enabled by a certain kind of new and radical *individualism* that in turn depends upon an almost uniquely transitional moment in the history of European modes of production. The peculiar overdeterminations of the

40. Christopher Kendrick, "More's Utopia and Uneven Development," *boundary 2*, 13, nos. 2–3 (1985): 233–266.

absolutist period, when classical feudalism is on the decline but full-fledged capitalism has not yet emerged into clear view, allow the class of small independent producers, for whom More speaks, to imagine their own class position as a universal one: that is, an (ideological) space of individual freedom is created by the fact that they are partly detached from the body of a dying feudalism—and are therefore in a position to adopt a critical stance toward the latter—while they have not yet come into their own historical destiny as subjects of a properly bourgeois hegemony. During this moment (which in historical retrospect is seen to be a very transient window of opportunity, but which from the perspective of 1516 must have seemed a stable and even "natural" situation), the class of independent petty producers, and especially their Humanist cultural representatives like More, can in relatively good faith understand their own counterfeudal and protobourgeois individualism as the universal interests of free and skillful production.

Accordingly, the estrangement that More's text effects of a still largely feudal England and Europe is based on just this atomized (but relatively progressive) sense of individuality, rather than on Blochian images of futurity and unalienated collectivity. And this is true even with regard to the feature of More's island that has drawn the highest socialist praise: its apparent economic collectivism. As Kendrick demonstrates in considerable detail, Utopian communism is grounded in "an attempt to body forth a cohesive society based upon the primacy of petty production and the hedonistic work ethic which forms its organic accompaniment" ("More's Utopia" 251). Kendrick coins the term "petty communism" (251) to describe the Utopian mode of production, a formulation whose deliberately paradoxical quality corresponds to the contradictions inherent in the notion of free, non–class-bound individualism that More's transitional moment enables.

The foregoing analysis of More's founding text of the utopian generic tradition is, I think, largely true of the genre as a whole, at any rate in its pre–science-fictional phase. But the ideological critique of ideology tends to become more problematic as bourgeois ideology becomes increasingly hegemonic and thus, so to speak, increasingly itself and increasingly *contradictory*. In other words, the (proto-)bourgeois individualism that in More's period can still function, despite its somewhat illusory character, in an essentially progressive way and in good faith, is riven by increasingly intolerable incoherence; it thus often assumes a more reactionary and irresponsible posture, as the dominance of capitalist social and ideological relations deepens. For one thing that capitalism as the dominant mode of production tends to make clear is the extent to which the notion of the free independent individual—a notion ultimately based, of course, on the "free" wage contract between the producers and the expropriators of surplus value—is actually dependent on a radically unfree and oppressive system of property relations: a system that is, indeed, frequently repellent to the most articulate of individualists, notably to those within the Humanist and neo-Humanist traditions. Therefore, the pre–science-fictional literary utopia after More continues to estrange mundane actuality; owing to this central insupportable contradiction, however, it typically does so in a *less* critical and cognitive way, and thus with even fewer prefigurations of utopia in the philosophical sense, than in the case of More's founding text. Accordingly, an effect of the grotesque often assumes increased literary importance.

The chief instance here is *Gulliver's Travels*. The two centuries that separate it from *Utopia* witness the establishment of capitalist dominance in the economic, the political, and, less securely, the cultural and ideological spheres. Swift's text is certainly no less individualist than More's. But More's individualism, in its relative coherence and at least moderate optimism, contrasts strikingly with the wild self-contradictions and bitter misanthropy that characterize Swift's. Orwell's diagnosis remains definitive: "He [Swift] is a Tory anarchist, despising authority while disbelieving in liberty, and preserving the aristocratic outlook while seeing clearly that the existing aristocracy is degenerate and contemptible."[41] The greatest joke of the text is that Gulliver, the prototypical bourgeois subject and hence the spokesman for common sense, is a naive fool (as his name implies) who proves hopelessly inadequate to the world that the bourgeoisie have created. But Gulliver's position is to a considerable degree Swift's own. Though no fool, Swift is caught in the intolerable dilemma of being intellectually dependent, as a bourgeois individualist, on the very system that he violently and often acutely despises. His quite authentic hatred combines with literary genius to produce the most powerful estrangements of English and European society achieved since More: these range from topical, local satire, through such more general estrangements of capitalist society as the great attacks on colonialism and militarism, to metaphysical estrangement of *homo sapiens* as a disgusting species (an element of the text that reaches its culmination in book 4 but is present from the early pages of book 1). Yet in all these negative representations there is very little genuine *criticism*. Cognitive pre-illuminations of any unalienated, collective alternative to actuality are, if not completely lacking, at a remarkably low level for literature of such stature. Irretrievably opposed to the status quo, Swift cannot render his opposition concrete; for reasons of both historical moment and personal inclination, he possesses few resources on which to draw save his own sense of individuality. This is perhaps especially true of those points in the text at which Swift, in direct emulation of More (the only modern figure who is presented, in the voyage to Glubbdubdrib, as comparable to the noblest heroes of antiquity), does attempt to delineate positive alternatives. For such representations—the King of Brobdingnag, Lord Munodi of Balnibarbi, the

41. George Orwell, "Politics vs. Literature," in *The Collected Essays, Journalism and Letters of George Orwell*, ed. Sonia Orwell and Ian Angus (Harmondsworth: Penguin Books, 1970), 4:253.

Houyhnhnms themselves—are even more monologic and abstract than More's own, more dependent upon the accumulated details of an individual preference (Munodi may simply be Swift's personal friend Bolingbroke), and so less open to the historical Blochian potentialities of a utopian future.

If, then, utopia as a literary genre tends to be (in a merely verbal paradox) less utopian in the philosophical and hermeneutic sense than science fiction, it is only to be expected that the invention of science fiction in the nineteenth century will have major implications for the older but more limited genre. Such is indeed the case. The new generic tradition, founded early in the century by Mary Shelley and consolidated in its final decade by H. G. Wells, partly grows out of the older one: for every science-fictional text is, after all, a representation of a place that is no place. But the advent of science fiction also, and in more fundamental ways, reinvents the older genre and energizes it with the kind of concrete utopian potentiality now available in the age when the future has, so to speak, finally come into existence. As one might expect, Wells himself is the first key figure in the synthesis of science fiction and the literary utopia. Before turning to him, however, I shall first consider a slightly earlier text, *News from Nowhere*, which I take to be the last great pre–science-fictional utopia and the only one, at least in English, comparable in literary importance to More's and Swift's.

But *is* it pre–science-fictional? Mere chronology is ambiguous on this matter; the more important point is that such a designation would seem to imply a precritical status for Morris's text—a curious characterization indeed for the most notable literary utopia of explicitly Marxist cast in the language. Morris is said to have been the first English reader of Marx's *Capital*, and his own magnum opus, in its attempt at a plausible depiction of working-class socialist revolution and the resulting communist society, seems definitively oriented toward the future and the Blochian (or proto-Blochian) utopia. Now, Morris's Marxism is indeed crucial to the text, mainly as a means of short-circuiting the pattern of precritical regression observable in the development of the literary utopia from More to Swift. By the late nineteenth century, the contradictions and oppressiveness of capitalism have become so overwhelmingly evident, and the oppositional resources of mere individualism so obviously inadequate, that some definite (and often overt) commitment to socialism becomes almost mandatory for really significant utopian literature. The major examples include not only the Marxist Morris himself but also his antagonist, the Christian Socialist Edward Bellamy of *Looking Backward* (1888). Though there are many specific points in *News from Nowhere* that offer comparatively noncognitive estrangements directly reminiscent of Swift and More (for instance, the transformation of Parliament House into Dung Market), the text as a whole does, on one level, attempt to offer a militantly critical and collective alternative to a materially wasteful, morally repugnant, and aesthetically disgusting Victorian capitalism.

Morris carefully delineates a postrevolutionary society where alienation has been overcome. His purely communist Nowhere is rationally and rigorously connected to its bourgeois prehistory through the terms of Marxist theory, while in some instances Morris actually goes beyond Marx, rendering explicit certain of Marxism's utopian elements (in the Blochian meaning) that Marx himself leaves mainly (not totally) implicit. Examples include the stress on art, on the revival of precapitalist handicrafts, on the beauties of nature, and on human plenitude and fulfillment generally: "Revolution having brought its foredoomed change about, how can you prevent the counter-revolution from setting in except by making people happy?"[42] As this acute and prophetic comment by one of the protagonist's informants suggests, Morris's Nowhere contrasts sharply with More's island and Swift's land of the Houyhnhnms not only in its critical Marxist vision of collectivity but also (what in the end, however, may come to much the same thing) in stressing the importance of concrete psychic desire and engaging the problem of boredom in utopia.

Yet the question of boredom, if engaged, is not exactly solved by this text, whose own monologism of style and manner is similar to that in *Utopia* and *Gulliver's Travels*. The relationship of Morris's text toward the problematic flatness and overexplicitness of the literary utopia (or toward the ideological character of the genre, as Marin would say) can be expressed by saying that the problems that are thoroughly solved on the purely intellectual level persist on the generic level. To put it another way, the disjunction we noted in the pre-science-fictional utopia between relatively strong estrangement and relatively weak cognition is here partly translated into an immense gulf between theoretical content and generic form. The false freedom of the literary utopia—which allows it to exhibit in great and often somewhat monotonous detail the utopian vision that Bloch insists can only be truly apprehended in fragments of pre-illumination—constitutes a *structural* problem that Morris's Marxism can complicate and in some ways ameliorate but that it cannot remove or wholly solve. The boredom often associated with utopia is itself a strictly generic phenomenon, resulting as it does from the monologic delineations that owe far more to the private fancies of the individual author than to genuinely critical anticipations of a collective future. Though it might seem strange to say so of a work as militantly communist and anti-individualist in overt theoretical orientation as *News from Nowhere*, the individualism associated with the genre is on one level stronger than Morris's (very strong) political intellect; the paradoxical result is that, in strictly formal terms, Marxism itself becomes something very like a private fancy of the author. In other words, Morris accepts the generic format established by More—the basically homogeneous system of detailed delineations and explanations that largely occlude narrative

42. William Morris, *News from Nowhere*, in *Three Works by William Morris* (New York: International Publishers, 1968), 275.

and characterization—and gives it a brilliantly critical, Marxist content. Yet the generic format retains its own determinate force, giving the text's Marxism a somewhat abstract character and limiting the degree to which *News from Nowhere* can really concretize the radically utopian futurity that it schematizes with such brilliant lucidity. Abundantly and creatively critical in Marxist content, Morris's text remains predominantly precritical and pre–science-fictional in monologic form.

Essentially the same point can be made by saying that *News from Nowhere*, for all its achievements, remains pre*novelistic*. The critical resources of science fiction, while greater, as we have seen, than those of the novel generally, are, as we have also seen, inescapably tied to the novelistic mode of fictionality; that is, to the dialogic and dialectical multiaccentuality of novelistic style theorized by Bakhtin, and to the critical historical insight that Lukács describes as a potentiality within novelistic representation. These are the elements that, to a very great degree, enable the critical power of the novel and *a fortiori* of science fiction, which is almost invariably fiction in the novelistic sense (understanding this category to include the briefer subnovelistic forms like the short story and the novella, as well as the post-Balzacian *roman fleuve*). Utopia in the philosophical and hermeneutic meaning is a version of critical theory, and might, indeed, almost be defined as the version of critical theory concerned with stressing the element of positivity always implicitly intrinsic to critique in the negative sense of demystification. It is hardly surprising then that utopia tends to function more strongly in the more critical and novelistic genre of science fiction than in the older (and, in specifically Bakhtinian terms, quasi-poetic) genre of the literary utopia, which necessarily lacks novelistic resources.

Indeed, the very characteristics of the literary utopia that limit its hermeneutic construction of utopia as collective unalienated futurity are precisely those that distinguish the genre from the novel. The detailed schematization of an alternative society—the ready-made representation of a no-place that is generated as if directly *willed* from the brain of the author as individual—amounts, on the one hand, to a generally monologic authorial style that tends to foreclose any properly novelistic clash and heterogeneity of different voices, and, on the other hand, to a largely static and spatial form of narrative construction inhospitable to historical temporality and characterological typicality. By contrast, the novel, and particularly the science-fiction novel, involves a much higher level of dialectical complexity. It is thus precluded from any comprehensive or absolute representation of utopia, and so is all the more capable of construing utopia truly—that is, in the kind of fractional pre-illuminations theorized (and practiced) by Ernst Bloch.[43]

43. Cf. the most classic aphoristic defense of the novel: "The novel is a great discovery: far greater than Galileo's telescope or somebody else's wireless. The novel is the highest form of human

Accordingly, the great vitalization of the literary utopia made possible by the advent of science fiction and the synthesis of science fiction with the older form amounts to the transformation of utopia into the utopian novel, which might also be designated (here I borrow and somewhat adapt Tom Moylan's useful term)[44] the *critical* utopia. In a sense, it seems absurd to deny that characterization to *News from Nowhere*. In self-conscious theoretical stance, no literary utopia before or since, at least in English, exhibits more acute critical insight. But Morris, though not barred by mere chronology from the novel and the possibility of the science-fictional utopia, remained decisively committed, in the matter of literary form, to poetry and other less dialogic genres. It remained for Morris's younger contemporary H. G. Wells (also, significantly, a socialist, though not a Marxist) to fuse the generic tendencies of utopia and science fiction and thereby to produce a literary utopia that is critical (and so philosophically utopian) not only in its didactic content but also in its novelistic form. The first key text here is *The Time Machine*. Not only does this novel inaugurate the science-fictional utopia; it is also (and not coincidentally, as we recall) the first text in which the crucial temporal and historical dimension of science fiction becomes completely explicit. Indeed, one might argue that, if science fiction is invented by Mary Shelley with *Frankenstein*, it is practically reinvented with Wells's pioneering text. The synthesis of science fiction with literary utopia produces the most critical utopia, in formal terms, to date, and, at the same time, establishes new utopian potentialities for science fiction itself.

In *The Time Machine*, of course, the alternatives to empirical actuality have a mainly *negative* utopian value. The novel opens with an image of smug middle-class British society—typified by such representatives of English positivism and conservative Liberalism as the Medical Man, the Psychologist, and the Editor—and then estranges this mundane reality by means of the several scenarios formulated by the Time Traveller as he attempts to understand the future of the Eloi and the Morlocks. The world of the year Eight Hundred and Two Thousand Seven Hundred and One A.D. first seems to him the decadence of a purely communistic society (there is perhaps some deliberate satire here of Morris's pastoral vision); it then seems a rigidly and stably hierarchical society in which class differences have been biologically naturalized; finally it seems an unstable hierarchical society in the midst of active class warfare. What most distinguishes this utopian novel from earlier utopias is the much higher level of critical *concreteness* attained. The alternative socialities are not presented as if ready-made by authorial fiat.

---

expression so far attained. Why? Because it is so incapable of the absolute. In a novel, everything is relative to everything else, if that novel is art at all"; D. H. Lawrence, *Reflections on the Death of a Porcupine*, in *Phoenix II*, ed. Warren Roberts and Harry T. Moore (New York: Viking, 1970), 416.

44. Tom Moylan, *Demand the Impossible* (New York: Methuen, 1986), passim.

Instead, they are novelistically produced through a properly temporal, historical narrative that exhibits, on the one hand, a protagonist more like a typical character than the heroes of earlier literary utopias and, on the other, a style more nearly dialogic. Accordingly, a more substantial apprehension of utopia in the Blochian sense is achieved. Such pre-illuminations are partly located in the negative utopian scenarios themselves. Every negativity, as we have discussed, conceals its own implicit positivity; the various privations of Wells's imagined future suggest corresponding (but antithetical) possibilities of collective fulfillment—just as, for Bloch, anxiety is as much a future-oriented and utopian emotion as hope itself (the two emotions are in fact inseparable from one another).

A more direct prefiguration of utopia, however, is to be found precisely in the heroic middle-class individualism of the Time Traveller, which recalls bolder and more affectively rich phases of capitalist cultural history than Victorian Liberalism, and which contrasts the Time Traveller so sharply with his timid and incurious friends. In this way, *The Time Machine* might be described as the exact opposite of *News from Nowhere*. Morris's text explicitly celebrates communist collectivity, but does so in a monologic, prenovelistic form that depends heavily on individualist ideology. Wells's science-fictional utopia devotes some of its energy to celebrating a certain kind of bourgeois individualism that (as the Time Traveller's isolated work habits suggest) had been largely occluded by capitalism's corporate phase; the celebration, however, is done with sufficient novelistic concreteness that the attractive qualities of the protagonist's courageous and intelligent curiosity attain a utopian and hence collective value.

With Wells, the theoretical description of science fiction and utopia (in both the philosophic and generic senses) is in many ways complete. I do not, of course, mean that he exhausts the generic possibilities of the science-fictional utopia, nor that his work provides a complete, definitive instance of the utopian pre-illuminations achieved by science fiction. I do think, though, that, as the inventor of the science-fictional utopia, and as the consolidator or second founder of science fiction itself, Wells establishes the basic terms of the dialectic between science fiction and utopia as it will operate during the century following *The Time Machine*. He is the preeminent and direct inspiration (though by no means always an object of uncritical admiration) for most of the British authors who follow him in producing important science-fictional utopias: Olaf Stapledon, C. S. Lewis, Aldous Huxley, George Orwell, Arthur C. Clarke, and others. It is noteworthy, of course, that much of this work emulates *The Time Machine* by recasting More's genre not only in science-fictional but in emphatically negative terms. Indeed, the negative utopia—the no-place that estranges the status quo mainly by attempting to extrapolate from the worst tendencies of the latter—is the most significant version of utopian literature in the first half of the twentieth century.

After midcentury, and especially after the 1960s, major science-fictional utopias are produced more often in North America than in Britain, and the positive utopia largely regains its traditional priority over the negative variety. These shifts notwithstanding, the terms of the utopian novel or critical utopia established by Wells continue to be decisive. He remains an essential precursor, on a level with More and Mary Shelley, and it is owing to Wells more than to any other particular author that nearly all significant literary utopias are now science fiction as well. Outstanding examples include Theodore Sturgeon's *Venus Plus X* (1960), Ursula Le Guin's *The Word for World Is Forest* (1972) and *The Dispossessed* (1974), Joanna Russ's *The Female Man* (1975), Marge Piercy's *Woman on the Edge of Time* (1976) and *He, She and It* (1991), Samuel Delany's *Triton* (1976) and *Stars in My Pocket Like Grains of Sand* (1984), the Mars trilogy of Kim Stanley Robinson (1993–1997), and Howard Hendrix's *Lightpaths* (1997) — not to forget that notable revival of the negative utopia, Margaret Atwood's *The Handmaid's Tale* (1985). There is no question here of attempting even a cursory survey of the contemporary science-fictional utopia, although two of the texts just named will be treated at some length in chapter 3 (where utopia will function as a key critical category generally). It is nonetheless worth reiterating the main point in general terms. The genre invented by More in 1516 does not truly come into its own, does not become a privileged form for utopia as Bloch conceives it, until more than three and a half centuries later, when it is able to avail itself of the critical resources of the novel and, above all, of science fiction.

There is one major issue yet to be discussed: the political-economic sense of utopia and its relationship to science fiction, as well as to utopia in the two other meanings we have considered. Just because utopia in this sense has the most indirect bearing on science fiction, it is only at this point in the argument that we are finally in a position to appreciate that oblique but important relationship. In his treatise on the Marxian distinction between utopian and scientific socialism, Engels argues, with vintage Marxian sarcasm, that for Fourier, Owen, and the utopian socialists generally, "socialism is the expression of absolute truth, reason and justice, and has only to be discovered to conquer all the world by virtue of its own power."[45] Utopian socialism, that is, understands itself as "an accidental discovery of this or that ingenious brain," and attempts "to manufacture a system of society as perfect as possible" (52). Engels allows — and Marx and Engels elsewhere give the same point greater stress[46] — that utopian socialism does contain genuine value in describing and exposing the horrors of the status quo. While the utopians, however, are perfectly capable of criticizing (in a loose sense) capitalism and capitalist society, "they

45. Frederick Engels, *Socialism: Utopian and Scientific*, trans. Edward Aveling (New York: International Publishers, 1978), 43. Further page references are to this text.

46. See Karl Marx and Friedrich Engels, *The Communist Manifesto* (New York: Monthly Review, 1968), 57.

could not *explain* them, and, therefore, could not get the mastery of them" (52; my emphasis). By contrast, the scientific socialism of Marx and Engels themselves is based on a precise rational analysis of the capitalist mode of production—most notably on the discovery of surplus-value and its extraction as the essential driving force within the system as a whole.

This rational grounding, then, allows Marx and Engels to formulate a theory of socialist revolution that assigns a historically determinate and privileged role to the proletariat, as the only social collectivity with both an inescapable interest in overthrowing capitalism and the (potential) ability to do so. Though the utopians may trenchantly revile bourgeois society, their inability to understand the latter in a rigorously critical way leaves them without any means of theorizing the *transformation* of actuality into the utopias of which they dream. Accordingly, and despite the personal good faith of many of the utopians (especially among the original giants of the movement like Fourier and Owen themselves), utopian socialism always risks conservatism. Lacking a scientific concept of collective social transformation, it must inevitably be tempted to imagine that utopia can be achieved through such essentially individualist means as tricks, reforms, personal fiats, and self-contained enclaves of social virtue, without any need for the revolutionizing of society as a whole.[47] For Marx and Engels, *only* such a radical revolutionizing could be sufficient to establish socialism, and such a total transformation of society is dependent upon the scientific understanding of capitalist society as a totality. It should not, however, be thought that the scientificity of Marx and Engels has anything philistine or pedestrian about it. They are indeed suspicious of those utopian socialists who claim to predict in great detail what the postrevolutionary society (that is, utopia in Bloch's sense) will be like. Nonetheless, they regard *some* vision of what may lie beyond alienation to be indispensable. Of the many passages in the Marx-Engels canon that might be selected for illustration, one of the best descriptions of achieved communism is from *Socialism: Utopian and Scientific* itself. It ends with this famous peroration: "Only from that time will man himself, more and more consciously, make his own history—only from that time will the social causes set in movement by him have, in the main and in a constantly growing measure, the results intended by him. It is the ascent of man from the kingdom of necessity to the kingdom of freedom" (73).

In other words, for classical Marxism pure communism is precisely the same thing that utopia is for Bloch (whose own emphatic claim to be squarely within the central Marxist tradition is far more justified than most of his Western interpreters have understood). It is an ultimate horizon beyond the alienations of class society that, because it lies on the far side of a revolutionary social

---

47. Though Proudhon is not to be counted as one of the original leaders of utopian socialism proper, perhaps the most elaborate and convincing deconstruction of the fundamental logic of utopian socialism remains Marx's reply to the French socialist's *Philosophy of Poverty*; see Karl Marx, *The Poverty of Philosophy* (New York: International Publishers, 1963).

transformation, can only be glimpsed in anticipatory bits and pieces of pre-illumination, but that nonetheless must be kept in view as much as is truly possible. The Marxist objection to utopian socialism is strictly parallel to the Blochian objection to the traditional literary utopia. Both claim to know too much too soon. Both produce impossibly detailed abstract maps of a place (or rather a no-place) in which no one has ever stepped. Accordingly, both versions of utopia suffer from a certain metaphysical flatness or hollowness, from a failure of genuine concreteness. Both tend to present themselves as, in Engels's phrase, the "accidental discovery of this or that ingenious brain." Though both manifest expressly collective concerns, both covertly depend on the perspective of individualism. Above all, utopian socialism and the utopian genre as invented by More are both weak with regard to the crucial category of *transition*. Whatever the strong points of an Owenite commune or of More's imagined island, it is impossible to understand how those strong points could ever be translated into the general condition of social actuality as a whole. In other words, what is true of the too schematic cartographies of the literary utopians in contrast to the Blochian hermeneutic of utopia is equally true of utopian as contrasted to scientific socialism: both are finally *precritical*.

In this perspective, then, it should be easy to see that the verbal resemblance between science fiction and scientific socialism, which might appear to be a mere accident, a near-pun, actually express a deep theoretical affinity. Science fiction, and, even more precisely, the science-fiction utopia, stands to the traditional literary utopia very much as scientific socialism stands to the utopian variety. The original Marxist claim, after all, is not simply to negate the social visions of the utopians, but rather to sublate the real value in their work—the passionate and often acute opposition to the oppressive empirical realities of the status quo—into a more concrete and fully critical theory of society and social transformation: a theory capable of negotiating and even practically guiding the transition from actuality to something better; that is, something closer to utopia in the strong Blochian sense. In a strictly similar way, science fiction vitalizes the pre–science-fictional literary utopia by making the genre of utopia more concrete and novelistic, and therefore more critical in theoretical stance. Whereas the estrangements of the older utopian fictions tend to be only weakly cognitive, and sometimes (like the wilder imaginings of the utopian socialists) approach the borders of fantasy itself, science fiction provides, in literary effect, estrangements of an authentically cognitive, critical nature that are therefore capable, at least in principle, of suggesting a rational means of transition from the mundane actuality of the author's environment to something radically different.

In sum, science fiction and scientific socialism both participate in the utopian hermeneutic theorized by Ernst Bloch to a much greater degree than (despite their names) classic utopian fiction and pre-Marxian utopian socialism. Accordingly, Bloch's vision of Karl Marx as the greatest of all utopian

thinkers was not (as it has often been misunderstood to be) a mere tactical gesture toward the authorities of the old German Democratic Republic. On the
contrary, we can now clearly see it to be at one with the fundamental logic of
his hermeneutic philosophy. Furthermore, from the main perspective of the
current essay—which is concerned with stressing the critical and utopian energy of science fiction—Marx is something else as well. If science fiction is indeed privileged with regard to critique and utopia, and if Marx remains preeminent among critical theorists and utopian visionaries, then, like Mikhail
Bakhtin, like Georg Lukács, like Bloch himself, Marx must inescapably be
counted as (if implicitly and even unconsciously) one of the major theorists of
science fiction.

Science Fiction and the Canon

The image of Marx as a theorist of science fiction *avant la lettre* provides a
suitable culmination to the preceding three sections of this chapter, which
have detailed the affinity between critical theory and science fiction in order
to substantiate the central claim of this book: that science fiction functions as
a privileged generic object for critical theory. Of course, I have only sketched
the major lines of conceptual force. This chapter, like this book as a whole,
makes no claim to being exhaustive, even with regard to those topics—style,
the historical novel, and utopia—that seem especially pertinent in delineating
the special relationship between science fiction and critical theory. Yet I believe that the foregoing analyses of this affinity are sufficient, when taken with
the definitional discussion of critical theory in chapter 1, to explain the consistent marginalization of science fiction by the dominant canons of literary
value. If science fiction indeed occupies a privileged position in relation to dialectics and the dialogic, to historical thinking and to critical demystification,
to the concept of totality and to the practice of radical social transformation—
if, in fine, science fiction enjoys a unique affinity with Marxism as well as with
other varieties of critical theory—then it is virtually self-evident why the literary ruling class, who ultimately determine questions of canonization, have not
wished to elevate the social and ideological status of so subversive a genre.

All genuine critique must expect such conservative resistance, and even the
faintest suspicion that science fiction has been keeping such dangerous theoretical company may be enough to motivate the belittling and ghettoization
that science fiction generally suffers at the hands of those who exercise great
influence in literary matters. So it is (in part) that such weakly, if spectacularly,
science-fictional sagas as *Star Wars* and *Star Trek*, and even their precursor
texts in the most primitive achievements of the original pulp tradition, are
made to figure more largely, in the public perception of science fiction, than
such authors as Asimov, Clarke, Heinlein, or Frank Herbert—and so it is also
that these and other, comparable authors figure more largely than Stapledon

or Wells or Mary Shelley. The intent of the dominant canonizers (though not necessarily in any conspiratorial sense, of course) is thus to encourage a superficial understanding of the genre while discouraging serious attention to those authors who could most consequentially refute such mystifications. The general effect is to insinuate a notion of science fiction as an almost *intrinsically* negligible literary kind, and this effect is achieved without even the labor of formulating an explicitly dyslogistic definition.

In much the same way, celebrated modern works in which the tendency of science fiction is strong or even, arguably, dominant—but which are not explicitly packaged or marketed as science fiction by their authors and publishers—tend to be handled so as to repress the issue of science fiction altogether. Convenient examples include Kafka's *The Trial* (1925) and Beckett's *Endgame* (1957), two of the more securely canonical texts of literary modernity. Though Kafka's novel is probably not to be considered a predominantly science-fictional work—the tendencies of (somewhat displaced) historical realism and of allegory are, I think, stronger than science fiction—there is no question that a science-fictional element does strongly operate here. The arrest of Joseph K. works to some degree like a science-fictional Novum, totally reconfiguring the mundane environment of empirical reality and thus (in partly the same manner as Frankenstein's creature) critically estranging the latter. K is plunged into an effectively new world, whose relation to the old one that he thought he knew is often in fact confusing but always remains cognitively explicable in principle. The text, indeed, clearly signals the functioning of cognitive estrangement from the earliest pages: "K. lived in a country with a legal constitution, there was universal peace, all the laws were in force; who dared seize him in his own dwelling?"[48] The world of baffling bureaucratic repression and violence turns out to be all too closely and logically connected to the world of apparent normality.

In *Endgame*, the science-fictional tendency is even stronger, and constitutes the dominant generic tendency of the text. Beckett's play ranks as probably the most notable science-fiction drama since Capek's *R.U.R.* (1921), and ought to be understood in company with the other science-fictional extrapolations about life after nuclear holocaust that are roughly contemporary with it: works, that is, like Pat Frank's *Alas, Babylon* (1959), Walter M. Miller's *A Canticle for Leibowitz* (1959), and (the finest of the postnuclear novels) Philip K. Dick's *Dr. Bloodmoney* (1965). *Endgame* is probably a greater work than any of these novels; like them, however, the drama of Hamm and Clov is concerned less with factually forecasting the details of human existence on the far side of thermonuclear devastation than with employing a postnuclear scenario as a Novum that, in a powerfully critical and cognitive manner, estranges the Cold War present in which novels and plays are still read. The point of Beckett's play, in other words, is to foreground the terrible banalities of a world that has

48. Franz Kafka, *The Trial*, trans. Willa and Edwin Muir (New York: Schocken, 1968), 4.

consciously and deliberately made nuclear holocaust into a concrete potentiality.[49] Yet the commentary that has been most influential in granting approved canonical status to Kafka and Beckett has, overwhelmingly, functioned to erase from public view the science-fictional character of their work. This is true to such a degree, indeed, that any criticism that seeks to understand *The Trial* or *Endgame* in science-fictional terms must itself involve a certain shock of defamiliarization. Such canonical erasures serve repressive political ends in two different (though certainly related) ways. On the one hand, of course, science fiction as a named genre is not permitted to share in the literary glory associated with certifiable Modern Masters. But equally, the most interesting and subversive aspects of the approved texts themselves are largely conjured out of view. Instead of being read, science-fictionally, as critical investigators of mutable and historically specific social totalities, Kafka is domesticated as a negative theologian and purveyor of metaphysical anguish, while Beckett is reassuringly dressed up as the individualist showman of merely existential absurdity. To efface the science-fictional is, to a considerable degree, to purge that which is fundamentally *threatening* to the normative middle-class order.

But, of course, a defense of that order is scarcely the project of Mikhail Bakhtin, or Georg Lukács, or Ernst Bloch, to say nothing of Marx himself. It is now time to engage the second of the two questions posed at the end of the first section of this chapter: If critical theory privileges science fiction, why has this been, in the main, an *unconscious* privileging, of which most critical theorists seem to have been unaware? If authors like Bakhtin, Lukács, and Bloch are as central to the theorization of science fiction as I have claimed, then why are overt references to science fiction so few and far between in their writings? None, after all, was chronologically disqualified from explicit and detailed examination of the genre. If science fiction, in sum, has a special importance for critical theory, why have critical theorists been so remiss in resisting the marginalization of science fiction by the canonizing practices of hegemonic literary ideologies?

To be sure, the oversight is far from total, especially in recent years. It is not by accident that the analysis of science fiction has for some time now constituted one of the most critically informed areas of literary studies generally. It is instructive, in this regard, to contrast the conceptual level attained in a typical issue of *Science-Fiction Studies* during the late 1970s with the (much lower) conceptual level in a typical contemporary issue of *PMLA*, the flagship journal of professional literary studies in North America, or *ELH*, which is generally considered its closest rival in general academic prestige. Even today, when

49. Cf. Adorno's commentary on *Endgame*, perhaps the most dialectical and critically informed to date: "The play's setting . . . is none other than the earth upon which 'there's no more nature.' The phase in which the world is totally reified, in which nothing is left that is not made by man, the permanent catastrophe, becomes indistinguishable from a supplementary, man-made catastrophe, in which nature is destroyed and after which nothing grows any longer"; Theodor W. Adorno, "Towards an Understanding of *Endgame*," in *Twentieth-Century Interpretations of "Endgame*," ed. Bell Gale Chevigny (Englewood Cliffs, N.J.: Prentice Hall, 1969), 86.

concerns proper to critical theory are much more widely shared within the literary academy than was the case two decades or so ago, there are few specialties in which genuinely critical perspectives are so influential as in the study of science fiction. This situation is, indeed, one of the enabling, or at least favoring, conditions of this book—whose claims to originality (as I have already noted) by no means include any boast on my part to be the first critical theorist, or even among the first critical theorists, to read science fiction seriously. Nonetheless, if the manifest neglect of science fiction by critical theory is—finally—being somewhat remedied, that neglect itself still remains in need of explanation.

To some extent, the explanation is historical in a very specific way. Indeed, it is largely *philological*. It would have been extremely difficult (or more likely impossible) to define the generic tendency of science fiction clearly and with particular regard to its deep affinity with critical theory in the post-Kantian and post-Hegelian sense until that tendency was strongly embodied in a large, varied body of work explicitly published and marketed as science fiction—a condition that, as we shall see, has been met only in the fairly recent past. As we have already seen, science fiction was not even securely consolidated as a distinct genre until the appearance of H. G. Wells's pathbreaking novels of the 1890s, and did not acquire a name or the degree of self-consciousness attendant upon such denomination until the advent of Gernsbackian pulp in the 1920s. The pulp tradition then went on to exercise an influence on the general perception of science fiction that cannot be wholly attributed to deliberate conservative resistance to the potentialities of science-fictional radicalism. The mere fact that pulp did, after all, originate the name itself was enormously consequential. It helped enforce the near-monopoly that the conceptually weak products of pulp—in its original magazine form, and later as translated into books, films, and television programs—enjoyed, at least in some quarters, over science fiction as a self-conscious literary enterprise.

The aesthetic and theoretical weakness of pulp is itself, of course, a phenomenon that requires explication, but is in fact readily explicable. Pulp science fiction quickly developed into a moderately successful publishing industry, with its own internal sociology and political economy. A profitable routine was soon established on the basis of a readership that was overwhelmingly male and middle-class, often adolescent or slightly pre-adolescent, and generally characterized by technocratic identifications with academic science, commercial engineering, and the military.[50] It was a readership often quite intense and, within its own limits, quite intelligent. But the interests of its members were largely technical, and the readers of pulp were not generally noted for being *widely* read, especially in modern literature, history, and philosophy.

---

50. Data to support these generalizations can be found in Albert Berger, "Science Fiction Fans in Socio-Economic Perspective: Factors in the Social Consciousness of a Genre," *Science-Fiction Studies* 4 (1977): 232–246, and in William Sims Bainbridge, *Dimensions of Science Fiction* (Cambridge, Mass.: Harvard University Press, 1986).

Even leaving aside the effects (often quite significant) of overt, formal censorship, the overall ideological atmosphere of the world generally taken to be the world of science fiction was, therefore, inhospitable to the kind of radical criticism associated with the generic tendency of science fiction in the strong sense of cognitive estrangement. In these circumstances, with so degraded a meaning attached to the name of science fiction, it was often difficult to construct as genuinely science-fictional even such direct precursors or relatives of pulp science fiction as Mary Shelley, Wells, or Olaf Stapledon—even though these very authors were often explicitly acknowledged as kindred within pulp science fiction itself. Conservative efforts to marginalize science fiction thus enjoyed powerful, though generally unwitting, support from those exercising proprietary rights over the name of science fiction itself.

The philologically based connection between pulp and science fiction retains considerable force to this day, and so continues to obscure the critical vitality of the genre. Thus it is, as we have seen, that the science-fictional character of such authors as Beckett and Kafka remains for the most part occluded, however frankly *Endgame*, for instance, may project a scenario of the (postnuclear) kind generally recognized to be classically science-fictional. To take another instance, even less widely understood is the way the Joycean method, especially in *Finnegans Wake*, incorporates something of the science-fiction tendency in its radical estrangement of the apparently smooth surface of everyday perception and consciousness. Though none of Joyce's texts counts as *predominantly* science-fictional, the multiaccentual linguistic play of *Finnegans Wake* effectively creates a new but cognitively explicable world out of the unconscious itself, a virtually utopian space that works to estrange the settled mundane constructions of centered personal, gender, and national subjectivity—thus giving the text an indispensable, if subordinate, element of science fiction. Yet the residual pulp associations of the term may seem, in many contexts, to create an unbridgeable gap between science fiction and James Joyce, the author established as perhaps the most securely canonical of the twentieth century. Let us consider yet another instance. The general affinity between science fiction and critical theory makes it unsurprising that specifically science-fictional devices should find a place in the rhetoric of critical theory itself, especially in the more speculative moments of the latter: for example, the theoretical fictions with which Freud expounds his final description of psychic drives in such late works as *Beyond the Pleasure Principle* (1920) and *The Ego and the Id* (1923). Yet to designate the idea of the pleasure principle and the death drive as in any way science-fictional would, in most forums, inescapably suggest connotations of a precritical and anti-Freudian stance.[51]

51. But such a designation finds a close parallel in Freud himself: "The theory of the drives is so to say our mythology. Drives are mythical entities, magnificent in their indefiniteness. In our work we cannot for a moment disregard them, yet we are never sure that we are seeing them clearly"; Sigmund Freud, *New Introductory Lectures on Psychoanalysis*, trans. James Strachey (New York: Norton, 1965), 84; translation modified.

Nonetheless, though it may still be difficult to formulate the science-fictional dimensions of Kafka or Beckett, Joyce or Freud, the fact that it is now *possible* to do so may ultimately be attributed to the appearance, in relatively recent years, of strongly critical work openly and unambiguously presented as science fiction: that is, the work (the great majority of it not antedating the 1960s and much of it a good deal later than that) of such writers as Stanisław Lem, Philip K. Dick, Alice Sheldon, Ursula Le Guin, Samuel Delany, Marge Piercy, Thomas Disch, Norman Spinrad, Joanna Russ, J. G. Ballard, Brian Aldiss, Octavia Butler, Gregory Benford, William Gibson, Bruce Sterling, Kim Stanley Robinson *et alii et aliae*. In pure abstract principle, critical theorists ought not, perhaps, to have "needed" the current, immensely creative era of science fiction in order to appreciate the importance of the genre. In historically concrete terms, however, it is nearly impossible to imagine that the most dialectical potentialities of science fiction could be grasped before the term itself had been heavily inflected by that upsurge in creativity whose early stages are conveniently marked by the British journal *New Worlds* and by Harlan Ellison's anthology *Dangerous Visions* (1967). In the last analysis, it is the work of aesthetically and conceptually advanced novelists, overtly and self-consciously appearing as science-fiction writers, that has finally made it possible—against all philological inertia and all conservative obstruction—to break the semantic stranglehold of pulp over science fiction, and so to define the link between science fiction and critical theory.

But this semantic stranglehold, however important, does not completely account for the relative neglect of science fiction by critical theorists. If the latter have on the whole been more at home with Sophocles or Shakespeare or Balzac, the reason also lies partly in the nature of canonization itself. The discussion of the levels of canonization in the first section of this chapter should have made it clear that canon-formation is an essentially *conservative* process. I do not mean that canon-formation is an entirely dispensable category to which an unproblematically "radical" alternative exists. To be simplistically "against" canonization is puerile and self-defeating; one must in some sense "accept" the process of canon-formation as Margaret Fuller accepted the universe. To conserve and privilege what seems of value from a particular point of view is, at the very least, a practical necessity: no individual has the time to read all—or even a substantial fraction—of the texts available. Indeed, nearly all the questions that concern the inclusions and exclusions of the canon tend to assume a sharper and more urgent form when discussion turns from the canon as such—which, in all its three phases, is considerably, though by no means infinitely, flexible—to the much less flexible institutional embodiments of canon-formation. It is in this latter context that such unavoidable questions of canonization present themselves as which texts are to be included in a thirteen-week syllabus, or in the current acquisitions list of a library suffering severe financial cuts. Such questions are finally *political*, of course, and they must be engaged. They cannot be waived in the name of an ultra-left pseudo-utopianism that would demand a strict formal equality of all texts.

On the other hand, the conservatism of canon-formation—whose first and most decisively conservative phase, it should be remembered, separates the literary from the nonliterary—is, if to some degree necessary, also something of which critical theorists should be wary. The procedure is intrinsically repressive, and, given the inevitable hegemony of precritical thought in class society, the repressions involved are by no means random or unselective. On the contrary, actually existing processes of canon-formation are nearly certain, in the main, to exhibit a bias toward the status quo and against genuinely critical thought that might undermine the taken-for-granted verities of empirical reality. To be sure, this bias is far from absolute. Literary canonization is a process that takes place at a high level of mediation from the ultimately determining processes of socioeconomic reproduction; consequently it enjoys, for the most part, considerable autonomy from the crudest repressions of the ruling order. But it would be naive to think that some measure of conservative prejudice can ever be completely eradicated from the construction of literary canons.

Unfortunately, critical theorists have not, on the whole, been sufficiently alert to this danger. Perhaps at least partly because the political issues at stake in literary canon-formation *are* so highly mediated—as well as because of the inescapable pragmatic need for some canonical hierarchization of texts—they have, on this matter more than on most, been swayed by the socially normative conservatism into which even the most rigorously critical mind is bound sometimes to lapse (and which, indeed, is not completely separable even from the basic constitution of individuals as the centered subjects of a repressive society).[52] Accordingly, critical theorists of literature, like their precritical colleagues, have tended to work mainly within the received literary canons, though critical theorists have necessarily added the proviso that canonical texts need not be read in received ways. Now, there is no question that the radical rereading of the established cultural monuments of the past is, in itself, not only legitimate, but indispensable to the critical project as a whole. The commentaries of Bakhtin on Dostoevsky, of Lukács on Balzac, of Bloch on Goethe—and, for that matter, of Marx and Engels on classical idealist philosophy—are especially noteworthy examples. Yet such focus on canonically approved masterworks becomes illegitimate to the extent that it leads theorists (Adorno probably remains the most eminent or notorious such instance) to neglect the ideological function of canon-formation and the ways in which the latter is wont to stigmatize those texts distributed from marginalized sectors of the literary market (or even, in some cases, denied direct access to the market altogether). For such texts may, as in the case of science

52. The classic reference here is, of course, to Louis Althusser, "Ideology and Ideological State Apparatuses," in *Lenin and Philosophy*, trans. Ben Brewster (New York: Monthly Review, 1971), 127–186.

fiction, contain much material of the highest importance from a critical-theoretical point of view.

Accordingly, though the canonization of science fiction and the construction of canons within science fiction are certainly to some degree implicit in this study, I must stress that these (practically unavoidable) processes are potentially in conflict with the most radical intent of my argument. If science fiction is read seriously, then science fiction will inevitably have its internal canons and its place within the general canon as a whole. But the danger will always exist that science-fiction canonizing may repress much that is genuinely new and critical within and beyond the genre. In this context, there is a definable grain of good, correct sense (though there certainly happens to be a great deal more of reactionary anti-intellectualism) in the alarm that many older science-fiction writers and editors, especially survivors of the Campbell era, often express at the increasing though still rather slight academic respectability that science fiction enjoys. There is, after all, a clear and ominous precedent in the reception of the great modernisms of the early twentieth century. Originally the stuff of canonical exclusion and conservative denunciation, the innovations of such works as *Ulysses* (1922) and *The Waste Land* (1922) were in only a few decades transformed into thoroughly respectable grist for the routine academic mill, on the one hand, and, on the other, into the inspiration for such dull epigones of literary modernism as Saul Bellow and the Eliotic poets of the 1950s. It is impossible to predict exactly what sort of similar fate might befall science fiction. Yet it cannot be denied that the cutting edge of science fiction may be blunted to the extent that the genre becomes at all official. There is no question that any project like the current essay is intended, in part, to make the question of the canon a less unhappy one for science fiction. But if that question ever becomes completely happy and unproblematic for science fiction, there will be good reason to suspect that science fiction will have changed for the worse more than the canon will have changed for the better. As happens so often in the history of repressive tolerance, the smile will be on the face of the tiger.

3. Excursuses

In this chapter, I offer substantial analyses of five major science-fiction novels. My aim is to demonstrate, in more detail than has previously been feasible, some of the different ways that science-fiction texts resonate strongly with concerns proper to critical theory. I do not attempt exhaustive readings, partly for reasons of economy, but also in order to warn against the imbecile empiricism that the notion of "practical criticism" often implies and the concomitant naïveté that holds the minute examination of particular texts to be the ultimate test or telos of literary theory. These readings are not proposed precisely as "examples" of the argument in chapter 2, and still less as *proof* (in any positivistic sense) of it. Rather, I am continuing the argument in a different register—the "molecular" register (as Deleuze and Guattari might say) of individual novels.

I should say a few words about the principles of selection at work below. As we have seen in the final section of chapter 2, the contemporary era in science fiction—the era whose early years are roughly marked by *New Worlds* and *Dangerous Visions*—deserves a privileged position in a project like this book. It is in the past forty years or so that we have witnessed the production of the largest distinct body of work that *strongly* incarnates the generic tendency of science fiction and is explicitly and unambiguously published under the name of science fiction. Especially insofar as the American and British traditions are concerned, this great increase in the critical sophistication of science fiction as a named genre can be correlated with the more general increase in critical thinking—that is, in dialectical, historical, and utopian thinking—that characterizes the general cultural phenomenon known as "the Sixties." Of the four American authors discussed below, only Philip K. Dick produced major work before the advent of the most fateful decade of the post–World War II era, and it is no accident that Dick became a science-fiction author largely because most forums for other fictional genres were closed to his subversive imaginings in the dreadfully conformist America of the 1950s. Furthermore, despite his important early work, Dick produced his best fiction during the

Sixties and immediately afterward; and Ursula Le Guin, Joanna Russ, and Samuel Delany are all literary children of the Sixties in an even more direct and obvious way. As will become evident from the detailed readings to follow, such radical currents of the Sixties as the civil rights and Black Power movements, the movements against the Cold War and the war in Vietnam, the youth counterculture, the environmentalist movement, feminism, gay liberation, and the various New Lefts generally supply the conditions of historical possibility for the major work of authors like Dick, Le Guin, Russ, Delany and their best colleagues and followers. If one were to seek a single descriptive historical phrase to characterize this body of science fiction, one could not do better than "the Sixties and after."

Accordingly, there is good reason that all the authors discussed at length below should belong to this—admittedly very large and diverse—cohort of current science-fiction writers. In fact, all but one of them are at this writing still alive, and any generalizations about their careers must be qualified by the recognition that they are still capable of somewhat redefining the overall shape of their own work. It seems obvious to me that all are among the most accomplished novelists of their—our—age. Though all belong to (very roughly) the same chronological group, I have made my selections on the basis of the importance of the particular novelistic texts, not with a purpose of picking five writers who might "represent" in any very specific ways the larger number of writers who could appropriately be discussed in this chapter. Nonetheless, it does not seem to me completely fortuitous that four of the five writers considered below are Americans and that two of the five are women. Probably these proportions do very approximately suggest some valid generalizations about where the critical and creative energy in contemporary science fiction is mainly coming from (though I do not mean to deny the continued importance of British science fiction nor the possibility that women writers may, by now, have achieved something like, or something better than, parity with their male colleagues). With regard to the particular titles I have chosen, the importance of at least three—the texts by Stanisław Lem, Le Guin, and Dick—is pretty widely acknowledged; the comparable importance of Delany's finest science-fiction novel must, I think, be generally recognized sooner or later; and, though *The Female Man* might seem the obvious and appropriate work by Russ to consider, I am convinced that the later novel I have picked is one of the secret masterpieces of contemporary fiction.

On the general matter of representation, there is one further point to be made with regard not only to the current chapter but to the book as a whole. As should be fairly evident by now, science fiction is for me primarily an Anglo-American phenomenon, and in a more minor way a French one. This amounts to a confession that the important Russian and East European traditions lie—to a considerable extent and above all linguistically—outside my professional competence, and are consequently underrepresented in the current study. But it does not seem right, even allowing for the deliberate selectivity of my approach throughout, that only a few scattered references *en passant* should represent the entirety of science fiction in Russian, Polish, Czech, and other languages that flourish east of Paris. Thus, although I picked Lem's masterpiece as one of the five novels to be treated because of its own general interest and for the specific conceptual reasons discussed below, Lem's presence in this chapter should also be taken as a somewhat more than token recognition on my part of the importance, for science fiction, of what used to be called the Second World. Doubtless the particular circumstances of postwar Poland make Lem less of a "Sixties" writer than his Anglo-American colleagues; but then, as we will see, Lem has had at his disposal the immense dialectical resources of Central European modernity.

Solaris: *Stanisław Lem and the Structure of Cognition*

A convenience of beginning with Lem's *Solaris* (1961)[1] is that in this novel cognition and estrangement figure not only as conceptual and aesthetic qualities but as overt themes as well. One way to define much of the novel's achievement is to note that it represents the fusion of two and in some ways almost antithetical tendencies within Lem's work. On the one hand, Lem—the heir, in this respect, of both Voltaire and Kafka—is a master of high-spirited and militantly arealistic philosophic satire, satire that, among other things, attempts to problematize the epistemological assumptions of unreflective, precritical common sense. An example of such (largely parabolic and even allegorical) work is *The Cyberiad* (1956), a series of science-fictional fables that work to estrange many of the most taken-for-granted assumptions that govern everyday life, perhaps most notably by foregrounding the constitutive, constructive function of language and the indispensable role that difference plays within representation itself. Another is *The Futurological Congress* (1971), a paranoid and frequently hallucinatory tale that again and again insists upon the extreme difficulty, or indeed the impossibility, of establishing any unproblematic baseline "reality."

On the other hand, Lem seems equally at home with a certain kind of precise, sober, understated factual (or rather pseudofactual) solidity. In *Return*

---

1. All references (given parenthetically by page number) are to Stanisław Lem, *Solaris*, trans. Joanna Kilmartin and Steve Cox (New York: Berkley Books, 1971). The Kilmartin-Cox translation presents some peculiar problems: it is made from a French translation rather than from Lem's original Polish, and has been said to be less than wholly reliable in exact verbal detail. This inexactness is unfortunate, as other Lem translations (notably by Michael Kandel) rendered directly from the Polish suggest Lem to be a stylist of some precision, and this impression is reinforced by reports from those capable of reading him in the original. In the current instance, however, it seems prudent (especially for one, like myself, who cannot read even a menu or a headline in Polish) to base no weighty arguments on particular formulations in the text.

from the Stars (1961), for example—a text that displays the strong influence of Hemingway in both technique and theme—Lem records the "homecoming" of a conventionally rugged masculine astronaut to the nonviolent hedonistic utopia that earth has become in his absence. The tone is laconic, and the observation of minute detail is calm and exact, so that the general literary effect of the novel in many ways approximates that of prosaic travel literature. This aspect of Lem—who, in this mode, might well be described as the supreme quasi-realistic observer of places and processes that do not, as a matter of fact, actually exist—is perhaps even more abundantly illustrated in *Tales of Pirx the Pilot* (1968), a cycle of stories about the almost routine "realities" of advanced space travel. Lem's ability to bring to such subject matter the same kind of close, unsensational realization that a more mundane author might achieve in writing about a fishing trip, say, or the boxing ring, is virtually unparalleled. It is easy to believe reports of Lem's popularity among the Soviet cosmonauts: he does give the almost uncanny impression of enjoying personal familiarity with forms of experience that only a tiny handful of human beings have known (and they only to a relatively small degree) at first hand.

In *Solaris*, both of these Lemian approaches are strongly at work and are skillfully synthesized. The detailed realism of presentation is worthy of that in the Pirx stories, to which, in its remarkable "knowledge" of interstellar travel, the text is often closely allied. For example, as the protagonist-narrator Kris Kelvin is approaching the planet of Solaris, he notes, "I had passed that imperceptible frontier after which we measure the distance that separates us from a celestial body in terms of altitude" (9)—an observation so casual yet so cogent as almost to convince us that we are indeed personally familiar with exactly that experience. Lem's pseudofactual invention is even more in evidence in his construction of the imaginary science of Solaristics, the study of the vast sentient ocean that covers the surface of the planet and with which human scientists are endeavoring to establish contact. Lem (the author, it should be remembered, of *A Perfect Vacuum* [1971], a series of reviews of twenty-first-century books, and *Imaginary Magnitude* [1973], a series of introductions to twenty-first-century books) so convincingly establishes the material reality of the science—its greater and lesser names, its research articles and encyclopedic tomes, its scholarly controversies and vulgar popularizations, its shifting orthodoxics and occasional heresies, its many well-trained professionals and few inspired amateurs, and above all its sheer *weightiness*—that large stretches of the novel (notably in the second, eighth, and eleventh chapters) bear the generic imprint of scientific and intellectual history. This is so strongly true, indeed, that it is with something of a shock that the reader remembers that Solaristics does not, after all, really exist.

This factological solidity in *Solaris*—the establishment, in and by the text, of a counterfactual yet quasi-factual locus that is cognitively plausible in immense detail—ultimately works, however, to enforce and embody an estranging conceptual fable at least as radical and intellectually ambitious as anything in *The Cyberiad* or *The Futurological Congress*. Indeed, we may note in passing that Lem illustrates, more richly than probably any other science-fiction author since Stapledon, the capacity of the genre to incorporate unabashed philosophical speculation: a novelistic element common in major classical realism (think of George Eliot, or Tolstoy) but that in the twentieth century has been largely confined to science fiction (the heir, as we have already seen, of much of the critical historical sense of classical realism). But the philosophical thrust of *Solaris* is not merely to estrange. It also takes as its very subject matter the category of estrangement, the relationship, that is, between the familiar and the other, between identity and alterity; and it explores the function and limits of cognition itself in coming to terms with this relationship. At the same time, the elaborate pseudorealism of the text concretizes these wide-ranging speculations in a genuinely novelistic manner. The result is one of the most *radically* science-fictional texts that we possess—in contrast, for example, to the tales in *The Cyberiad,* which might better be described as relatively abstract parables and allegories *about* themes familiar to science fiction than as science fiction proper in the strongest sense.

The point made most emphatically by Lem's invention of Solaristic science is the dialectical *provisionality* of all genuine knowledge and cognition, most definitely including even the physical or "hard" sciences.[2] From the Lemian standpoint, the chief philosophical enemy is positivism; that is, the dogmatic assumption of an unproblematic and invariably positive adequation between knowing subject and known object. It is indicative only of the widespread confusion of science with positivism (a confusion that, as Lem recognizes, is shared by a good many working scientists) that numerous readers have interpreted the novel as an attack on, or at least a demystification of, science. It is characteristic of Lem's rigor, however, that the antiscientific viewpoint is represented and engaged within the text itself, in the work of the anti-Solarist Muntius. Muntius has denounced Solaristics as a religious faith camouflaged as science; he would, at least implicitly, deconstruct the distinction between religion and science in general. He invents a series of ingenious analogies between Solaristics and traditional Western religion—for instance, the central Solarist goal of contact between humanity and the mysterious ocean recalls mystical communion or the Second Coming—and on this basis offers to conflate the one with the other: "Solaristics is a revival of long-vanished myths, the expression of mystical nostalgias which men are unwilling to confess openly" (180).

2. Darko Suvin usefully makes a similar point in "The Open-Ended Parables of Stanisław Lem and *Solaris*," an essay printed as an afterword to the edition of the novel cited above: "Lem's major novels have at their *cognitive core* the simple and difficult realization that no closed reference system, however alluring to the weary and poor in spirit, is viable in the age of relativity theory and post-cybernetic sciences" (220; emphasis in original).

The text does consider this view seriously and to some degree sympathetically. Muntius's analogies are perfectly valid in themselves, and it need not be denied that science and religion, as interpretive modes by which human beings grapple with the largest questions confronting their species, may well display points of resemblance. Nonetheless, Muntius's position is decisively rejected—not because it is offensive, but because it is simplistic. Muntius neglects salient differences between different forms of interpretation and thus naively equates partial, if striking, resemblance with total identity: Kelvin is clearly endorsed by the novel itself when he decides that his Solarist mentor Gibarian "was right to characterize Muntius's strictures as a monumental simplification which ignored all the aspects of Solarist studies that had nothing in common with a creed, since the work of interpretation based itself only on the concrete evidence of a globe [Solaris] orbiting two suns" (182).

In other words, Lem's view of science is not particularly scandalized by Muntius's—as any positivistic view would be—but it is considerably more *complicated*. The Lemian rejection of positivistic dogmatism is made not in the name of an epistemologically nihilistic relativism like Muntius's (which, after all, is just the reactive and undialectical obverse of dogmatism) but in order to enforce an authentically critical view of scientific rigor in all its complexity. Science, as Lem constructs it, has little to satisfy those precritical minds (a category that, of course, includes at least some part of *all* minds) that hunger after certainty and finality. For example, the great second chapter of the novel, in which Kelvin summarizes for himself (and the reader) much of the history and current state of Solarist studies, insinuates a mood of intense frustration, a frustration motivated partly by the occasional degeneration of science into dogma as different schools of Solarists establish varying degrees of institutional hegemony, but more fundamentally by the refusal of genuine science to yield definite onto-theological answers. Even a scientist like Kelvin himself (ironically named after the inventor of the temperature scale on which *absolute* zero is foregrounded) is not immune to the nostalgia for absolutes. He can, indeed, be momentarily overwhelmed by revulsion at the unavailability of final and certain conclusions:

> Lifting the heavy volume with both hands, I replaced it on the shelf, and thought to myself that our scholarship, all the information accumulated in the libraries, amounted to a useless jumble of words, a sludge of statements and suppositions, and that we had not progressed an inch in the 78 years since researches had begun. The situation seemed much worse now than in the time of the pioneers, since the assiduous efforts of so many years had not resulted in a single indisputable conclusion.
> The sum total of known facts was strictly negative. (28–29)

Yet, as Kelvin himself knows well enough, progress *has* in some sense been made—his own presence in the experimental station suspended above Solaris is a testimony to the continuing, if problematic, viability of Solaristics—even though the scientific endeavor is always necessarily provisional, and even though its effort to construct a rational framework for evidence may proceed by a negative dialectic that yields no indisputable conclusions. Indeed, Solaristics, in its relative paucity of consensus and lack of positive conclusions, may best be seen as an extreme case among sciences, a pure textbook model of science as contradistinguished from positivistic triumphalism. But this very extremity foregrounds the fundamental epistemological dialectic of scientificity in general. Science is ultimately a matter of interpretation in the critical post-Kantian sense. Scientific progress, as Lem conceives it, consists more in the provisional elimination of unworkable hypotheses and the evolving consideration of central problems from a variety of angles than in any arrival at final resolutions. Nor can science enjoy any pristine autonomy from ideology. As in all dialectics, much depends upon the position of the observer: Solarists with different methodological leanings—mathematical, cybernetic, biological, psychological, and so forth—frame the problem in different ways. Even the scientific community as a whole is not so intellectually autonomous as it might choose to believe. At one point Kelvin goes somewhat out of his way to recall for us a European opinion poll that "demonstrated that the changes in lay opinion were closely correlated to the fluctuations of opinion recorded in scientific circles" (176). Science, in sum, is an immensely difficult project, and this difficulty is novelistically crystallized in the *supremely* difficult science—almost the metascience—of Solaristics.

Nonetheless—and this remains one of Lem's fundamental conceptual points—difficulty does not render the scientific project vain. As the protagonist of the novel, Kris Kelvin is a Promethean scientific investigator in a specifically science-fictional tradition that goes back to *Frankenstein* (1818) itself (subtitled "The Modern Prometheus," it may be recalled), though this tradition is of course also allied to the much older Western tradition of the heroic humanistic quest for knowledge. (It is not by chance that the ship aboard which Kelvin arrives at Solaris is named the *Prometheus*.) As so often in this tradition, the ultimate result of the quest is radically ambiguous, amounting more to the discovery of unexpected complexities than to the simple success or failure of the quest as originally formulated. As we shall consider, Kelvin becomes involved in "communication" with the ocean in ways extremely unlike anything for which his training has consciously or specifically prepared him; by the end of the novel—as he makes his first actual visit to the surface of Solaris—he attains what some commentators have construed as a moment of unprecedented empathy or psychological breakthrough with the ocean. The text thus allows the possibility that Kelvin may be the greatest of all Solarists in history, at least in the sense that he may be the first to achieve the long-awaited goal of contact. He himself feels that sufficient communication has been established that he decides to abandon earth permanently and to remain on Solaris. Yet neither Kelvin nor the reader can be certain, and the last two sentences

of the novel strike a note of pointed ambiguity: "I did not know what achievements, what mockery, even what tortures still awaited me. *I knew nothing* [my
emphasis—this clause of course condenses one major aspect of the various
long expositions of Solaristic science that precede it in the text], and I per-
sisted in the faith that the time of cruel miracles was not past" (211). As always,
it is the provisionality of the quest that is most important and that possesses essential epistemological dignity. The quest is sufficiently worthwhile that Kelvin (who, at least by the end, has arguably evolved into a cognitive spokesman
for the author) is willing to devote his life, in several senses, to it. But he can
expect no reward in the form of onto-theological certainty.

Yet what, precisely, are the alternatives to such certainty? Philosophically,
perhaps the most nagging specter that haunts any properly critical perspective
is the problem of solipsism. If positivistic finality is unavailable, if cognition is
fundamentally a matter of provisional interpretation that is itself always subject to revision, correction, and elaboration, then how are different interpretations to be evaluated? (This is the problem of solipsism in the form of theoretical relativism.) How can any such interpretation ultimately claim to be more
than the projections of the single thinking mind? (This is the problem of solipsism proper.) Characteristically, Lem does not evade this crux, but explicitly
incorporates it into one of the most conceptually interesting—if problematic—episodes in the text. Shortly after arriving at the experimental station
above Solaris, Kelvin is plunged, with almost no preparation or helpful explanation, into the apparently weird goings-on that, as we later learn, are precipi-
tated by the visits of the Phi-creatures. One of his first responses is to conclude,
not unreasonably, that he may be going insane and that the strange sights he
has witnessed may therefore be the hallucinatory inventions of his own dis-
eased mind. Proceeding in classically scientific fashion, Kelvin attempts to test
this hypothesis by designing a controlled experiment that will measure the objective reality or unreality of his perceptions. It is precisely at this point, however, that the merciless logic of solipsism makes itself felt: "I was going around
in circles; there seemed to be no escape. It was not possible to think except
with one's brain, no one could stand outside himself in order to check the
functioning of his inner processes" (57). As it is Kelvin himself who must construct and interpret the experiment, how can the results of the latter be epistemologically distinguished from his original perceptions that the experiment is
designed to verify or falsify in the first place? But then he does think of a way.
He constructs a complicated problem in interstellar mapping, and compares
the empirical answer given by the station's satellite to the answer he derives
through laborious calculations that require the aid of the station's computer. If
the two sets of figures jibe, then, he reasons, it will follow that his calculations
have been sound and that his mind is therefore healthy: "My brain might be
unhinged, but it could not conceivably compete with the Station's giant
computer and secretly perform calculations requiring several months' work.

Therefore if the figures corresponded, it would follow that the Station's computer really existed, that I had really used it, and that I was not delirious" (58). In these terms, the experiment does succeed to Kelvin's satisfaction, and he ceases to doubt his own sanity.

Yet once the issue of solipsism has been introduced, the logical slippage in the passage just quoted is evident. Kelvin cannot know that the figures *do* correspond except by trusting his own readings, whose reliability the hypothesis of insanity must put into question in the first place. On the other hand, the only real alternative to accepting Kelvin's verification of his lucidity is to read the entire novel as the tale told by someone hopelessly and irretrievably demented—an approach that would offer few rewards in general and that, in particular, can only with great difficulty be made to cohere with the novel's calm, precise, understated realism of presentation. What the entire episode most interestingly conveys, I think, is a properly dialectical response to the problem of solipsism, or, in more general terms, the problem of verification itself. Once (positivistic or other) dogmatism has been rejected, verification can never be unambiguously attained on the purely logical level; on that level the solipsistic hypothesis can never be rejected with complete certainty. But authentic cognition is not, for critical theory, a matter of purely formal (and hence, in the long run, contemplative) logic. On the contrary, it finds its ultimate test in what the Marxist tradition calls *praxis*; that is, the synthesis of thought with creative and self-creative material production. In a way somewhat parallel to that of therapeutic practice in Freudian psychoanalysis (which may indeed be considered one of its versions), praxis pragmatically grounds concepts by testing and actualizing them within actual historical processes. Praxis is thus to be understood not as the opposite or antithesis of (critical) theory, but as the latter's completion and as that which allows thought to transcend the (solipsistic and relativistic) vicious circles and infinite regresses of logical formalism. Such is precisely what Kelvin's experiment achieves. Though it does not allow him (or us) to refute solipsism on the merely contemplative level, the act of scientific experimentation does provide him with a practical verification of his own sanity, thus allowing him to reject madness as a sufficiently unlikely hypothesis. Correlatively, it also allows us to regard the novel as essentially readable—which it would hardly be if Kelvin were to be construed as so mad as to be incapable even of reading a line of numbers.

It is just at this point in *Solaris*, however, that the (pragmatically resolved) problem of solipsism opens out onto a related but much larger problem, one that constitutes the most prominent cognitive issue of the novel: the hypothetical *collective* solipsism of humanity as a whole, or, in other words, the question of whether the radically other is by definition beyond the power of the human mind to grasp. This is, of course, the philosophic crux that haunts the entire science of Solaristics, with its goal of establishing contact with the strange ocean; and it is this mystery that, in various ways, most threatens

Kelvin's balance after he has succeeded in reassuring himself about his own personal mental health.

Indeed, it is in this context that the conceptual superiority of Lem's novel to many more weakly science-fictional texts is particularly evident. Contact with extraterrestrial beings is a familiar literary motif. But contact has most often been silently and simplistically equated (or nearly equated) with mere *meeting*. In *Solaris*, however, meeting has occurred almost a century before the time present of the novel, and by no means simply or inevitably implies genuine contact. Interposed between the two is the problem of collective solipsism, which manifests itself in many and various ways, no matter how the Solaristic project is formulated. For example, if contact is defined as communication between humanity and the alien life form, then it must be questioned whether the category of communication itself—all known models of which derive from the relations among humans and, to a lesser degree, other earthly life—has any meaning when dealing with a nonhuman and nonterrestrial intelligence. For that matter, is it disqualifyingly anthropocentric to apply the category of intelligence to the living ocean? Or is even the category of life, in this context, unacceptably biocentric? (For that matter, is the category of ocean unacceptably geocentric?) In fine, is the project of establishing contact with the ocean merely difficult, or is it intrinsically meaningless from the start? Is there, in other words, any form of praxis capable, in this instance, of short-circuiting or somehow transcending the collective solipsism of the human race?

Characteristically, the novel offers only partial, tentative, and provisional answers to this question. At some points, Lem's text inclines toward epistemological pessimism, implying (in a way that strongly suggests certain tendencies within poststructuralist philosophy) that the ocean is so utterly other as to be quite ungraspable through any variety of dialectic whatever.[3] For example, the scientist Snow, Kelvin's Solarist colleague on the station, is led to abandon the goal of Solaristics altogether. In what has become probably the most widely quoted passage in the novel, Snow insists that humanity can never seek anything other than itself: "We think of ourselves as the Knights of the Holy Contact. This is another lie. We are only seeking Man. We have no need of other worlds. We need mirrors. We don't know what to do with other worlds. A single world, our own, suffices us; but we can't accept it for what it is" (81). Snow's words are persuasive. In one of his surveys of Solarist literature, Kelvin finds that much the same argument has been made in print by the eccentric autodidact Grastrom, who maintains that all science is irredeemably anthropocentric and that "there neither was, nor could be, any question of 'contact' between mankind and any nonhuman civilization" (178). This point should

---

3. At this point I must acknowledge conversations with Steven Shaviro, who suggests to me that, read in this way, *Solaris* reveals an unexpected kinship to the novels of Maurice Blanchot. I suspect that detailed comparison might reveal several specific points of similarity between Lem and Blanchot, both heavily philosophical European novelists of the World War II generation.

be taken with particular seriousness in view of the fact that Grastrom's pamphlet has, evidently, been placed in the station's library on the personal authority of Gibarian (the same mentor who, as we have seen, decisively rejects the simpler and more conventionally relativistic Muntius, who had conflated science with religion).

Furthermore, *Solaris* sometimes emphasizes the basic and evidently ungraspable otherness of its title "character" in imagistic as well as discursive ways. One of the most remarkable activities of the ocean is its creation of "mimoids," huge and immensely complex formations thrown up from the surface of the planet, and which Solarists have interpreted as sensory organs, as limbs, as means of communication, and in various other ways, without being able to attain verification of any of these hypotheses. Kelvin synesthetically describes one variety of mimoid as "a symphony in geometry, but we lack the ears to hear it" (130). And this sort of deliberately paradoxical, almost antivisual imagery informs the extensive physical descriptions of the mimoids themselves—descriptions that often seem quite lucid and detailed in their particulars but that, when taken as wholes, turn out to be effectively impossible to visualize or remember. Though certainly spectacular, the mimoids are, it seems, just too different from anything in our earthly experience to assume for us any clear or even approximately stable meaning. Not by coincidence is one of the first explorers of the mimoids—the pilot André Berton—given almost the same name as the avowed artistic enemy of representational cognition. Contact may indeed be an impossible goal.

But the text allows more positive interpretations as well. Kelvin's moment of apparent empathy with the ocean at the very end of the novel is the culmination of an elaborate psychological narrative that features one sort of possible "communication" between the ocean and the scientists, and that, in classically dialectical fashion, highlights the necessary involvement and active participation of the scientists themselves. Most of the actual plot of *Solaris* concerns the creation by the ocean of the Phi-creatures, phantom humans who appear in the experimental station as simulacra of people from the earlier private lives of the scientists. It is never clear whether they are designed as the ocean's instruments of communication, or of study, or beneficence, or torture, or even amusement (all these interpretations have some plausibility), or for some other purpose altogether—if, indeed, the notion of purpose itself can meaningfully be applied to the ocean at all. In any case, these phantoms, though products of the ocean, attain some degree of autonomy from it and seem more and more human as the tale progresses. But, of course, it is at this moment that the overfamiliar category of the "human" is estranged and problematized. Kelvin is haunted—or "visited," as he himself generally puts it— by the duplicate of his dead wife Rheya, whom he had loved but had also treated shabbily, even helping (though unintentionally) to drive her to suicide. Though at first horrified by the appearance of the new Rheya, Kelvin gradually comes to love her with an intensity that clearly surpasses that of his earthly marriage to her original; she, in her turn, seems to become capable of the ultimate expression of human love, as she is willing to sacrifice her "life" for the sake of Kelvin's happiness. Before entering into this passionate communion with the phantom Rheya, Kelvin (though professionally trained as a psychologist) had generally appeared to be a cold, rather unempathic person. As he finds within himself unexpected capacities for love and commitment, he perhaps attains the kind of *self*-knowledge that has so often been one of the outcomes of the traditional humanistic quest.

The entire novel may thus be read as essentially a love story. And it may be simply in love itself that Kelvin attains the only sort of contact with the ocean (whose creature Rheya is, after all) that supremely matters. In this way, Kelvin's decision to remain on Solaris after Rheya's "death" suggests a virtually Dantean vision of the ultimate identity of love and cognition, as Kelvin decides that the ocean is finally to be understood as a kind of evolving, imperfect god. Forswearing earth, he remains full of expectation and confident that the ocean's "activities did have a purpose," even while characteristically adding that he cannot be "absolutely certain" (211).

This basically humanistic reading of the novel—which amounts to one version of epistemological optimism concerning the Solaristic goal of contact—is, however, powerfully challenged within the text itself. To see Kelvin as a lover in the grand Dantean and Renaissance Neoplatonic traditions is attractive, but it may also be quite groundless. Snow (whose own relation with a Phi-creature, though clearly harrowing, is never shown in any detail) finds Kelvin's passion genuinely moving and impressive; he insists nonetheless that it is also rather idiotic: "She is willing to give her life. So are you. It's touching, it's magnificent, anything you like, but it's out of place here—it's the wrong setting" (162). Snow adds, ominously but irrefutably, "You are going around in circles to satisfy the curiosity of a power we don't understand and can't control [that is, the ocean], and she is an aspect, a periodic manifestation of that power" (162). Mark Rose has added this useful gloss to Snow's argument:[4]

Lem has employed the sentimental codes of the literary love story and thus encourages us to sympathize with Kelvin's passion only to lead us into a trap that illustrates how difficult it is to avoid inappropriate patterns of thought. Snow is correct. In embracing Rheya as completely human, Kelvin has adopted a position no more adequate than that of Sartorius [another of the Solarists at the station, in general the type of the petty bureaucrat], who merely wishes to obliterate the visitors.

Indeed, the Solarists do discover that the Phi-creatures are radically inhuman on the submolecular level—where they are compounded of neutrinos rather

---

4. Mark Rose, *Alien Encounters* (Cambridge, Mass.: Harvard University Press, 1981), 92.

than atoms—and this physical otherness may be an apt figure for their irre-trievable alterity (despite some appearances) in every important sense. In that case, the reading of *Solaris* as a love story is overthrown. Kelvin's devotion to the phantom Rheya may be only the illusory simulacrum of love—and a pa-thetically hopeless attempt on his part to redeem the earthly guilt that the death of the actual Rheya has placed forever beyond redemption. However noble his erotic impulses by the canons of earthly psychology and morality, they may in this particular context (in "the wrong setting," as Snow says) sim-ply be inappropriate.

If such is indeed the case, then the meaning or purpose of the ocean's pro-cess of phantom-creation remains opaque; and the whole "love" story of Kel-vin and the Phi-creature may amount—in scientific or epistemological terms—to nothing more than a particularly intimate and unusual encounter or meeting between a Solarist and the ocean, with no real contact achieved. In this antihumanistic reading, then, Kelvin's ultimate abandonment of earth signifies not the fulfillment of his Solaristic quest, but his excruciating defeat by the quest's insuperable difficulty. Yet the novel does not allow us to repose in the epistemological comforts of pessimism. Lem's text is deliberately am-biguous and provisional in its conclusions, and the tension between humanis-tic and antihumanistic readings remains a subtle and delicate dialectic.[5]

The dialectic of otherness with which Solaris—and *Solaris*—present us may, however, be deepened if we consider the problem from a somewhat dif-ferent angle. The most sophisticated and useful conceptualization of other-ness known to critical theory is, I believe, to be found in the psychoanalysis of

5. It may be relevant at this point to consider the cinematic version of *Solaris* made by the So-viet director Andrei Tarkovsky eleven years after the book's publication. Tarkovsky's *Solaris* de-serves some attention in its own right; it remains one of the few masterworks of science-fiction film (a relatively unfruitful genre, for reasons discussed in Carl Freedman, "Kubrick's *2001* and the Possibility of a Science-Fiction Cinema," *Science-Fiction Studies* [July 1988]: 300–318). Nonethe-less, the alert reader of Lem's novel cannot fail to notice that Tarkovsky responds to the tension between humanistic and antihumanistic readings by pretty much abolishing the latter side of the Lemian dialectic. For Tarkovsky, Kelvin's romantic passion is an unqualified good that helps him attain a greater realization of his own humanity. To elaborate on this theme, the filmmaker de-parts completely from Lem's text by inventing a whole earth-based plot in which Kelvin is contrasted unfavorably with his father, who is represented as an earthier and more "authentic" type than his technocratic son. The son's moment of empathy at the end takes on a decidedly mys-tical quality, and involves not only or even mainly the ocean itself, but instead an imagined recon-ciliation with the father. Accordingly, the fusion of love and cognition that is but a tantalizing pos-sibility in the novel becomes an achieved certainty in the movie. In this way, Tarkovsky domesticates (literally and figuratively) Lem's whole problematic of radical otherness, and turns a multidimensional and radically ambiguous narrative into a fairly linear tale of self-realization and the humanistic development of personality. The philosophical problems posed by the ocean are mostly elided, and the mimoids—whose visual representation, one might have thought, would offer interesting challenges to the film director's art—are mostly (though not totally) ignored. For Tarkovsky, Solaris, with its possibly irrecuperable alterity, becomes a comparatively minor pres-ence in *Solaris*. Tarkovsky's *Solaris* is certainly as successful, on its own terms, as Lem's. But the relatively simplistic religious humanism of the Soviet filmmaker may serve to accent by contrast the dialectical complexity of the Polish philosopher-novelist.

Jacques Lacan.[6] Though heavily indebted to the Sartrean category of the other as a key determinant factor in subject-formation, Lacan goes beyond the problematic of existential humanism by *radicalizing* the nature of the other and thus sharply problematizing the possibility, even in principle, of any recuperation of otherness within the precincts of the self. For Lacanian psychoanalysis, the Other (the capital letter plays a specific role in the Lacanian scheme that need not be detailed here) is no sort of humanistic antiself or alter ego, but is finally to be identified with what Lacan calls the symbolic order; that is, the entire system of language and of signification generally. The symbolic is in no way analogous or opposed to the self or individual subject; the symbolic is that which gives rise to the formation of subjectivity in the first place. To be a subject, to be capable of speech and the articulation of desire, is, by definition, to be placed within the symbolic order, which thereafter speaks through us, or, more precisely, speaks us.

The point, for Lacan, however, is not only that each of us is, in our subjecthood, an effect of the symbolic, of the whole transpersonal order of signification. It is also that the process of subject-formation is—not contingently but constitutively—a process of subject-*alienation*. To be situated as a speaking subject within the symbolic order is to be irretrievably sundered from the as-if-unmediated wholeness and plenitude of primary narcissism. Accordingly, desire is always, in Lacan's familiar phrase, the desire of the Other—in the sense that desire (defined as the margin opened up when verbalized or otherwise signified demand surpasses mere biological need) necessarily proceeds from the place of the Other, namely, from the symbolic itself. For Lacan, as for all Freudian analysis, it is the unconscious that is the locus of desire par excellence; and it is in this way that the unconscious must be understood (as Lacan's single most celebrated formula has it) to be the discourse of the Other.[7] Accordingly, what Lacan achieves is to produce a concept of otherness that is at once radical and yet still meaningful: a concept that exists on a kind of dialectical borderline between the graspable and the ungraspable. The Lacanian Other is supremely difficult of access, not because it is obscure or distant, but precisely because it is too *close* to us, in the sense of setting the constitutive conditions of everything that we say, think, do, and are. Its discursive expression is strictly unconscious, and though the unconscious is (in another famous Lacanian axiom) structured as a language, it is not directly readable. On the contrary, the unconscious must be understood as a metalanguage that,

6. For a quite different application of Lacanian thought to Lem's text—but one that helped to inspire my own—see Elyce Rae Helford, "We Are Only Seeking Man: Gender, Psychoanalysis, and Stanisław Lem's *Solaris*," *Science-Fiction Studies* 19 (1992): 167–177.

7. One of the most important discussions of the significance of these formulations—that the unconscious is the discourse of the Other and that desire is desire of the Other—and of the whole general Lacanian problematic of otherness may be found in one of Lacan's most remarkable essays, "The subversion of the subject and the dialectic of desire in the Freudian unconscious"; see Jacques Lacan, *Ecrits*, trans. Alan Sheridan (New York: Norton, 1977), 292–324, esp. 312.

just because it enables any and all particular acts of signifying, is thereby itself beyond signification. Nonetheless, the metalanguage of the unconscious may be and regularly is *translated* into readable signs, as Freud himself explicitly recognized in his theorization of dreams, parapraxes, and neurotic symptoms as imperfectly but meaningfully legible effects of unconscious desire. The radically Other of Lacan can, therefore, never be unproblematically symbolized (for it is at one with the entire symbolic order), but it may be fragmentarily and provisionally understood: above all, for Lacan, in that psychoanalytic version of praxis that is the analytic situation of psychotherapy.

The pertinence of these Lacanian categories to *Solaris* should be evident. The point is not to document actual "influence," though it would not be at all surprising to find evidence of specific influence running in either or both directions between Lacan and Lem. It is rather to recognize an affinity generated by the presumably independent attempts of two philosophically powerful European minds of roughly the same generation to produce, in the specific context of scientific practice, rigorously radical conceptualizations of the other. Both Lem and Lacan, one might say, are concerned to take otherness *seriously*, avowedly contradistinguishing themselves from the superficial notions of otherness to be found in pulp science fiction and in ego-psychology, respectively. If the ocean of Solaris is read as a figure of otherness in the Lacanian sense, then much in Lem's novel may be clarified. In particular, the links between the (classically novelistic) psychological narrative of Kelvin and the text's larger epistemological concerns—which have seemed a little tenuous to some readers—are revealed to be even closer and more intricate than our discussion has suggested thus far. If the unconscious is the discourse of the Other, then the latter can be most radically engaged only on the unconscious level. To attempt contact with the radically other is thus to involve one's own unconscious desires, as the Solarists discover when the Phi-creatures are materialized out of their most painful and repressed memories. The scientific project of understanding the ocean is not, it turns out, a positivistic process of mastery occurring on a high level of conscious resolution—as their conventional training had led the Solarists to expect—but is much more like the psychoanalytic situation as theorized by Freud and, even more, by Lacan. Just as the analyst (perhaps the very paradigm of the scientist in Lacan's view) can achieve no authentic cognition without engaging his or her own repressed desires in a complex practice of transference and countertransference, so Kelvin (a Solaristic *psychologist*, it should be remembered) achieves what degree of contact he can with the ocean mainly through a painful psychic agon that involves the unconscious itself. His is a struggle that may produce a certain degree of knowledge and self-knowledge, but that leaves him, at the end of the novel, in a position that is the very reverse of mastery. He cannot coolly analyze the other from any secure Archimedean point, but must commit himself to an emotionally and intellectually devastating analytic *practice*.

Indeed, Kelvin's impossible passion for the simulacrum of Rheya may, in one aspect, be read as perhaps the most remarkable literary representation of countertransference since the one that Freud (somewhat unwittingly) left behind in his case history of Dora. If Kelvin, as he says in the novel's final sentence, *knows nothing*, it may be partly in the Socratic sense that Lacan rather admired. But the plain sense of the words is only partly qualified by irony. The other—the ocean—can never be fully or confidently known, and its unconscious discourse can be glimpsed only very provisionally as the latter is translated into various and always ambiguous signs, from the mimoids to the Phi-creatures themselves. Perhaps at no point is Lem more at one with Lacan than in his insistence on a dialectical rather than a merely binary model of cognition. In *Solaris*, the familiar science-fictional problem of contact with the alien, with the other, is posed, but Lem distinguishes himself from weaker treatments of the theme not only by stressing the immense (might one say, the Lacanian?) difficulty of the problem, but also by refusing to give an unequivocal answer as to whether such contact can succeed or not. As we have seen, a selective culling of evidence from the novel can produce a reading congenial to either epistemological optimism or pessimism—to humanism or poststructuralism, as it were—but the text as a whole transcends both options, suggesting that the quest for contact is not wholly vain, but also that contact can be attained only in such tentative, fragmentary, ambiguous, oblique, and *unexpected* ways that the notion of contact itself is in serious need of rethinking. Is Kelvin at the end of the novel a successful quester who has attained hard-won knowledge? Or is he a man broken and rendered rather absurd by the encounter with the sheerly other? The only adequate answer is that (like the Lacanian analyst) he is both, or neither. A genuine dialectician of the unconscious, he is thus perhaps, in some sense, the most accomplished of all Solarists who have ever lived. But his accomplishment is one that nobody could possibly envy.

Solaris must therefore be seen as not only a deeply and strongly science-fictional text, but virtually a meta–science-fictional text as well. A work of profound cognitive estrangement, what it cognitively estranges with greatest force is precisely the nature of cognitive estrangement itself. The encounter of the Solarists with the fundamentally other estranges for them the taken-for-granted category of the human, as Kelvin in particular (perhaps also, though to a lesser degree, Snow, though presumably not Sartorius) gains fragments of new insight into himself by way of his scientific attempt to come to terms with the Phi-creatures and so to make contact with the ocean. In addition, such illumination as this estrangement provides is cognitive in the strongest dialectical sense, growing out of a kind of concrete transformative praxis and remaining radically interpretive and provisional. It remains only to stress that, for all its weighty philosophic intent, *Solaris* is by no means a narrowly didactic work, using that term here to mean a work concerned merely with displaying a certain conceptual "content" while remaining indifferent on the level of literary form. On the contrary, Lem's text not only fuses a fully novelistic concreteness of presentation with the most ambitious and radical epistemological interrogations; it also formally doubles its own themes of cognition and otherness in the interpretive problems it sets for the reader.[8]

Indeed, this doubleness is no mere literary gimmick. It is not an instance of what Yvor Winters would have called the fallacy of imitative form but is instead an essential aspect of the whole Lemian project of presenting the radically other. An otherness that baffles novelistic characters but is more or less transparent to the reader could hardly, after all, motivate a serious examination of the other. It could function only by what *would* be a mere gimmick; namely, the artificial withholding of knowledge from the characters, a device that may indeed be found in many weakly science-fictional texts of the pulp sort. But if Solaris is really to confront Kelvin and his colleagues with all but insuperable interpretive problems, then *Solaris* must do something of much the same sort for and to the reader. One may well think, in comparison, of the sibylic difficulty of Lacan's prose style, which is designed to mimic the fitful and flickering illumination that psychoanalysis may achieve into that other discourse known as the Freudian unconscious. Thus, for example, in the literary interpretation of *Solaris*, the properly generic question of whether and to what degree Lem's text may be considered a love story cannot, as we have seen, be disentangled from the epistemological question of whether and to what degree Kelvin's passion for the phantom Rheya involves him in meaningful contact with the ocean.

More generally, the construction of the fundamentally other ocean that, like the unconscious for Lacan, can be known only obliquely and through its effects requires, on the plane of literary representation, what Carl Malmgren (writing specifically about *Solaris*) has usefully termed "alien effects."[9] The extreme otherness of the ocean cannot be directly shown but must function as the relatively blank center of the novel whose nature the reader tries, with considerable difficulty, to infer from what the other *does*. Accordingly, literary criticism of Lem's novel is a particularly fascinating yet also frustrating activity; the text itself is unusually insistent upon the provisionality and partiality of every reading and especially upon every construction of the ocean itself. The dialectical humility enforced on Kelvin is a lesson for us as readers also. But a certain epistemological modesty—the sine qua non of science as Lem (and

8. Perhaps the most detailed reading of the way that the form and content of *Solaris* reflect each other has been offered by the German semanticist Manfred Geier in his *Kulturhistorische Sprachanalysen* (Cologne: Pahl-Rugenstein, 1979), 67–123. In English-language *Solaris* criticism, this theme was, so far as I am aware, first introduced in Istvan Csicsery-Ronay Jr.'s article, "The Book is the Alien: On Certain and Uncertain Readings of Lem's *Solaris*," *Science-Fiction Studies* 12 (1985): 6–21. I am indebted to both analyses.

9. See Carl D. Malmgren, "Self and Other in SF: Alien Encounters," *Science-Fiction Studies* 20 (1993): 29.

Lacan) see it—is not in the least, as we have considered, the same as nihilism. And Lem's text should not be read as nihilistic. Both Solaris and *Solaris* suggest that the largest questions of the universe may time and again baffle the best efforts of dialectical reason—but also that only dialectical reason is capable of genuinely posing such questions at all.

The Dispossessed: *Ursula Le Guin and the Ambiguities of Utopia*

The epistemological concerns that dominate *Solaris* are also very much present in *The Dispossessed* (1974),[10] which, in one of its aspects, is, like Lem's text, a novel about the practice of science and hence about cognition itself. The protagonist is the physicist Shevek (based, evidently, on Robert Oppenheimer, one of the most genuinely heroic figures in the history of physics since Galileo).[11] And the scientific problem that occupies him throughout most of the novel is his attempt to resolve an immensely difficult dichotomy between the opposed physical theories of simultaneity and sequency. What is at stake here—though translated into the cosmological physics of a no-place in the far future—is a quite actual theoretical problem, notably in modern linguistic and historiographic discourse: namely, the problem of reconciling synchrony and diachrony, of formulating a theory capable of describing existing structures in all their determinant force while also accounting for the processes of historical change. In one of the climactic scenes of the novel, Shevek solves his problem after extensively pondering the ancient Terran physics of "Ainsetain" and of the quantum physicists whom Ainsetain, with his search for a unified field theory, had opposed. Shevek decides that both sides in that old earthly controversy had been right in the long run, though in ways that can be grasped only with much more recent (for us, of course, nonexistent) mathematical tools. In this way, he is inspired to resolve the most daunting scientific conundrum of his own era and (more fortunate than Einstein) successfully to produce his own unified theory of the cosmos as a rationally accountable totality: "The coexistence of succession could be handled by a Saeban transformation series; thus approached, successivity and presence offered no antithesis at all. The fundamental unity of the Sequency and Simultaneity points of view became plain; the concept of interval served to connect the static and the dynamic aspect of the universe" (225).

10. Ursula K. Le Guin, *The Dispossessed* (New York: Avon, 1975). All page references will be given parenthetically in the text.
11. "He [Shevek] was still lanky, with big hands, protruding ears, and angular joints, but in the perfect health and strength of early manhood he was very beautiful. His dun-colored hair . . ." (48). Physically, this is a portrait of Oppenheimer; and, as we shall see, Shevek's values strongly recall Oppenheimer's radical and nonconformist humanism.

Though a nonexistent mathematical physics is (at least in detail) perhaps the one concept even more resistant to literary representation than a nonexistent musical composition, the fundamental point here is clear enough: Shevek succeeds in moving beyond the impasse constituted by the binary dichotomy of synchrony and diachrony by recasting the entire problem in specifically dialectical terms. There ought to be no question of choosing between simultaneity and sequency. Each is true in the sense of yielding genuine insights; equally, however, each becomes a reified dogmatism to the degree that it is abstracted from the other. A properly unified approach critically engages both viewpoints, sublating them in the classically Hegelian sense of canceling them on one level while, on another, preserving them in a higher and more complex synthesis. And, as with all authentic dialectics—including, as we have seen, science as understood by the Lem of *Solaris*—the cognitive project must be an ever-provisional and radically *interpretive* one that abjures the dogmatic certainties of positivism. Shevek attains knowledge of "the foundations of the universe" (226) only when he ceases to demand " a security, a guarantee, which is not granted, and which, if granted, would become a prison" (225). Physics does not, after all, exist in some metaphysically sealed realm of certainty beyond the overdeterminations of dialectical speculation. *The Dispossessed*, like *Solaris*, insists that the critical, dialectical approach is so radically valid as to encompass the epistemology even of the physical sciences.

Indeed, the dialectical epistemology that *The Dispossessed* is concerned with enforcing manifests itself not only in the theme of Shevek's scientific work but also (here again there is a parallel with *Solaris*) in the structure of the novel itself. The difficult doublet of sequency and simultaneity is replicated in one way by the double planets—Urras and Anarres—on which nearly all the action of the novel takes place. But it is more elaborately replicated by a fundamental doubleness of the plot. In one of its aspects, the novel focuses on the Anarresti Shevek's visit to Urras; although, strictly speaking, this visit is an event that unfolds over time, its function in the text is relatively synchronic, as it takes place in the time present of the narrative, is of relatively brief duration, and, above all, is thematically defined less by any evolving story than by the synchronic discontinuity between the simultaneously present values of Urras itself, on the one hand, and of Shevek on the other. Yet the meaning of Shevek's visit could not be fully intelligible without a properly historical understanding of Anarresti society in general and of the diachronic narrative of Shevek's biographical development in particular. In having to weave together these two plot strands, Le Guin is, then, in a position comparable to Shevek's own as he attempts to produce a unified theory out of the competing viewpoints of sequency and simultaneity (just as Lem's project of representing the radically other is in some ways parallel to Kelvin's project of making contact with it).

Le Guin's *solution* is also comparable to Shevek's. She acknowledges the ultimate indispensability and inseparability of the two approaches, however incompatible with each other they may at first appear. The two plot strands are presented in alternating chapters, and initially the gap between diachrony and synchrony seems immense. The journey of the eminent scientist Shevek to Urras cannot be easily or unproblematically adequated to the early boyhood development of Shevek the child. As the novel progresses, however, the two levels of the narrative become more and more closely allied to one another, as Shevek's biographical evolution points more and more clearly to his contro-versial decision to visit the other planet. By the end, the synthesis is complete: Shevek returns to Anarres, and the completion of his encounter with Urras is at one with the completion of his biographical narrative to date. In the final sentence — "His hands were empty, as they had always been" (311) — the dis-crete state of being that is expressed by the simple past tense of the first clause is grammatically conjunct with the sequential narrative implied by the pluper-fect tense of the second clause. Le Guin thus suggests, on the micrological level of syntax, the ultimate dialectical unity of the novelistic plot and, beyond that, of synchrony and diachrony in general. It is no accident that Shevek, though generally very sympathetic to "Ainsetain," is repelled by the "wall-building" (or, as we might say, reifying and positivistic) intellectual imperial-ism of Terran thought, from which even the great theorist of relativity was not wholly free: as witness the latter's "warning that his physics embraced no mode but the physical and should not be taken as implying the metaphysical, the philosophical, or the ethical" (224). For both Shevek and Le Guin, such intel-lectual walls are to be transcended, and the same dialectical epistemology is valid in fields from mathematical physics to the construction of novels — and to politics itself.

In the context of *The Dispossessed* as a whole, indeed, the specifically epis-temological function of the Le Guinian dialectic is finally subordinate to (while closely related to) much more directly political concerns. It is in the text's alliance to the dialectical critique of politics and political economy that the parallel with *Solaris* finally breaks down. For Le Guin is, generically, a uto-pian artist in a way that Lem is not and would presumably not wish to be (just as Shevek is a political radical in ways that would never occur to Kris Kelvin). In fact, the importance of *The Dispossessed* for the whole utopian generic tra-dition has, I think, yet to be fully appreciated — partly, no doubt, for reasons of historical perspective, though also because of the continued stigmatization of overt science fiction by the most influential arbiters of aesthetic value. Le Guin's stature *within* science fiction is widely familiar (*The Dispossessed* made her the first author twice to win both major science-fiction awards — the Hugo and the Nebula for Best Novel — simultaneously), as are her access to "main-stream" forums (for example, *The New Yorker* and *Critical Inquiry*) and the re-spectful attention accorded her by influential critics, like Harold Bloom, who evince little real interest in science fiction generally.[12] It is not yet a common-place, however, that *The Dispossessed* is not only the central text in the post-war American revival of the positive utopia, but, arguably, the most vital and politically acute instance of the positive utopia yet produced, at least in the English-speaking tradition.[13] Its only rivals in this respect are, I think, *Utopia* itself (which, though actually composed in Renaissance Latin, also belongs to the larger Anglophone culture) and *News from Nowhere*. As the discussion, in chapter 2, of the passage from the utopia proper to the science-fictional uto-pian novel would lead us to expect, Le Guin's achievement is considerably more concrete than More's or Morris's. The psychological depth and com-plexity of Shevek as a protagonist and the intricately dialectical plot construc-tion far surpass the equivalent aspects of the earlier texts, and this novelistic so-phistication is, as we shall see, integral to the text's critical achievements.

The political critique implemented by *The Dispossessed* may best be ana-lyzed as comprising three distinct theoretical moments: the positive utopian value of the anarchist society of Anarres; the complex estrangements effected by the Urrasti societies, especially that of A-Io, which are presented as alterna-tive to Anarres; and, finally, the self-critique of anarchism itself. This tripartite scheme has a specifically logical value, but it does not, of course, correspond exactly to the presentational method of the narrative itself. For the dialecti-cal—and radically novelistic—elegance of the narrative that we have already observed enables Le Guin to fictionalize what I shall analyze as a logical *se-quence* of political concepts in as nearly *simultaneous* a fashion as possible: thus making formally possible an almost incomparable (within the utopian ge-neric tradition) richness of conceptual nuances, comparisons, contrasts, and juxtapositions. It is in this way that the epistemological dialectic of the text ul-timately functions not so much for its own sake (as is the case with *Solaris*) but in the service of a more specifically political dialectic. Or, the point might be better made by saying that on this level—the level of utopian speculation— the Le Guinian dialectic is fundamentally epistemological, political, and novelistic-formal, all at once; which is also to say that it is on this level that Le Guin's deepest methodological affinity with Shevek himself lies.

It is what I have designated the first theoretical moment of *The Dispos-sessed*—the construction of a positive anarchist utopia—that is probably the most widely appreciated aspect of the book. This is also the aspect that allies it

12. Bloom judged Le Guin worthy of a volume in his Modern Critical Views series (New York: Chelsea House, 1986). His introduction, which praises Le Guin as "the best contemporary author of literary fantasy" (1), as one who commands "absolute rhetorical authority" (2), and as perhaps the "pur[est] storyteller writing now in English" (3), combines a few interesting insights with an appalling ignorance of science fiction in general.

13. Though I find a number of her conclusions dubious, Carol McGuirk, "Optimism and the Limits of Subversion in *The Dispossessed* and *The Left Hand of Darkness*" (originally published in Bloom's volume on Le Guin [see note 12], 243–258) offers an interesting and well-informed dis-cussion of Le Guin's relation to the ideological foundations of the utopian generic tradition.

most closely to the general upsurge of American utopian fiction in the mid-1970s. Two almost exactly contemporary works—Joanna Russ's *The Female Man* (1975) and Marge Piercy's *Woman on the Edge of Time* (1976)—are particularly noteworthy in being also partly devoted to portraying anarchist utopias. Neither does so, however, in nearly so ample and rigorous a fashion as Le Guin's text. Russ's Whileaway looms much less large than Le Guin's Anarres (it is only one of four worlds in the novel), and Russ does not attempt to convey the detailed texture of everyday life in utopia as Le Guin does. And, for all its genuine strengths, Piercy's construction of Mattapoisett's utopian future displays, as we shall see, relatively little of Le Guin's theoretical sophistication, almost wholly lacking the element of dialectical reflexivity and self-critique that, as we shall also consider, contributes so much to the ultimate strength of Anarres.

Anarres is a physically bleak world that, more than a century before the time present of the novel, was colonized by a group of followers of the Urrasti anarchist thinker Odo. Hostility was high between the governments of Urras and the Odonians, and the latter welcomed the opportunity to leave their home planet altogether and to build their own liberated society from the ground up. Though Odo does not appear to be closely based on any actual anarchist leader (Emma Goldman may be a distant parallel), the world that her followers make is guided by principles familiar with the European and North American anarchist traditions. The Odonians are faithful to the original insight of Michael Bakunin (probably the most original theorist of anarchism) that anarchism must be (to use a vocabularly slightly later than Bakunin) anarcho-*communism*, and that, as Bakunin maintained in his bitter controversy with Marx, the struggle for collectivist ends must be waged exclusively through anarchist means. Whereas Marx postulated a transitional postrevolutionary stage during which the victorious proletariat would replace the existing dictatorship of the bourgeoisie with a dictatorship of their own, Bakunin insisted that a "workers' state" was a contradiction in terms and that any attempt to impose one would corrupt the revolution irredeemably.[14] On Anarres, accordingly, the collective ownership of all property has been safeguarded and concretized from the outset by collective control and decision-making. Democracy is direct, and there is no specialized state machinery—no laws, no police force, no military, no judiciary—distinguishable from the population as a whole. With the abolition of private property, the very concept of possession itself is considerably weakened—

14. Shortly after the publication in 1874 of Bakunin's major work *Statism and Anarchy* (in which criticism of Marx and Marxism plays an important part), Marx copied out in a notebook substantial extracts from the volume and interspersed them with his own comments in rebuttal. The resulting conspectus thus provides a convenient overview of this controversy, one of the most important in the history of socialism; see Karl Marx, *Political Writings*, vol. 3, *The First International and After*, ed. David Fernbach (New York: Random House, 1974), 333–338. Marx's critique of anarchism has some affinity with his and Engels's critique of utopian socialism that was discussed in chapter 2.

even to the point that singular possessive adjectives (and singular personal pro-nouns in the genitive case) are rarely used—and has been largely replaced, as an organizing principle of everyday life, by the concept of sharing. This achievement amounts to the at least partial realization of the most famous of all Bakuninite maxims, "I do not want to be I, I want to be We," which, indeed, is echoed in Odo's saying, "To be whole is to be part" (68).

Unlike Bakunin, however, the Odonians are resolutely nonviolent. Though they can enjoy a good fistfight, their principles condemn any lethal or seriously injurious use of force, especially as an organized means of addressing social contradictions. Here the chief influence seems to be Peter Kropotkin,[15] who broke with Bakunin's emphasis on violence and largely succeeded in re-placing it (in anarchist theory, though not always in working-class anarchist practice) with the pacifist conviction that political violence is intrinsically counterrevolutionary. Though the Anarresti do not completely exclude the occasional possibility of legitimate self-defense, they are certain that any rou-tine practice of force, or of coercion ultimately sanctioned by force, is both in-efficient and an irretrievable betrayal of communal solidarity.

Among later theorists of nonviolent anarchist collectivism, Paul Goodman seems a particularly important presence in the philosophy of Odo. His stress on the importance of education and creativity are much in evidence on An-arres, where education is conducted in Goodmanite fashion; that is, in as de-centralized and nonhierarchical a way as possible, and where the dichotomy between the aesthetic and the functional has, to a large extent, been broken down. In addition, the Anarresti balance a Bakuninite emphasis on collectiv-ity with a Goodmanite insistence on the sanctity of the individual conscience as the sine qua non of liberation.[16] For the Odonians as for Goodman, a spe-cial importance attaches to individual freedom in the sexual realm, and An-arresti adolescents routinely experiment, openly and without shame or guilt, with heterosexual and homosexual copulation. Adults too are free to follow their (noncoercive) sexual impulses, and neither sex nor sexual orientation

15. For a detailed examination of the relevance of Kropotkin for Le Guin, see Philip E. Smith II, "Unbuilding Walls: Human Nature and the Nature of Evolutionary and Political Theory in *The Dispossessed*," in *Ursula K. Le Guin*, ed. Joseph Olander and Martin Harry Greenberg (New York: Taplinger, 1979), 77–96. It is worth noting that, although source studies by Smith and others (as well as Le Guin's own scattered comments) have made clear the *direct* influence on Le Guin of such anarchist leaders as Kropotkin, Goldman, Paul Goodman, and Herbert Read, the name of Bakunin is, for the most part, conspicuous by its absence in such discussions. Presumably Bakunin's passion for violence has alienated him from Le Guin's personal sympathies. But it seems to me that Bakunin is so fundamental to the theory and practice of anarchism generally that his influence is, willy-nilly, crucial to any properly anarchist problematic like Le Guin's.

16. As Shevek thinks in one of the key expository passages of the novel: "With the myth of the State out of the way, the real mutuality and reciprocity of society and the individual became clear. Sacrifice might be demanded of the individual, but never compromise: for though only the soci-ety could give security and stability, only the individual, the person, had the power of moral choice—the power of change, the essential function of life. The Odonian society was conceived as a permanent revolution, and revolution begins in the thinking mind" (267).

plays any part in the social division of labor. Though marriage in the earthly sense can hardly exist in a world without laws or patriarchy, Odonianism does subtly encourage (though it does not prescribe) monogamy; and the happiest Anarresti seem to be those who choose "partnerships," long-term mutual commitments with, however, no legal or economic significance. Le Guin neatly suggests her own solidarity with the principles of the Anarresti in the dedication of the novel, "For the partner." In earthly terms, of course, this means *For my husband*; but neither the possessive adjective nor the legalistic noun is acceptably Odonian.

Of course, Le Guin's achievement in constructing Anarres as a positive utopia lies not simply in her skillful weaving together of various doctrinal strands from anarchist theory, but also in her novelistic dramatization of how daily life in such a society is actually felt and how subjectivities evolve in such an environment. The main point about the Odonian Anarresti is that they not only subscribe to pacifist and anarcho-communist principles, but that they have been wholly formed by a society founded on such principles. Anarres is therefore not only a utopian construction in the generic sense, but one especially rich in utopian moments in the Blochian sense—moments of a deeply resonant peace and freedom beyond the alienations of class society. Admittedly, a historical memory (reinforced by deliberate propaganda) of the horrors of Urrasti class society does live among the Anarresti. *Profiteer* and *propertarian* remain the vilest and most contemptuous insults in their language, and, interestingly, *altruist* is also a pejorative epithet—a reminder that altruism is merely the undialectical inversion of greed and is equally a violation of authentic socialist solidarity. For the most part, however, the Anarresti have achieved a considerable degree of taken-for-grantedness in their revolutionary Odonianism, and it is in a number of quite nondoctrinal, as-if-incidental passages that Le Guin most compellingly depicts the utopian workings of Anarresti subjectivity.

For example, once when Shevek is at dinner during his visit to Urras, he observes his hostess chastising her young son for a breach of manners, and thinks how such reprimands (as in the case of his own daughter) sound much alike in all tongues: "*Sadik! Don't egoize!* The tone was precisely the same" (119; emphasis in original). Yet if the tone is similar, the content, of course, is not. Only in a profoundly collectivist society could childish "egoizing," as a small betrayal of the Bakuninite We, be the most typical rudeness that parents try to discourage in their young. Or consider this delineation of the paradigmatically "private" experience of sexual ecstasy—a description of the lovemaking that Shevek and his partner Takver enjoy after a long separation: "The first time they both came as Shevek came into her, the second time they struggled and cried out in a rage of joy, prolonging their climax as if delaying the moment of death, the third time they were both half asleep, and circled about the center of infinite pleasure, about each other's being, like planets circling blindly, quietly, in the flood of sunlight, about the common center of gravity, swinging, circling endlessly" (258). In one sense, this passage is situated in a tradition of sexual description that derives directly from D. H. Lawrence, most notably from *Women in Love* (1920) and perhaps *The Plumed Serpent* (1926). Precisely what distinguishes it from Lawrence and immensely enhances its Blochian value, however, are its completely unforced quality and its as-if-normal freedom from hierarchy, coercion, and phallocracy. The image of the lovers as circling planets is presumably a common astronomical figure for people who in fact live on a twin planet; it is at the same time a fitting metaphor for sexual union as the free and equal community of lifelong anarcho-communists.[17]

It is largely in this way, in the portrayal of ordinary aspects of daily living, that the Odonian planet assumes a novelistic concreteness and solidity unprecedented in the generic tradition of the positive utopia. The rather abstract and merely posited quality that we have noted in More's Utopia and even Morris's Nowhere are highlighted with special clarity if we think, in contrast, of the three-dimensionality and, so to speak, the imaginative elbow-room of Le Guin's Anarres. At the same time—and here the intricate inter-inanimation of what we have called the first and second theoretical moments of *The Dispossessed* becomes evident—many of the text's most illuminating delineations of Anarresti life and thought are achieved not directly but by way of contrast with the Urrasti alternatives, which, in their close similarity to earthly societies of the 1970s, are thereby estranged with great cognitive and affective force. Indeed, one especially shrewd strategy of Le Guin's novel lies in its reversal of the hero's journey customary to utopian fiction. Traditionally, the utopian protagonist—like Raphael Hythloday or Morris's dreamer—functions as a mundane Everyman, a stand-in for the reader, whose own reactions to the discovered no-place of the text may help to guide our own. Here, however, it is the hero himself who represents the no-place, and the strange land to which he journeys (there may well be a deliberate allusion here to Heinlein's most famous title, *Stranger in a Strange Land* [1961]) turns out to be very much like our own empirical environment. The latter is thus estranged in an unusually powerful and complex way. For Shevek's responses, however foreign to our own actual habits of thought, do enjoy the axiological normality that the utopian text customarily grants to its protagonist. At the same time, while Urrasti human nature is revealed to be anything but natural,

17. It is passages such as those discussed in the foregoing paragraph that provide the strongest justification for Darko Suvin's description of Le Guin's work as "parables of de-alienation." See "Parables of De-Alienation: Le Guin's Widdershins Dance," in Suvin's *Positions and Presuppositions in Science Fiction* (Kent: Kent State University Press, 1988), 134–150. Suvin usefully notes that the title of *The Dispossessed* refers to the Anarresti as people who have not only dispossessed themselves of private property but are also thereby no longer possessed, in Dostoevsky's sense, by the demon of propertarianism. Dispossession in Le Guin's usage thus amounts to what Suvin calls de-alienation or what I would call a moment of utopia in the Blochian meaning of the term.

the quality of the Odonian Anarresti is effectively condensed in the very different human nature—Shevek's own—that has been wholly shaped by anarcho-communist culture and society: and this despite the fact that, as we shall later consider, Shevek is very far from being a statistically typical Anarresti and hence is in that sense not even an *Anarresti* Everyman.

The most powerful civilization on Urras, and the only one that Shevek actually visits, is that of A-Io, which is predominantly a figure for the monopoly-capitalist United States during the period of the novel's composition. The correspondence does not amount to a perfect identity, however, as certain features of A-Io are regressive from the standpoint of the 1970s. The formal subordination of women, for example, and also the great general strike and insurrection at the end of the novel belong to an earlier phase of capitalism, one located somewhere between Victorian liberalism and the Great Depression of the 1930s. On the other hand, at least one important characteristic of A-Io—its substantial avoidance of ecological pollution, at any rate within its own national boundaries—is more advanced than what any major capitalist nation has actually managed to achieve, though it is perhaps not an intrinsically unattainable achievement for a bourgeois civilization. While mainly a representation of Le Guin's America, then, A-Io also functions as a figure for capitalism in general, one that contains a plausible cross-section of the potentialities that society may actualize under the dictatorial rule of the bourgeoisie.

It is this metafigure, as it were, for capitalism that constitutes the alien environment into which Shevek is plunged. Much of his mental energy during his trip to Urras is devoted to trying to understand the Iotic profit economy and the culture based upon it, and rarely since the incomparable opening chapters of volume 1 of Marx's *Capital* (1867) has the sheerly *unnatural* character of capitalism been so powerfully estranged, so thoroughly defamiliarized. For example, Shevek's attempts to penetrate the mysteries of finance capital lead mainly to bewilderment and revulsion:

He could not force himself to understand how banks functioned and so forth, because all the operations of capitalism were as meaningless to him as the rites of a primitive religion, as barbaric, as elaborate, and as unnecessary. In a human sacrifice to deity there might be at least a mistaken and terrible beauty; in the rites of the moneychangers, where greed, laziness, and envy were assumed to move all men's acts, even the terrible became banal. (105)

The allusion, in the last line, to the Arendtian concept of the banality of human evil is presumably not accidental. Yet even more revolting to Shevek than high finance—to the point, indeed, of making him feel almost physically sick and giving him nightmares for months to come—are the (to us) ordinary realities of an elegant retail shopping district. The intense degree of reification—the effacement of production, the triumph of the wholly commodified spectacle, and the unbridled riot of pure quantity—are here seen as if for the first time.

The general effect is to give the classic Lukácsian critique of reification in *History and Class Consciousness* (1922)[18] something like a tangible aesthetic form:

And the strangest thing about the nightmare street was that none of the millions of things for sale were made there. They were only sold there. Where were the workshops, the factories, where were the farmers, the draftsmen, the miners, the weavers, the chemists, the carvers, the dyers, the designers, the machinists, where were the hands, the people who made? Out of sight, somewhere else. Behind walls. All the people in all the shops were either buyers or sellers. They had no relation to the things but that of possession. (107)

Such a passage not only presents the actualities of capitalist reification in a new and demystifying light, but also, of course, reveals much about the (strictly utopian) subjectivity and aesthetic taste of someone, like Shevek, who has been constituted by a society in which the making and using of things, rather than the buying and selling of commodities, enjoys economic centrality. Employing the specific terms of Marxian economics, one might say that Shevek not only advocates but *incarnates* the triumph of use-value over exchange-value.

A similar kind of cognitive estrangement operates in many of Shevek's encounters with the noneconomic aspects of Iotic bourgeois society as well. Perhaps the clearest picture of Odonian education, for example, is found not in any of the numerous direct descriptions of schooling on Anarres, but rather in Shevek's bewilderment when, after assuming a professorial position at the most prestigious university in A-Io, he is confronted by students outraged by his refusal to impose formal academic requirements or to distinguish among them by means of the grading system. He simply cannot imagine why anyone would choose to study except for the intrinsic joy of learning. Shevek, however, is no Candide, and it would be a mistake to think that his anarcho-communist upbringing necessarily places him in the position of the naïf vis-à-vis the culture of generalized commodity production. When, for instance, he meets with the commodification of eros in the person of Vea—the type of the sexy cock-teaser and wealthy courtesan—he at once sees through her pseudo-sophisticated claims to be quite happy and even to exercise immense secret power over men. He correctly perceives that her whole elegant way of life is based upon the degradation of women and has accordingly left her weary, restless, and alienated: an effortless insight that perhaps tells us more about the achieved utopian quality of Odonian sexuality (and more about what the text constructs as its essential *normality*) than even the direct description of Shevek and Takver's lovemaking.[19]

18. See Georg Lukács, *History and Class Consciousness*, trans. Rodney Livingstone (Cambridge, Mass.: MIT Press, 1971), esp. 83–222.

19. That Shevek at one point finds Vea sufficiently attractive to make a drunken pass at her does, however, seem to be a slip in view of the overall sexual logic of the novel. For a powerful (if not, in my view, necessarily persuasive) argument that Anarres and *The Dispossessed* are not nearly so progressive on issues of gender and sexuality as they may appear to be—and one that specifically engages the matter of Shevek's brief attraction to Vea—see Samuel Delany's brilliant,

The various degradations of Iotic capitalism—from the sadness of Vea or the cynicism of the university students to the murderous physical force with which the general strike of socialist workers is suppressed—do not, however, completely exhaust the Urrasti contrasts with Anarres. Shevek encounters on Urras at least two ideological systems distinct from that of the bourgeoisie. One is that of the authoritarian socialism of Thu, a transparent figure of the Soviet Union, whose values are represented mainly by one of Shevek's colleagues, the Thuvian physicist Chifoilisk. By the end of the novel, the Thuvian standpoint has in fact been rather more vindicated than most readers seem to have noticed. For one thing, Chifoilisk's warnings to Shevek turn out to be thoroughly justified, as the latter reflects much to his own chagrin. Whereas Shevek had hoped to open mutually productive relations between Anarres and Urras, his profiteering Iotic hosts have been wholly cynical and manipulative, as Chifoilisk insisted they would be, gambling that Shevek is on the verge of breakthroughs in theoretical physics that may yield technological developments of great military and commercial value to them. Furthermore, Shevek finds that the coalition leading the general strike includes not only anarcho-communists like himself but also a large pro-Thuvian faction: suggesting that, as Chifoilisk had maintained, the genuinely revolutionary-socialist dynamic of Thu may not be wholly exhausted after all. Still, for the most part, the text's attitude toward Thu amounts to the classic anarchist critique of Soviet Communism. "But you are archists," as Shevek tells Chifoilisk, "The State of Thu is even more centralized than the State of A-Io. One power structure controls all" (110).[20]

Even more unacceptable in the long run, but equally opposed to the middle-class Iotic ethic, is the aristocratic mind-set of another of Shevek's scientific colleagues, Atro. Atro's passion for blood, race, and martial glory clearly has a certain protofascist quality, and he becomes the very type of the raving jingo after A-Io becomes involved in a military intervention patterned after the Vietnam War. Even so, initially Shevek does feel a certain bond with the old man. Both are deeply hostile to capitalism, though from opposite sides, and

meticulously detailed, and often maddeningly idiosyncratic essay, "To Read *The Dispossessed*," in his *The Jewel-Hinged Jaw* (New York: Berkley Windhover Books, 1978), 218–283. Delany's reading has been quite influential among those who consider Le Guin's feminism, at least in *The Dispossessed*, to be insufficiently radical; see, for instance, Tom Moylan's extensive discussion of the novel in his *Demand the Impossible* (New York: Methuen, 1986), 91–120.

20. Because Marxism is represented in *The Dispossessed* mainly by Thu, Le Guin has, unsurprisingly, cast the ongoing debate between Marxism and anarchism very much in favor of the latter. Accordingly, she has quite elided the fact that, as Fredric Jameson has pointed out (see Jameson, "World Reduction in Le Guin: The Emergence of Utopian Narrative," *Science-Fiction Studies* 2 [1975]: 230), Marxism has its own tradition of the withering away of the state and is by no means adequately represented by Thuvian authoritarianism. (But I must strongly dissociate myself from Jameson's suggestion—unacceptable, I think, even in 1975—that the Maoist Cultural Revolution in China had anything to do with the antistatist dimension of Marxism or, indeed, much to do with Marxism at all.)

Atro's contempt for money and bureaucratic power is both genuine, and, in the Iotic context, somewhat refreshing. The ideological affinity between the anarcho-communist and the reactionary aristocrat thus amounts to a miniature version of the whole set of shadowy resemblances between the opposed yet somewhat parallel anticapitalist perspectives of revolutionary socialism and Burkean conservatism generally. And the partial symmetry of Shevek and Atro is personally deepened by the fact that each, evidently, is to be regarded as the greatest theoretical physicist of his own generation.

The central contrast of the text between Anarres and A-Io is thus somewhat complicated by the quite different further alternatives represented by Chifoilisk and Atro. Yet the text's rejection of both Stalinism and aristocratic conservatism is finally as unambiguous as its rejection of bourgeois capitalism, and the anarcho-communism of Anarres is clearly superior to all three. At this point, however, we must consider the third theoretical moment of *The Dispossessed:* the *self*-critique of anarchism. Though the text upholds anarcho-communism against the opposition of A-Io or Thu or the eccentric Atro, it nonetheless stages its own interrogation of its own official ideology and of its own anarchistic utopian project—thus fulfilling the subtitle's promise of an *ambiguous* utopia. Despite Le Guin's own anarchist convictions, the chief critical-theoretical affinity here is, willy-nilly, with a thinker far more dialectical than any that anarchism itself has yet produced: Trotsky. And a quick review of certain elements in Trotskyist political theory will help to illuminate Le Guin's novel.

In common with the entire tradition of classical Marxism, Trotsky had assumed that socialism could only be built in—or, at least, in cooperation with—countries that had achieved the highest levels of material production under capitalism. But, after his own expulsion from the Soviet Union in 1929 signaled both the dwindling prospects for international revolution and the achieved Stalinization of the Soviet regime, he set himself the task (among many others) of analyzing the fate of socialism under conditions of scarcity. The kernel of his whole elaborate theory is contained in a previously little-noticed hypothetical comment of the young Marx that Trotsky unearthed and made famous. As a result of any serious attempt to establish socialism on a low productive and technological basis, "only want will be generalized," Marx predicted, "and with want the struggle for necessities begins again, and all the old crap must revive."[21] In other words, material privation not only sets quantitative limits to the achievements of socialism; it may qualitatively deform socialist values at their very core. At one point Trotsky neatly summarizes such deformations by way of a concise parabolic figure: "The basis of bureaucratic rule is the poverty of society in objects of consumption, with the resulting struggle of each against all. When there is enough goods in a store, the purchasers can

21. Quoted in Leon Trotsky, *The Revolution Betrayed*, trans. Max Eastman (New York: Pathfinder, 1972), 295.

come whenever they want to. When there is little goods, the purchasers are compelled to stand in line. When the lines are very long, it is necessary to appoint a policeman to keep order" (112). For classical Marxism fully as much as for anarchism, the policeman is, of course, the paradigmatic type of the enemy. Although Trotsky came to acknowledge that socialism of a sort might be constructed in the absence of the overwhelming material abundance presupposed by Marx, his analysis does suggest that the inevitable reemergence of competition, privation, and bureaucracy must foreclose the development of socialism in the strongest sense of an egalitarian and noncoercive society. The socialist project under conditions of economic underdevelopment must, in fine, be a decidedly ambiguous one.

To a considerable degree, such is precisely the case on Anarres. The latter is a harsh world, poor in most natural resources and desperately underdeveloped, so that extreme scarcity and even the threat of full-fledged famine are not unusual. Despite genuinely heroic efforts by many Anarresti to maintain the Odonian principles of freedom and nonviolence under the most adverse circumstances, the "old crap" that Marx foresaw does indeed return. Economic emergency requires that the Anarresti be assigned urgent jobs around the planet without regard to their personal circumstances, thus causing great disruption in people's lives and in one case separating Shevek and Takver for several years. Technically, of course, these postings are voluntary, and no legal machinery exists to enforce them. But the indisputable fact of emergency creates an atmosphere of regimentation powerful enough to control almost everyone. The assignments do not, for the most part, *feel* voluntary, either to the characters who suffer them or to the reader. In addition, the jobs to which individuals are posted often take on a quasi-bureaucratic character themselves, and outbreaks of violence are not uncommon. For instance, during a conversation shortly after an especially terrible period of scarcity, Shevek hears of a train-driver, who, attempting to deliver grain to a region where it was desperately needed, used his train to kill several members of a starving crowd that was trying to get at the foodstuffs. Shevek, in turn, tells of his own posting during the same emergency. The devout anarchist and pacifist was charged with calculating food rations, in effect deciding who should starve to death so that other healthier and stronger people might have a chance to live. Shevek finds this job so intensely distasteful that he eventually quits it. But he knows that, even on Anarres, it is the kind of job that is easy to fill. "There's always somebody willing to make lists" (251), he comments, almost as though consciously echoing Trotsky's critical theory of underdevelopment as the basis of bureaucratic power under socialism.[22]

Trotsky's closely related critique of the Stalinist doctrine of Socialism in

---

22. And compare these thoughts of Shevek's, which echo Marx's and Trotsky's words quite closely: "It was easy to share when there was enough, even barely enough, to go round. But when there was not enough? Then force entered in; might making right; power, and its tool, violence, and its most devoted ally, the averted eye" (206).

One Country is also of direct relevance in understanding Le Guin's Anarres, which is an insular world as well as a poor one. For Trotsky, world revolution was the indispensable condition of fully successful revolution, and he strongly refuted Stalin's claims that the Soviet Union was capable of building not only socialism but pure classless and stateless communism under conditions of autarky. For such a project, Trotsky insisted, the economic and cultural resources of the more advanced nations were essential; and he maintained that Stalin's path would lead not only to continuing economic backwardness but also the cultural narrowness and chauvinism that are always antithetical to the true spirit of socialist internationalism. Le Guin shows that this is, to a considerable extent, very much the trap into which the Anarresti have fallen. Indeed, the text suggests that even the most heroic generation of the Anarresti—the original settlers—may have made a serious mistake in allowing themselves to be isolated on a barren planet rather than remaining on Urras to fight there for socialism and democracy. One leader of the general strike in A-Io insists, "But they've got no Moon [that is, Anarres] to buy us off with this time. We make justice here, or nowhere" (237).[23]

In any case, after accepting their removal to Anarres, the settlers and their descendants proceed to deepen their own isolation as much as possible. There is some limited trade—in one economic aspect the whole Odonian utopia, which happens to possess certain valuable metals, is but a mining colony of Urras—but in general the Anarresti try to restrict connections with their mother world as much as possible, so fearful are they of the profiteering corruption of A-Io. The danger of such capitalist corruption is quite real; even Shevek, after witnessing the depths of Iotic poverty and the full horrors of violent Iotic repression, comes somewhat to sympathize with his compatriots' isolationism, despite his earlier wish to establish contact between the two planets. Nonetheless, the project of building Socialism in One World not only ensures that the Anarresti will never share in the wealth and natural beauty of Urras, but also guarantees extreme intellectual isolation (notably hurtful in Shevek's own field of mathematical physics) and a concomitant attitude of

23. There is a very interesting parallel here (which may or may not amount to a deliberate allusion on Le Guin's part) with the emigration scheme put forward by the nineteenth-century French communist leader Etienne Cabet. Cabet proposed that some twenty or thirty thousand communist militants should abandon the corruptions of Europe in order to found a classless colony elsewhere, probably in the Americas. Marx honored Cabet for his sincere revolutionary fervor but denounced his emigration project as folly. Among the specific reasons that Marx gives for opposing Cabet, the following are of particular interest for a reading of The Dispossessed: if the best people should leave Europe, the power of the worst there would only be strengthened; a better material base for the construction of communism exists in Europe than anywhere else; an isolated communist colony would be troubled by internal discordance; the harsh physical environment of Cabet's colony would inhibit the development of socialism; it is impossible to move democratically from a society of private property to one of communal property without a period of democratic transition. For a convenient account of the Cabet-Marx controversy, see Louis Marin, Utopics: Spatial Play, trans. Robert Vollrath (Atlantic Highlands, N.J.: Humanities Press, 1984), 273–280.

ignorant nativist prejudice. Shevek's boyhood friend Tirin—an even more militantly principled anarchist than Shevek himself—notices at a very early age how he and his schoolfellows are encouraged to *hate* the Urrasti in a way that seems contrary to true Odonianism. Such bigotry reaches its grotesque and unbearably ironic culmination when, in a full betrayal of Odonian principles, the Anarresti deny entry to a group of latter-day Odonians from a "Third World" nation on Urras. For Odonianism, wall-building—the violation of wholeness and collectivity—is the primary social and intellectual sin. Yet the novel notes from the outset how the Anarresti, by walling the universe out, have walled themselves in: "Looked at from the other side, the wall enclosed Anarres: the whole planet was inside it, a great prison camp, cut off from other worlds and other men, in quarantine" (2). A prison camp, needless to say, makes for a very ambiguous utopia indeed.

There is one further dimension to the self-critique by the text of its own utopian project. This dimension relates not so much to any specifically Trotskyist dialectic. Instead, it amounts to a serious qualification of the traditional Bakuninite critique of legality and state machinery. The problematic features of Anarresti society do not result wholly from its poverty and isolation. Some of them seem to be largely intrinsic to the pure anarchism of Odonianism itself. The elimination of all governmental and legal systems opens the way to an elaborate tyranny of public opinion and informal pressure, a tyranny that in some ways is all the more difficult to fight against precisely because it is officially nonexistent. What is at stake here is the dialectical character of law itself. The anarcho-communist indictment of law in class society as an instrument of class coercion is by no means invalid. Indeed, it is amply illustrated in A-Io itself, where law is devoted mainly to the sanctity of private property and the state. Because, however, the anarchist critique ignores what the Marxist tradition would call the relative autonomy of law as a form of social production, it fails to understand how law may also possess a progressive character in the degree of protection it offers from arbitrary power. Accordingly, anarchism fails to foresee the problems attendant upon the abolition of legality. George Orwell, whose interest in the relations between law and power was ultimately expressed in somewhat obsessive form in *Nineteen Eighty-four* (1949), succinctly makes the point in one of his most acute critical insights:[24]

In a society in which there is no law, and in theory no compulsion, the only arbiter of behavior is public opinion. But public opinion, because of the tremendous urge to conformity in gregarious animals, is less tolerant than any system of law. When human beings are governed by "thou shalt not," the individual can practise a certain amount of eccentricity: when they are supposedly governed by "love" or "reason," he is under continuous pressure to make him behave and think in exactly the same way as everybody else.

24. George Orwell, "Politics vs. Literature," in *The Collected Essays, Journalism and Letters of George Orwell*, ed. Sonia Orwell and Ian Angus (Harmondsworth: Penguin Books, 1970), 4:252.

Orwell's words find a remarkably close parallel toward the end of *The Dispossessed*. When Shevek, his partner Takver, their friend Bedap, and a few other dissident Anarresti set up the Syndicate of Initiative to challenge the prevailing isolationism and, ultimately, to lay the groundwork for Shevek's voyage to Urras, they provoke angry opposition that first threatens violence and finally does turn violent indeed. When Takver remarks to Bedap, "I'm a coward, Dap. I don't like violence. I don't even like disapproval!" Bedap replies: "Of course not. The only security we have is our neighbors' approval. An archist can break a law and hope to get away unpunished, but you can't 'break' a custom; it's the framework of your life with other people" (292). The truth of Bedap's explanation is indicated by the fact that the ugly jingoism that threatens the impeccably Odonian Syndicate of Initiative is but the culmination of an extensive pattern throughout the text by which what Orwell called the totalitarian side of anarchism manifests itself. The pattern extends back to Shevek's childhood, when the first stirrings of his mathematical genius are condemned by his uncomprehending teacher as mere "egoizing" and an unwelcome deviation from normal childlike behavior. Though he is at first reluctant to see it for what it is, he encounters instances of this pattern in quite various forms: when his scientific career is frustrated and sabotaged by his senior but uncreative colleague Sabul; when the musical ambitions of Bedap's friend Salas are baffled by vulgar artistic conformism and by a current of philistine utilitarianism that has somehow managed to survive the Odonian stress on the aesthetic dimension of all departments of life; when Tirin, appropriately grown into a satiric playwright, is driven into a madhouse by ignorant and bigoted responses to his work; perhaps most poignantly of all, when Shevek and Takver's daughter Sadik is harassed and persecuted by her peers because of her parents' freethinking. On one level, of course, all such small and large tyrannies represent a betrayal of Odonianism, with its Goodmanite stress on individual autonomy and the free spirit. Yet on another level these tyrannies are actually encouraged by Odonianism itself. The Bakuninite liquidation of law and government leaves no court of appeal from the despotism of popular prejudice.

Le Guin's critique of anarchism is, then, remarkably thoroughgoing. Indeed, *The Dispossessed* may well constitute the most devastating and rigorous dissection of anarchist thought and practice ever undertaken, in either discursive or narrative form, by an author committed to anarchist principles. Yet it must be stressed that the critique is, after all, a *self*-critique. Though the anarchist utopia constructed by the text may indeed be ambiguous, the text's ultimate commitment to that utopia (and to anarcho-communism) is not. Shevek returns home convinced that Urras is Hell and that Anarres, for all its imperfections and even for a "misfit" like himself, is overwhelmingly superior to any feasible alternative, Iotic, Thuvian, or otherwise. (He also, however, returns home with the knowledge that his equations will make possible the construction of the ansible—a device for instantaneous communication across light-years—that should help to alleviate provincialism and isolation generally).

The superiority of Anarres ultimately lies above all in its dialectical character, its self-reflexive capacity for self-correction. Shevek's rebellion against Anarresti conformism is, after all, itself thoroughly Odonian in character. It is thus enabled by the fact that the Anarresti do keep the Odonian ideals constantly in view, however imperfectly they may adhere to them and despite certain problems in the ideals themselves. Whereas A-Io has never acknowledged the claims of justice at all, and whereas Thu has acknowledged but *systematically* betrayed them, the betrayals of Anarres are comparatively contingent and always subject to rectification by the very sort of person—like Shevek—that Anarres is bound to produce. In Sartrean terms, one might say that Anarres is a somewhat degenerated and problematic *group* but a group nonetheless; that is, a revolutionary collectivity that is still vitally, if by no means unproblematically, felt to be such by the individuals that compose it. The societies of A-Io, on the contrary, operate by the logic of the *series*; that is, the mere plurality of atomized individuals bound together by the external and quantitative relations of domination and exchange.

The dialectical complexity of *The Dispossessed* should not, therefore, be confused with a refusal to take sides. Indeed, far from resolving into any sort of Olympian apoliticism that would affect a liberal-individualist position "above" politics, Le Guin's text is able to enforce its anarcho-communist political vision with special power precisely because of its theoretical self-critique, and it is perhaps here that the novel's greatest achievement is located. Like all authors in the utopian generic tradition, Le Guin is in some measure a didactic writer. Although, as Brecht would remind us, the didactic impulse is a perfectly legitimate component of artistic production, and is devalued only by the precritical prejudices of a naively contemplative middle-class aesthetic, it is also true that narrowly didactic art is weakened by being didactic in an insufficiently *critical* way, by failing to be strictly dialectical. The result is the kind of text that seems to make things too easy for itself, to argue its case in a way that causes the outcome to appear rigged in advance. Le Guin, by contrast, is distinguished by her willingness to make things *difficult* for herself, to incorporate into her own text as many rigorous objections to her own viewpoint as possible. The result is the kind of text that achieves a genuine critical victory, not just a formal win by default. Like the greatest didactic writers—Brecht and Ibsen come readily to mind—Le Guin, at her best, prefers on intellectual and aesthetic principle to make her case as strong as possible by not flinching from the most cogent counterarguments that might be mounted.

A few pertinent examples may make the point clearer and serve as a kind of coda to our discussion of *The Dispossessed*. As I mentioned earlier, the utopian Mattapoisett of Marge Piercy's *Woman on the Edge of Time* is a socialist and anarchist project of the future and, as such, has a number of affinities with Le

Guin's Anarres. But Piercy largely evades the kind of problems that Le Guin confronts. For example, the informal despotism of public opinion to which a lawless society is vulnerable does indeed emerge in Piercy's Mattapoisett (even to the point, for example, that the correctness of personal feelings can be subjected to quasi-judicial proceedings), but it does so, as it were, around the margins of the text, and is never really incorporated into the novel's self-consciousness. Accordingly, the text seems unaware of its own antinomies, thus rendering Piercy's anarchism more naive and less critical than Le Guin's; in that way, *Woman on the Edge of Time* fails to make as powerful a statement of its political project as one sympathetic to the latter might wish. It remains, to be sure, an outstanding achievement nonetheless. But it does not, when placed beside Le Guin's fully critical utopia, present itself as one of the most *intelligent* versions of the utopian genre.

This kind of comparatively weak didacticism may be found in some of Le Guin's own work. I am thinking, for example, of *The Word for World is Forest* (1972), in many ways a superb tale of interstellar imperialism and genocide clearly designed to figure the American invasion and occupation of Vietnam. Though the novella possesses considerable power, it suffers from a failure of dialectical rigor. A whole range of potential contradictions within the project of imperial conquest is simply effaced, and a starkly binary ethical opposition is established. The peaceful attractive Athsheans are shown in such paradisal innocence, and the bloodthirsty invaders appear as so one-dimensionally evil in their cruelty, stupidity, arrogance, and sexual perversion, that the text seems to have programmed its ideological dynamic somewhat too neatly and seamlessly, and thus to have evaded any possible complexities. The abstract absolutism suggests (rather as in *Woman on the Edge of Time*) a theoretical weakness behind the overconfident facade. On the other hand, such weakness is precisely what Le Guin avoids in *The Lathe of Heaven* (1971), one of her best novels though unfortunately neglected. This text implements a critique, rather after the tendency of the Frankfurt School, of the traditional Western drive toward mastery and the domination of nature. The real dialectical subtlety of Le Guin's intelligence, however, is expressed here in the fact that the functionalist and utilitarian drive for power is embodied not in a simplistically megalomaniacal engineer of destruction, but in a cultivated and well-intentioned *psychiatrist* (there is some Foucauldian as well as Adornian resonance). Dr. Haber seeks not personal gain but such entirely praiseworthy goals as world harmony and the elimination of racism. Le Guin's (impeccably anarchist) point seems to be that the dialectic of domination is so corrupting as to be unacceptable even in pursuit of the most admirable ends. Whether one finally agrees or not, the argument is immensely strengthened by being directed at domination in its apparently best, rather than in a transparently evil, version.

This, then, is the kind of didactic power that *The Dispossessed* displays supremely. The text's dialectical interrogation of its own project and ideology sounds almost incomparable depths of complexity and earned self-confidence in its own political standpoint. The effect is immensely to strengthen, not to weaken, the cognitive integrity of the novel's utopian (in both the generic and Blochian senses) impulse. The result is perhaps the most enduring and unavoidable landmark in modern American science fiction.

The Two of Them: *Joanna Russ and the Violence of Gender*

This is not the place to elaborate on (or much enter into) the controversies that have focused on the degree or quality of Ursula Le Guin's feminism. But the matter may at least be broached, if only because these discussions often involve the name of Joanna Russ as well. The basic contrast frequently adduced is between the gentleness of Le Guin's feminism and the angry militancy of Russ's. This rather simplistic dichotomy is then, in many cases, further oversimplified by being given polemical value in quite opposite ways: the reasonable, broad-minded, humane Le Guin is championed over the shrill, narrow, terroristic Russ; or the fearless, incisive, radical Russ is celebrated in contrast to the soft, accomodationist, perhaps even faintly treasonous Le Guin. Such reductive binary oppositions, in which one author is merely used as a foil to the other, do a serious disservice to both, and offer little more than a caricature of their work. (One would not guess, for instance, that Russ is one of the *funniest* of current novelists, while humor is rarely to be counted among Le Guin's many strengths.) Still, since Russ and Le Guin are among the most accomplished of women authors in modern science fiction—indeed, perhaps *the* two preeminent female writers in the genre since Mary Shelley[25]—some sort of comparison is probably inevitable.

Suffice it here to say that since the composition of *The Dispossessed* Le Guin's feminism has become a more pronounced presence in her writing (most notably, perhaps, in *Always Coming Home* [1985], that remarkable achievement of what might be called archaeological science fiction). Even among her earlier work, *The Dispossessed* foregrounds specifically gender and sexual issues less prominently and insistently than some of her other texts (above all *The Left Hand of Darkness* [1969], where the ambisexuality of the Gethenians estranges and destabilizes what earthly common sense assumes to be one of the most

25. Perhaps the only other female science-fiction author (at least in America) who has attained a stature truly comparable to that of Le Guin or Russ is Alice Sheldon, who wrote mostly under the alias of James Tiptree Jr., and was publicly discovered to be a woman only in the latter part of her literary career. Her reputation may, in the long run, be limited by the fact that most of her best work is in short-story rather than novel form. But she remains a major presence in modern science fiction (and in modern fiction generally), a notable presence in the later work of Russ in particular, and quite possibly the *last* major woman writer to adopt, after the manner of George Eliot and George Sand—and the Brontë sisters, who originally appeared as Currer, Ellis, and Acton Bell—the cover of a masculine pseudonym.

secure components of personal identity). Accordingly, for a more thoroughly and complexly feminist inflection of science fiction than any that the foregoing analysis of Le Guin has engaged—for a more intricate examination of the dialectic of sex—we may appropriately turn to Russ and, in particular, to the novel that I take to be her most powerful and complex, *The Two of Them* (1978).[26] First, however, I must offer a few introductory reflections on the affinities between science fiction and that rather special variety of critical theory known as feminism.

Some general attempt to examine how feminism and science fiction can be articulated with relation to each other is especially germane because the dominant project of Russ's fictional work (to a greater degree, probably, than in the case of any other author) can be described as the fusion of science fiction with feminism. But the term *fusion* is potentially misleading here. The viability of Russ's project depends upon certain possibilities always intrinsic to science fiction, but rarely exploited until recently, and largely occluded by the almost exclusively masculine and (in overt terms) sexless ethos that dominated magazine science fiction from the Gernsback through the Campbell eras. Indeed, Russ's literary reputation—which is clearly in the ascendant today but remains lower, in my view, than her achievement would warrant even *after* one has allowed for the continuing marginalization of science fiction in general—has suffered from the two distinct sets of ideological stumbling blocks that any feminist science fiction must confront: those presented by the internal sociocultural mores of the science-fiction establishment *and* those presented by American feminist criticism as well. The former, with its spiritual roots in the pulps (and, to some degree, its directly material roots there too), has never been able wholly to eradicate its traditional suspicion of even women and sexuality as such, let alone feminism so radical and uncompromising as Russ's.[27] As we have seen in chapter 2, science fiction as a named and self-conscious literary enterprise has often failed to actualize the radical potential of the genre. This failure has been especially true with the issue of gender—probably because the technocratic and quasi-military values so integral to pulp and postpulp science fiction are more *directly* challenged by the critique of phallocracy than by almost any other form of radical criticism. Though such science fiction can make a small and subordinated place for women characters, it is particularly allergic to any undermining of overall masculinist assumptions.[28]

26. Joanna Russ, *The Two of Them* (New York: Berkley Books, 1979). All page references will be given in the text.

27. But, for a pathbreaking argument that pulp science fiction, despite its massive sexism and misogyny, contains elements of genuine value for feminism, see Robin Roberts, *A New Species: Gender and Science in Science Fiction* (Champaign: University of Illinois Press, 1993), 40–65. In the Blochian terms that I myself favor, Roberts locates utopian moments of a specifically feminist character within what would appear to be unpromising forms of cultural production.

28. One small but, I think, telling example: David Hartwell, who is generally considered the leading science-fiction editor in America today, and who, as it happens, has been publicly praised

As to the mores of American feminism, the latter has on the whole re-mained attached to naturalistic fiction of the sort that has flourished since the latter half of the nineteenth century (in sharp contrast to its French counter-part and despite the powerful example of Virginia Woolf). The dominant aes-thetic of the U.S. feminist academy has generally understood naturalism as a kind of indispensable truth-telling. Correlatively, it has often regarded devia-tions from such putatively straightforward reflectionism—most prominently the formal experimentations of modernism and postmodernism—as dispens-able, and perhaps even intrinsically undesirable, luxuries. One convenient index is that, in America, Kate Chopin's *The Awakening* (1899) has served as the sort of touchstone feminist fiction exemplified in France by Monique Wittig's *Les Guérillères* (1969). This pro-naturalist bias has resulted in a dis-trust of science fiction generally and in particular of science fiction that—like much of Russ's and unlike at least the earlier Le Guin's—explicitly incorpo-rates modernist literary techniques.[29] And, of course, this feminist distrust of science fiction has only been deepened by the clear sexism of the most charac-teristic pulp and "Golden Age" products. Accordingly, what I take to be the fundamental generic point of Russ's work—the rendering manifest of feminist potentialities latent within science fiction—has had to contend not only with simple incomprehension but with active ideological resistance from substan-tial sections of what ought to have been the two natural audiences for feminist science fiction.

Nonetheless, what Russ's work can help us to understand is that science fic-tion is an especially appropriate form for feminism. Feminism is unique among varieties of social radicalism because of the peculiar nature of the social contra-diction that it addresses. It is not only that the dialectic of sex and gender—unlike that of class, race, or ethnicity—is grounded in actual and nontrivial biological difference. The point is also, and more importantly, that the tradi-tional biological requirements for the preservation of the human species, and the affective structures of feeling ultimately based upon these requirements of

by Joanna Russ for his support of feminist science fiction (see the interview with Russ in Charles Platt, *Dream Makers* [New York: Berkley Books, 1983], 2:199), includes this sentence in his introduction to one of Russ's short stories: "By the mid-1970s Russ had become, as both critic and writer, the most forceful advocate of feminism in the field [i.e., in science fiction], much admired and often feared"; see Hartwell, ed., *The World Treasury of Science Fiction* (Boston: Little, Brown, 1989), 906. I have no doubt that Hartwell's estimate is correct. But *feared?* Joanna Russ—an author and academic? Russ's work does contain some graphic de-scriptions of violence, but male authors, from Homer to William Gibson, have seldom been feared for that reason. Nor has a capacity for astringent commentary—which Russ certainly possesses—normally inspired much terror of the countless male critics who can also write acerbic prose. But the mere fact that Russ's talents have been devoted to attacking sexist ideol-ogies is quite enough to make her, for much of the science-fiction community, very frighten-ing indeed.

29. For an interesting feminist discussion of naturalist and modernist (or postmodernist) ten-dencies *within* science fiction, see Veronica Hollinger, "Feminist Science Fiction: Breaking Up the Subject," *Extrapolation* 31 (Fall 1990): 229–239.

biology, have usually made it unfeasible to *segregate* women in quite the same (physical) way that subordinated class, racial, and ethnic groups have normally been segregated away from the living space of the oppressors. Women are thus the sole subaltern group whose members typically live with members of the corresponding dominant group; the typical woman enjoys (roughly) the same socioeconomic status, and, in particular, (roughly) the same level of material consumption, as that claimed by the male members of her own household.

Accordingly, male dominance manifests itself by unequal divisions of labor and power *within* the household, and also by the structurally socioeconomic threat aimed at any woman who would disrupt the domestic status quo (so that, for example, the married woman of apparently secure middle-class station may be quickly proletarianized by divorce). This crossing of oppression with domestic intimacy and mundane routine makes such oppression in some ways difficult to visualize and hence to conceptualize. In contrast to other forms of counterhegemonic struggle, feminism knows no privileged public loci—no factory floors or municipal squares, no plantations or segregated lunch counters—where social contradiction is, metaphorically or otherwise, condensed to its very paradigm. Sexism and the struggle against it take place literally everywhere, but thus, in a certain sense, nowhere in particular. Gender oppression is dispersed and defused throughout virtually all levels of all known societies, and this extreme decentralization creates both organizational and conceptual problems for oppositional movements. To put the matter in slightly different terms, the domain of erotic and familial connection that may provide a partial haven from the battles centered on class or nation is in gender terms itself a battleground. The clear definition of the issues and space to be contested is, of course, an important a task in any social struggle; but this task is especially, and perhaps uniquely, difficult for the struggles of feminism.[30]

Feminist theory is therefore of all forms of critical theory the most concerned with the ideological inscriptions of everyday life, with the imbrication of the political in the empirical and the personal. Everyday life, however, remains one of the most problematically theorized moments of the social field, and discursive feminist theory, for all its achievements, has only partially made up the deficiency. The problem is not, perhaps, one to be fully solved by further research and reflection. Feminist theory must begin as the analysis of women's oppression; and it may be that the unique character of such oppression, and the correlative enormity of an empirical moment more intricate and more extensive than that with which any other major form of theory has

30. I am indebted to the considerations on gender oppression in comparison with class oppression offered by Perry Anderson, *In the Tracks of Historical Materialism* (London: Verso, 1983), 89–93. Anderson underestimates the importance of the state as a coercive apparatus for the repression and regulation of women; it is symptomatic, in this regard, that his discussion includes no mention of abortion.

to deal, presents *intrinsic* obstacles to the elaboration of discursive feminist theory at a level of methodological abstraction comparable to that familiar within most versions of critical theory. It is probably no accident that much (including much of the best) feminist intellectual work has been undertaken in explicit or implicit alliance with at least one other variety of critical theory, most notably Marxism, psychoanalysis, or poststructuralism. Yet none of these "marriages" has been altogether happy, and the persistence of unresolved and unproductive tension in such syntheses can be explained in ways discreditable to neither side. If, for example, the project of a Marxist feminism remains—despite much invaluable work toward that end—somewhat problematic, it is not because Marxism is irretrievably phallocentric or feminism irretrievably middle-class (though there are, of course, versions of each that might seem to justify such a charge). The problem is rather that Marxist theory, as the analysis of capital and class, and feminist theory, as the analysis of gender, address themselves not merely to different objects but to different *kinds* of object; they thus require verbal formulation at somewhat different levels of abstraction. In other words, it is not just that feminist imperatives may be somewhat incommensurate with the normal generic requirements of Marxist theory. The point is also that feminism, profoundly engaged as it must be with the empirical intricacies of the *vécu* (of "authentically" lived experience), may to some degree be incommensurate with the discursive and abstract forms that have generically characterized critical theory; therefore feminism must, for at least some of its strongest critical-theoretical expressions, find alternative modes of discourse.

The most important of these other modes is that of narrative itself. It may be that concrete narration, with its necessary attention to the details of living, and its representational approximation to the temporal rhythms of the diurnal (and nocturnal), is capable of a more adequate critique of everyday life than can ever be attained, even in principle, by discursive theory. In particular, the novel—with its Bakhtinian commitment to inclusive, heterogeneous, dialogic style, and its Lukácsian sensitivity to historical processes as registered in the lived experience of ordinary people—would thus appear to be a privileged vehicle for those rigorous and nuanced investigations of the *vécu* that must constitute one of the major objectives of the feminist critical-theoretical project. From this point of view, indeed, the level of achievement (as gauged even by the more conservative canons of literary value) of women novelists from the nineteenth century onward does not look like an accident.

Insofar as feminist theory is concerned, then, I propose an at least provisional reversal of the Hegelian valorization of philosophy over art—a reversal that may help to revive the ancient etymological kinship between narrative and knowledge. Whereas for Hegel art could offer only brilliant glimpses of the critique that philosophy alone might display in a fully adequate manner, feminism may find the abstract generic forms of philosophical discourse too coarse-grained and, as it were, too ready-made to achieve so thorough and agile a criticism of gender relations and women's experience as can be achieved in the form of fiction. Feminist fiction would thus function as the "completion" of discursive feminist theory, rather than the other way around. I further suggest that, of all the varieties of fiction, the forms of narrative art specific to science fiction—with its special resources for estranging the familiar and suggesting alternatives to the given—may be particularly well suited to deal with the penetration of sexism into the quotidian world. The oppression of women is so closely woven into the fabric of daily experience that the strongest cognitive estrangements (those of which science fiction is uniquely capable) may be required in order to display such oppression as it cannot know or display itself. In addition, the critique of actually existing gender relations that feminist science fiction is capable of implementing must, of course, also involve, explicitly or implicitly, some properly utopian view of what may lie beyond the mundane. "Only in science fiction," as Robin Roberts has neatly put it, "can feminists step outside the father's house and begin to look around."[31] At once committed, in the most fundamental formal and epistemological terms, both to the centrality of the everyday sphere and to a radically critical perspective on the latter, science-fictional narration may well be capable of demystifying the structures of gender oppression with unique force and clarity.

Such is the achievement of *The Two of Them*. As Russ's work in general has been undervalued and certainly underdiscussed, so *The Two of Them*, within the Russ canon, has been unfairly overshadowed by some of her other work (above all, by *The Female Man*, easily her most celebrated book). *The Female Man* deserves its celebrity, but it is important to understand that *The Two of Them* attempts something quite different from and in some ways more difficult than the project of the earlier text. Of the four parallel worlds of *The Female Man*, one—Janet's anarchist utopia of Whileaway—is exclusively female and hence has *no* relations between the sexes. Another—Jael's world, in which men and woman live separately and are literally at war with one another—assumes radically different relations between the sexes from those that we empirically

31. Roberts, *New Species*, 2. Similar points have been made by other feminist scholars of science fiction. For instance: "Speculative fiction in the best cases makes the patriarchal structures which constrain women obvious and perceptible. . . . Speculative fiction is thus a powerful educational tool which uses exaggeration to make women's lack of power visible and discussable. It can motivate women to avoid handicapping themselves by conforming to the demands of femininity"; Marleen Barr, *Alien to Femininity* (New York: Greenwood, 1987), xx. Or again: "Unlike other forms of genre writing, such as detective stories and romances, which demand the reinstatement of order and thus can be described as 'closed' texts, science fiction is by its nature interrogative, open. Feminism questions a given order in political terms, while science fiction questions it in imaginative terms"; Sarah Lefanu, *Feminism and Science Fiction* (Bloomington: Indiana University Press, 1989), 100. Probably the most wide-ranging development of the view shared here by Roberts, Barr, and Lefanu is Barr's later *Feminist Fabulation* (Iowa City: University of Iowa Press, 1992).

know; in particular, Jael's world features the virtual absence of heterosexuality in any familiar sense. The other worlds—Joanna's (nearly) actual America of the late 1960s and Jeannine's America of the same time in an alternative reality where the Second World War was never fought and where the Great Depression never ended—do display a great deal of sexism and "compulsory heterosexuality" (Adrienne Rich's resonant phrase) of the sort familiar in actuality, but, for the most part, in fairly *blatant* forms. Indeed, in Joanna's world especially, the gross details of gender oppression are frequently estranged in some of Russ's finest effects of satiric humor.

By contrast, *The Two of Them* is, as we shall see, ultimately concerned with estranging liberal patriarchy and normative heterosexual relations *at their best*, or in any case at what initially appear to be their best. The target here is the subtlety as well as the grossness of sexist oppression, and (in the kind of intellectual maneuver that we observed in Le Guin's best work) the text provides one of the most radical and radically intelligent feminist inflections of science fiction by staging its argument with regard to the most difficult as well as the easy cases. Irrevocably militant, *The Two of Them* is capable of interrogating feminism itself in a feminist way, thereby laying bare the complicity with oppression of any (feminist or other) essentialism—while not, however, necessarily denying that praxis itself may require essentialistic risks. The text is estranging from the first, but the initial discontinuities ultimately serve as comparatively simple terms in a more complex and more revolutionary narrative of cognitive estrangement.

The novel is structured on two theoretical moments: first, an essentially precritical liberal feminism, and, second, the transcendence of the latter in dialectical or radical feminism.[32] The liberal moment is represented primarily by the relations between the Trans Temp agents Irene Waskiewicz and Ernst Neumann and by their encounter with the society of Ka'abah. The latter is a strategically important but culturally regressive planet to which Irene and Ernst are dispatched on a secret mission; its dominant sexual ideologies and general accouterments are based upon those of the Islamic, especially the Arab, world. As time- and space-traveling operatives of Trans Temp (the

32. By dialectical or radical feminism I mean a feminism that is allied to a radical critique of the status quo generally. I thus intend to distinguish it from liberal feminism (that is, a feminism that demands only reforms in the direction of formal gender equality within the limits of the dominant socioeconomic order) but also from what has been called *cultural* feminism (that is, a feminism that largely waives general socioeconomic questions and instead concentrates on the construction and maintenance of a female counterculture as the central project of the feminist movement). The terminological situation is potentially confusing, as many cultural feminists have described their own position as one of radical feminism. It seems to me, however, that cultural feminism—like any other culturalism—is incapable of genuine radicalism, since the latter must involve a dialectical and hence *total* critique of the status quo, rather than the reification of a single social determinant (like gender) or a single level of social production (like culture). For an excellent discussion of these issues, to which I am here indebted, see Alice Echols, "Cultural Feminism: Feminist Capitalism and the Anti-Pornography Movement," *Social Text*, no. 7 (1983): 34–53.

Trans-Temporal Authority, a highly professional and technologically sophisticated bureaucracy that combines elements of a military service, an intelligence agency, and a diplomatic corps), Irene and Ernst appear, in the novel's
early pages, to relate to one another on a basis of rough equality, as partners
and fellow professionals—despite the fact that Ernst is not only Irene's lover
and her senior by some twenty years, but also her immediate superior (in fact
if not in nominal rank) within the Trans Temp hierarchy. (He is also the man
who once rescued her from an oppressive and unbearably boring teenage life
in the lower-middle-class conformist America of 1953.) Ka'abah, by contrast,
is a hotbed of overt, unabashed sexism, whose ideologies of formalized gender hierarchy are deeply at odds with the apparently free-and-easy relations of
Ernst and Irene. Interestingly, Ka'abah's civilization is *not* ancient, but very
recent. It has reached its third generation during the time present of the
novel, and has been self-consciously constructed according to Arab models
(notably *The Thousand and One Nights*, which is several times mentioned by
name in the text).

The living spaces of Ka'abah exist not on the planet's surface but have
been carved out of its interior; this exquisitely claustrophobic image figures
the suffocatingly "closed" character of Ka'abite society, particularly with regard to women, who are generally confined within small places literally as
well as figuratively. Irene is appalled, as the reader is meant to be, by the oppression of women on Ka'abah, and, in particular, by the desperate plight of
the young would-be poet Zubeydeh, a twelve-year-old girl whom the novel
presents as a typical case study of victimization by manifestly cruel sexism.
Poetry on Ka'abah is a manly, publicly respected occupation and as such is
closed to women. For them, the serious attempt to pursue a poetic career can
be extremely dangerous—as in the case of Zubeydeh's maternal aunt Dunya,
who in her girlhood cherished poetic ambitions and who consequently
spends her adulthood confined and medicated as a lunatic. In contrast to
such bigotry and repression, the yuppie liberalism represented by Ernst and
Irene appears progressive and even seems to justify the open and rather un-
diplomatic contempt for Ka'abah that Irene's martial prowess and Trans
Temp status allow her to exhibit with impunity. Designed and constructed by
men as a practical utopian project of totalitarian male rule (and in this way
rather like the Republic of Gilead in Margaret Atwood's *The Handmaid's
Tale* [1985], which may well have been directly influenced by *The Two of
Them*), Ka'abah at first functions as a negative utopia that contrasts sharply
with Trans Temp liberalism.

The crucial point, however, is that Irene's outrage and sympathy on behalf
of Zubeydeh and the women of Ka'abah are initially framed by the secure
sense of superiority with which liberal metropolitan feminism typically regards the gender relations of postcolonial—especially Middle Eastern—societies. The Arab model is of course highly significant, for probably no other

nation or culture is so consistently denigrated in North American and Western European discourse. Credited neither with the otherworldly wisdom of the Indian, nor with the civilized refinement of the Chinese, nor with the attractive earthiness of the African, the Arab—but more particularly the Arab male—is constructed, in hegemonic ideology, as a mass of repellent contradictions, lecherous yet unmanly, violently aggressive yet weak and cowardly, crafty yet stupid. In his already classic study of Orientalist discourse (published in the same year as *The Two of Them*), Edward Said notes:[33]

In the films and television the Arab is associated either with lechery or bloodthirsty dishonesty. He appears as an oversexed degenerate, capable, it is true, of cleverly devious intrigues, but essentially sadistic, treacherous, low. . . . In newsreels or newsphotos . . . the pictures represent mass rage and misery, or irrational (hence hopelessly eccentric) gestures. . . . Books and articles are regularly published on Islam and the Arabs that represent absolutely no change over the virulent anti-Islamic polemics of the Middle Ages and the Renaissance. For no other ethnic or religious group is it true that virtually anything can be written or said about it, without challenge or demurral.

To a considerable degree, the stereotype that Said identifies of the "sadistic, treacherous, low" Arab man applies to Zubeydeh's father, 'Alee. Though he is not, perhaps, a completely unsympathetic character—there may be some disinterested love for his daughter in his concern about the possible consequences of her poetic ambitions—he is in general presented as a figure of unctuousness and self-satisfaction. In the classic sadomasochistic way, 'Alee combines a smug tyranny over those who enjoy less social power than he does (mainly, the women of his household) with a toadying servility toward those who might possibly enjoy more (mainly, Ernst and Irene).

Of course, Orientalist mythology also includes images of Arab femininity, so that the bullying yet cowardly Arab man ('Alee's physical cowardice is noteworthy) is complemented by the pathetic figure of the oppressed but resigned and helpless Arab woman. In *The Two of Them* this stereotype is represented primarily by 'Alee's wife and Zubeydeh's mother, Zumurrud. Massively conditioned (in pharmaceutical as well as ideological ways) to internalize the official sexist doctrines of Ka'abah, she generally functions—with the exception of one memorable moment of lucid, honest insight—as an obedient mouthpiece for "false" (that is, un- and antifeminist) consciousness. In models of femininity as well as masculinity, the production of sexist Ka'abite ideology is, then, inextricably bound up with the (re)production of Orientalist myths.

Accordingly, Irene's initial anti-Ka'abah standpoint combines antisexism with quasi-imperialist essentialism vis-à-vis the non-Western cultural other. Implicitly taking the story of her own personal rise from bored, marginalized teenager to privileged Trans Temp operative as a universal model of gender liberation, Irene can recognize Ka'abah sexism only at the price of a studied

---

33. Edward Said, *Orientalism* (New York: Pantheon Books, 1978), 286–287.

insensitivity to the specific cultural forms within which it operates. Thus, for example, her refusal to be constrained by or respectful of official Ka'abite ideology is, on one level, a proud and thoroughly justified gesture of feminist liberation. Yet, because her feminism is at first directed *only* toward the blatant sexism of a culture technologically and politically weaker than her own, her negation of one form of domination (and this pattern is paradigmatic of the feminism of the liberal bourgeoisie) is inseparable from her affirmation of another. Her challenge to Ka'abite sexism, in other words, is based directly on an unquestioned presupposition of Trans Temp superiority and privilege.

Perhaps the central instance of Irene's unreflective sense of superiority to the Ka'abites is her easy certainty that, after a matter of days, she understands Zubeydeh's real interests incomparably better than Zumurrud ever could. To be sure, the novel does ultimately seem to justify Irene's instinct on this matter, which is momentarily endorsed even by Zumurrud herself in her single flash of lucidity.[34] But, under the circumstances—given the advantage over the Ka'abites, male and female, that Irene claims on the basis of a liberal Western ethnocentrism—it is impossible to disentangle her admirable impulse to rescue Zubeydeh from the more general sense of epistemological privilege that the colonizing culture arrogantly grants itself with respect to the colonized culture. This sense of privilege, moreover, invariably involves a relatively uncritical attitude toward the colonizing culture itself. In this way, Irene's superior knowledge of Zubeydeh's needs seems to present itself as part of a general sense of quasi-imperialist superiority that is certainly essentialistic and indeed almost racial in character. Given such an ideological context, it does not even feel entirely accidental that, as is repeatedly made clear, the Ka'abites are physically much *smaller* than Irene and Ernst.

The notion of metropolitan superiority and generalizability is precisely the kind of ideological blindness that Gayatri Chakravorty Spivak has described as the failure of metropolitan feminist deconstruction to be sufficiently deconstructive (or, indeed, sufficiently feminist):[35]

Feminism within the social relations and institutions of the metropolis has something like a relationship with the fight for individualism in the upwardly class-mobile bourgeois cultural politics of the European nineteenth century. Thus, even as we feminist critics discover the troping error of the masculist truth-claim to universality or academic objectivity, we perform the lie of constituting a truth of global sisterhood where the mesmerizing model remains male and female sparring partners of generalizable or universalizable sexuality who are the chief protagonists in that European contest.

34. After Irene indicates her intention to take Zubeydeh away with her, Zumurrud attempts to dissuade her daughter from going. At one point she seems to have succeeded, and Zubeydeh announces her willingness to remain on Ka'abah. Then: "Zumurrud stares. The cat speaks out of her: 'Oh, take her away before she believes it!' and she turns her back on them. She adds, 'Fool!' and then, 'Get out.'" (101).

35. Gayatri Chakravorty Spivak, "Imperialism and Sexual Difference," *Oxford Literary Review* 8, nos. 1–2 (1986): 226.

In order to claim sexual difference where it makes a difference, global sisterhood must receive this articulation even if the sisters in question are Asian, African, Arab.

Yet (as Spivak would certainly agree) the mere "inclusion" of colonial and postcolonial experience within the discursive apparatuses of metropolitan feminism may result in little more than a trivial and ultimately racist exoticism unless it results in—and is thoroughly integrated with—a critical interrogation of *metropolitan* gender relations: especially, perhaps, the gender relations of those liberal-professional sectors of the metropolitan nations that constitute the typical provenance of feminism itself. In other words, if the liberal feminism represented by the initial attitudes of Irene Waskiewicz is to be genuinely transcended, the requisite dialectical process must involve not only greater "understanding" of the non-Western other but a higher level of *self*-understanding as well.

It is just this level of genuine dialectical critique—of feminist deconstruction—that *The Two of Them* does enact. Ka'abah does not, indeed, become measurably less opaque than it appears in the early parts of the novel. But this opacity is to a considerable extent justified through one of the cognitive conveniences provided by the world-invention specific to science fiction. After all, where Ka'abah most significantly *differs* from actual terrestrial Arab civilizations is in possessing almost no historical depth. As a recent, artificially contrived social experiment, Ka'abah need not be credited with the pseudo-organic processes of subject-formation that a more profoundly historical culture would involve.

This depthlessness—this *really* postmodern condition, as one might say—by no means justifies Irene's liberal Orientalism, for it is in the very nature of the latter to erase historical depth and specificity in any case. It does, however, justify the final use to which the novel puts its own invention of Ka'abah. The latter ultimately functions as a science-fictional and radical-feminist heuristic mechanism that illuminates the operations of sexism in Irene's own metropolitan and liberal-professional sphere. In this context, it is relevant to note that there is an interesting affinity (at one point almost explicitly acknowledged by the text itself) between Ka'abah and *The Two of Them*. If Ka'abah is in a sense a postmodern *fiction*, an artificially constructed experiment designed to embody and promote certain social values, the same is of course true of Russ's novel, even though the values of the latter are antithetical to those of the Ka'abites. Indeed, Russ, with her unaffected use of modernist and postmodernist techniques, quite insistently foregrounds the constructed, nontransparent quality of her own text. Not only does the novel feature the free use of literary allusion and of prose that is often self-consciously layered and ornate. Still more important, the "fourth wall," so to speak, of the narrative is frequently broken by interventions from the authorial persona addressed directly to the reader (and, in one case, almost directed to Irene herself): interventions that openly discuss matters of genre and reader-response and that sometimes even offer different fictional versions of the "same" event. Such devices convey a rigorous Brechtian estrangement and highlight the text's character as a thought experiment, as a narrative study in feminist critical theory. But they also suggest the novel's kinship with that somewhat differently constructed experiment that is Ka'abah, whose inhabitants are significantly described as enjoying "the ritual feeling of being inside a play or story" (12). By thus stressing the artificiality of Ka'abah as part and parcel of its own artificial or deliberately constructed quality, *The Two of Them* emphasizes its habitation of an epistemological level sharply different from that inhabited by its heroine; the text therefore distances itself from the precritical Orientalism that she initially displays. At the same time, the novel also makes clear that Ka'abah is finally to be understood as a critical *device* that works toward the transcendence of yuppie Trans Temp liberalism and the attainment of a genuinely radical-feminist perspective.

The moment of the text that most decisively inaugurates the transcendence of liberalism occurs when Irene moves beyond attitudinal sympathy and takes action to rescue Zubeydeh, removing her from Ka'abah. Despite his tacit liberal approval of Irene's general antisexism (or, at least, the absence to this point of any overt disapproval on his part), Ernst seriously doubts the prudence of such direct action. Confronted with Irene's new militancy, he even begins to appear as something of a Burkean conservative. "I am beginning to wonder about the wisdom of remaking cultures or even people's lives" (121), he comments. But Irene is—quite uncharacteristically for her—stubborn on the importance of the rescue, and her insistence carries the day. After this break, Irene's relationship with Zubeydeh, though never clearly defined in any familiar terms—Irene functions as Zubeydeh's adoptive mother, though in some ways she seems more like an elder sister—begins to become more interesting and important to her than her well-established relationship with Ernst (and thus the significance of Russ's title is shifted).

Even more importantly, though not unrelatedly, Ka'abah, as it geographically recedes through countless miles of space, begins to function less as a mere cipher of otherness and unabashed sexist evil, and more as a negative utopia that now does not so much *contrast* with yuppie liberalism as effect a cognitive estrangement of the subtle but pervasive sexism that dominates Irene's own liberal-yuppie sphere of Trans Temp. Irene's bond with Ernst becomes increasingly unsatisfactory, as the condescending and fundamentally oppressive character of many turns of phrase, tones of voice, and large unspoken assumptions becomes clear to her for the first time. In fact, Russ has provided, much earlier in the text, numerous clues to the informal but powerful gender hierarchy that has always governed relations between Ernst and Irene. Shortly after their arrival on Ka'abah, for example, Irene is in a characteristically apologetic mood and, somewhat masochistically confessing her professional shortcomings, allows, "Why you hired me I'll never know." The next line of the novel is, "He smiles. 'For your beautiful eyes'" (21). It is only, however, after the experience of Ka'abah and Zubeydeh (who perceives the gender hierarchy between Ernst and Irene before Irene herself does) that the political meaning of such apparently contingent moments of everyday life is manifest—for Irene, and perhaps for the reader as well. She is eventually able to tell Ernst, "You act like a Ka'abite" (132), and to construct a reasonably clear analogy between the earlier domination of Zubeydeh by her father and her own domination by Ernst: a domination in both cases backed, in the last instance, by the threat of administrative sanction, whether that of the Ka'abah authorities or of Center, the Trans Temp headquarters with which Irene begins to voice open dissatisfaction.

There is, indeed, good reason to suspect that Center and Ka'abah have always had more in common in their treatment of women than one would initially have guessed. Irene turns out to be the *only* female field agent in Trans Temp, and her unique status is closely bound up with her personal attachment to Ernst. As Ernst watches Irene going off the professional rails, he foresees that "Center will use the incident as an excuse never to recruit women again" (159). Evidently it is not, after all, *much* easier for a woman to become a Trans Temp agent than to achieve the roughly equivalent status of a poet on Ka'abah. Irene's rage at her subordination grows, and her subordination is in a sense made all the more infuriating by the fact that, in contrast to gender oppression on Ka'abah, it refuses to call itself by its proper name. For example, as Irene proposes outright disobedience to Center, Ernst secretly cancels the Trans Temp I.D. codes that she needs for computer access—literally undermining the identity of one who, like Ernst himself, knows no "home" outside of Trans Temp—and openly threatens Irene with administrative punishment. "They [the authorities at Center] won't be as indulgent" (142), he warns her. Yet, almost literally in the same breath with such an ominous threat, he can "playfully" allow that *if* there is a difference between men and women, "I'm glad of the difference" (143). *Vive la différence* has, of course, always been a more appealing motto to the gender for whom difference means power. But it is power in the rawest form that provides the climax of the novel: Irene is finally provoked not only to leave Trans Temp but, in a scene of graphic violence, to kill Ernst.

The attitude of the text toward the killing is extremely complex. Is Irene to be seen as a proto–radical-feminist heroine striking a fundamentally defensive blow for freedom? Or is she a murderer? Or has she simply gone mad? The first answer is finally the most compelling and plausible; but the novel—insisting on the complexity and importance of the issues by deliberately framing them in a difficult way, by making things *hard* for itself—refuses to justify her action in any easy, obvious, or unproblematic way. Ernst is an attractive character—physically, and, within the ideological limits of liberal patriarchy, in other ways as well—and the relatively short time during which Irene goes from questioning his ultimate beneficence to shooting him dead constitutes an undeniably shocking presence in the text.

For this reason, I think, the killing of Ernst has proved something of an interpretive crux for readers. John Clute, whose general view of the novel is hostile, seems to find Ernst's death especially disturbing, given "his humanity and his lack of any avowedly sexist tendencies." Sarah Lefanu, though arguing against Clute and for the novel's success, nonetheless allows that "for me it is not just his 'humanity' that makes the shooting of Ernst distressing; it is also his sexiness." Kathleen Spencer, in perhaps the most perceptive reading of *The Two of Them* to date, suggests, "We genuinely *like* Ernst, and it is initially hard to feel that his death is justified" (emphasis in original).[36] But (as Spencer does go on to argue) the killing is not so illogical, nor is Ernst quite so likable, as may superficially appear. It is not simply that Irene's single decisive act of gender-based violence has for its context a massive and indeed all but universal structure of systemic violence against women: a structure of which Ka'abah provides an especially plain example but which is also, as we have seen, typified by Trans Temp itself. Nor is it only that Ernst, the genial liberal, has all along maintained a subtle regime of domestic and professional control over Irene, a regime usually more humane than 'Alee's over Zumurrud and Zubeydeh but, in its own way, no less absolute and manipulative. It is also that Ernst's amiable liberalism contains—as is indeed characteristic of liberalism in general—its own submerged threat of violence, and that Irene, when she kills Ernst, is being directly threatened by the repressive iron fist within the liberal velvet glove. After all, Ernst, for all his charm and sexiness, clearly chooses loyalty to Trans Temp over loyalty to Irene; and she stands to lose everything— not only her privileged status, but perhaps also her freedom and not inconceivably even her life—if he makes good on his threat to report her to the Center authorities. As a practical matter, indeed, it is not clear that Irene could succeed in leaving Ernst and Trans Temp and fleeing with Zubeydeh unless she *does* kill him. Once he discovers what she is up to, Ernst does try to stop Irene, and while alive he would probably possess the power to do so. Accordingly, not only does the death of Ernst neatly figure the text's cancellation of liberal feminism and of liberalism generally. Even on the more literal level, a certain defense of Irene's lethal action against him can be made by the ethical logic of the preemptive strike.

Yet here, as usually, the logic of the preemptive strike is somewhat problematic. For *The Two of Them* never does make completely clear just what the alternatives to killing Ernst might have been. And there is no question that Irene's slaying of Ernst—whom she thinks of, even toward the end, as "one of

---

36. John Clute, review of *The Two of Them*, *Foundation*, no. 15 (1979): 105; Lefanu, *Feminism and Science Fiction*, 194; Kathleen Spencer, "Rescuing the Female Child: The Fiction of Joanna Russ," *Science-Fiction Studies* 17 (1990): 178.

the few men she's ever met who likes women" (144)—remains a deliberately disturbing presence in the novel. Of course, the easiest way for the reader to avoid a verdict of either justifiable homicide or second-degree murder would be to find Irene not guilty by reason of insanity. But to dismiss Irene as mad and thus to find her killing of Ernst merely inexplicable is perhaps the worst possible capitulation to the ideology of phallocracy against which the novel is oriented. Madness—feminine madness—is in fact a persistent theme of *The Two of Them*, which, in one of its aspects, claims as precursor-texts such fictions as *Jane Eyre* (1847) and *The Yellow Wallpaper* (1892). Among the women characters who can be regarded as to one degree or another insane are the usually medicated Zumurrud; her sister, the incarcerated would-be (or would-have-been) poet Dunya, Russ's science-fictional version of The Madwoman in the Attic; Irene's long-suffering mother Rose; her girlhood friend Chloe; as well as Irene herself. As Zubeydeh, who is young enough to be considered unambiguously sane, puts it, "The gentlemen are always calling the ladies crazy and that's wrong" (138).

The point here is a kind of Foucauldian feminism. If, as Foucault argues,[37] madness is a cultural invention necessary in order that reason may by binary contrast know itself securely, Russ would add that this particular and fairly recent binary is deeply connected to the oldest binary of all. If reason is to be represented as masculine, as it almost invariably has been, then madness, in hegemonic phallocratic ideology, is virtually by definition feminine. The consequent privileged relation between insanity and femininity thus helps to constitute feminine subjectivity itself—so that (as Russ's gallery of female characters helps to illustrate) after a certain point there are few, if any, possibilities for feminine development that can wholly escape the taint of madness. Madness, then, is as much a political as a clinical issue, and the refusal to accept the hegemonic clinical binary of sickness and health is an indispensable feminist moment. Irene herself, as her rage toward Ernst grows, does indeed question her own sanity, but she is also politically astute enough to question her own questioning: "It occurs to her that they may even be right, that nothing in her life accounts for the intensity of her anger, that Center is not Ka'abah, that Ernst is a man who loves and respects women. He has good judgment; once he judged her worthy and now he judges her mad. *The gentlemen always think the ladies have gone mad*" (147; emphasis in original). What Russ helps us to see is that the psychiatric category of madness is among the most important of those putatively liberal and thus gender-neutral tools actually used to perpetuate the subordination of women. Perhaps with regard to no other particular issue does *The Two of Them* more powerfully demonstrate the complex gender

37. The main reference is of course to Michel Foucault, *Madness and Civilization*, trans. Richard Howard (New York: Random House, 1965). For a specifically feminist treatment of the matter, and one explicitly indebted to Foucault, see Phyllis Chesler, *Women and Madness* (Garden City, N.Y.: Doubleday, 1972).

relations that link social power, everyday details of routine and intimacy, and the formation and deformation of subjectivity itself.

It remains to ask, however, exactly what kind of liberation Irene, having killed Ernst and successfully escaped with Zubeydeh to the American Southwest, has really achieved by the end of the novel. Her own experience has blown to bits the unreflective liberal feminism of her earlier self, and has at least begun to indicate the necessity for much more radically feminist perspectives. Nonetheless, it would be misleading to describe even her final stance as one of achieved radicalism. Irene remains—and here the basic organizational problems of feminism, with its roots firmly in the personal and the *vécu*, are manifest with a vengeance—an isolated struggling individual with almost no orientation toward collectivity and collective struggles. Only a few pages from the end of the novel, a direct intervention by the authorial persona describes Irene's situation in clearly unpolitical and hence rather pessimistic terms: "A nobody. An unimportant and powerless person. She has no idea yet that she can find other unimportant and powerless people" (178). The adverb *yet* might, of course, be taken to suggest the possibility of a more hopeful and more political future. But the general situation at the end of the novel makes such hope rather tenuous at best. Kathleen Spencer is surely right to describe *The Two of Them* as having "a dark ending."[38] Irene is not only displaced and almost certainly proletarianized—"a thirty-year-old divorcée with a child to support" (176), and with no money, no job, and no usable connections—but is on the run from the authorities as well. Indeed, the authorities who have most reason to pursue her are those of Trans Temp itself; so that the organization that for virtually all Irene's adult life has been not only her employer but her home and family also—"The Gang," as she used to call it—must now be considered her enemy. Sarah Lefanu is also surely right when, perhaps with some understatement, she describes *The Two of Them* as "a more pessimistic novel than *The Female Man*."[39] For the range of structural gender relations in Irene's universe seems to run approximately from Ka'abah on the right to Trans Temp on the "left"—the two models of sexist practice are another of the pairs alluded to by the novel's title—and to lack any all-female anarchist utopias like Whileaway or even such models of autonomous women's organization as Jael's world could supply. Whereas, in the earlier novel, Jael and Janet and the worlds they represent play an important pedagogic and inspirational role for Joanna and Jeannine, Irene at the end of *The Two of Them* is very nearly alone.[40]

38. Spencer, "Rescuing the Female Child," 178.
39. Lefanu, *Feminism and Science Fiction*, 192.
40. In passing, it is worthwhile also to compare Russ's downbeat novel with Suzette Hayden Elgin's comparatively upbeat 1969 short story, "For the Sake of Grace" (see Elgin, *Communipath Worlds* [New York: Pocket Books, 1980], 224–247), on which some of the details of *The Two of Them* are based (Russ explicitly acknowledges the debt in the dedication of her novel to Elgin). The story is set on an elaborately and virulently sexist pseudo-Arab planet that is clearly the model

Very nearly, but not quite. Zubeydeh is not, after all, merely a child to be supported. She is also Irene's intelligent and courageous partner, who, chronologically located at the frontier between late childhood and the first stirrings of grown-up identity, is sometimes capable of combining the unabashed clearsightedness of the child with an increasingly sophisticated protopolitical perspective. The two of them—Irene and Zubeydeh—do perhaps constitute a potential collectivity, albeit a small one. Though their only accomplishment to date is strictly negative—the rejection of both Ka'abite and Trans Temp versions of patriarchy—it may not be inconceivable that, motivated in part by the memory of those older women, like Dunya, who could never get even so far as such rejection, they will be able to build some more positive women's space for themselves and perhaps for others too. Though no mechanism seems to be at hand for the realization of such a project, this is nonetheless the hope on which the novel finally insists. Its last pages are devoted to a somewhat abstract and poetic allegory of hope presented in the form of Irene's dream. Even within the dream the reality of despair (in forms that partly recall that magnum opus of Western patriarchal despair, T. S. Eliot's *The Waste Land* [1922]) cannot be denied: "And Irene must answer with all her heart, *It is impossible*, for even the old sorcerers and wizards could not make something out of nothing; for an ocean there must be a drop of water, for a human being the paring of a nail, for a forest a blade of grass. But here there is nothing" (180; emphasis in original). Yet, if despair and nothingness are inescapably real, they are not the only reality, and they certainly do not have the final word. *The Two of Them* concludes thus:

You can barely see it. You can barely hear it. From autumn leaf to autumn leaf goes the message: something, nothing, everything. Something is coming out of nothing. For the first time, something will be created out of nothing. There is not a drop of water, not a blade of grass, not a single word.
But they move.
And they rise. (181)

Very far from being, like *The Female Man*, a positive utopia in the generic sense, *The Two of Them* concludes with one of the purest and most desperate affirmations of utopia in the Blochian sense that can be found in modern fiction. The nothingness, the *all but* absolute negativity that defines the situation at the end of the novel, registers the depth and subtlety of actually existing sexist oppression and the correlative difficulty of formulating—not to say enacting—any liberatory program. For the true hermeneutic of utopia, however, every negativity may be taken, as we have seen, to imply a corresponding positivity.

---

for Ka'abah. Real possibilities for female advancement do, however, seem to exist, but through individual excellence rather than collective political action. Generically, Elgin's story, though partly science-fictional, is also allied to the fairy tale—and specifically to the fairy-tale convention of the happy ending—in ways that Russ's novel is not.

Utopian hope is ultimately grounded not in a pragmatic analysis of strategic and tactical details, but in the hope *principle* that irresistibly drives us to imagine something better than actuality. There could be no more fundamental and far-reaching revolution, at least in some ways, than that which would decisively overthrow patriarchy: and utopian hope is most fully itself when it envisions and demands the most radical and most completely unprecedented reconfiguration of the social totality.[41] Generically, the dream vision is precisely appropriate for the expression of utopian hope at the end of *The Two of Them*; it discourages us from asking exactly how, pragmatically, something may for the first time be created out of nothing. What is instead to be stressed is that somehow there will be—because there must be—movement and rising toward an *almost* unimaginable utopia.[42]

Stars in My Pocket Like Grains of Sand: *Samuel Delany and the Dialectics of Difference*

To a considerable degree, the more important critical themes of this chapter thus far—the nature and limits of cognition, particularly with regard to the problem of radical otherness; the indispensability and the contradictions of utopian construction; the problematics of sex, gender, and social marginality—all converge in an analysis of Samuel Delany's most recent science-fiction novel to date, *Stars in My Pocket Like Grains of Sand* (1984).[43] Sometimes

---

41. Cf. the French slogan from May 1968 with which Russ concludes her next novel after *The Two of Them*: "Let's be reasonable. Let's demand the impossible"; Russ, *On Strike Against God* (Trumansburg, N.Y.: Crossing Press, 1980), 107.

42. I should acknowledge that, in response to a much earlier version of this section (which was given as a talk at a couple of professional conferences), Joanna Russ generously sent me a quite long, detailed personal letter in which she discussed *The Two of Them* and my analysis of it. I am grateful to Professor Russ for taking the time and effort, and I found her comments useful while revising and expanding my analysis into its current form. To avoid misunderstanding, I should emphasize two points as strongly as possible. First, I learned much from Professor Russ's comments not because they happened to come from the author of the novel but because they came from an intelligent and sensitive *reader* of the novel. Second, my account of *The Two of Them* is in no way "authorized" by Professor Russ, and she bears no responsibility for any of my positions or formulations.

43. Samuel Delany, *Stars in My Pocket Like Grains of Sand* (New York: Bantam, 1985). All page references will be given in the main text. One slight peculiarity of attempting to come to terms with the novel is that, when it was originally published, it was announced as the first half of a diptych, the second half to be entitled *The Splendor and Misery of Bodies, of Cities* and to be published within a year or two. The second novel did not appear on schedule, and by the late 1980s rumors were current around the science-fiction community to the effect that it might never appear. In a new afterword to a 1990 reprinting of the edition cited above, Delany, however, insisted that he was "still working on it" (385), and estimated a new publication date in about 1993. He tantalizingly added that *The Splendor and Misery* was a "more dangerous book" than *Stars in My Pocket*, as well as a harder one, because it "looks more at the more oppressive aspects of the relation between the mirage of centrality and fragmentation" (385). At this writing, *The Splendor and Misery* has still not been published. But *Stars in My Pocket* is, in any case, more than worthy

praised as Delany's masterpiece—though not yet so amply represented in the secondary literature on Delany as such earlier works as *Babel-17* (1966), *Nova* (1968), *Dhalgren* (1974), or *Triton* (1976)—*Stars in My Pocket* may well be the most intellectually ambitious work in the entire range of modern science fiction. Like *Solaris*, it seriously attempts to represent otherness (or rather a considerable range of othernesses) and to engage some of the intellectual problems that the attempt to understand otherness raises. Indeed, Delany actually goes beyond Lem in the extent to which he registers these problems not only as manifest content but also in the formal structures of the novel. The result is perhaps the most thoroughgoing use of modernist and postmodernist technique in any major science-fiction novel thus far (with the possible exceptions of several works by J. G. Ballard and of Delany's own *Dhalgren*). Delany, however, is a political artist in a sense in which Lem is not and in which Le Guin and Russ are. Like *The Dispossessed*, Delany's *Stars in My Pocket* is devoted to the wholesale creation of entire worlds and societies notable both in political comparison with and in political contrast to our own. But his text does not present itself as didactic in quite the same way as Le Guin's. Indeed, the phrase that Delany composed, in overt riposte to *The Dispossessed*, as a subtitle for *Triton*—"an ambiguous heterotopia"—applies to the later novel too. For *Stars in My Pocket* is less concerned with the interrogation of particular political theories like anarchism than with the more general critical consideration of ambiguity and heterogeneity as political issues. Like *The Two of Them*, it thereby gives considerable attention to the politics of gender and to specifically feminist concerns. Delany, in this respect, however, casts his conceptual net more widely than Russ, also pursuing a close examination of the politics of sexual orientation and of that entire complex of social marginalities designated in earthly terms by such rubrics as race, ethnicity, and nation. Very few novels, within science fiction or beyond it, have ever tried to do as much as Delany's magnum opus. If the personal interest—strongly expressed in *Stars in My Pocket Like Grains of Sand*—that Delany has maintained in the texts of critical theory makes his work an inevitable or at least "natural" reference point for a study like the current essay, the immense scope of his finest novel makes it an extremely difficult text with which to come to terms.[44]

---

of being considered a major work by itself. If the sequel should appear, it may well suggest by back-illumination many insights into its predecessor that are unavailable to us now; it would not, I trust, actually cancel anything in the reading I offer here.

44. In this context it is worth recalling Delany's stature as a critical theorist (in the discursive sense) himself, especially with regard to the study of science fiction. Given the general thesis of my study here, it does not seem coincidental that Lem, Le Guin, and Russ have all also written criticism of more than routine interest. But Delany's nonfictional prose establishes him as, of these four, by far the most accomplished scholar of critical theory; he is the only one whose criticism is of really first-rate importance in its own right (that is, even if it were unsupported by an accompanying body of major fiction). Delany's nonfictional (like his fictional) output is extensive, but see especially his first major collection of essays, *The Jewel-Hinged Jaw* (New York: Berkley, 1977), and, in more recent years, his frequent critical contributions to *The New York Review of Science Fiction*.

If there is a single category of critical theory that might help us to comprehend *Stars in My Pocket*, it is one that must necessarily problematize the very idea of comprehension itself: namely, difference. The major theoretical provenance of this category, especially with regard to its epistemological sense, is of course the structural linguistics of Saussure. The founder of the synchronic study of language noticed that, because the linguistic sign bears neither natural nor metaphysical connection to its referent—because the sign is, in this sense, unmotivated and conventional—the whole edifice of linguistic signification is guaranteed not by any principle external to itself but rather by the immanent principle of difference that allows one sign to be distinguished from another. A sign like *sand*, for example, is capable of maintaining a reliable, if conventional, relationship to its referent simply because it differs from such alternative signs as *band* or *Sanka*.[45] It is, however, in a specifically post-Saussurian and indeed poststructuralist problematic that rather more radical and extensive implications of difference have been traced. Though numerous current instances (and philosophical filiations that reach back to Heidegger and Nietzsche) could easily be adduced, perhaps none remains more consequential than Derrida's deconstruction of Saussure himself.

Derrida effectively criticizes Saussure for failing to draw the most fundamental consequences of his own privileging of difference as a linguistic category. Derrida argues that, far from ensuring the stability of any structure of signification, difference is that which ruthlessly destabilizes all such structures and renders any unproblematic or securely self-identical meaning impossible. In linguistic terms, the point is not only that, as Saussure saw, the sign can never fully adequate itself to its referent. Even more important, the internal composition of the sign by signifier (the acoustic or graphic image) and signified (the psychological concept supposedly tied to the signifier) is also, as Saussure did *not* see, irretrievably problematic. Difference is, in Derrida's famous coinage, always *différance*. Not only does every signifier differ from every other; it also thereby *defers* to every other, in the sense that the differential determination of its own meaning is always to be found elsewhere. Accordingly, meaning—and therefore all thought and all identity—cannot be securely achieved in any particular act of signification. On the contrary, it operates in a fitful, problematic way throughout the entirety of the signifying system—the

45. Cf. this important summary passage from Ferdinand de Saussure, *Course in General Linguistics*, ed. Charles Bally and Albert Sechehaye, trans. Wade Baskin (New York: McGraw-Hill, 1966), 120: "Everything that has been said up to this point boils down to this: in language there are only differences. Even more important: a difference generally implies positive terms between which the difference is set up; but in language there are only differences *without positive terms*. Whether we take the signified or the signifier, language has neither ideas nor sounds that existed before the linguistic system, but only conceptual and phonic differences that have issued from the system" (emphasis in original). Saussure immediately goes on to add that the parallelism between the differences of the signifier and those of the signified does, however, make for a positive and stable "system of values," and, indeed, constitutes "the distinctive function of the linguistic institution" (120–121).

very systematicity of which is thereby undermined and put into question (or put *sous rature*, "under erasure," in Derrida's own favored phrase). It is important to stress that, contrary to certain widespread misunderstandings, the implications of Derridean difference do not result in any simple skepticism or metaphysical nihilism. The blank absence of meaning and identity would be as suspect a notion for Derrida as their full presence. Meaning and identity do inescapably continue to operate, but in a flickering, unreliable, and necessarily uncertain fashion that eludes any confident mastery or total comprehension.[46]

At this point, then, and especially in the context of Delany's science fiction, it may be tempting to construct a suggestive parallel between the cognitive uncertainties of poststructuralism and those of quantum physics, particularly with respect to the Heisenberg uncertainty principle.[47] At least as specifically and technically grounded, in its attention to the measurement of certain subatomic particles, as Derrida's deconstruction of Saussurian linguistics, the uncertainty principle is also at least as far-reaching in its epistemological implications. In maintaining that, on the subatomic level, certain pairs of variables, such as position and velocity, cannot be simultaneously attributed to the same particle in any completely meaningful way, Heisenberg in effect places *sous rature* the entire Newtonian and post-Newtonian project of attaining precise mathematical comprehension of the physical universe. Though we should, perhaps, be somewhat wary of such audaciously interdisciplinary analogies, Derrida and Heisenberg do seem to have at least this much in common: for both poststructuralist philosophy and quantum physics, difference and uncertainty cannot be understood as contingent failures of precision, but are irreducibly intrinsic to the natural and human sciences and thus to the objects that the sciences (problematically) study.

Because difference and uncertainty critically interrogate the stability of meaning, identity, measurement, and representation, any attempt to register the Derridean or Heisenbergian problematic by means of novelistic representation is bound to be riven by contradiction of the most urgent and unavoidable sort. Yet such is—quite self-consciously—the achievement of *Stars in My Pocket Like Grains of Sand*. The central construction of the novel is an almost unimaginably immense world (or rather, universe) of difference. The environment assumed and conveyed by the text comprises about six thousand planets inhabited by intelligent species, each planet at least roughly as large and varied a collection of distinct cultures as our own earth, so that the total

46. My discussion of Derrida draws, to some extent, on his early work generally, but especially on Jacques Derrida, *Of Grammatology*, trans. Gayatri Chakravorty Spivak (Baltimore: Johns Hopkins University Press, 1976), 27–73.

47. For an interesting discussion of the relevance of quantum physics to Delany's work, see Martha Bartter, "The (Science-Fiction) Reader and the Quantum Paradigm: Problems in Delany's *Stars in My Pocket Like Grains of Sand*," *Science-Fiction Studies* 17 (1990): 325–340. Bartter does not substantially engage the matter of poststructuralism, though she does mention it in passing.

amount of cultural difference is staggering. Even something as apparently straightforward as a reliable census of the whole seems to be unobtainable; and, in such a vastness, many familiar concepts that may be reasonably precise in other contexts become, in quasi-Heisenbergian fashion, inherently fuzzy and indeterminate. (For instance, one cannot meaningfully ask for the exact number of survivors of a world that has been destroyed in an era when space travel and interplanetary colonization are routine). The dialectical point here is one that has long been ignored by many weakly science-fictional texts of the pulp and post-pulp sort, which have posited galactic and even intergalactic civilizations whose size is assumed to present merely technical and quantitative problems. What Delany shows is that quantity and quality are intimately connected, and that size on such an order of magnitude as this text suggests must involve a literally awesome *complexity*. The attempt to think and, even more, to imagine such a huge field of difference is almost impossibly daunting and can result in a sort of mental vertigo. "The Universe is overdetermined" (164), as a quotation apparently familiar to Delany's characters has it.

Communication is of course radically problematic in such a universe; the coexistence and sometimes collision of an almost countless number of signifying systems—so that, to take a small example, the gesture of an upraised hand may suggest "halt" or "full speed ahead" or "I have to go to the bathroom" (180)—results in a riot of *différance* that, among other things, makes political and economic relations among the various worlds extremely difficult. Whereas even a masterwork like Asimov's Foundation trilogy finds the administration of a Galactic Empire to be a *relatively* straightforward project, much of *Stars in My Pocket* is devoted to rigorously confronting the all but insuperable problems posed by any attempt to manage such a nearly unthinkable degree of difference.

The text indicates that such management can be attempted in two antithetical ways: the macrological and the micrological. The former project enjoys some official sanction under the auspices of the Federation of Habitable Worlds, which seems to be the largest superplanetary political structure in the novel. Though the name suggests an allusion to the United Federation of Planets in *Star Trek*, Delany's Federation displays no clear-cut quasi-military organization; its powers and principles remain shadowy and nebulous. It does, however, seem to be the sponsor of the Web, an only somewhat less shadowy interstellar intelligence corps devoted to the control and distribution of information about the worlds in the Federation. It is never clear just what all the functions and aims of the Web may be, but its most widely accessible project is the maintenance of GI, or General Information: a kind of ultracomputerized system that can wirelessly broadcast a constant encyclopedic barrage of facts about the various cultures of the Federation directly into the brain of anyone whose planet chooses to avail itself of the service. One asks questions of GI simply by thinking them, and GI may superficially appear to be the wonderfully utopian achievement of an information age that far transcends our own computerized environment. But things are not so simple as that. GI is no disinterested technical marvel; it is deeply implicated in the various commercial interests and political conspiracies of the Web. There are numerous gaps in the information available through GI, some of which seem to be deliberate and tactical, but others of which probably result more from the positivistic and undialectical model of knowledge on which GI, with its shotgun blasts of discrete facts, is based. It is, for instance, quite early that we learn that, most tellingly, "History is one area that General Info is notoriously poor in imparting" (68). GI is, I think, best understood as the science-fictional apotheosis of the traditional Western project of undialectical reason: the project, that is, epistemologically to colonize the world through a reductive empiricist mastery grounded in mere facticity. In its Gradgrindian one-dimensionality, GI is, indeed, an exquisite figure of all positivistic, contemplative, ruling-class knowledge. Delany's text is composed in full awareness of the Foucauldian interconnections of such knowledge with power, and it is in both specific tactical ways and large structural ways that GI is always implicated in the vague but evidently ruthless power politics of the Web.

But *Stars in My Pocket* also portrays a more micrological attempt to manage and grasp, to some degree, the immense differences of the universe—a project considerably more modest in scope, and more dialectical and praxis-oriented in character, than GI. This kind of project can be found in the profession of the Industrial Diplomat, or ID, an evidently freelance consultant who is hired on a case-by-case basis to facilitate particular economic and cultural exchanges among the worlds of the Federation. In contrast to the attempts at Olympian comprehension by the Web, the ID works "on the ground," so to speak, both figuratively and (for the most part) literally, in an ad hoc and personally involved way. The Web, which, with its totalistic aims, generally discourages interstellar travel outside its own ranks, takes a particularly dim view of the IDs, who nonetheless seem to have little choice but to maintain a wary but tenable working relationship with the masters of GI.[48] The central character of the novel (and its narrator after the opening prologue) is the ID Marq Dyeth, who describes his task, in neatly dialectical fashion, as involving not Web-like comprehension of difference (the metaphor implied by the arachnoid image is of course significant) but rather self-reflexive recognition that no such comprehension is feasible: "During my first three years as an ID, I thought my job₁ [that is, primary undertaking] was not to be surprised at the universe's human variety. Later I realized that it was not to be surprised that nonstop surprises would henceforth be my life" (215).

---

48. There is some analogy here (and one probably not inadvertent on Delany's part) with the relationship between the private detective and the official forces of law and order in the classic American hard-boiled detective story—a genre in which Delany has expressed considerable interest.

The ID is, indeed, most aptly understood as a *reader*—an "explicit cultural semiotician," as Scott Bukatman has noted in passing[49]—who can only hope to be as sensitive as possible to the never securely graspable changes of *différance*. "Words, the Web, woman, world—all of these," as Marq says, "have their nebulous position in a cloud of shifting meanings" (366); and the ID must struggle to make as much sense of these shiftings as possible. Accordingly, the ID may be wiser than the Web merely in the Socratic—and, as we have seen, Lacanian and, indeed, in some ways generally dialectical—sense of knowing total or final knowledge to be unattainable.

Indeed, Marq is a quite self-consciously unreliable narrator, who can often do little better than to guess at some of the most intriguing problems that the text presents. What happened to Rhyonon, a somewhat primitive inhabited world that seems to have been destroyed in toto? Why is the Web using various methods, including death threats, to discourage curiosity about that disaster? Was Rhyonon perhaps destroyed by Cultural Fugue? And what exactly *is* Cultural Fugue anyway? We know it to be some sort of very rare but widely feared planetary catastrophe, and an object of considerable concern on nearly every world that Marq visits. He can describe it as what occurs when the socioeconomic pressures on a world "reach a point of technological recomplication and perturbation where the population completely destroys all life across the planetary surface" (70), and he claims to be able to recognize some of the signs of its approach. But it is not at all clear that he understands either the actual mechanisms by which Cultural Fugue operates or its underlying causes. Maybe the Xlv are somehow involved. But who *they* are constitutes the most obscure problem of all. Marq knows them to be the only nonhuman species to have developed interstellar travel; beyond that curious fact, however, the unpronounceability of their name figures a quite opaque otherness. Though the universe of *Stars in My Pocket* is far more information-saturated than that of *Solaris*—given its GI, its brilliant translation machines, and its other like marvels—reliable communication with the Xlv has proved as elusive as with Lem's strange ocean. Yet, in the immensity of Delany's inhabited universe, even such a tantalizing mystery cannot interest (relatively) many. One sense in which knowledge is problematic is simply that in such a vastness there is impossibly much to know. As an ID, Marq is aware that the Xlv are "truly alien" (93), but he also realizes that their very existence "is simply another little-known fact—because in our human universe, of necessity, *all* facts are as little known as the works of great poets" (141; emphasis in original).

If even Marq Dyeth, with all his professional expertness—he is not only an ID but, from all one can gather, a highly accomplished one—remains ignorant on many important matters, the same is even more true of the reader. The

49. Scott Bukatman, *Terminal Identity: The Virtual Subject in Postmodern Science Fiction* (Durham: Duke University Press, 1993), 275.

principles of difference and uncertainty do not merely describe the "content" of the novel's central creation (its universe of six thousand inhabited worlds) but so thoroughly structure the composition of the text itself that, in rigorously Derridean fashion, the traditional binary opposition between form and content is radically problematized and deconstructed. There is virtually no exposition in *Stars in My Pocket* and no didacticism of the Le Guinian sort. Delany is (with the exception of Ballard) virtually the first science-fiction novelist whose principal literary roots are firmly grounded in classical modernism: and *Stars in My Pocket* should be understood as less a conventionally narrative story than a neo-Joycean (or perhaps neo-Proustian) unfolding of extremely various and problematic situations and states of being. If it does not, as we shall see, wholly lack a "plot," neither, after all, do *Ulysses* (1922) or even *Finnegans Wake* (1939).

Perhaps a more directly pertinent precedent is suggested—or rather invented—by the novel itself. I mean the "participatory works" (130) of Vondramach Okk, a bloodthirsty tyrant and great poet who lived several generations before the time present of the novel. Vondramach, who served as patron to one of Marq Dyeth's ancestors, and who continues to touch his life in other (perhaps coincidental) ways, used a private language to compose works that demand the maximum attention and participation of the reader. The operative aesthetic maxim seems to be *Poetry is what is avoided as it is surrounded by translation* (130; emphasis in original). Applied to the interpretation of *Stars in My Pocket* itself, the notion of the participatory work helps to illuminate Delany's all-important handling of *detail* and to indicate how the reader occupies a position analogous to that of the ID.

Perhaps the most relevant contrast here is with more conventionally generic utopian fiction (like *The Dispossessed* or even, to some degree, *The Female Man*) in which all or at least the great majority of details that structure the text's invented world are carefully selected by the author according to the text's didactic function, and are thus more or less easily grasped by the reader in light of their expository significance. But in a more radically modernist and, as Delany might encourage us to say, heterotopic fiction like *Stars in My Pocket*, the details of the text are—in a way that resonates strongly with the Derridean logic of supplementarity—frequently in excess of any clearly controlled logical significance. It is not just that some details may be significant and others not (though that is to some degree true). It is also that, to a considerable extent, the distinction between significant and insignificant detail is itself deconstructed—so that the text solicits the reader's active participation in significantly accounting for each detail as best she or he can and in making what connections he or she finds most relevant.

Delany, in other words, declines to impose the kind of overarching logical structure that would straightforwardly guarantee the meaning of each microunit of the novel. Instead, we are left to be overwhelmed by a massive amount of exceedingly various detail, and we must collaborate with the author in building up the image—or rather images—of this vast universe of difference. A few details, perhaps (such as the functioning of GI, for example) can be pretty securely grasped by an attentive reading—or, more likely, rereading. But even the most attentive reading is bound to find much meaning (perhaps above all that of the Xlv) irrecuperably uncertain and problematic. The text is, in this sense, virtually inexhaustible.[50] As we have seen, some difference is integral to the process of cognitive estrangement that defines science fiction in general. But it would be difficult to name another science-fictional text that more insistently and micrologically confronts us with difference on a sentence-by-sentence and paragraph-by-paragraph basis. Cognitive estrangement not only functions as an overall effect of the novel; it is infused into the very temporal process of reading. Paradoxically, however, one result of this thoroughly modernist and radically science-fictional literary project is to create a powerful sense of *reality* itself. It has occasionally been noticed how modernism may be in a sense more "realistic" than realism. Just as the transcription of a tape-recording of actual conversation is almost certain to bear a much closer generic resemblance to the dialogue of Beckett or Ionesco than to that of Ibsen or Arthur Miller,[51] so the process of dealing with and trying to decode actuality is much more like attempting to make sense of *Stars in My Pocket Like Grains of Sand* than it is like reading a more conventionally realistic novel. None of us, after all, ever does attain total certainty. We all really do live in a world of difference, and each of us is, in important ways, precisely an ID. Indeed, the abbreviation neatly suggests how the project of cultural semiotics that defines the Industrial Diplomat is inseparable from the (necessarily problematic) construction of identity itself.

But how, exactly and in detail, does the ID manage to comprehend difference with any degree of success at all? What is the dynamic at work that allows the ID's dialectical approach to work more adequately (or less inadequately) than the positivism of the Web's GI? However much Marq Dyeth may be doomed to operate in the universe of Heisenberg and Derrida, the very title of Delany's text does seem to promise that, in some way, comprehension may be achieved. In light of our earlier discussion of *Solaris*, it seems appropriate to suggest that *desire* must play a crucial cognitive role in a dialectical praxis that

50. Cf. Seth McEvoy, *Samuel R. Delany* (New York: Ungar, 1984), 3: "One can speculate that Delany's structure is a dyslexic view of prose. In some of Delany's more difficult work, such as *Dhalgren*, there are gaps. Certain facts are missing from the narrative that are usually part of a standard prose text. It is up to the reader to supply these facts. This method of co-creation (where the reader must supply the missing parts of the story, sort of a literary partnership) appears in every book by Delany to a certain extent." The derivation of the concept of the participatory work from Delany's personal struggles with dyslexia is, I think, reductive, but it is also illuminating; and it is doubtless not without validity on the biographical level.

51. This analogy was suggested to me by Theodor Adorno, "Towards an Understanding of *Endgame*," in *Twentieth-Century Interpretations of "Endgame*," ed. Bell Gale Chevigny (Englewood Cliffs, N.J.: Prentice-Hall, 1969), 102.

aims to attain some purchase on a world of difference. But, as we prepare further to address this question directly, it is necessary first of all to give our discussion of difference more concreteness by constructing it not only in the strictly epistemological terms suggested by quantum physics and Derridean poststructuralism, but in overtly political terms as well.

Here, I think, the most useful critical-theoretical reference is to the negative dialectic of Adorno—perhaps the greatest of all philosophers of difference and a remarkably prescient forerunner of poststructuralism.[52] Whereas, however, actual French poststructuralism—whether in Derrida or even in apparently more "social" theorists like Deleuze and Foucault—has generally thought difference in epistemological or, at most, ethical ways, Adorno's perspective is unswervingly political from the outset. For Adorno, the eradication of sociopolitical difference in the triumph of totalitarian domination has been the principal, if largely secret, tendency of Western civilization since its Homeric dawn; and this tendency, which is designated, for certain purposes, as the dialectic of enlightenment, reaches its unimaginably horrible but perfectly logical culmination at Auschwitz. Indeed, it is explicitly as a philosopher of the Holocaust that Adorno, in one of his finest meditations, most tellingly delineates the significance of integration as the antithesis of difference and nonidentity:[53]

Genocide is the absolute integration. It is on its way wherever men are leveled off— "polished off," as the German military called it—until one exterminates them literally, as deviations from the concept of their total nullity. Auschwitz confirmed the philosopheme of pure identity as death. . . . Absolute negativity is in plain sight and has ceased to surprise anyone. . . . What the sadists in the camps foretold their victims, "Tomorrow you'll be wiggling skyward as smoke from this chimney," bespeaks the indifference of each individual life that is the direction of history. Even in his formal freedom, the individual is as fungible and replaceable as he will be under the liquidators' boots.

The antithesis to genocide—the antithesis to the ultimate uniformity and elimination of difference—would amount to the Adornian utopia; this, in turn, would be a social formation in which individual freedom and desire are accorded maximum dignity in ways consonant with the achievement of social solidarity. The integrity of the whole would not require the leveling of difference among the component members, and this scrupulous respect would extend not only to all men and women but to nonhuman aspects of the social totality

52. Cf. Terry Eagleton, *Walter Benjamin* (London: Verso, 1981), 141: "The parallels between deconstruction and Adorno are particularly striking. Long before the current fashion, Adorno was insisting on the power of those heterogeneous fragments that slip through the conceptual net, rejecting all philosophy of identity, refusing class consciousness as objectionably 'positive,' and denying the intentionality of signification. Indeed there is hardly a theme in contemporary deconstruction that is not richly elaborated in his work."

53. Theodor W. Adorno, *Negative Dialectics*, trans. E. B. Ashton (New York: Continuum, 1983), 362.

as well (among Adorno's many prescient moments were his anticipations of the movements against environmental pollution and for animal rights).

To a remarkable degree, such an Adornian utopia is just what the universe of *Stars in My Pocket* offers. To be sure, the Federation is not in the least politically programmatic. Its various planets are governed by a large variety of political systems, from syndicalist communism to industrial fascism, and most planets do not even have worldwide government at all. Yet on the average—and most notably on Marq Dyeth's home planet of Velm, which is organized according to a predominantly though not purely socialist, egalitarian system known as bureaucratic anarchy—an extraordinary (by earthly standards) amount of sociopolitical difference is able to flourish, especially with regard to the politics of gender, sexuality, and sexual orientation. Adorno, it may be remembered, was one of the first male thinkers since Engels to stress the political importance of gender and sexuality; and his resolute nonidentitarianism bears a strong affinity to the celebration of gender equality and polymorphous perversity that is one of Delany's central themes in much of his fiction and nonfiction, and that is never more powerfully represented than in *Stars in My Pocket*.

Marq's environment is one in which gender differentiation (into three rather than only two genders for some species) is structured, for the most part, by no hierarchy or division of labor, and implies no stigmas or stereotypes of the earthly sort. Indeed, in one of the novel's most cunning strategies of uncertainty, the reader often finds it difficult even to be sure which characters are male and which female, for the very language of gender has undergone a radical transformation. *Woman* is the gender-neutral noun for an intelligent being, with *she* the corresponding pronoun; while *he*, interestingly, is reserved for anyone, regardless of gender, who is considered by the speaker as an object of sexual desire. For the reader, of course, this usage is bound to carry strong connotations of homosexuality, which, while not necessarily predominant in Marq's universe, is generally accepted in a quite taken-for-granted way. Marq himself is almost exclusively homosexual (the first such major character in Delany's science fiction, though homosexual experience is represented in some of his earlier work, notably *Dhalgren*), and his sexual habits, especially with regard to the "runs" on his home world of Velm, are largely based on the gay male subculture of urban America during the 1970s and early 1980s—an environment that Delany evidently regards as containing (to put the matter in Blochian terms) important utopian pre-illuminations of liberated sexuality. For example, shortly after Marq is introduced, a casual sexual encounter he experiences while on an interstellar diplomatic mission is described in quite emphatically estranging language. The sexual play includes "low-amperage high-voltage electrodes that he had me play across his handsome, lithe body," and Marq sums up the one-night stand in this way:

All I can say is that, like some diplomat himself, he was as obliging to me as I was to him, with only one or two quizzical and good-natured inquiries, while I managed to drink his semen and induced his rectum to drink, as it were, mine—he held me with hard arms and legs and said: "Oh . . ." And, minutes later, "You're a very interesting woman." (76)

Deliberately disturbing to actually hegemonic notions of compulsory hetero-sexuality, such a passage succinctly encapsulates the acceptance of difference in a radically sexual and polymorphous utopia. That which is shocking to most of the pertinent ideologies in our world is merely routine in Marq's.

Nor is the politics of difference in *Stars in My Pocket* limited to issues of sexuality and gender. Marq's environment is also noteworthy for the connec-tions (sexual and otherwise) among different species, and this theme is clev-erly deployed so as to estrange ideologies of race, nation, and ethnicity, but also of earthly interspecies relations and animal rights. Especially important in this context is Velm, by far the most closely described planet in the novel. Designed to strike the earthly reader as an especially alien locus in many dif-ferent ways (for example, the planet has five directions instead of the earthly four, and taste is the supreme and hence frequently metaphorized sense in the way that sight is for us), Velm is home to two intelligent species, humans and evelmi. The latter are physically quite other—they possess scales, claws, six legs, wings, and multiple tongues—but are at least as intelligent as hu-mans and in some ways might be considered socially more advanced. Before meeting humans, the evelmi had "no concept for uneven-distribution-of-exchange-power" (108).

Despite such differences, humans and evelmi freely and peacefully inter-mingle, at least in the southern part of the planet. Not only do they cooperate in technical and political matters, and frequently enjoy sexual relations across the line of species, but humans and evelmi are capable of building stable ex-tended families together, like Marq's own well-established line of the Dyeths. Indeed, these families—actually called streams—are not biologically based (in that case they would be structured by some degree of sameness) but, in a maximization of heterogeneity, are wholly adoptive. And the Dyeths (the only stream portrayed in detail) therefore constitute a relatively small but powerful utopic space of "racial" difference—which is managed and regarded not with positivistic liberal toleration but in terms of sexual and familial *desire*. The mixed marriage is, perhaps, the only fully satisfactory (that is, the most radi-cally nonidentitarian) way to deal with ethnic and national otherness.

The cognitive estrangements effected by the representation of cross-species relations are considerably deepened and complicated by one of the most re-markable inventions in the whole of *Stars in My Pocket*: the extraordinary scene of the dragon hunt in chapter 10. Dragons are flying animals native to Velm, who, though not intelligent in the manner of evelmi or humans, are biologically closely related to the evelmi (in much the same way, presumably, that apes are related to humans). Dragon hunting is a widely popular and respected sport among evelmi and humans alike. And Delany describes the preparations for the hunt and the early stages of the hunt itself with the kind of loving, meticulous detail familiar from such classic hunting literature as that of Hemingway or Faulkner: we see the careful selection of weapons and other equipment, the valued encounter with the sage and experienced master hunter, the patient tracking of the quarry, and so forth. The reader, however, is bound to be somewhat puzzled at this point. We already know Marq's society to be vegetarian ("meat" is produced synthetically, not harvested from dead animals), and hunting seems generally incoherent with the nonviolent Velmic ethos. The moment of the hunt when the first "hit" is scored is a masterstroke of estrangement and ironic reversal. It turns out that the radar-bows of the hunters do not kill the dragons or harm them in any way. Instead, a hit precisely registers the dragon's sensations and viewpoint at that moment, and, by broadcasting them directly into the brain of the hunter, gives the latter the sensation of inhabiting for a few seconds the dragon's body and consciousness. One almost *becomes* a dragon, temporarily, thus really attaining the kind of quasi-mystical empathy with a member of a different species that is sometimes claimed by apologists for earthly hunting. Like the sexual relations between humans and evelmi, the dragon hunt is a utopic figure of difference: and difference, once again, that is not simply tolerated in what Adorno would call formal freedom, but is actively *desired*, sought, and embraced.

Yet, however rich in utopian moments *Stars in My Pocket* may be, the text can by no means be classified as an unambiguously positive utopia in the generic sense. Even the Dyeths, who provide the most warmly endorsed environment in the novel, may be slightly suspect for enjoying a kind of aristocratic prestige and privilege that somewhat conflicts with the officially egalitarian values of bureaucratic anarchy. Beyond Dyethshome—their ancestral estate, which, it should be remembered, the stream possesses because of the largesse of the terrible Vondramach Okk—the ambiguities multiply. The peaceful relationship between evelmi and humans is a fairly recent achievement and even in the time present of the novel is not yet complete; in the apparently more primitive northern regions of Velm, far from Dyethshome, actual violence between the species still occurs. Beyond Velm altogether, the universe of the Federation, however progressive on the whole, still contains numerous reminders that the philosopheme of pure identity—the ultimately genocidal attitude toward difference—lives on. The Thants, for instance, are an offworld family who for many years have been on close and friendly terms with the Dyeths; toward the end of the novel, they surprisingly turn up for a formal banquet at Dyethshome and behave with abominable rudeness and hatred. In accents that clearly recall Christian fascism, they denounce the Dyeths as sick and criminal, especially for enjoying sexual relations within the same gender and between different species, and their general attitude toward the evelm members of the stream (whom the Thants deride as mere "animals") amounts to the equivalent of unabashed Ku Klux racism.

Though the reasons for the Thants' unexpected hostility remain somewhat uncertain, it seems to involve the recent political situation on their own planet and to be somehow connected to the largest political conflict within the Federation, that between the Family and the Sygn. Though the nature of this struggle is also far from completely clear, it appears to be at least in part a battle between identitarian and nonidentitarian viewpoints, particularly with regard to a running controversy over which approach is most effective at preventing Cultural Fugue. The Sygn is differentially structured, as the Saussurian and Derridean connotations of the word itself imply, and is "committed to the living interaction and difference between each woman and each world from which the right stability and play may flower" (86). Family values, by contrast, stress the eternal over the temporal and do not regard stability as at all compatible with mutability and free play; instead, the Family promotes "the dream of a classic past as pictured on a world that may never even have existed in order to achieve cultural stability" (86). The Sygn seems to be the more powerful of the two factions and is certainly more coherent with the "modernity" of the epoch. But the Family is a far from insignificant force, and its ahistorical, totalistic identitarianism remains—as the Thants' descent into raving bigotry illustrates—a very real threat. The values of Dyethshome as a utopic space of difference may have succeeded to a degree almost unimaginable in our own world, but they remain frequently assaulted and far from invulnerable. As such, their particular quality and appeal are highlighted by contrast. The utopian character of difference apprehended in desire appears more forcefully than might be the case in a more triumphalist—and so less heterotopic—text.

In other words, the utopian power of the novel is enhanced by its incorporation of counterutopic loci. The most closely described such counterutopic locus in *Stars in My Pocket* is Rhyonon, which the text critically positions, with regard both to the Velmic ethos and to the ethos of our own actual environment, in particularly complex ways. Rhyonon is the planet on which the prologue to the novel is set and which is destroyed (perhaps by Cultural Fugue) at the prologue's end. The prologue is the only portion of the text not narrated by Marq Dyeth; indeed, not only does Marq himself not appear in it, but the whole cosmopolitan galactic environment through which Marq freely moves is hardly visible save in a few fleeting glimpses. This formal disjunction between prologue and main text corresponds to the general social and technological backwardness of Rhyonon, a harsh world only tenuously connected to the galactic system of the Federation. Owing to what seems to be some sort of religious obscurantism, Rhyonon even declines to participate in GI, functioning *beneath* its positivistic level as the ID functions, or can function, above it. Worse still, actual slavery exists on Rhyonon. Though only institutions are officially permitted to own slaves, private individuals can illegally contrive to buy them. The slave class is not racially structured in its origins, but is composed of those—generally neurotic and impoverished social misfits—who have agreed to become "rats" by undergoing a lobotomy-like procedure called Radical Anxiety Termination. The latter produces a dull passivity and greatly diminishes mental capacity, although, contrary to promises made, it does not give any evidence of producing happiness. After undergoing the procedure, the newly made slaves, while not drawn from any particular racial group, are henceforth generally regarded with a bigoted contempt that is quasi-racial in character. As their name implies, the rats are dehumanized by the attitudes of those around them, and, in the general manner of slaves, they are almost unconditionally subject to the whims (including the sexual whims) of their masters.

Most of the prologue is devoted to chronicling many unhappy and not particularly eventful years in the life of one such unfortunate, Rat Korga, whose story at several points shrewdly alludes (as Robert Elliot Fox has noticed)[54] to actual chattel slavery and its aftermath in African-American history. Despite such allusions, however, the open buying and selling of human beings and the formal subordination of the rats may well seem to distance Rhyonon from the actual social context of the American reader in 1984. Indeed, Rhyonon—with its bleak research stations, its relatively sparse population, and its rigid but somewhat insecure technocratic hierarchies—is in many ways a fairly conventional science-fictional environment: and the somewhat routinely alien scenery combines with its social regressiveness to emphasize its general otherness vis-à-vis our own world. After we begin to learn about Velm, however, and about the universe of the Federation generally, our perspective begins to change. As the liberated ethos of Marq Dyeth's environment more and more estranges our own taken-for-granted assumptions, much of the identitarian repressiveness of Rhyonon seems (especially with regard to matters of sex and gender) uncomfortably closer and closer to mundane earthly actuality. We learn, for instance, that on Rhyonon several forms of consensual sexual intercourse were actually illegal, and that the ancient diction of *man* and *woman* in the sense familiar to us, with such attendant variations as *bitch* for woman, was still the current jargon.

54. See Robert Elliot Fox, *Conscientious Sorcerers* (New York: Greenwood, 1987), 118–119. Fox is noteworthy for being one of the few scholars of African-American literature to have recognized Delany's important place in that tradition. The general neglect is, of course, yet another instance of the marginalization of science fiction; but it is particularly ironic and depressing to find such marginalization practiced by those whose own field has suffered from a closely similar denigration and malign neglect by hegemonic literary canons. Comparing Delany with Amiri Baraka and Ishmael Reed, Fox rightly judges Delany to be "the most profoundly imaginative and intellectual of the three" as well as "the most meditative, the most self-conscious craftsman" (ix). I myself would go still further and claim Delany as the most original and accomplished male novelist to have emerged in the African-American tradition since the era of Baldwin and Ellison. But look for any reflection of that achievement in the mainstream forums of Black Studies, and you will, with few exceptions, look in vain.

This complex triangular estrangement of Marq's world, Rat Korga's world, and our own world is greatly facilitated by the "resurrection" of Rat Korga in the main text of the novel. Rescued by the Web from Rhyonon's planetary catastrophe and his brain partly healed, Rat is united with Marq on Velm and to some degree begins to function (since so many of his own assumptions are much closer to earthly than to Velmic norms) as a kind of utopian Everyman in the manner of Raphael Hythloday. This aspect of *Stars in My Pocket* reaches its climax at the banquet where the repressive dogmatism of the Thants is revealed. Marq complains to Rat that the "idiotic statements" of the Thants have "made me feel as if I were living on some world out of history where all that we do here was against the law!" (337). But Rat replies that it is really *he*, not Marq, who has been made to feel that way; and when Marq at first fails to understand, Rat explains, "You didn't grow up on such a world. You didn't spend your childhood and make your transition to maturity on a world where bestiality and homosexuality were legally proscribed. So you do not possess the fund of those feelings to draw on. I do" (337). But so, of course, does the reader, regardless of gender or sexual orientation. Marq's reactions bring home to us that our own earth, fully as much as Rhyonon or the society implied by the Thants' bigotry, is, in effect, some idiotic world out of history—in estranging contrast, that is, to the progressive nonidentitarianism of Marq Dyeth's universe of difference.

To consider Marq Dyeth and Rat Korga together brings us, finally, to the "plot" of *Stars in My Pocket*. And we are now in a position to consider more closely how desire functions as cognition in the comprehension (in some sense) of difference. The chief narrative line of the novel is, in fact, a love story (like *Solaris* in one of its aspects). Acting from typically obscure political motives, the Web rescues Rat and brings him to Marq on Velm after determining—in a riot of positivistic precision—that, to seven decimal places in one direction and to nine in the other, each of these gay males is the other's "perfect erotic object" (179). Only a day after uniting the lovers, the Web takes Rat away again—also for unclear reasons, though it does appear that Rat (who is eerily associated with the long dead Vondramach) is somehow inspiring instability on Velm that might even lead to Cultural Fugue. During the heartbreakingly brief interval during which Marq and Rat are together, Marq experiences desire and its fulfillment with an intensity that far exceeds anything he has previously known, extensive and varied as his sexual and diplomatic careers have been. The erotic union of the two represents a negotiation of difference in many different ways—from the apparently trivial fact that Rat is much taller than Marq (which would have made their liason illegal on Rhyonon), to the far from trivial fact that Marq, the ID, is one of the more privileged, well-traveled, and generally well informed beings in the Federation, while Rat Korga is a former slave and a "hugely informatively deprived individual from a generally informatively deprived world" (165). Yet such differences, far from being obstacles to the sexual coming-together of Marq and Rat, are precisely what their union is based on: not through any attempt to *reduce* difference, nor to accept it with liberal toleration, but in an active embracing of difference with unimaginably keen enthusiasm.

So radical are the differences to be thus engaged that, in attempting novelistically to concretize the process (which is sexual, cognitive, and diplomatic, all at once), Delany is trying to represent that which lies at the very frontier of representability. Whereas the *(relatively)* humanistic description of Shevek and Takver's lovemaking in *The Dispossessed* can borrow heavily, as we have seen, from a preexisting Lawrentian tradition, Delany must invent a new language—almost literally—to convey the sexual solidarity of Rat and Marq:

We lay on the bed; and his hand on my chest was a stone outcrop on uneven giltgorse. His rough hair, with something reddish in it, was the hue of split tolgoth pith. . . . My own breath against his neck came back to strike my face like a hotwind eroding the prehistorical escarpments of the oest to their characteristic roundness. The line between his arm and my chest was the crevice of some sunken -wr, the near bank, mine, heavy with growth, the far one, his, notably sparse. (213)

Yet, however remote in one sense this differential balance and union—this secular apotheosis of difference—may be, there is another, Blochian sense in which it is a strongly utopian achievement and thus not finally alien to us at all ("The alien is always constructed of the familiar" [143], as one poem by Vondramach Okk begins). The comprehension of difference through fulfilled desire in some ways amounts, in Blochian terms, to *Heimat*, or home, which the novel itself, in self-consciously Blochian language, defines as "the place you can never visit for the first time, because by the time it's become 'home,' you've already been there" (100). But an even more pertinent reference is—yet again—to Adorno. In one of his rare explicit statements of a positive alternative to the philosopheme of identity and domination, Adorno holds up the ideal of "peace among men as well as between men and their Other," defining peace as "the state of distinctness without domination, with the distinct participating in each other."[55] There is no more illuminating gloss on what Marq Dyeth and Rat Korga achieve.

To engage and comprehend difference through a desire that (as with the Biblical connotations of *knowing*) amounts to cognition as well as gratification has, of course, been a large part of Marq's modus vivendi since long before he ever heard of Rat Korga. As an ID, Marq can quite literally claim peace to be his profession, and diplomacy may ultimately resolve into nothing other than love itself—the same kind of erotic desire that, as we have seen, animates the Dyeths as a viable stream and gives the dragon hunt its special zest. Yet it

55. Theodor Adorno, "Subject and Object," in *The Essential Frankfurt School Reader*, ed. Andrew Arato and Eike Gebhardt (New York: Urizen Books, 1978), 500.

seems to be only after his extraordinarily intense and all-too-brief encounter with Rat Korga (and motivated, no doubt, not only by the encounter itself but by his subsequent mourning for its loss) that Marq can give a thorough theoretical account of how he negotiates the universe and manages, despite its immensity, to comprehend it, to keep stars in his pocket like grains of sand. It is, he says, a matter of "the structure of desire I negotiate every day as I move about in" (368) the universe, a beautiful universe in which all faces and hands are luminous, even the ordinary and ugly ones, as they too "still belong to the categories where the possibility of the sexual lies" (368). Though he of necessity must use the external and positivistic coordinates of GI and the Web, he more profoundly relies upon "my own map of the universe" (368), a map based on the ad hoc contingencies of desire but nonetheless organized into "information, some of it logical, some of it mythical, some of it in error, and much of it, yes, no doubt merely wrong or right" (369). But it is, he goes on, nonetheless "information beautiful yet useless to anyone but me, or someone like me, information with an appetite at its base as all information has, yet information to confound the Web and not to be found in any of its informative archives" (369).

Such information—the sine qua non of diplomacy and the synthesis of wanting and knowing—may, in fact, ultimately be all that stands between survival and Cultural Fugue. The latter, which Marq defines as "the perpetual and unremitting destruction of both nature and intelligence run wild and without focus" (373), may really amount only to *pure* difference, which, by a recognizable dialectical paradox, turns out to be exactly the same as no difference at all: it turns out, that is, to be the same as the genocidal violence of total identity and absolute integration in the Adornian sense. The only finally viable alternative may well be the peaceful negotiation and management of difference through the praxis of desire—in other words, love. Love, for Dante, was the force that moved the sun and other stars; the antithesis of that state, characterized by both violence and stasis, he termed Hell. There is a real sense in which Delany is at one with Dante—his science-fictional and highly theoretical precursor—in suggesting an erotic nonidentitarianism to be all that can save us from the Holocaust (as Adorno might term it) of Cultural Fugue.

In a kind of epilogue to this reading of *Stars in My Pocket*, we may note that the novel does not, then, ultimately conform to the doctrines of poststructuralism in the most orthodox sense. Like so much of Delany's fiction and criticism—but more powerfully, I think, than any other of his texts—the novel explores themes crucial to poststructuralism, above all, the great determinant theme of difference. Yet it also finally resists the tendency of the most influential poststructuralist canons to abjure totalization in *all* its forms. Orthodox poststructuralism repudiates not only those idealist and contemplative varieties of totalization implicated by Adorno in the dialectic of enlightenment, but even those engaged and ad hoc materialist varieties organic to praxis itself. In *Stars in My Pocket*, the totalization—using the term now very much in its core Sartrean sense of a personal project that sums up or make sense of the various contingencies of existence—of difference is achieved, as we have seen, through desire in the praxis of the ID. (The Freudian connotations of the abbreviation—the id emphatically appearing in all capitals—should not be missed.) Since, as we have also seen, the structural position of the ID like Marq Dyeth is in many ways analogous to that of the reader, it should come as no surprise that the reader's encounter with this highly participatory text is best described as a work of praxis too, and one that cannot possibly be viable unless totalized through some degree of desire invested in the text. "The text you write must prove to me *that it desires me*,"[56] writes the later, poststructuralist Barthes in a slight lapse of his own from poststructuralist orthodoxy. Barthes immediately goes on to say that the proof exists and is simply writing itself. Perhaps of no science-fictional text is this more true (perhaps, in other words, no other science-fictional text is, as Barthes might also say, more *writerly*) than *Stars in My Pocket*. In its scrupulous respect for difference, which is totalized in desire—in its wholehearted invitation to the reader to take part in the construction of this participatory work—Delany's novel proves that it indeed desires us.

Or, more precisely, it proves that it desires our desire, which can be concretized and fulfilled only in the self-consciously participatory and constructive process of reading itself. Not every reader will return desire for desire, of course. There are those who read science fiction but who profess to find Delany's later work unreadable, just as there are those who read fiction in general but who still profess to find Joyce and Proust unreadable. Yet—again as with Joyce and Proust—the reader who is moved to participate, by reading, in the radical textualization of difference and desire will find in *Stars in My Pocket Like Grains of Sand* an intensity of interest that very few other works can begin to match. The novel may or may not turn out to be Delany's farewell to science fiction. What is certain is that, whether he returns to the field or not, Delany has, with *Stars in My Pocket*, transformed it forever.

The Man in the High Castle: *Philip K. Dick and the Construction of Realities*

I conclude this series of excursuses with Philip K. Dick—the author who, as I have already indicated, remains for me the finest and most interesting writer in the entirety of science fiction—and *The Man in the High Castle* (1962).[57]

56. Roland Barthes, *The Pleasure of the Text*, trans. Richard Miller (New York: Hill and Wang, 1975), 6.
57. Philip K. Dick, *The Man in the High Castle* (New York: Berkley, 1981). All page references will be given in the text.

The choice of a particular novel is in this case particularly difficult. Dick—owing mainly, one suspects, to the working conditions that economic necessity forced upon him during most of his career—never produced the kind of overwhelming and singular masterpiece that Le Guin achieved with *The Dispossessed* or Delany with *Stars in My Pocket Like Grains of Sand.* On the other hand, he did write more genuinely first-rate novels than any other science-fiction author or, indeed, than any other American novelist of any kind during the second half of the twentieth century. Any of the three novels discussed mainly in terms of style in the preceding chapter—*Do Androids Dream of Electric Sheep?* (1968), *Ubik* (1969), and *A Scanner Darkly* (1977)—might appropriately be discussed at greater length here. The same can be said of *Time Out of Joint* (1959), *Martian Time-Slip* (1964), *The Simulacra* (1964), *Dr. Bloodmoney* (1965), *The Three Stigmata of Palmer Eldritch* (1965), *Flow My Tears, The Policeman Said* (1974), *The Transmigration of Timothy Archer* (1982), and arguably two or three other novels. Such a multiplicity of masterworks is unprecedented in science fiction and rare in fiction altogether; and it is made all the more astonishing by the fact that many of these texts were (as the dates above suggest) written at a furious pace, one right after the other. Of course, Dick (who composed nearly fifty novels) had his failures too, from the amateurish *Solar Lottery* (1955), to the perfunctory *The Zap Gun* (1967), to the pretentiously tedious *Valis* (1981) and *The Divine Invasion* (1981). But even Dick's worst novels are never without elements of genuine interest, while his middle-level work—typified by such texts as *Clans of the Alphane Moon* (1964), *The Penultimate Truth* (1964), and *We Can Build You* (1972)—would be major achievements by the standards of most good novelists.

If, out of all the material available, I choose here to focus on a text that has received more than its share of commentary already (*more*, that is, not in proportion to its own intrinsic merit, but simply in comparison to the relative neglect suffered by many other Dick masterpieces), it is mainly for two closely related reasons. First, *The Man in the High Castle* contrasts with the four novels analyzed earlier in this chapter in that it does not seem emphatically and obviously to present itself as science fiction. *Solaris, The Dispossessed, The Two of Them,* and *Stars in My Pocket Like Grains of Sand* all prominently feature the most typical science-fictional motif—space travel—and all, as we have observed, elaborately delineate scientific and technological developments far in advance of the empirical circumstances in which the texts were composed. In Dick's novel, by contrast, the setting is the apparently mundane one of postwar America (mostly the San Francisco Bay area) and no technical advances appear as anything more than incidental background details. In fact, *The Man in the High Castle* was not at first marketed as science fiction,[58] and probably

58. See Paul Williams, *Only Apparently Real: The World of Philip K. Dick* (New York: Arbor House, 1986), 91.

never would have been if what modest reputation Dick had then established had not been almost exclusively within the science-fiction field. Yet science fiction is, as I shall maintain, indeed the dominant generic tendency of the text: Dick's novel can thus be analyzed in a sort of case study of how cognitive estrangement may operate without the most familiar trappings of science fiction as a named genre. My second reason for considering *The Man in the High Castle* here is that the novel is a metageneric work, one of whose chief aims is both implicitly and explicitly to interrogate the definitional structure of science fiction itself. I therefore conclude this chapter with the reading of a text that, partly through superficially appearing to be only dubiously or not at all science-fictional, critically estranges the question of just what science fiction really is.

As with any novel of alternative history, the founding critical strategy of *The Man in the High Castle* lies in its uncoupling of the necessary from the actual, and thus in its defamiliarization of the historical status quo. In historical actuality, the status quo of Dick's America (which is still, to a considerable degree, our own) was based largely on the Allied victory over the Axis in the Second World War: a literally epoch-making military triumph that led to the integration of the world's capitalist economies into a single bloc dominated by the United States and to the concomitant Cold War between the capitalist bloc and the always much weaker Stalinist bloc led until its defeat and collapse by the Soviet Union. So momentous was the outcome of World War II, and so crucial to U.S. supremacy, that hegemonic American ideology during the postwar era (and especially during the three decades of most intense U.S. triumphalism, that is, the American "century" that lasted from the unconditional surrender of Germany and Japan in 1945 until the beginning of the long economic decline around 1973) has generally represented the Allied success as inevitable and almost metaphysically sanctioned. And this representation has been greatly facilitated, of course, by the extreme evil of Nazism and the correlative "unthinkability" of an Axis victory. Composed at the high noon of postwar American success and self-confidence, Dick's novel—set in an America contemporary to the text's composition but in an alternative historical line in which Germany and Japan triumphed in World War II—undertakes, then, precisely to think the unthinkable.

To a considerable extent, however, the "unthinkable" turns out to be surprisingly familiar. In the Pacific States of America (a new country carved by the Japanese victors out of the western United States and, though nominally governed by a collaborationist clique in Sacramento, actually ruled by Tokyo through occupying Japanese authorities), social and psychic life display what Dick's fiction in general suggests to be the "normal" alienations and conundrums of human existence in the monopoly-capitalist America of his own era. It is symptomatic in this regard that Frank Frink, the structural and ideological center of this multiplotted text, is a quintessentially Dickian protagonist.

Cut very much from the same cloth as Rick Deckard in *Do Androids Dream of Electric Sheep?*, Joe Chip in *Ubik*, or Bob Arctor in *A Scanner Darkly* (to take several of the more memorable examples), Frank is a well-intentioned and reasonably competent man who nonetheless ultimately functions, for the most part, as a somewhat hapless hero of sheer ordinariness—a congenial but much harried proletarian who is buffeted by powerful transpersonal forces (sexual, economic, and political) far beyond his control or even his full understanding.

Sexually, for instance, he is defined by his lonely estrangement from his ex-wife Juliana, whose stunning physical beauty combines with a certain ominous air (she is a judo expert and eventually kills a man) to constitute a recognizably Dickian femme fatale. (But Juliana is probably the most benign representative of the type in Dick's fiction, just as Pat Conley in *Ubik* is the most sinister.) The unattainability (or irrecoverability) for Frank of the intensely desired Juliana amounts to one version of sexual alienation. The latter is equally, though differently, manifest in Juliana's own weary restlessness and lack of erotic clarity—traits that lead her, somewhat against her better judgment, into a brief affair with an overbearingly macho truckdriver who turns out to be a Gestapo assassin in disguise.

If such sexual alienation is as prominent in the PSA as in Dick's own world, the same is true of alienation on the economic level. Economic alienation is displayed in several varieties: most brilliantly, perhaps, in the elaborate portrait of Robert Childan, the owner of a small but expensive store that specializes in (mainly bogus) American handicrafts, and who, in his avarice, his bigotry, his cruelty, and his toadying servility toward the powerful, amounts almost to the paradigmatic subject of fascism. The shopkeeper Childan can, indeed, be read as a classical Marxist representation of the petit bourgeois at his worst. But it is Frank Frink who is, again, more central to the novel's structure. A skilled if not necessarily brilliant machinist employed by the Wyndam-Matson Corporation—a vast and powerful company owned by a hedonistic multimillionaire who counts as yet another of Dick's familiar character types—Frank loses his job after showing disrespect to his boss. In partnership with a friend, he then attempts to earn a living as an independent jewelry-maker (incidentally one of Philip Dick's own various occupations). It never becomes clear just how much economic success his tiny company Edfrank will finally have, but its initial vicissitudes (which include being manipulated and cheated by Robert Childan) are always difficult and often discouraging: so that Frank amounts to a case study of the alienation and vulnerability of the common man both as industrial proletarian in the strict sense and as independent artisan. Yet, in economic as in sexual matters, what Frank suffers is, after all, nothing more nor less than what any ordinary man might be forced to endure in Dick's own America. When Childan, smarmily attempting to ingratiate himself with an affluent Japanese couple, solemnly proclaims that the world would be "much worse" (106) if his own country had won the war, the reader cannot but reflect that, insofar as the PSA itself is concerned, the quisling Childan is wide of the mark—just as wide of the mark as those who would guess a Japanese-controlled America to be the kind of terroristic nightmare implied by such historical Japanese atrocities of the World War II era as the rape of Nanking or the Bataan death march. The differences between the 1962 California of actual history and that of *The Man in the High Castle* are simply a good deal less striking than one might have supposed. Paradoxically, part of the estranging effect of Dick's alternative America is that its Japanese sector does not seem so very strange at all.

Indeed, the Japanese hegemony in the PSA is represented as in many respects quite praiseworthy. The militaristic Tokyo government of the war years has been replaced by a regime more concerned with trade and commerce than with martial conquest, and the Japanese have established a Co-Prosperity Pacific Alliance: a successful state-directed capitalist framework in which (in a sharp contrast to Japan's actual Greater East Asian Co-Prosperity Sphere during the war) the Americans appear to function more as authentic (though junior) partners than as exploited subjects of imperialism. The prevailing Japanese civil code is known for being harsh but fair, and the Japanese officials who administer it enjoy an enviable reputation for personal incorruptibility. In a nice defamiliarization of actually existing racism, Caucasian Americans must learn to live without the kind of racial privilege they once enjoyed, as a yellow skin is now more likely to be the signifier of power. The Japanese, however, do not seem to have sponsored any systemic racism of their own. To be sure, life in the PSA is characterized by a certain austere discipline, inevitable given the presence of an occupying foreign power. But everyday existence is comparatively tolerable, and the Japanese authorities themselves—especially the one who appears most prominently, Mr. Nobusuke Tagomi, head of the San Francisco trade mission—are represented as humane and cultivated individuals.

In only one instance does Frank Frink suffer any misfortune in the PSA that would have been unthinkable in Dick's own United States: his brief imprisonment simply and solely on account of being Jewish, an identity he had tried to camouflage by altering his name from its original form of Fink. Yet the point here is that such anti-Semitic persecution is instigated not by the Japanese themselves but by their German allies; and Frank is released because of the personal intervention of Mr. Tagomi. More generally, in fact, the formal alliance between Germany and Japan is experiencing considerable strain: much of one of the novel's several plots concentrates on the tensions that have developed between the Axis superpowers. We learn that, despite the requirements of diplomatic politesse, Mr. Tagomi and his colleagues have long harbored considerable private contempt for their German counterparts and even a good deal of sympathy for the Jewish victims of Nazism, whose offense, after all, was to be—like the Japanese themselves—non-Aryan. It eventually comes as little surprise that the top Nazi rulers in Berlin are in the planning stages of Operation Dandelion, a nuclear attack intended to obliterate the home islands of Japan itself, leaving the overseas possessions of the Japanese empire to be taken over by the German Reich.

It is, indeed, the contrast between Germany and Japan that forms one of the main organizing conceptual principles of the novel. Whereas the Tokyo regime has developed from sanguinary Tojoist militarism to a robust semiliberal commercial capitalism that in many ways resembles the actual American-dominated economic system of Dick's own 1962, the post-Hitler Nazi hierarchy has remained intact and preserved its terrorist and genocidal nature (though it now commands the general respect and respectability that victors normally enjoy). The mass murder of the Jews has been nearly completed, and has been accompanied or followed, against equally little opposition or outrage, by the even more enormous Nazi projects of massively reducing the Slavs and virtually depopulating Africa. Germany is also pursuing a vigorous space program, and is widely admired as the world's technological leader in both military and civil matters. Further, the Germans have imposed their rule on the eastern portion of the old United States; and (unlike the PSA) the new society they establish there contrasts very sharply with Dick's own empirical environment. Though *The Man in the High Castle* declines to offer any direct representation of the German-controlled sector of America (no actual scenes of the novel are set east of Colorado and Wyoming), all reports suggest life there to be dominated by a Nazi terror similar to that which many European countries actually experienced. In marked contrast to the relative decency of the PSA, Americans nearer the Atlantic coast are said to live under a murderous totalitarianism in which the will of the secret police is almost absolute. The only dissenting voice at all widely heard is, evidently, the ineffectual one of Bob Hope, broadcasting mildly satiric anti-Nazi jokes from an insecure haven north of the Canadian border.

Yet, however thorough the terrible efficiency of the Nazi regime may be, what the Germans seem to lack is any genuine telos comparable to the peaceful commercial affluence pursued by the Japanese. Even as their pursuit of global (and, through the space program, even extraglobal) domination becomes more and more successful, and their subjugation or extermination of "lesser" peoples more and more complete, the question remains (troubling Frank Frink, for instance) as to what the real goal of such incessant and mainly destructive activity can be. The Nazis seem to have won as unconditional a victory as they could have hoped for. But what, from the Nazi viewpoint, is the *point* of victory? The clearest answer in the text is provided by Captain Rudolf Wegener, a highly placed but secretly anti-Nazi operative of the regular German military, and the only morally decent German that we see or hear about in the novel. Wegener's chief textual function (above and beyond the purely narrative role he plays in alerting the Japanese authorities to Operation Dandelion) is, in anthropological terms, that of the native informant, shedding light on the inner workings of the German mind: "Suppose [thinks Wegener] eventually they, the Nazis, destroy it all? Leave it a sterile ash? They could; they have the hydrogen bomb. And no doubt they would; their thinking tends toward that Götterdämmerung. They may well crave it, be actively seeking it, a final holocaust for everyone" (233). The allusion to the culminating opera of *The Ring of the Nibelung* (1874) is quite pertinent, just as the similarity of Wegener's name to that of the author of *The Ring* amounts to a slyly ironic joke by the musically erudite Dick. What he suggests here about the Nazi Germans is the same as what Nietzsche, in effect, maintained about the musical dramas of his hated contemporary, who fittingly became Hitler's favorite composer and the central figure of the Nazis' artistic pantheon: namely, that beneath the massive pomp, the mighty technical achievement, and the "Wagnerian" grandiosity and self-conceit, there lurks an essential nihilism and opposition to life.[59]

The philosophic and aesthetic terms with which Wegener attempts to make sense of his own culture register the way that the sociopolitical contrast that *The Man in the High Castle* draws between Germany and Japan resolves into what the text takes to be a more fundamental and determinant *spiritual* (that is, cultural and ideological) opposition: an opposition in which Germany and Japan function, at least in large part, as instances of the Western and Eastern value systems generally. The Eastern way, with its stress on enduring values, on fate, and on received nonutilitarian wisdom (this last concretized by the *I Ching*, which the Japanese and the sympathetic American characters, but not the Germans, frequently consult) is represented as naturally moderate and humane. If there is one term that sums up what the text upholds as the essence of Oriental spirituality, it is probably *wu*: a word whose origins, like those of the *I Ching* itself, are Chinese rather than Japanese (so that the ideological unity and continuity of the East, of which Japan is but the most politically powerful representative, are stressed). The novel never offers a precise translation of *wu*—perhaps because no Western language could exactly render so alien a concept—but it seems to be a kind of wisdom that is both worldly and otherworldly at once, an achievement of peaceful balance and proportion, and a true sense of fitting properly and without strain or force into the universe as a whole. *Wu* is not quite the exclusive preserve of the Orient; there are individual Westerners, especially, it appears, those of artistic achievement, who may have some grasp of the principle. For example, the young Japanese businessman Paul Kasoura credits some Edfrank jewelry with possessing *wu*. But only in the East, evidently, is *wu* the central value that drives

59. For Nietzsche's devastating critique of Wagner, see especially his final work, *Nietzsche Contra Wagner* (1888), conveniently available in English in *The Portable Nietzsche*, ed. and trans. Walter Kaufmann (Harmondsworth: Penguin, 1976), 661–683.

entire societies. One logical result is that Eastern societies will tend to be more humane than Western ones, for implicit in *wu* is the understanding that all life has value and a right to its own place in the cosmos. So deep-seated is *wu* that, for instance, Mr. Tagomi is seriously unbalanced and suffers something like a nervous breakdown when he is forced to take human life, even though he does so in a wholly justified defensive operation against Gestapo thugs.

Opposite to *wu* is the German—and generally Occidental—principle of will and domination (a principle subtly alluded to in the very name of Operation Dandelion, since the dandelion is the flower that constantly expands its dominion). In a way that strongly resonates with what Horkheimer and Adorno call the dialectic of enlightenment,[60] the novel sees Nazi atrocity as the extreme but perfectly logical extension of something typically and profoundly Western: the valorization of ceaseless activity, of agency, of expansion and acquisition and domination—in sum, of that relentless imperialism of the subject, which would conquer and colonize all that is not itself, even at the ultimate and paradoxical price of reducing itself to insubstantiality and at last to nothingness. For the inflationary, expansionist subject, having consumed everything other to itself, and so having drained the world of all objective solidity, must thus logically undermine its *own* objective reality and in the long run its own existence. It is not despite but rather *because* of the fact that the Nazis can have no definable goal short of universal holocaust, that they express more completely than anyone else in Western history the common but fatal preference for doing as against being, for the active as against the passive or copulative. Whereas Eastern *wu* partakes of the subtlety, the indirection, and the (in some ways) autotelic poise of art, the Western principle of willfulness depends on a ruthlessly instrumental and literal-minded logic of domination.

One especially noteworthy example in the novel is that, in the mistrustful geopolitical maneuvering between the superpowers, the Japanese often resort to codes based on metaphor and poetic allusion, having found that these work to "baffle the Reich monitors—who could crack any literal code, no matter how elaborate" (18). It is pertinent once again to quote from the thoroughly Dickian ruminations of Captain Wegener: "They [the Nazis] want to be the agents, not the victims, of history. They identify with God's power and believe they are godlike. That is their basic madness. . . . It is not hubris, not pride; it is inflation of the ego to its ultimate—confusion between him who worships and that which is worshiped. Man has not eaten God; God has eaten man" (38). Yet this ultimate egoism, this mad quest for total agency, cannot be dismissed as the aberration of a particular regime in a particular nation; it is but the purest and most uncompromising version of a tendency deeply woven into the

60. See Max Horkheimer and Theodor W. Adorno, *Dialectic of Enlightenment*, trans. John Cumming (New York: Seabury, 1972), esp. 3–42.

entire fabric of Western history—a tendency that, it can be argued, is at work at least as far back as the dominative (but finally self-denying) ruses of Odysseus in one of the founding documents of our culture.[61] History from Homer to Hitler and beyond can be understood as consisting largely in the progress of variations on this fundamental theme. For Dick—as for Horkheimer and Adorno—the association of the quintessential Western will to domination with the horrors of genocidal Nazism serves as a forceful estranging device to highlight just how lethal our Occidental civilization really is.

Especially our *American* civilization—as this, I think, is the most urgent point of Dick's cultural typologies. For the elaborate historico-philosophical scheme by which *The Man in the High Castle* contrasts Germany and Japan, West and East, should not, of course, be accepted uncritically. Both sides of the theory obviously suffer from at least some degree of essentialism (a charge to which Horkheimer and Adorno themselves are by no means immune), and Dick's attitude toward the Orient may be suspected of a certain naive (and, in the long run, unconsciously racist) sentimentalism born of relatively superficial knowledge. In particular, the notion of a sanely balanced and *wu*-filled East does not really cohere with the novel's representation of a thriving Japanese capitalism. Capitalism, after all, is necessarily driven by an expansionist and dominative dynamic, and even in its most liberal versions is inescapably dependent upon violence—though it is certainly true (and relevant to the novel's theoretical slip here) that in liberal capitalism of the sort that Dick portrays the violence may be largely *displaced*, geographically and otherwise, as the violence of fascism typically is not.

But Dick's most compelling interest is not in the Orient as such or in the (quite presciently) protohippie mysticism that centers on the *I Ching*.[62] The real focus, rather, is on his own country, and the prescience of *The Man in the High Castle* may also be located in certain anticipations of the New Left (with which Dick was, indeed, to become somewhat involved) and the latter's critique of America. Geographically located between East and West, between Asia and Europe, and in that sense perhaps irrevocably committed to neither, the United States is nonetheless clearly a part of Western civilization, with all the attendant dynamism and willfulness. Indeed, at the time of the novel's composition America was overwhelmingly the most powerful nation of the West, and of the world at large, and so approximated to the position of Germany in Dick's alternative history. Furthermore, not only was the United States politically and technologically supreme, but it was increasingly showing itself capable of its own atrocities. It is no accident that the novel was

61. Ibid. 43–80.
62. For an account of the typological scheme of *The Man in the High Castle* that does, however, lay greater stress than I do on the *I Ching* (and on Taoism generally), see Patricia Warrick, *Mind in Motion: The Fiction of Philip K. Dick* (Carbondale: Southern Illinois University Press, 1987), 40–58.

originally published during the early days of the American assault (which was always genocidal in at least one of its basic tendencies)[63] against Vietnam. It was thoroughly within the spirit of Dick's diagnosis that one fashion among New Left antiwar activists of a few years later was to give the name of America a German spelling.

In this sense, then, Dick's text may be interpreted as a plea for his country to *change course*, to abandon the path of dominative will, to be guided, as it were, more by its Pacific than by its Atlantic coast. Whatever precritical romanticism may inhere in Dick's view of Asian culture and society, this view must be understood first and foremost as a powerfully estranging heuristic device with which to foreground the terrible affinity between German fascism and the imperialist activism of American monopoly capitalism. It should further be noted that Dick's concern stems not only from sympathy for the prospective victims of American militarism but also, and perhaps even more urgently, from a quite direct patriotism. Dick's representation of a conquered and divided America memorably expresses the paradox always inherent in the dialectic of enlightenment. Just as the destructive will to control is inevitably self-destructive as well, so in the German-controlled sector of America the German principle of domination, which is also the American principle, has horribly transformed America almost beyond recognition. In the PSA, by contrast, the alien, Eastern values of *wu* have largely preserved America, so that life in the PSA resembles the still fairly tolerable American condition that Dick himself experienced in 1962. In its subtextual but important polemical aspect, *The Man in the High Castle* amounts to a petition not only against genocide but against national suicide too.

We are now in a position to appreciate just how profoundly and in what ways Dick's novel must be considered science-fictional, despite the fact that it generally eschews the futuristic science and technology so prominent in most of the work (including most of Dick's own work) self-consciously produced within the science-fiction tradition. *The Man in the High Castle* is constituted as science fiction at the point of the latter's closest affinity with the tradition of the historical novel in the Lukácsian sense. Though it is difficult to guess what Lukács himself would have made of this particular text (which he probably never saw), few novels of its era more powerfully express the critical sense of historicity—the sense that historical societies are complexly determined and mutable totalities, that historical actuality never possesses any transcendent ontological fixity but is always subject to dialectical interrogation and to the processes of material change—that Lukács understands as definitive of the

63. A truly adequate gloss on this parenthesis would amount to a full-scale account of the Vietnam War itself. But the fundamental principle relevant here is the one first formulated by Sartre in his critique of the French war in Algeria. Whenever a technologically sophisticated army tries to wipe out a guerrilla force that enjoys the overwhelming support of—and blends imperceptibly into—its own civilian population, then genocide is intrinsic to the logic of the situation.

genre of historical realism. We might say that, for Dick, the device of an alternative present serves much the same function, in the critical estrangement of the actual present, that is served by the actual past in the historical novel proper. Like most of Dick's fictions, *The Man in the High Castle* is concerned with the construction of different realities; in few of his other works, however, is the historical character of plural realities quite so compellingly stressed.[64]

The resulting estrangement of historical actuality—the demystification that the text implements of the sense of taken-for-grantedness that tends to congeal around the historical fait accompli—proceeds on several different but complexly related levels. In the first place, merely by tracing a history alternative to the Allied victory in the Second World War (and thus by showing an America not, as in the reality of 1962, self-confident and globally supreme, but defeated and dismembered instead) the text works to denaturalize the American arrogance of power. For American success is displayed as the reverse of inevitable. Far from finding the key to world leadership in any fixed metaphysical essence of the American character (the object of such triumphalist apotheosis in the most popular civic ideologies of the time), Dick humblingly stresses the degree to which the outcome of epochal historical contests may be determined by sheer chance. For the novel attributes America's military failure in large part to one pure contingency. The bullet that in fact missed Franklin Roosevelt in Miami in February 1933 is here imagined to have hit its target, thus sending the weak, conservative Southern Democrat John Nance Garner to the White House, to be succeeded in 1940 by the reactionary Republican Senator John Bricker. America was thus wholly unprepared for Pearl Harbor in 1941, and, with its allies, eventually succumbed to the combined might of Japan and Germany. On such details, Dick suggests, may the fate of empires turn.

But Dick does not critically estrange the America of 1962 only by showing that great events might have happened otherwise. He also estranges the character of victory and world domination; more specifically, he forces a cognitive reexamination of actual historical events by questioning, as we have seen,

---

64. Of course, Dick's work often regards the multiplicity of realities in metaphysical (and sometimes even theological) as well as in historical ways, and *The Man in the High Castle* is no exception: a significant portion of the novel is devoted to pondering the ultimate ontological status of alternative time lines and such closely related matters as the nature of authenticity itself (with regard, for instance, to the artifacts in Childan's shop). I am the more willing to deemphasize such questions in my own reading because this aspect of the book has thus far received much greater attention in the secondary literature on Dick than has the problematic of historical critique that I am pursuing here. See, for instance, Mark Rose, *Alien Encounters* (Cambridge, Mass.: Harvard University Press, 1981), 119–127; John Huntington, "Philip K. Dick: Authenticity and Insincerity," *Science-Fiction Studies* 15 (1988): 152–160; despite its title, George Slusser, "History, Historicity, Story," *Science-Fiction Studies* 15 (1988): 187–213; and—in my view the most conceptually agile and wide-ranging of these commentaries but one that largely shares the same concerns—John Rieder, "The Metafictive World of *The Man in the High Castle*: Hermeneutics, Ethics, and Political Ideology," *Science-Fiction Studies* 15 (1988): 214–225.

whether America *did* win World War II after all—in the sense, that is, of really triumphing in the name of those values of freedom and peace most widely upheld in postwar American nationalism. Because, in popular ideology, the ultimate moral sanction of the American-dominated postwar order always lay not only in anti-Communism but, even more definitively, in the totally successful and ethically unambiguous crusade against the Axis, *The Man in the High Castle* deeply subverts America's moral credentials for world leadership by locating Nazi evil within the larger Western phenomenon of the dominative will. The latter is not only something that America shares but (as the mere name of Vietnam can remind us) something that is, in 1962, making itself more and more manifest in American policy in murderous ways. A novel constructed on the counterfactual premise of Axis victory may run the risk of allowing the reader a considerable measure of escape and lazy intellectual comfort simply through the relief with which one can turn from fiction to real life—but not so easily if, as in this case, the novel forces one to ponder whether the actual America is, so to speak, in danger of really becoming Amerika.

The portrayal of Robert Childan, after all, reminds us that America is not without its own home-grown fascists, or potential fascists. And Dick compels us to consider the implications of such a character when we turn from the novel to a contemporary political reality in which America's national leaders happen to include Childan's phonetically and psychically similar counterpart, Richard Nixon.[65] On the other hand, it is also true that neither a potential fascist like Childan nor a contented fellow traveler of fascism like Wyndam-Matson (with his boyish hero worship of General Rommel and his happy acceptance of Nazi victory generally) constitute the whole story of America. America is also defined by Frank Frink, not only Jewish and hence necessarily anti-Nazi but a principled antiracist as well; by Ed McCarthy, Frank's brave and generous partner in the jewelry business; by Juliana Frink, whose anti-Nazism leads her to kill the Gestapo operative with whom she has been sleeping before he can complete his mission of assassination; and by the intended victim whom Juliana thus saves, the title character of the novel, Hawthorne Abendsen (whose role we shall consider shortly). Such morally admirable Americans—most of whom, it should be noted, allow themselves to be taught and their lives to be guided, to a considerable degree, by the *I Ching*—remind us that the United States is still a Pacific as well as an Atlantic nation. The text thus performs a third level of estrangement by suggesting that, if America's victory in the Second World War was not inevitable, neither

65. Nixon, in fact, seems to have been a figure of special loathing and contempt for Dick, as for so many other American radicals of his generation. The elegantly subtle hint of Nixon in *The Man in the High Castle* (for Childan does not really count as even a disguised portrayal) is counterpointed by the obvious and elaborate treatment of him, under the name of Ferris Fremont, in Dick's posthumously published novel *Radio Free Albemuth* (1985).

is its complete self-transformation into Amerika. In one way, the image of an America divided between its German and Japanese sectors is, paradoxically, a symbol of hope. It implies that America is not yet monolithic, that its fate is not yet sealed, that the values of *wu* may yet be within the American grasp.

This brings us, however, to the issue of sociopolitical change and more specifically to the role of human agency within sociopolitical change. The question is extremely difficult, for at this point the historical—or, in the Lukácsian sense, historicist—problematic of *The Man in the High Castle* is in some conflict with its metaphysical problematic, and especially with its Asian (or pseudo-Asian) mysticism. On the one hand, the insistence upon historical mutability is crucial to any novel of alternative history, and particularly, as we have seen, to a novel that engages historical alternatives so complexly and compellingly as Dick's text. On the other hand, when we ask exactly how change is to be *effected*, any positive answer seems to be blocked by at least two elements of the Dickian worldview. First, the very possibility of purposeful and consequential historical action is problematized by the importance that Dick assigns to chance, to sheer meaningless contingency. The Miami assassin who either succeeded or failed (depending upon the historical line) in murdering Roosevelt could hardly have predicted the coming of the Second World War, and surely never meant to determine his country's fate in the most important war of the century. If so momentous an outcome can be traced to the random and unintended, to the exact path of a single bullet, then it is unclear how anyone, whether in individual or collective action, can hope to exert a significantly intentional impact on the march of history.

Even if, however, this epistemological problem could be solved and the character of effective action for change could be clarified, there would still remain the second—and ethical—problem. Even assuming that we *know* how to alter events, are we *justified* in doing so? Does not the very attempt (and especially when it involves violence) necessarily participate in the will to dominate and so violate the principle of *wu*? Unlike some who have been attracted by Eastern quietism, Dick takes no comfort in the illusion that evil, if unresisted, will somehow wither away or transform itself into something more tolerable. Certainly the global Nazi regime in *The Man in the High Castle* shows no sign of doing anything of the sort. But can we really fight the Nazis without becoming like them? This is, as a matter of fact, precisely the agonizing dilemma that grips Mr. Tagomi, nearly costing him his sanity and even his life, after the shoot-out in his office. His protection of Captain Wegener from the Gestapo is in itself morally impeccable, and no means other than direct lethal force could possibly have achieved that end. Yet, for a man so committed to the noninstrumental ethic of *wu* as Tagomi, the use of force remains dreadfully culpable nonetheless. Though the typical Western reader finds it easy to justify Tagomi's action and even to applaud it as heroism, Tagomi himself remains bitterly upset and divided; when the novel leaves him he has still not succeeded in resolving his terrible conundrum.

To a considerable degree, this conundrum—how to become part of the solution without also becoming part of the problem?—is the novel's own. "We do not," as Wegener himself thinks, "have the ideal world, such as we would like, where morality is easy because cognition is easy" (236). But the question of purposeful action, though difficult, is not entirely unanswerable, and *The Man in the High Castle* is not completely without some sense that human beings can intentionally change the world for the better. For example, far less ambiguous, morally, than Tagomi's armed defense of Wegener is his pacific rescue of Frank Frink. To be sure, this rescue hardly counts, in any obvious way, as a world-historical action; Frank, as the typical Dickian protagonist, is not the kind of person whose name is likely ever to appear in a history book. But the implication may be that it is precisely *not* by grand and hence inevitably egoistic schemes, but by such apparently small projects of kindness and human solidarity—projects undertaken by and on behalf of fairly ordinary people—that the human race can hope to make genuine progress.

There seems to be another, though related, avenue to such progress as well. For the most part, the text displaces hope for effective change from the directly sociopolitical realm to that of the *aesthetic*. Because the true work of art is not driven by the egoistic greed to dominate, but is, on the contrary, perfectly balanced within itself and in that sense autotelic, it may be that art has a power to transform that need not be implicated in the imperialist activism of the dialectic of enlightenment. The creation of art is after all itself a process of transformation—"Yes," thinks Mr. Tagomi, as he contemplates a piece of Edfrank jewelry, "that is artist's job: takes mineral rock from dark silent earth transforms it into shining light-reflecting form from sky" (220)—but one that, far from continuing incessantly in a downward spiral toward nihilism, instead finds a peacefully achieved goal in the artwork itself. The successful creation of art, one might say, amounts to a version of mastery and purposeful action that remains innocent of domination and violence. Tagomi draws real spiritual sustenance from the small silver triangle, and there is a more general implication throughout the text that the artistic production of Frank Frink and Ed McCarthy may amount to the stirrings of a new American renaissance, of a movement toward new creativity and moral health. The mundane ordinariness of Frank and Ed—the fact that they appear as anything but world-historical figures in the grand Hegelian fashion—in this way seems almost to take on a Joycean celebratory quality. Part of the point may be that the importance of art lies in its humble, proletarian character—just as, according to Paul Kasoura, *wu* itself "is customarily found in least imposing places" (168).

The most prominent aesthetic achievement that we meet in Dick's novel is an instance of the particular art that was Dick's own: Hawthorne Abendsen's novel, *The Grasshopper Lies Heavy*. Within the world of *The Man in the*

High Castle, this is a counterfactual tale of alternative history, one in which the Allies defeated the Axis in the Second World War (though the details of Abendsen's text are different in many ways from those of real history). Although banned by the German authorities wherever they can impose their will—the Japanese, significantly, allow it to circulate freely—*The Grasshopper Lies Heavy* has become a wildly popular bestseller, constituting, indeed, the specific interest most widely shared among the diverse characters of *The Man in the High Castle*. Just as the jewelry produced by Edfrank is suffused with *wu*, so does Abendsen's novel possess a special affinity with the values of balance and wise passiveness: an affinity hinted at in the very title,[66] and confirmed when we eventually learn that the book was written with the assistance of the *I Ching*. *The Grasshopper Lies Heavy* also possesses—again like Edfrank's jewelry—a genuine transformative power, at least in the sense of touching people directly and awakening them to new possibilities. When Tagomi insists that "many books are actually alive. Not in metaphoric fashion. Spirit animates it" (65), he is speaking specifically of the *I Ching* and also of the Bible. His words, however, apply to Abendsen's novel as well, which is written in collaboration with one and named after the other of the texts he mentions. For the novel is not only popular in the strictly commercial sense, but seems to be gripping numerous readers and providing them with new insights into the noninevitability of the actually existing global hegemony of the Reich, thus critically defamiliarizing and demystifying the latter. Even the German consul in San Francisco—a quite unexceptional and bureaucratically thuggish minor Nazi official—cannot resist Abendsen's narrative. He is amazed by "the power of fiction, even cheap popular fiction, to evoke" (119), and well understands why his superiors think the book dangerous enough, from the Nazi viewpoint, to deserve suppression.

But the character who is most impressed by *The Grasshopper Lies Heavy* is undoubtedly Juliana Frink, who is also one of the text's sharpest readers. She comes to understand how Abendsen's novel (like any work of cognitive estrangement, it might be added) has as its ultimate concern not an invented world but a real one: "He told us about our own world . . . ," she thinks. "He wants us to see it for what it is. And I do, and more so each moment" (238). Mightily impressed by the possibility of, as she later puts it, a "way out" (244)

---

66. The enigmatic phrase comes from a Western rather than an Eastern religious source, but resonates strongly with what Dick regards as the essential Eastern attitude. The reference is to the Book of Ecclesiastes (12:5), and the immediate context is concerned mainly with describing old age. "The grasshopper lies heavy" has been variously interpreted to mean that the grasshopper is heavy with food, in contrast to the abnormally thin old man; that the grasshopper, who would not generally be thought of as heavy, nonetheless seems heavy when compared to the extremely light old man; and that the grasshopper is a metaphor for the old man, who is heavy only in the sense of being a burden to himself. (I am indebted here to *The Interpreter's Bible*, vol. 5 [New York: Abingdon, 1956].) What all these readings have in common is the stress on human helplessness and vulnerability, on the opposite of virile mastery.

of the status quo, Juliana not only kills her Nazi lover before he can assassinate the novel's author, but then herself pays a visit to Abendsen. Appropriately enough, he turns out to be a quite ordinary person, without the kind of grandeur or charisma that Wyndam-Matson attributes to Rommel. In fact, he is somewhat reminiscent of Juliana's ex-husband Frank, to whom she considers returning. Similarly, Abendsen's Cheyenne home turns out to be not the heavily armed fortresslike "high castle" of widespread gossip, but an ordinary middle-class dwelling; and Abendsen himself, as a student of the *I Ching* and a man in touch with the values of *wu*, declines even to carry a revolver. Because Abendsen appears as an onstage character only in the final few pages of *The Man in the High Castle*, it may seem odd that Dick accords him such centrality in his title. But an artist is to be judged by his art, and Abendsen earns his centrality through the achievement of *The Grasshopper Lies Heavy*. Though we cannot know what the ultimate effect of the book will be (such things cannot be predicted in advance), the evidence suggests that Abendsen's text, far from being dismissable as a mere bit of "cheap popular fiction," may well be the most remarkable counterhegemonic project that a conquered America has yet produced.

Of course, Hawthorne Abendsen is the exact counterpart of Philip K. Dick himself, at least in the sense that *The Grasshopper Lies Heavy* estranges the world of *The Man in the High Castle* in just the same way that *The Man in the High Castle* estranges our own world. Accordingly, the beneficent transformative capacity that Dick's novel suggests for *The Grasshopper Lies Heavy* is also something that it implicitly claims for itself. But the claim is compelling not only with regard to one particular text, but also with regard to that entire generic tendency, so often stigmatized, known as science fiction. If Abendsen's tale is, as Juliana finds, capable of telling us about our own world and even of suggesting a way beyond the status quo—if, in sum, it effects an estrangement of the sort that this entire essay has argued to be in close affinity with critical theory itself—then it is clear that the genre in which Abendsen writes may be more intellectually and politically serious than those wont to scorn it as cheap popular fiction could suspect. In one memorable passage, indeed, the metageneric function of Dick's novel becomes virtually explicit. When Paul Kasoura and his wife Betty are at dinner with their guest Robert Childan, *The Grasshopper Lies Heavy*, about which so many people in the PSA are talking, comes up in conversation. Since Robert has not read it (and, significantly, has no interest in so doing), Paul politely tells him what the novel is like:

"Not a mystery," Paul said. "On contrary, interesting form of fiction possibly within genre of science fiction."

"Oh no," Betty disagreed. "No science in it. Nor set in future. Science fiction deals with future, in particular future where science has advanced over now. Book fits neither premise."

"But," Paul said, "it deals with alternative present. Many well-known science fiction novels of that sort." To Robert he explained, "Pardon my insistence in this, but as my wife knows, I was for a long time a science fiction enthusiast." (103)

Betty presents the commonsense or philistine view of science fiction, Paul a more critical one. Betty sees science fiction exclusively as narratives of the future, with the future itself understood in progressivist and positivistic terms that foreground the linear advance of "science" (that is, the physical sciences) and technology—a view of science fiction that, perhaps not incidentally, happens to be fairly widespread in Germany. Paul, on the other hand, understands (what Dick himself demonstrates throughout the novel) that the character of the genre lies neither in chronology nor in technological hardware, but in the cognitive presentation of *alternatives* to actuality and the status quo. Though it may seem ironic that Dick won his only major science-fiction award for a novel that its original publisher did not even consider science fiction, the irony is in fact much finer: namely, that Dick won his Hugo for a novel that demonstrates how the fundamental conceptual structure of the genre may be preserved while discarding the superficial trappings with which Hugo Gernsback tried to identify it. In its critical estrangement of Dick's own America, *The Man in the High Castle* is not only authentic science fiction but one of the crowning masterpieces by the most endlessly fascinating master of the genre.

Coda
Critical Theory, Science Fiction, and the Postmodern

A s we have seen, it is in the nature of both critical theory and science fiction to speculate about the future. It seems appropriate, then, to conclude this book with some speculations about the future of critical theory and science fiction themselves. In order to do so, it is necessary to coordinate each of these categories with our current historical moment, which is usually designated the moment of the postmodern. First, however, we must try to get some sense of just what this very widespread but often ambiguous term can usefully be made to mean.

The first difficulty of any discussion involving the postmodern is the lack of any clear and comprehensive sense, at all widely shared, of exactly what the postmodern is. The self-contradictory structure of the word itself no doubt invites confusion, since, strictly speaking, *nothing* is postmodern. By definition, nothing is subsequent to the modern—except, of course, those things that have not yet happened, though when they do happen they will be modern too. Every actual use of the term therefore requires a deliberate straining beyond its literal sense, and there have been so many such uses significantly different from one another that no particular usage has been able to establish itself securely. To make matters yet more complicated, the general condition of the postmodern is designated by two distinct nouns that have by no means always functioned as exact synonyms: postmoder*nity* and the more familiar postmoder*nism*. The latter term is not only more frequently encountered but somewhat simpler and less imprecise in its general connotations, and to it I will first turn.

Postmodernism may seem a comparatively manageable concept because it has most often been used with regard to fairly specific matters of artistic style and form—originally, of course, in architecture, though more commonly now in connection with literature (as well as with those partly literary and partly visual arts enabled by the development of film and television technology). Although in strict terms there may be nothing after modernity, there is certainly a flourishing literature that postdates the moment of classical modernism: the moment, that is, of that once scandalous and now securely canonical body of literature that was produced around the time of the First World War (as the long liberal reign of entrepreneurial capital was coming to a close and the dominance of monopoly capital was making itself felt) and that is most famously instanced by such names as W. B. Yeats, Paul Valéry, T. S. Eliot, Marcel Proust, James Joyce, Ezra Pound, Virginia Woolf, Rainer Maria Rilke, Vladimir Mayakovsky, and D. H. Lawrence. Of course, there have been many literary tendencies in the decades since these authors emerged, and most—for example, the realist (or perhaps, in Lukácsian terms, naturalist) revival of the 1930s that is represented by diverse authors from Graham Greene to Dashiell Hammett—have rarely been described as postmodernist. Usually, the category is reserved for work that not only comes after literary modernism (and, more specifically, after the Second World War) but that is held to respond to the modernist aesthetic directly, intensely, and ambivalently.

In this understanding, postmodernist work avails itself of all the revolutionary technical innovations of the great modernists but deploys them in essentially different ways and with different aims in view. The basic contrast generally adduced is that modernism tends toward the monumental and the mythic, while postmodernism works to undermine such totalizing structural principles, favoring instead a protodeconstructive stress on the marginal, the fragmentary, and the heterogeneous. According to this view, the characteristic modernist tone is lofty and not infrequently tragic, while postmodernism inclines more readily toward the ribald and comic, and sometimes toward a certain flattening of affect altogether. Modernism upholds the traditional authority of high art, while postmodernism revels in a scandalous mixing of high and low, of traditional humanistic culture with the culture of mass society. Modernism, in fine, remains, for all its sense of irony, committed to the classic aesthetic project, whereas postmodernism strives to break decisively with the category of the aesthetic. Although (and perhaps significantly) the central names of the postmodernist pantheon are not quite so obvious as is the case with modernism, most commentators would agree that, if there is a postmodern literary canon, it must include such work as the drama of Samuel Beckett and the French *nouveau roman*, the novels of Thomas Pynchon and of William Burroughs, the poetry of Frank O'Hara and the journalism of Tom Wolfe.

This formal description of postmodernism, in contrast to modernism, seems, then, to be fairly clear. Unfortunately, it is also of extremely limited usefulness. If it seems plausible, and if it has attained a certain degree of acceptance, that is, I think, because it does incisively describe the relations that obtain among a relatively small number of widely familiar texts. The stylistic opposition adumbrated above does seem to hold so long, for example, as we think of modernism in terms of the drive toward ahistorical mythic totalization and the protoreligious solemnity of *The Waste Land* (1922), and of postmodernism in terms of the humorous pop-cultural satire, the celebratory antinomianism, and the stress on the fragment irrecuperable into any totality that characterize such William Burroughs texts as *Naked Lunch* (1959) or *Cities of the Red Night* (1981).

In the great majority of concrete instances, however, the opposition breaks down hopelessly when pressed at all. What of *Ulysses* (1922), a text as central to the modernist canon as any one could name, which, however, prominently exhibits nearly every formal characteristic ever held to distinguish postmodernism? Even the elaborate system of Homeric parallels functions (at least among other ways) as a kind of immense running joke, a humorous demonstration that in the age of newly intensified commodification and of the floating signifier—an age marked by Leopold Bloom, the wandering canvasser of newspaper advertisements—almost anything can be made to mean almost anything else. What of so major a figure as William Carlos Williams? His dates (1883–1963) suggest him to be a modernist, and the architectonics of *Paterson* (1946–1958) can be interpreted so as to make that belated epic appear to be a modernist survival in a predominantly postmodern age. Yet his lyrics, early and late, have much more in common with postmodernist form as the latter is most widely understood; and Williams has doubtless been the leading influence, among poets of his generation, on American verse during the era of postmodernism. What of Brecht? Chronologically (1898–1956) more modernist than postmodernist, he scandalously abuses the whole category of the aesthetic and celebrates the irreverences of plebian humor in ways that may seem to align him with postmodernism. At the same time, however, he maintains an unswervingly one-sided political commitment that would seriously embarrass that decorum of indeterminacy often associated with the postmodern. What, indeed, of Pynchon, who might well be considered the most typical of all postmodern novelists (at least in English), yet whose postmodernism coexists, in such works as *The Crying of Lot 49* (1966) and *Gravity's Rainbow* (1973), with a sense of literary architecture and an attention to the totally *wrought* character of the literary artifact that beautifully cohere with the highest standards of high modernism? These are but a few instances of the confusion inherent in the conventional opposition between modernism and postmodernism. Examples could easily be multiplied.

It seems to me, then, that any merely formal or stylistic distinction—any properly *aesthetic* distinction—between modernism and postmodernism must come to grief. Ingenious attempts can be—and have been—made to "save the appearances" (as Owen Barfield would say); that is, to preserve the distinction by greater and greater complication, by admitting instances of modernist survival and postmodernist anticipation, of modernist elements in predominantly postmodernist work and vice versa (just as the Ptolemaic model of the solar system can be preserved by introducing a greater and greater complexity of variables). But such efforts are unconvincing. It is not a matter of admitting a reasonable number of qualifications to a basically valid generalization, but of the "qualifications" becoming so extensive as to undermine any such validity in the first place. The examples above are taken from literature. A similar deconstruction of the binary opposition between modernism and postmodernism could, however, be offered with regard to music (where, for instance, serious consideration of Alban Berg and perhaps even of Stravinsky would undermine the superficially plausible idea of a progression from Schoenbergian modernism to the postmodernism of John Cage or Philip Glass) and to the plastic arts (where, even leaving aside the astonishing case of the uniquely proto-postmodernist Marcel Duchamp, one could, for example, argue that the cartoon quality that seems so quintessentially postmodern in Warhol or Roy Lichtenstein is prefigured almost in toto in high Cubism itself).

As for the newer arts, here the same sort of formal and stylistic complexities are further complicated by considerations of a more specifically historical sort. If one insists upon imposing a (merely aesthetic) periodization of modernism and postmodernism on film, then one is presented with an art whose very advent is inseparable from the moment of modernism: an odd notion, since the modernism of the more traditional arts presupposes—on the most immanent, formal level—older and more familiar aesthetic practices (the realist narrative, the sonata form, the representational portrait) to estrange and supersede which is precisely the modernist vocation. Television and rock music present still odder cases, as these arts do not come into being until the postmodernist era; they thus suggest the possibility of a postmodernism that is posterior to no modernism of its own. Oddest of all, perhaps, is the situation of the music video—sometimes considered the most thoroughly postmodern kind of artistic construction—which makes its first appearance more than a generation after the advent of postmodernism, and which thus may call for yet newer terminological contortions (post-postmodernism?).

At this point, then, one may well be tempted to jettison all oxymoronic prefixes and to declare that there is simply *modernism*. We may conclude that modernism is characterized by a complex heterogeneity of styles across many arts old and new, and that, though it first came clearly into view at the moment of Joyce and Proust and Eliot and Schoenberg and Picasso, it is—like so much else that also first emerged at approximately that moment, from the automobile to the sexual revolution—still very much with us today. The most efficient, and by no means the least plausible, solution to the problem of the postmodern is to pronounce it a false problem in the first place.

Yet this solution, though preferable to nearly all attempts to construct a rigidly aesthetic (or anti-aesthetic) theory of postmodernism, does fail to account for some genuine distinctions. The example of the music video, in fact, supplies a useful clue. It is not only that this artistic practice seems to lack any clear formal prehistory—in the sense, that is, that the prehistory of Pynchon is in Joyce, or that the prehistory of Joyce and Proust is in the nineteenth-century realist novel. The more salient contrast is that the music video, born near the dawn of the Reagan era, springs to life full-grown, so to speak, from the collective head of several immensely wealthy and powerful multinational corporations. There is practically no gradual evolution or progress from appreciation by an intense coterie to wider acceptance. Almost literally overnight, the music video passes from nonexistence to instant availability throughout the cable television systems of the United States. This postmodern situation could hardly differ more sharply from, say, the poverty and neglect in which *Ulysses* was composed, not to mention the reception that Joyce's novel received upon publication: a reception that for many years was marked both by literary (and legal) condemnation and by commercial failure. Respectable—especially academic—opinion seemed uncertain only as to whether *Ulysses* was to be regarded more as disgusting, obscene, and degraded, or merely as mad and unreadable. The contrast here is not only with the sometimes controversial but nonetheless safe and profitable videos of MTV and its imitators. It is also with, for instance, *Gravity's Rainbow*, which (despite the famous difficulties of a Pulitzer jury) was virtually a secure academic classic on the day it was published, assured of respectful literary attention and steady sales in collegiate bookstores.

Once, then, we cease to direct our attention myopically upon matters of immanent aesthetic form alone, and begin also to consider questions of reception and socioeconomic "context," a reasonably tenable distinction between modernism and postmodernism does begin to become clear. Modernism represented an artistic revolution whose specifically formal aspect found its "social equivalent" in the actual biographical and historical struggles of the great modernists and their work—struggles conducted largely in *poverty*, the most pervasive, stubborn, and unglamorous signifier of ruling-class disapproval. The modernist project amounted to rebellion in something more than the conventionally figurative sense, and was generally a lonely enterprise, undertaken without the support, and often against the active opposition, of established social networks and institutions. Even Eliot, with his high-toned family background and his impeccably genteel, right-wing viewpoint, found that being attacked by conservative literary opinion as a "literary bolshevik" and as a "drunken helot" could entail isolation and even some measure of the material deprivation that actual helots have experienced. In postmodernism, this moment of struggle and poverty has for the most part been absent. The great postmodernists have been able to enjoy—with big capital and with the dominant institutions of bourgeois society generally—a relationship more congenial than would ever have been thinkable in the modernist era proper. Whatever the political claims that may be made for certain particular works of postmodernist art, the general conditions of postmodern cultural production have displayed relatively little antagonism vis-à-vis the centers of social and economic power. The half-starving Montparnasse painter producing modernist masterworks for an indifferent or hostile world, though by now a cultural stereotype, was originally a real enough figure. The postmodernist successor is likely to be adequately fed and even to be receiving lucrative commissions from banks and high-tech firms interested in decorating the walls of their corporate headquarters.

To some degree, of course, postmodernism has received a kinder and gentler reception precisely because of the modernist revolution in aesthetic taste. The essential stylistic continuity between modernism and postmodernism allowed the former to clear the socioaesthetic ground, as it were, for the latter. Not the least prominent feature of the postmodern era that opened shortly after the Second World War was the canonization (academic and otherwise) of the modernist classics, no longer experienced as outrages against decorum. I do not offer that, however, as the most important point of comparison between modernism and postmodernism. Nor do I mean to imply some crudely political contrast between a heroically revolutionary modernism, bravely resisting the dominant forces of the time and paying dearly for such integrity, and a cowardly, collaborationist postmodernism, eagerly embracing a cozy relationship with the masters of the status quo. The basic flaw that vitiates such a scheme is not so much its moralism as the fact that it finally amounts to yet another version of the vain attempt to draw a decisive distinction between modernism and postmodernism on immanent and formal grounds. Like other such versions, it may appear valid in some instances but is far too simplistic for general applicability.

In order to draw a really tenable distinction between modernism and postmodernism, it is necessary to *historicize* the terms of the comparison radically. What is crucial here is not the postmodern aesthetic (or anti-aesthetic), but, instead, the situation of the aesthetic itself in the postmodern age. We might say that what really counts for an understanding of postmodernism is not the relationship of postmodernism to capital but—a not unrelated but nonetheless very different thing—the relationship of capital to postmodernism. In other words, the character of postmodernism, or of postmodern cultural production, is inseparable from the specifically socioeconomic condition of postmodern*ity*.

Postmodernity, in turn, must be understood in connection with that particular period of modernity responsible for modernism as such. I have already identified this period as the time around the First World War, the era distinguished in economic terms by the early stages of monopoly capital (or what Lenin described as the imperialist phase of capitalism) and in technical terms by that moment of industrialization marked by the preeminence of automotive and electrical technologies. What now needs to be stressed about the modernist era is that—as scholars in several fields and from various points of view have begun to emphasize[1]—modernism sprang from a socioeconomic

1. For instance, I am here indebted to Marshall Berman, *All That Is Solid Melts into Air* (New York: Simon and Schuster, 1983) and, even more, despite certain particular disagreements and differences in terminology, to Perry Anderson's major critique and reworking of Berman's argu-

matrix in which the power of essentially *pre*modern survivals was still considerable and in many ways even dominant, and in which the struggle between the modern and the premodern was especially intense. It is thus hardly surprising that tendencies on the cutting edge of modernity, such as the aesthetic masterpieces of modernism, had to struggle against strong resistance. From the social dominance of an agrarian ruling class in the France that formed Proust to the ideological dominance of the Roman Catholic Church in the Ireland that formed Joyce, from the Junkerdom of Brecht's Germany to the Czarist semifeudalism of Mayakovsky's Russia, modernism was produced by a modernity that still had many of its decisive battles yet to win against the forces of aristocracy, agrarianism, royalism, and religious reaction.

Modernism, in other words, arose as the extremely various and internally heterogeneous aesthetic of a curious temporal conjuncture that combined the most regressive social trends with those of progressive modernization (whether towards socialist or increasingly capitalist goals). All historical moments, of course, are moments of struggle and transition. But this commonplace applies to the moment of modernism in an especially powerful and thoroughgoing way. The peculiar complications of the historical moment help explain not only the wildly differing political connotations of modernist art (from Yeats, Eliot, and Pound on the far right to Brecht, Mayakovsky, and Hugh MacDiarmid on the far left), but also the unusually furious opposition against which the modernist project was conducted. The conservative rear guard was able to sense that the battles of which *Ulysses* and *The Waste Land* gave evidence could by no means be confined to the aesthetic realm alone. It is surely no coincidence that the nation in which modernism found its readiest and warmest welcome was the one in which the process of social modernization was most advanced and premodern survivals weakest, namely, the United States. And it is equally no coincidence that the most considerable modernist artist of American birth and residence—William Faulkner—was shaped by rural Mississippi, one of the few areas of North America that (mainly owing to a premodern agricultural order in the aftermath of chattel slavery) was socially structured by much the same sort of conflictual conjuncture that defined modernist Europe.

Least of all is it a coincidence that the global event (indeed, in most ways the *first* of all truly global events) that we have uncontroversially taken to mark the chronological border between modernism and postmodernism in art—namely, the Second World War—is also the epoch-making social upheaval that radically redrew the balance of forces between archaic survival

---

ment, "Modernity and Revolution" (in *Marxism and the Interpretation of Culture*, ed. Cary Nelson and Lawrence Grossberg [Urbana: University of Illinois Press, 1988], 317–338). Not the least valuable of Anderson's points is the importance he ascribes to Arno Mayer, *The Persistence of the Old Regime* (New York: Pantheon, 1982).

and deepening modernization, overwhelmingly to the advantage of the latter. The new era inaugurated in 1945—characterized by the increasing multinationalization of monopoly capital and by the growing preeminence of nuclear, electronic, and computer technologies—is thus one in which modernity has to an unprecedented degree come into its own: so that modernity is no longer so elaborately defined by a vital agon with its premodern other. This, the era of postmodernity, might therefore more usefully be called the era of *pure* modernity—which means, particularly within the metropolitan nations of what used to be called the First World, an era in which capital itself is now more untrammeled than at any previous point in history. Postmodernity, we might say, is the era in which capitalist modernization is so thoroughly triumphant that, owing to the lack of that contrast on which visibility depends, it becomes somewhat difficult to see.

The argument I am suggesting here is very close to that of Fredric Jameson, whose several treatments of the postmodern have some claim to be considered, at least for the time being, as the canonical account of the matter. The postmodern condition, Jameson writes, "is what you have when the modernization process is complete and nature is gone for good,"[2] or, in somewhat ampler terms, the situation "in which late capitalism has all but succeeded in eliminating the final loopholes of nature and the Unconscious, of subversion and the aesthetic, of individual and collective praxis alike, and, with a final fillip, in eliminating any memory trace of what thereby no longer existed in the henceforth postmodern landscape."[3] The most serious qualification that I would make to this description of postmodernity is to emphasize, more than Jameson himself does, the importance of the "all but" in *all but succeeded*. My point is not only the Habermasian one (maintained in chapter 1) that modernity to this day remains in specifically definable ways incomplete, especially on the cultural and ideological levels though not necessarily only there. Even in more general and abstract terms, it may be doubted whether any such fully achieved totalitarianism of the postmodern as Jameson evokes can ever really be attained, whether all traces of anything other than capitalist modernization can really be eliminated down the Orwellian memory holes.[4] We must leave open the possibility not only of authentic subversion (which may well be nearly impossible to imagine concretely today) but also, and more ominously, the possibility of a yet more postmodern—that is, a more completely

2. Fredric Jameson, *Postmodernism* (Durham: Duke University Press, 1991), ix.
3. Fredric Jameson, *Late Marxism* (London: Verso, 1990), 5.
4. Cf. Katherine Hayles in her critique of the Baudrillardian theory of simulation, often taken to be the quintessence of the postmodern: "Within contemporary culture . . . simulacra are unevenly dispersed, dominant in some places and scarcely visible in others. The Iowa farmer who has spent the day inspecting his seed corn, feeding his hogs, and spreading manure on his garden will not be easily persuaded that he lives in a world where it is no longer possible to distinguish between simulation and reality"; Hayles, "The Borders of Madness," *Science-Fiction Studies* 18 (November 1991): 321.

modernized and commodified—age than our own. At the same time, Jameson's description powerfully registers not only the momentous socioeconomic shift after the Second World War, but also the properly postmodern structure of feeling, the sense we do sometimes have of living in a wholly modernized environment, especially, perhaps, when we look back with some nostalgia to the modernist era itself (though it is not inconceivable that our own era will one day be the object of a similar *Heimweh*).

Accordingly, the postmodernity of art, or that which is manifest on the aesthetic level as postmodernism, is defined by the penetration, by capital, of artistic production, as of other varieties of social production, to a degree previously unprecedented. If much postmodern art has been able to maintain a relationship with big capital that may seem, by strictly modernist criteria, to be shockingly cozy, this nexus must be understood not in primarily moralistic or stylistic terms, but in the context of a general historical situation in which all departments of life are structured by capitalist modernization—by the ruthlessly quantitative and external ratios of exchange-value—in ways and to a degree hitherto unimaginable. It cannot, of course, be denied that such a socioeconomic matrix of art must leave its imprint on the properly formal and stylistic level. Yet, as we have seen, it remains impossible to bring any generally valid aesthetic discrimination between modernism and postmodernism into clear focus: partly because the processes of capitalist modernization are themselves very unevenly structured and already powerfully at work during the era of modernism, but also because of the extreme internal variousness of modernist style inherited by the postmodernists, itself doubtless an overdetermined effect of the unusually high degree of socioeconomic complexity that characterizes the modernist period. Though a more exhaustive formal inventory of modernist and postmodernist art than has yet been attempted might well suggest certain aesthetic tendencies to be somewhat more typical of one or the other, the aesthetic dimension alone cannot characterize postmodernism with any real rigor. Such characterization can be achieved only when postmodernism is situated within postmodernity; we may note that it is in this sense, rather than in any more narrowly stylistic one, that certain of the newer art forms can be usefully analyzed as privileged examples of postmodern cultural production. In television, in rock music, and perhaps above all in the music video (though not, in the same way, in the older medium of film), postmodernism is directly and inextricably bound up with some of the defining features of postmodernity, most clearly on the merely technological level but also (when one considers the political economy of the major media corporations) on the socioeconomic level as well.

The question of postmodernism—of postmodern art—should not, however, be engaged without also raising the more fundamental question of the general situation of art in the era of postmodernity. And here again a certain historical perspective of the sort discouraged by postmodernity itself is necessary. For at least two centuries capitalist modernization has tended to determine the status of art in antithetical ways. On the one hand, the regime of capitalist exchange works to marginalize all aspects of social production that do not directly contribute to the extraction and realization of surplus-value (to the "bottom line," in the jargon of current popular economics). In this way, the tendency of capitalism is to eliminate art altogether; and the contempt that the bourgeois philistine has for the "uselessness" of art is deepened and complicated by the suspicion that art may be not only useless but dangerous, that it may harbor a potential for social subversion. On the other hand, the blankly an-aesthetic condition that this tendency seems to imply has never proved ideologically feasible for any actual capitalist society. However pointless or suspect the realm of feeling may be according to the strict logic of capital, practical capitalist dominance has never been able to manage completely without it. Indeed, as capitalism melts into air all that is rich and solid in social life generally, the importance of art, and of the aesthetic as a specialized department of life, is in some ways actually *enhanced:* the aesthetic becomes one of the few oases available in the general affective aridity. This contradictory social situation is the matrix not only of postmodernism and of modernism before it, but also, of course, of realism and of Romanticism itself—in sum, of all the tendencies of aesthetic production under the fully dominant regime of exchange-value.

Capitalism, then, cannot exactly accept or exactly reject art. But it can exactly *colonize* art, sponsoring and shaping in one way what it strives to obliterate utterly in another. Postmodernity, as the apex (thus far) of capitalist modernization, thus represents the most extreme point to date of *both* contradictory tendencies inherent in the rule of capital. On the one hand, the postmodern condition, with its increasing homogeneity of commodification and its destruction of historical memory, and with its desperately single-minded devotion to the expansion of the global capitalist market, is in some ways as an-aesthetic a condition as humanity has yet achieved (a development not unrelated to the hostility toward the idea of the aesthetic sometimes found within postmodernist aesthetic production). Yet, at the same time, this very anaesthesia creates an unparalleled need for works of art, a need met in unparalleled abundance. Postmodernity is at once the least and the most aestheticized of all eras. If capital has with one hand squeezed the aesthetic most completely out of social life in general, it has with the other hand saturated society with an unprecedented number of individual artworks. Once again, the newer electronic forms probably have a special importance in this regard (one thinks, for example, of the degree to which a hit rock song or a successful television situation comedy can penetrate our social consciousness), though we should not underestimate the vast continuing importance of print itself, which is much more widely disseminated now than at any prior moment of history. Furthermore, postmodern art is not only, as we have seen, uniquely colonized by capital and thus frequently on friendly terms with it; artistic production is also becoming an increasingly significant fraction of multinationalized capitalist economic production itself. The most urgent paradox inherent in the situation of art under postmodernity, however, is also the most thoroughly political. It is clear that under postmodernity art must experience unique difficulty in establishing perspective on its social "context," in developing its potential for utopian prefiguration. But never, and for precisely the same reasons, has utopia in art been more desperately needed.

This consideration brings us, finally, to the coordination of the postmodern with the first term of this essay as a whole: critical theory. What we are now in a position to see is that the situation of critical theory under postmodernity resembles, to a considerable degree, that of the aesthetic itself, though with some significant differences that render the critical project even more difficult and problematic than the artistic one. Like art, critique is "useless" from the strict viewpoint of the extraction of surplus-value in the increasingly pervasive, globalized capitalist market. Even more than art, critique is also vulnerable to the further stigma of being potentially dangerous to the hegemony of the bourgeoisie. For, as we saw in chapter 1, critical thinking, with its insistence upon the dialectical interrogation of the given, can hardly adopt a wholly affirmative stance vis-à-vis any status quo. Furthermore, the somewhat compensating tendency of bourgeois society with regard to art—the practical ideological necessity for certain oases of affectivity and the correlative inflation of the aesthetic as a specialized and colonized terrain of social life—is almost entirely lacking in the case of critical theory. Indeed, it is not clear that the dominant middle-class order really requires any thinking at all above the level of mere technique, save perhaps in the very long run: and any long-term perspective that can encompass, for instance, the eventual social dangers (even from the capitalist viewpoint) of capitalist deindustrialization is likely also to encompass the unwelcome point that capitalism itself, as a necessarily expansionist system, must ultimately meet its own absolute limits. But the massive institutional and, as it were, formal hostility of postmodernity toward critical thought that is consequent upon such conditions does not exhaust the difficulty of the postmodern critical project. There are also problems of a more internal sort, problems that once again apply to art but impinge against critique with even greater force.

The point here is not only that the totality that must form the ultimate object of genuinely critical thought—the world capitalist system—becomes increasingly hard to conceptualize as it becomes increasingly comprehensive and unchallenged. It is not only that, consequently, the postmodern destruction of historical memory places special obstacles in the path of historical (and so of dialectical) thinking. It is also—and this is perhaps the most deeply anticritical tendency of the postmodern—that postmodernity, even while rendering the very category of totality difficult to grasp, renders *itself* into so increasingly smooth, self-sufficient, and perfectly rounded a totality that it becomes harder and harder to find a point of purchase from which to launch any praxis of the sort associated with critical theory. Such a project seems, to a greater and greater degree, to be like climbing a wall of glass. The most obvious (and in my view the central) example is the current lack of any properly postmodern strategic model that would concretize for our era the Marxist concept of revolution. Clearly, the Leninist concept of the revolutionary party, which may have fulfilled that need during the era of modernism, has been decisively overtaken by history—not so much by the collapse of the Soviet Union and of East European Communism, as by the same apparent irresistibility of global capital ultimately responsible for those Stalinist failures—and the resulting lack is still to be made good. Yet much the same pattern is observable in areas of critical theory and praxis far removed from the vicissitudes of Marxism-Leninism. In psychoanalysis, for instance, therapeutic practice may continue; it is increasingly compromised, however, not only by the socially conformist "neo-Freudian revisionism" that Marcuse shrewdly identified near the beginning of the postmodern era,[5] but, even more drastically, by the various pharmaceutical evasions of psychic desire available to a heavily medicated institutional psychiatry.[6]

Increasingly deprived, then, of a concrete grounding in actual praxis, critical theory increasingly loses ground to numerous and various versions of a precritical empiricism; while praxis itself tends to decompose into a miscellaneous collection of well-intentioned but more or less local and frequently myopic "activisms." The perspective of the dialectic becomes harder and harder to attain, while, in a pathetic irony, the weaker versions of postmodern positivism mindlessly proclaim the dialectic to be conceptually superseded. The overriding irony here is that—as in the case of art in its dimension of providing anticipatory illuminations of utopia—critical theory is made difficult by precisely the same forces that make it less dispensable than ever before. Critical thinking, despite all its problematic character, becomes one of the few alternatives to absolute capitulation before the commodified actuality of the postmodern. Once again, however, the critical may be in an even less privileged position under postmodernity than the aesthetic. Art—though certainly not without a major dimension of collectivity, as artists from Homer (presumably) to Brecht would remind us—has never depended upon the collective projects of praxis in quite the same way that critical theory has. Ac-

---

5. See Herbert Marcuse, *Eros and Civilization* (Boston: Beacon, 1955), esp. 238–274.

6. It is symptomatic that today, at least in North America, psychoanalysis is ordinarily considered as a part or variety of psychiatry, whereas Freud himself normally uses the two terms almost as antonyms.

cordingly, art can perhaps flourish under postmodernity to a degree that critique cannot; for art bears a somewhat less fraught relation to the limits of merely individual creativity.

One implication, then, would be that critical theory under the dominance of the postmodern must, at least in some ways, more nearly approximate the situation of art. This is not to announce, much less to celebrate, the aestheticization of thought, nor is it necessarily to propose as *generally* valid any counter-Hegelian supersession of philosophy by art. It is merely to accept (rather in that Carlylian sense in which one had better accept the universe) that the ultracommodified condition of postmodernity, having rendered the possibility of praxis extremely dubious at best, has necessarily cast the critical project into those largely individual terms traditionally more familiar to the project of the aesthetic. In such circumstances, critical theory can hardly attain the sort of confident collective sweep that distinguishes the writings of Marx or Freud themselves. Instead, critique is more likely to appear in the form of the individual intervention and to be characterized more markedly than ever before by the achievements of individual *style*. Yet it need not and indeed must not therefore lose its defining dialectical character, its stake in unyielding reflexivity and in the potential for emancipatory change of the social totality. On the contrary, a stubborn commitment to the radical potentialities of the dialectic becomes more urgent, as we have seen, precisely as it becomes more difficult and problematic.

Perhaps still the finest example in this regard is one of the first great works of postmodern critical theory, Adorno's *Minima Moralia* (1951). The very subtitle, *Reflections from Damaged Life*, proclaims the primacy of the individual standpoint—a primacy further consolidated by the generic form of the text, which is structured as a series of very brief essays on an immense variety of topics, and marked by a pungent, highly polished, and aphoristic style. The volume might in a sense be described as a triumph of postmodernist art itself. But Adorno's resolute insistence upon a dialectical perspective forecloses any possibility of conservative, empiricist aestheticism. On the contrary, *Minima Moralia* is first and foremost a meditation on its own postmodern conditions of possibility, on the damaging and distorting reduction of critique to the individual sphere where it nonetheless remains vital and may still bear, even if as a negative imprint, the memory and hope of praxis. "For the intellectual," as Adorno puts it, "inviolable isolation is now the only way of showing some measure of solidarity."[7] Or, in other words,

In the age of the individual's liquidation, the question of individuality must be raised anew. While the individual, like all individualistic processes of production, has fallen behind the state of technology and become historically obsolete, he becomes the

7. Theodor Adorno, *Minima Moralia*, trans. E. F. N. Jephcott (London: Verso, 1978), 26.

custodian of truth, as the condemned against the victor. For the individual alone pre-
serves, in however distorted a form, a trace of that which legitimizes all technifica-
tion, and yet to which the latter blinds itself. (*Minima Moralia* 129)

A great deal of Adorno's brilliance lies in his ability to take the full measure
of the reduced circumstances that constrict critical theory under postmodernity without succumbing either to undialectical defeatism or to an equally if
antithetically undialectical intellectualist hedonism—both lapses of rigor that
mark so many of the weaker versions of current poststructuralism (a poststructuralism to which Adorno, as we discussed in chapter 3, in other ways bears
much kinship). As the position of critique becomes more dubious, the importance of keeping the dialectical spirit alive is only increased. Without "the persistence of the dialectic" (Jameson's phrase), the triumph of postmodern reification would be genuinely universal. It is with no careless hyperbole that
Horkheimer—Adorno's closest colleague, whose construction with Adorno of
Critical Theory, as they called it, may in retrospect be viewed as the first (indeed, partly proleptic) and in some ways still the greatest attempt to forge a variety of critical theory proper to the unprecedented situation of the postmodern—goes so far as to insist, "The future of humanity depends on the existence
of the critical attitude."[8]

The discussion to this point should have prepared us, in several different
ways, for the final conceptual turn of this coda: the coordination of the postmodern with science fiction. Because science fiction is a form of art in which,
as we have seen, the Blochian prefigurations of utopia are especially important, and because science fiction generally enjoys, as this entire study has
taken care to establish, a special affinity with critical theory, it should be clear
that much of the foregoing argument on the situations of art and critique
under the commodified and commodifying regime of exchange-value must
have considerable direct application to the situation of science fiction today.
Before dealing with the matter in this way, however, I will approach the problem from a somewhat different angle: by considering the question of postmodernism, of postmodern aesthetic practice, *within* science fiction.

In addition to the general stylistic periodization of modernism and postmodernism that I have already tried to dismantle, some commentators have
proposed homologous but miniature and usually at least somewhat nonsyn-
chronous versions of the same scheme that have been intended to apply to
various specialized departments of cultural production. Thus, for example,
in film—which, as we have seen, does not even exist prior to the moment of
classic modernism in general—the work of Hitchcock and his great contemporaries (Bergman, Fellini, Ford, Kurosawa, Orson Welles, and others) can
be taken to represent a filmic modernism, with the passage to postmodernism

8. Max Horkheimer, *Critical Theory*, trans. Matthew J. O'Connell et al. (New York: Herder
and Herder, 1972), 242.

exemplified by the transition from Hitchcock to his own anxious ephebe, Brian De Palma. Or again, Raymond Chandler might be understood as the Joyce or Proust of the modernist detective novel, contrasted to the postmodernism of Ross Macdonald and especially of such current practitioners of feminist crime fiction as Sara Paretsky. Science fiction, as it happens, is especially vulnerable to this kind of superficially plausible chronology. Indeed, it is not difficult, in the case of science fiction, also to fill in the term anterior to modernism, and so to produce a tripartite design in which the "Golden Age" work typified by Heinlein and Asimov amounts to the science-fictional equivalent of realism, with modernism represented by such authors as Le Guin and Delany of the *Dangerous Visions* era, and postmodernism represented by that more recent science-fictional tendency known as cyberpunk. Though a specifically formal description of postmodernism is no more tenable within science fiction than anywhere else, it will be useful to substantiate this assertion through a brief consideration of cyberpunk itself. Indeed, though the latter does not, in my view, possess anything like the literary-critical importance that its current (though already fading) trendiness might suggest, this very trendiness ensures that any discussion of science fiction and the postmodern that did *not* acknowledge cyberpunk would look odd.

Cyberpunk is unanimously agreed to have its chief founding moment in William Gibson's 1984 novel, *Neuromancer*, which remains the undisputed paradigm and only generally recognized masterwork of the kind. The name itself (for which Gibson is not responsible) is something of a misnomer. A portmanteau word in the style of Lewis Carroll and Joyce, it suggests a preoccupation with cybernetic and computer technologies that is combined with a sensibility akin to that of punk rock, the most vital form of rock music during the late 1970s and early 1980s. But cyberpunk actually has little to do with punk. The overall structure of feeling of *Neuromancer* and its successors bears almost no affinity to that of the Sex Pistols or the Clash and very little (apart from a flattening of affect) to that of Talking Heads. Instead, cyberpunk displays a filiation to the much older tradition of hard-boiled detective fiction of the Hammett-Chandler type. In *Neuromancer* itself, the protagonist, Case the computer cowboy, is a hard-bitten professional and a lone individualist hero who has little in common with the various personae of Johnny Rotten, Joe Strummer, or David Byrne, but who is certainly reminiscent of Philip Marlowe or, still more, of the Continental Op. As his name implies, he exists, like them, primarily for the *case*, for the individual task at hand.

What makes Gibson's novel such a remarkable achievement is not the conventional action-adventure plot through which Case moves, nor the tediously cynical and sentimental attitude with which he orients himself to his environment. It is, rather, the delineation of that environment itself. The latter is a thoroughly commodified postmodern landscape, in which the mean streets of the old hard-boiled detectives are now to be found in an increasingly urbanized world that is also a world of increasing urban decay—a world, also, in which the power of the nation-state has been largely replaced by that of a few giant multinational corporations engaged in unceasing industrial espionage. This physical landscape has its supplement and analogue in the less tangible mean streets of cyberspace, that hallucinatory terrain that exists only electronically but in which computer cowboys like Case have exciting, dangerous adventures. Gibson's estranging projection of a cognitively plausible near-future is in the best science-fictional tradition, and holds considerable negative-utopian value. It may well be, however, that a great deal of the popularity that Gibson and his colleagues have enjoyed is due not to their genuinely innovative portrayals of the postmodern cyberpunk world, but rather to the conservative reassurances that tend to accompany such portrayals. For the future shock that Case's environment might provoke is softened and domesticated by the implication that the simple, old-fashioned macho attitudes that define Case (he is, indeed, a less complex character than any of Hammett's or Chandler's protagonists) are after all adequate to this brave new world. In any event, there is, even apart from such conservative nostalgia, nothing in particular that makes cyberpunk, in merely aesthetic terms, a decisively new postmodernist moment within science fiction. Here yet again the purely formal line between modernism and postmodernism cannot be clearly drawn, and Gibson, for all his distinctive brilliance, is in no definable way more stylistically "advanced" than, say, Delany or Joanna Russ—or even (reaching back still earlier in science-fiction history) Alfred Bester.

But this is not the place for a full-scale consideration of the artistic significance of cyberpunk. I have begun to indicate what seem to me its major strengths and limitations, though in fact a considerable critical literature on this matter already exists.[9] In summary terms, it seems clear that cyberpunk

9. My own brief comments on the significance of cyberpunk may be supplemented by the articles listed below (which represent a selection from the astonishingly large amount of serious commentary that cyberpunk has attracted). None is merely dismissive of cyberpunk or unappreciative of its real achievements, especially in *Neuromancer*; nonetheless the general tendency of nearly all these essays is deflationary of the many extravagant claims made by cyberpunk's apologists. The following essays are most conveniently found in Larry McCaffery, ed., *Storming the Reality Studio* (Durham: Duke University Press, 1991), the most useful single volume for any reader trying to come to terms with cyberpunk: Istvan Csicsery-Ronay Jr., "Cyberpunk and Neuromanticism," 182–193; Veronica Hollinger, "Cybernetic Deconstructions: Cyberpunk and Postmodernism," 203–218; George Slusser, "Literary MTV," 334–342; Darko Suvin, "On Gibson and Cyberpunk SF," 349–365. Roughly contemporary with the above is Peter Fitting, "The Lessons of Cyberpunk," in *Technoculture*, ed. Constance Penley and Andrew Ross (Minneapolis: University of Minnesota Press, 1991). The following are from *Science-Fiction Studies*: Terence Whalen, "The Future of a Commodity: Notes Toward a Critique of Cyberpunk and the Information Age," 19 (March 1992): 75–88; Nicola Nixon, "Cyberpunk: Preparing the Ground for Revolution or Keeping the Boys Satisfied?" 19 (July 1992): 219–235; Neil Easterbrook, "The Arc of Our Destruction: Reversal and Erasure in Cyberpunk," 19 (November 1992): 378–394; Claire Sponsler, "Beyond the Ruins: The Geopolitics of Urban Decay and Cybernetic Play," 20 (July 1993): 251–265. Of these essays, Hollinger's is especially noteworthy for providing one of the most sympathetic treatments of cyberpunk written from a nonetheless not uncritical point of view; Fitting's for giving perhaps the

has failed to produce a second author truly comparable to Gibson in importance—not even Bruce Sterling, the chief propagandist of the movement, with whom Gibson has been closely associated both personally and professionally—and that even most of Gibson's own later work has failed to fulfill the high promise of *Neuromancer*. Though it is too early to offer such judgments with full confidence, we may even speculate with some plausibility that, when the requisite perspective is attained, most of the finest science fiction produced in North America during the 1980s and 1990s (the era of cyberpunk) will be seen to be the work of authors, from Gregory Benford on the libertarian right to Kim Stanley Robinson on the socialist left, who are emphatically *not* to be counted among cyberpunk's practitioners. In the meantime, however, the huge popular impact of cyberpunk, and the centrality that some serious commentators have accorded it in the understanding of the postmodern,[10] deserve explanation in their own right.

The explanation is not far to seek. The success that cyberpunk has enjoyed (and it is, as we shall see, no accident that this success has been more intense and unqualified *outside* the normal readership of science fiction than within it) is based on the way it imaginatively registers perhaps the two most prominent features of late-capitalist society today: the multinationalization of both finance and industrial capital, and the growing technological importance of the computer. In other words, the radically postmodern quality of cyberpunk is to be found not in any specifically postmodernist aesthetic style, but in the use of generally well established literary techniques—some derivative of classic modernism and others as old as Homer—to capture with remarkable vividness the socioeconomic-technological horizons of postmodernity. The point, however, is not only that cyberpunk at its best (which is mainly to say *Neuromancer*) offers an unprecedently forceful picture of certain key features of postmodernity, displaying an ultracommodified global totality increasingly difficult to comprehend and increasingly resistant to the counterhegemonic projects of praxis. The enormous and virtually instant commercial success of cyberpunk (and of the *idea* of cyberpunk, which has proved captivating to many who may not have read a single page of Gibson's prose) is also, I think, due to the attitude of essential *acceptance* with which cyberpunk orients itself to the postmodern environment.

---

best general overview of cyberpunk available; Whalen's for bringing to bear a degree of economic literacy that is unfortunately rare in literary and cultural studies; and Nixon's for offering a feminist perspective badly needed in the study of this sometimes suffocatingly macho literature. For the reader seeking still more secondary work on cyberpunk, see George Slusser and Tom Shippey, eds., *Fiction 2000: Cyberpunk and the Future of Narrative* (Athens: University of Georgia Press, 1992).

10. I am thinking, for instance, of the paradigmatic role granted to cyberpunk in Brian McHale, *Constructing Postmodernism* (London: Routledge, 1992), and of Scott Bukatman, *Terminal Identity: The Virtual Subject in Postmodern Science Fiction* (Durham: Duke University Press, 1993), which makes liberal use of cyberpunk, especially *Neuromancer*, in a theoretical description of the structure of postmodern culture.

There is indeed a certain sense in which cyberpunk, for all its critical descriptive power, finally resolves into an uncritical conservatism. In *Neuromancer*, it is not just that the exciting but structurally inconsequential adventures of individual cowboys like Case seem to be the only means of negotiating the unimaginably overdetermined totality of postmodernity. On one level, this might be nothing more or less than a grim political realism. In addition to such genuinely critical realism, however—and condensed above all in the virtually pathological character of Case himself, who is hopelessly alienated from any vital connection whether political or erotic[11]—is what C. Wright Mills might have called the "crackpot realism" of sentimental cynicism: the attitude, in this instance, that takes a world resistant to praxis and apparently void of utopia as one in which the entire notions of praxis and utopia may be merely abandoned with hard-bitten "knowingness." Cyberpunk thus colludes with reification even while exposing it, and, accordingly, offers us the always comforting conservative assurance that, in counter-Leninist fashion, *nothing* is to be done. In this way, the success, especially the initial success, of cyberpunk has been very much a phenomenon of what Alexander Cockburn used to call the Age of Reagan. Rigorously critical in its indicative understanding of the postmodern condition, this literature offers, in its imperative mode, little but a banal, cringing surrender before the same actuality so lyrically celebrated by the apologists of capital.

It is thus not difficult to understand why cyberpunk has been so much more acclaimed by those largely indifferent to the history of science fiction than by those conversant with it. Many of the former have proclaimed that in cyberpunk science fiction finally becomes (this is intended as a compliment) part of "mainstream" literature.[12] But some understanding of the counterhegemonic conceptual resources of science fiction is required in order to evaluate this claim for what it really is: an admission that, in contrast to some earlier science fiction (and especially to much science fiction during the generation immediately preceding the Reaganite phase of postmodernity), cyberpunk is *less* radically critical and so less radically science-fictional. It would be foolish, however, to take this judgment merely as an occasion for

11. Of course, Case is not exactly celibate, and his sexual affair with Molly looms fairly large in the novel's plot. But Case's libidinal investments are mainly narcissistic ones in his own ego (as is especially notable in the text's Manichaean quality, its contempt for and desire to escape from the body, which is regarded as "meat"). Accordingly—and in line with Freud's crucial distinction between the transference neuroses and the narcissistic neuroses—the affair with Molly is really more psychotic than erotic. The text's final sentence—"He never saw Molly again" (William Gibson, *Neuromancer* [New York: Ace, 1984], 271)—neatly encapsulates this attitude with a memorable shrug.

12. This is a familiar attitude toward marginalized literatures. A couple of generations ago, many white critics imagined that they were being commendably broad-minded by allowing that African-American literature had finally joined the "mainstream"—as though Baldwin and Ellison should have been flattered by being permitted into the company of William Golding and Saul Bellow.

moral blame of the cyberpunk authors (not that such blame would in all cases necessarily be ill-grounded). The partial failure of cyberpunk should rather be taken as a sign of the growing totalism of the postmodern situation and the concomitant extreme difficulty of gaining a foothold from which authentic critique can be launched and, correlatively, from which science fiction can be written. Furthermore, since science fiction is of all forms of art the one most closely and profoundly allied to critical theory, it comes as no surprise to conclude of science fiction what we earlier maintained of critical theory and of art in general: that the very circumstances which most inhibit it also render it more urgently necessary than ever before.

It is, then, the general circumstances of postmodernity that necessarily define the status and importance of science fiction today. As I have already discussed, science fiction is, at least in our time, the privileged generic tendency for utopia; that is, for those anticipatory figurations of an unalienated future that constitute the deepest critical truth of which art is capable. More difficult to attain even than critique in its negative, demystifying dimension, utopia has never been so desperately needed as it is now, in our postmodern environment that ruthlessly tends toward total reification. Indeed, not since before the October Revolution itself (whose ultimate overthrow in 1991 constituted only the sickening final chapter of a downward narrative begun with bureaucratization and Stalinist betrayal almost six decades earlier) has it been harder and lonelier to imagine a social organization beyond alienation and exploitation, or to imagine sociopolitical forces more decisive than the regime of exchange-value (of "the market," in currently fashionable jargon). Such imagining, however close to impossible it may be, must now be the principal vocation of science fiction. To what degree science fiction will prove adequate to the task cannot be predicted.

Yet there is at least one sense in which science fiction is particularly well suited to the postmodern situation (however hostile, in most other respects, postmodernity may be to the critical and utopian power of science fiction at its most radical). Science fiction has, as we have seen, its general orientation primarily toward the future. Indeed, it should be remembered that the advent of science fiction during the moment of Mary Shelley is inseparable from the very invention of history and the future as these terms are now meaningful. Though this does not, as we have also seen, imply any sort of futu*rism* in the positivistic sense, it does mean that of all literary modes science fiction ought to be the least tempted by the kind of premodern regressivity whose strength still largely defines the moment of modernism itself. Accordingly, even more than the modernist fictionality—still very far from formally exhausted—of Joyce or Proust, science fiction must scorn the concept of regression to the premodern, even while encountering substantial difficulty with the kind of *progression* that postmodernity has in fact entailed. In other words, it is in the generic nature of science fiction to confront the future, no matter how unpromising a critical and utopian activity that may seem (as now) to be. "No one," as Nietzsche writes, "is free to be a crab. . . . One *must* go forward—step by step further into decadence (that is *my* definition of modern 'progress')."[13]

These words from *Twilight of the Idols* neatly describe the situation of science fiction today. The crablike nostalgia of going backward is unavailable, for it is contrary to the nature of science fiction. There is simply no choice but to go onward, even though that means progressing into a more and more commodified postmodernity—an apt equivalent indeed to the Nietzschean "decadence." Nietzsche himself, it might be remembered, was able, in his own terms, to see beyond decadence to a kind of utopia (though the heroic future aristocracy of the Overmen is a reductively individualist and thus drastically compromised version of utopia). Will the science fiction of a deepening postmodernity do better? Will it achieve pre-illuminations of a utopia more collective and actual? There can of course be no guarantees. But I trust that the history and structure of science fiction, as this essay has displayed them, give reason to conclude that such hope need not be abandoned.

13. Friedrich Nietzsche, *The Portable Nietzsche*, ed. and trans. Walter Kaufmann (New York: Penguin, 1976), 547.

Index

UNIVERSITY PRESS OF NEW ENGLAND

publishes books under its own imprint and is the publisher for Brandeis University Press, Dartmouth College, Middlebury College Press, University of New Hampshire, Tufts University, and Wesleyan University Press.

ABOUT THE AUTHOR

Carl Freedman is Associate Professor of English at Louisiana State University and the author of more than thirty articles and of *George Orwell: A Study in Ideology and Literary Form* (1988). In 1999 he received the Pioneer Award for Excellence in Scholarship from the Science Fiction Research Association.

LIBRARY OF CONGRESS CATALOGING-IN-PUBLICATION DATA

Freedman, Carl Howard.
 Critical theory and science fiction / by Carl Freedman.
   p. cm.
 Includes bibliographical references and index.
 ISBN 0-8195-6398-6 (alk. paper) — ISBN 0-8195-6399-4 (pbk. : alk. paper)
  1. Science fiction — History and criticism — Theory, etc. 2. Delany, Samuel R. Stars in my pocket like grains of sand. 3. Le Guin, Ursula K., 1929– Dispossessed. 4. Dick, Philip K. Man in the high castle. 5. Russ, Joanna, 1937– Two of them. 6. Lem, Stanis±lw. Solaris. 1. Title.
 PN3433.5 .F74 2000
 809.3'8762 — dc21   99–048532